The Jenische Stones

The Jenische Stones

Gregg Hammond

THOUSAND ACRES

Library of Congress Control Number: 2024930309

ISBN (paperback): 978-1-963271-03-4
(eBook): 978-1-963271-04-1

Elaina Robbins, editing
Angel L. Ivanov, Romani translations

THOUSAND ACRES

Thousand Acres is an imprint of Armin Lear Press, Inc.
Armin Lear Press, Inc.
215 W Riverside Drive, #4362
Estes Park, CO 80517

This book is dedicated to my loving, patient, and devoted wife.

Preface

This story is near to my heart in many ways. Both sides of my family immigrated to Indiana in the early 1800s. The characters in this book are loosely based on folks I have encountered throughout my life, including relatives I have known or been told of. Some of the surnames, including Beck, Mooney, and Kunkle, were derived from my lineage. One great-grandfather on the Tillett side of my family, for instance, immigrated to America in the 1840s. He became an early pioneer in our county, working as a canal boat captain and a circuit judge. He also assisted runaways in escaping from Southern states' slavery.

On my mother's side, my family drew its spiritual foundation from German Baptist Brethren and Dunkard Brethren roots. I would often sit and listen to my grandmother tell her family tales of Indiana farm life during the 1800s and 1900s—my uncle's secondhand war exploits, our ancestors' underground railway station, and visits from passing "Gypsies." Through her, too, I learned that in past times, the Anabaptist faithful from "peace churches" often fell prey to ridicule and discrimination. In one case, in 1918, a

1

drafted conscientious objector (CO) from Indiana was sentenced to hard labor at Fort Leavenworth for his war resistance. Another CO who refused to wear an army uniform died while at Fort Leavenworth after being subjected to physical abuse.[1]

Though not a German Baptist myself, I was raised in a Brethren tradition. I watched this interweaving of faith while I came of age in my small Indiana farm community, richly influenced by the simple and dutiful Schwarzenau Brethren practice. This book has taken creativity and examples from those who stood firm in their beliefs and guided Indiana spirituality for the generations that have followed.

My Irish paternal grandma's rich yarns contrasted starkly with my German Brethren side. She spoke of ghosts, spirits, and episodic Ouija board sessions. Those images also stuck in my mind. To me, they didn't seem to conflict with faith; instead, they seemed another side of the same coin.

Visiting Germany, I became fascinated by the Bronze Age Neolithic stone circles, especially one hidden in the forest near the village of Boitin. I initially believed such ancient monuments had been used only for astrology observations or burial rituals. However, later, I discovered there were also many legends surrounding these circles. They allegedly bore witness to passageways and portals into other worlds. Spirits, both good and bad, purportedly accessed these stone rings to travel from one dimension to another.

I've often wondered if these tales were based on observation or possibly even fundamental physical interactions. At any rate, I found the folklore intriguing enough to add another level of inspiration and imagination to this story. Thus, my travels and the

---

1   Elevationweb.org. "World War I: The Co Problem." World War I: The CO Problem | The Civilian Public Service Story. Accessed January 13, 2023. https://civilianpublicservice.org/storybegins/krehbiel/world-war-1.

influences of both branches of my early family have nourished this written journey.

Lastly, I wanted to address some of the content in this book that may cause reader concerns. This is a work of historical fiction, and as such, it contains ethnic slurs and terminology that are now considered offensive and inappropriate. The word Gypsy, for example, is used throughout this book to refer to the Jenische and Romani people; this is simply because of the period in which the book takes place and is not meant to offend.

This book also contains graphic images of violence, including war crimes. While these chapters are difficult to read, many of the scenes are derived from truth, based on actual accounts I've heard from veterans and my own experiences during the Vietnam and Iraq wars. May they serve as reminders of the horrific sacrifices made in battle and of why we as human beings must do whatever possible to keep "never again" a reality.

Introduction

A few stragglers genuflected and took their seats in the small Indianapolis Episcopal cathedral. Greta, seated in the second row of pews, took Oscar's hand. The elderly couple looked at each other.

"Time seems to have gone so quickly," Greta said softly, her English colored by a hint of a German accent.

"It feels like only yesterday I was downstairs, pacing and waiting for Fredrick to be born," Oscar said, his accent a bit heavier. Underneath his modest attire, his body, once physically strong from years of labor, had grown frail with age. However, when he smiled, his eyes glistened the same way they had when he'd first seen Greta in Hannover, Germany, all those years ago.

"And now Fredrick watches his son wed, as we once watched him be joined in matrimony," Greta said, looking fondly to her left. Fredrick and Lena were seated close together, hands clasped, their eyes riveted on the groom. Daniel stood in front of the priest at the foot of the sanctuary stairs, nervously glancing down the aisle.

"How handsome Daniel is," Greta said.

"He reminds me of you," Oscar said. "I would recognize those deep blue eyes anywhere."

"Perhaps the resemblance was clearer when I was fifty years younger," Greta said with a slight chuckle, squeezing Oscar's hand.

Closing her eyes, she remembered the old country and the life they had long ago left behind.

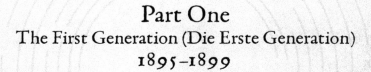

Part One
The First Generation (Die Erste Generation)
1895–1899

I

From Whence We Came
(Woher wir kamen)
1895

Westerly summer winds blew as Oscar and Greta stepped off the afternoon train. Oscar, in his collarless suit, and Greta, in her cape and white bonnet, scanned the Butzow train depot. The couple's religious garb, as usual, stood out in the crowd.

Neither of them saw Dieter until he gently touched Oscar's shoulder. Oscar turned to see a tall, broad-shouldered man in his early fifties clad in a gray, tattered military coat. His kind eyes shone in a face tanned and creased with furrowed lines, which was partially obscured by a thick, graying beard.

"Oscar," said Dieter, in his deep, rumbling voice. "It has been far too long, my boy. I'm happy you decided to visit." He looked at the young man's thick, wavy brown hair and chin strap beard and laughed, shaking his head.

"You look so much like Carl did once. I must look so old to

you," he said, holding out a hand. "The years have shown me no mercy, it seems."

"Uncle, you have aged well," Oscar said, shaking Dieter's hand.

"And Greta, you seem hearty and well," Dieter said. Greta, whose Germanic lineage was apparent from her blue eyes and gleaming red-blonde eyebrows, dipped her head in thanks.

Dieter helped gather the couple's modest luggage and loaded it into the waiting-covered carriage. Greta eyed him with concern, noticing he walked with a slight limp, but Dieter seemed used to his condition.

The forty-minute wagon ride over muddy and winding roads to Dieter's home near the Tarnow forest passed quickly as the three talked. The surrey was open to the air, and a pleasant breeze cooled Greta's face as she watched the buildings and people pass by in the early June sunlight.

"Thank you for coming such a long way." Dieter glanced over at Oscar and Greta.

"Of course. We were so happy when we got your letter," said Greta. "After all, this will likely be the last visit we'll have before we leave for America." She subtly adjusted her position on the lumpy carriage seat. As she had grown physically strong from her five years of farmwork and disciplined living, the uncomfortable accommodations did not bother her much.

"Oh! All the details for your trip are arranged, then?" asked Dieter.

"Yes," said Oscar. "We've got our tickets for ship passage, and our replacement tenant farmers will take over next month. Fredrick's invitation could not have come at a better time."

Fredrick. Greta had never met Oscar's paternal Uncle Fredrick, who had immigrated to America in the late 1850s, but she imagined that he must look much like Dieter. She may not have met the man, but she already knew much about him. According to Oscar, Uncle Fredrick heavily invested in wool purchasing during the American Civil War and became financially secure through what many called war profiteering. He had later secured military contracts for uniform manufacturing, an endeavor that made him even more wealthy. Fredrick had then used his fortune to buy farms in the rich lands of Pennsylvania, Ohio, and Indiana.

Fredrick had remained a hazy figure in Greta's imagination until recently when, one morning, the postman had dropped off a tattered letter. Greta, seeing the return address, had turned on her heels and ran.

"Oscar, a letter from America has arrived," she had called out, moving swiftly toward the pig pen. Oscar had set down the large cloth bag of ground feed and took the letter from her hand.

"It's a letter from Uncle Fredrick," he had said, holding the envelope up.

"Please read it," Greta had implored. "All the way from America! How exciting."

Oscar had stood silently reading the letter, then he had slowly turned and smiled at Greta, his eyes alight with hope. Greta would never forget that look.

"This is the opportunity my father never had," he had said. "Uncle Fredrick has asked if we would be willing to come live in America."

In the weeks following its arrival, Greta had read that letter so often she'd memorized portions of it. She could recall her favorite part even now:

I am advancing in years; my energy and time are fleeting. I

feel obligated to help my brother's family while I still can. Carl helped financially sponsor my voyage to America, for which I will always be grateful.

Though I have long since left the Brethren affiliation, I am still comfortable serving the German Baptist farmers here in America. While you make arrangements in Germany, I can process the trip to the United States through my contacts and acquaintances. I can also arrange a passage to the United States if you decide to come.

Carl sacrificed much to assist my journey to America. Paying back the debt now would give you a chance to leave Germany and start a new life.

This opportunity would change everything. Since they'd wed at the ages of twenty and twenty-one in 1890, Greta and Oscar had moved onto a German government-owned farm near Hannover with Oscar's father. Carl did not own any part of the farm other than six milk cows. Instead, he was allowed to live there in return for farm labor and a third of the profits. Many local German Brethren parishioners took part in this governmental arrangement while struggling to hold their shrinking church congregation together. The austere life of "usufruct," government land propriety, though better than a fiefdom, held no long-term hope of security. Caring for livestock and planting and harvesting grain only to have the government take the bulk of the profits disheartened even the most resilient of souls.

"I am very happy for you," Dieter said, guiding the surrey around a deep rut in the road. "When Carl began Bismarck's tenant farming, after your mother died, I knew he'd only end up exhausted and broken. It is hard, thankless labor, as you both have learned."

Greta and Oscar nodded in unison. The newlyweds had toiled selflessly, helping Oscar's father on the farm until Carl's untimely death barely a year prior. They kept little money and only had limited time for themselves. Greta's days on the farm were difficult: milking cows, raising swine, and tending to chickens while helping Oscar farm the controlled sections of land planted in accordance with governmental dictates.

"The required tithing may have made your situation even worse," Dieter said. Tithing was very much a part of the Anabaptist belief; the expected ten percent was a pillar of faith and means of church survival.

"Excuses or rationalizations for avoiding tithing are common, to be sure," Greta said. "But doing right by our Lord bears no price."

"'Lord, all my desire is before thee, and my groaning is not hidden,'" Oscar added.

"Nevertheless, that tenant farm took Carl's life," Dieter said, shaking his head. "I told him it would. The dust only worsened his disease, and the government and the church both helping themselves meant Carl never even saw the fruits of his labor."

Greta winced as she recalled Carl's slow and painful demise. Each day, Carl's breathing had become more labored. Emphysema from the early years of coal mining and, later, farm dust had taken its toll on his health. Some days, he had found it impossible to perform the simplest tasks on the farm; even collecting eggs or feeding the small brood of hens incapacitated him for hours. Greta was grateful that Dieter hadn't seen his brother in that state.

"I learned all that I know of farming from my father," Oscar said, barely audible over the clatter of the surrey. "I will always cherish my memories of his wisdom and patience." Greta leaned her head on Oscar's shoulder briefly; she had witnessed the relationship between the two men and knew how much Oscar loved and missed his father.

"Never mind all that now," Dieter said in a slightly clogged voice. He cleared his throat and adjusted his hold on the reins, looking over at them brightly. "Have you met the new tenant farmers yet?"

"Yes, they came to visit," Greta said. "They are German Baptists from a sister church. They are also concerned for the county's future given Germany's checkered history and state-mandated military conscription."

"Then why are they starting to farm now?" Dieter mused.

"Not many are blessed with an opportunity like the one we have been given," Oscar said. "They likely have no other options. We, for our part, are anxious to depart Germany."

"I know you will find America more lucrative," Dieter said, guiding the horse to the right. They were out of the city now. Cultivated fields dotted with forests, farmhouses, and patches of bog in the low areas stretched as far as the eye could see underneath the bright blue sky.

"We are more concerned with Germany's political unrest than our financial straits, to be frank," Oscar said. "The fear of the political unknown is the real problem. Farm labor under Prussian social control is trying, though I suppose it is still better than working under some godless, Marxist philosophy."

"That was certainly one reason we accepted an offer for a new life far from the uncertainty of Germany," Greta confirmed.

"The kingdom of Prussia's place in this reunified empire feels uncomfortable, to be sure," Dieter said grimly. "Who knows what will occur under the new chancellor? I only know that he seems quite chummy with the Kaiser, or so I've heard."

"Exactly. Given that and Germany's preferences, many of the brethren worry that more wars loom in the future," Oscar said, glancing over at Greta. Oscar and Greta, like most German Baptist Brethren, believed that killing and violence were wrong regardless of circumstances.

"Lucifer's favorite pastime is war," Dieter said. Greta looked at Dieter's weathered face, each premature line illuminated by the cheery sunlight. He seemed to feel her gaze, and his eyes darted to meet hers for a moment, his expression wistful.

"America holds many opportunities for both of you, more than our so-called unified Germany ever will," he said. "I only wish that when I was your age, I could have had the chance to go to America. It's agonizing when you know in your heart that you could have a better life if only the door were allowed to be opened. And yet, there are those who even now wish to deny you that chance." He shook his head sadly, and his horse snorted as if in agreement.

"What do you mean, Uncle?" asked Oscar as the wagon moved past birch and oak trees lining the marshy landscape.

"The church, of course," said Dieter. "I believe in God and a higher power, but I find the hypocrisy of the church reprehensible."

"Uncle Dieter!" Greta gasped.

"Be honest," Dieter said in a stern voice. "Haven't the church elders objected to your going to America? What have they said about the idea?"

"Well," Oscar said slowly, "they weren't all exactly in agreement. Some elders say leaving Germany is a 'betrayal of the fatherland.'"

"How so?" asked Dieter.

"'War conflicts with our moral beliefs, but there may come a time in which our national survival depends upon young men of faith willing to stand for Germany.' That's what another elder said, or something like it."

"But," Greta interjected, "as you know, our brethren, for the most part, do not believe in war. I believe our fellowship connection with the German Baptists in America helped sway their decision."

"Hmm," Dieter said.

"And, finally, Oscar and I have both been in the congregation for years," Greta said with conviction. "I believe the elders deeply care for us. They have watched us grow up and grow to love one another, after all. So, yes, they did agree in the end."

"Imagine that," Dieter said under his breath.

"They even agreed to grant us some financial assistance for the journey, which was much appreciated," Greta said, her eyes fixed stubbornly on Dieter's face. "Our savings clear only a few marks. We needed help, and they gave it to us."

"I will leave it at this," said the older man, holding up a hand in surrender, his face softening somewhat. "I find the indiscriminate decisions the church makes as to whom their rules apply and to whom they don't to be hypocritical. I am just happy that the two of you ended up on the right side of one of their so-called verdicts. Now, look! Here we are."

Greta looked up to see a small, sturdy home made of mortar and stone. The tan building was covered in budding leaves of vining ivy, and the dark green wooden trim and front door blended with the surrounding woods. Her indignation seemed to flow out of her at the sight.

"What a handsome home," she couldn't help but say.

"I found all the stones from the nearby fields," Dieter said proudly as they approached the structure. A small black herding dog barked happily at them as they neared.

"That's Isaiah," Dieter said.

"What happened to Ula?" Oscar asked.

"She died," said Dieter sadly. "She was quite old, nearing fifteen. Isaiah is still a young dog, so please excuse his manners."

Inside, after Oscar and Greta received a very enthusiastic greeting from Isaiah, Dieter set to work building a warm fire in the ashlar fireplace with its hand-hewn oak mantel. A badly rusted military bolt-action rifle rested above the hearth; Greta tried to avoid looking at it, gazing instead at the woodworking and masonry tools, axes of various sizes, and a few seemingly random religious paintings that decorated the pinewood walls. A few sticks of handmade furniture sat on the wide-planked floor, and oil glass globe lamps adorned nearly every surface. A shabby black violin case lay forlornly in one bare corner next to a rumpled, graying blanket covered in black fur.

This place desperately needs a woman's touch, Greta thought as she placed her weathered brown leather valise on the floor. Dieter lit the fire with a match, and as soon as he was sure it had caught, he turned and winked at the couple.

"I know it feels warm now, but as soon as the sun sets, we're going to need the fire. Now, come this way," he said, limping briskly up the stairs ahead of them.

Dieter showed Oscar and Greta to a small room with a stuffed feather mattress on a handmade wooden bed frame. Two straight-backed wooden chairs and a bureau furnished the space, though the walls were bare. Thin curtains fluttered around the window, which was cracked to air the spartan quarters. For the short visit, the room seemed more than adequate, Greta decided.

That night, as Greta and Oscar prepared for bed in the little guest room, Greta asked about Uncle Dieter's strange comments about the church.

"It almost seems like he hates them," she said quietly as she brushed out her long, shining hair. She kept the strawberry-blonde strands, which she rarely cut, pulled into a bun and tucked into her white cloth bonnet and prayer covering when she was in public. It always felt nice to loosen them at the end of the day.

"I should have warned you before we came," Oscar said, keeping his voice down. "The Danish War left Dieter scarred. As a young man and a member of the German Baptist Church, Dieter was drafted by the government to fight for the confederation in the war against Denmark. The church elders offered no real support to prevent Dieter's conscription."

"Oh," Greta said, her heart sinking.

"He was subsequently wounded during one of the battles he endured," Oscar said. "That's why he walks with a limp; he has ever since I can remember. Pa said that sometimes, Dieter cries out in his sleep as he dreams of the war, so be prepared to be awoken at night."

"Goodness. Poor Dieter."

"I know. It must have been both a terrible trauma and betrayal," Oscar said, his eyes sorrowful. "As for the church, Dieter told Pa that he no longer has any use for organized religion or the people who he feels failed him. Even after thirty years, he still holds bitterness. He is faithful to God in his way, but he seems obsessed with questioning the Brethren elders."

"Despite all that, he seems a good man," Greta said, setting her brush down.

"Are you ready for me to put out the lamp?" Greta asked.

As she got into bed, Greta said a silent prayer. *Lord, grant Dieter peace in his heart so he can come to forgive those who betrayed him,* she pleaded. Soon, she was asleep in Oscar's arms.

The visitors arose early the following day and spent their first-day completing farm chores and socializing. Dieter was impressed by Greta's strength, watching as she quickly heaved buckets of water and bags of grain around the farm. Isaiah, who seemed thrilled to have company, chased her around.

"Before my mother's death, she often told me how strong I was," Greta said with a laugh when Dieter complimented her over warm buttermilk that evening. The sun was getting low, and Dieter had lit all the oil lamps. A fire crackled in the hearth, giving the cabin a beautiful golden glow.

"Your mother has passed? I am sorry to hear that," Dieter said. He set down his glass on the table. "Greta, I realize now that I know so little about your background."

"I feel as though I know very little about you also, Uncle," Greta admitted.

"Well, you knew my brother Carl, so you do know something of me," Dieter said. He looked up at Oscar. "I'm sorry I didn't come to your wedding, Oscar. Or to Carl's funeral, for that matter. Frankly, the thought of seeing all the church hypocrites again was beyond my limits of tolerance." There was an awkward pause.

"It is well," Greta said. "Let's get to know each other now. I will start." She smiled, her eyes dark in the firelight.

"I'm a third-generation German Baptist Brethren," she told Dieter. "My grandparents reformed from the Lutheran faith while living in Sweden. They moved south to become part of the German Baptist movement."

"Which is how you met, of course," Dieter said. Greta nodded and took Oscar's hand under the table.

"Yes, I admired Greta from the day we first met," Oscar said. "That's when her grandparents brought her to church after her parents died." Dieter looked sharply at Oscar.

"Both of them?"

"Greta's parents were killed in a train crash at Hanau when she was fourteen," Oscar said in a somber voice, glancing at his wife. "They were going to visit a relative and had left Greta with her grandparents that weekend."

"I ended up living with my grandparents until we were married," Greta said, nodding. "I am lucky to have them. Oscar was a great comfort to me when I lost my parents."

"I am truly sorry," Dieter said. "I know your parents can never be replaced. I hope it is of some comfort that with your marriage, you have gained a new family that cares about you." Greta's eyes welled with tears, and she nodded slowly.

"It certainly is," she said.

"Well, now, let's refrain from serious talk," Dieter said, setting his glass down and standing. "I may be getting older, but I believe my singing is improving with time."

Greta surreptitiously wiped her eyes as Dieter limped across the room. Bending down, he flipped open the shabby violin case from the floor, prying out an equally shabby violin. Soon, his warbling baritone voice combined with his off-key violin playing had both Oscar and Greta laughing until they cried. Isaiah, who had been napping, woke up and howled along with his master.

The next few days were simple and pleasant, following the same pattern. The spoke of family, the weather, their labors, and Oscar and Greta's nearing immigration to America. The evening conversations with Dieter were comforting and often funny, and the violin usually made at least one appearance. There were times, however, when Dieter would sit and stare at the wall. The young couple knew that when this happened, Dieter was lost in thoughts of the war that had never entirely left his mind. They let him have a moment of peace, doing sundry tasks until he was ready to talk again. During the second night, Greta woke to hear a cry of distress from the next room, though the sound quickly disappeared. She didn't say anything about it the next day.

Finally, on their third evening, supper and the conversation seemed to mellow Dieter into talking about his wartime experiences. Greta and Oscar stayed silent as Dieter spoke. His face, lit with the flickering oil lamps and the firelight, seemed to take on a grim cast despite the bouquet of vibrant cornflowers Greta had placed on the table beside him.

"My mother's parents, as you know, were from Denmark," Dieter said heavily, his eyes fixed on a knot in the pine wood wall. "They were Lutherans who moved to Germany, drawn by the reform of the Anabaptists, much like your family, Greta. They opposed war and killing in any form and were angry that the church made no effort to contest my conscription."

Dieter's face contorted with grief, and he suddenly looked many times his age. "During a battle, I bayoneted a young, unarmed, and wounded Danish soldier. When I killed that helpless boy, I felt as if I had plunged the bayonet through my own heart. Every night, I see his face in my dreams."

The three sat staring into the fire together for a moment, the silence punctuated by the crackling of the fire and Isaiah's quiet snores.

"No one should ever have to go through that," Oscar said finally. "I am so sorry, Uncle."

"Well, Oscar, I am telling you this because I want you to understand fully why your decision to leave Germany is for the best," Dieter said, looking at his nephew. His dark eyes glittered with emotion. " being drafted into some stupid inevitable war would benefit no one. The division over military service within the church has become much too complicated; those who won't fight or who leave for America are often regarded by this government as criminals. However, despite the church split over conscripted service, I do not doubt that you are making the best possible decision."

Leaning back in his chair, Dieter surveyed his two visitors. "The political situation is much more stable in the United States. By leaving, you can avoid going through the hell that likely awaits if you stay here. That's one of the reasons I wish to financially support your journey to America by any means I can."

Greta's eyes widened. "We so appreciate your offer, Uncle, but it is not necessary," she said, looking at Oscar, who nodded. "With certainty, war can come to any country, but at least we will have greater opportunities in America."

"Yes, better opportunities for you and your children," said Dieter, his eyes shifting to Greta. "Have you two planned or thought of . . ."

Greta's earnest expression seemed to shutter from within.

"Excuse me," she said abruptly, standing and striding to the front door. Isaiah instantly leaped up and trotted at her heels, following her out into the darkness toward the privy. Dieter looked at Oscar quizzically.

"I hope I did not offend her," he said. Oscar sighed and closed his eyes.

"We have been married over five years, and we have yet to conceive a child," Oscar told Dieter. "We have prayed at church to no avail."

Dieter let out a heavy sigh. "Ah," he said.

"Papa often told me that a grandson was what he wanted more than anything else before he passed on," Oscar said sadly. "But despite all of our prayers, it did not happen."

"That is a shame," Dieter said. "The pair of you would make good parents. I can tell."

Oscar leaned an elbow on the table and propped up his chin with a hand. "I never thought we would both reach the age of twenty-five with no children," he said. "I'm twenty-six now, in fact, and we still have no heir." An expression of sadness tugged at his young, handsome face. "I believe the reality is that we are incapable of having a child together. In fact, we have basically given up even trying."

"What a trial God has handed you," Dieter said. "Greta is obviously very sensitive to the topic."

"Greta is hard on herself," Oscar admitted. "She is a good wife with strong integrity, and she takes her obligations seriously. She is trusted and admired by those in our church whose opinions matter. Our inability to conceive has shaken her confidence and made her feel incomplete, I fear."

"That isn't fair. Greta seems to be a godly woman."

Oscar glanced toward the window through which the little outhouse could be seen. "Greta has had a hard life, but she always keeps a smile on her face. She was an only child, and after she lost her parents, naturally, she wanted to create a family of her own."

"Of course." Dieter took a sip of his warm buttermilk. "Have you or Greta consulted a doctor?"

"We rarely have the privilege of seeing a physician," Oscar replied, staring into the dancing flames. "Our work on the farm is difficult and leaves us little time to concern ourselves with health. The thought that there are perhaps medical reasons for our lack of conception has crossed my mind, but without the financial means for medical examination, it is not realistic to be consumed with such things."

"I could—" started Dieter, but Oscar shook his head.

"Your moral support is more than enough, Uncle," he said. "Perhaps once we get to America, we can see a doctor. We have some money left over from the purchase of the steamship tickets—the money we made from selling Papa's cows helped. We can use that when the time comes."

Dieter looked questioningly at Oscar. "I thought Uncle Fredrick arranged a passage for you two," he said.

"He offered to, certainly," said Oscar. "But we thought it would be unfair to ask for too much of his generosity, especially since he has offered to help us buy a farm in America. That is why we decided to pay for the passage ourselves. However, that is another matter; for now, we need to focus on our journey. Nevertheless, we greatly appreciate your offer, Uncle."

Just then, the front door opened, and Greta came in, Isaiah close behind.

"Morning will be waking the chickens before we know it,"

she said. "I think I will prepare for bed." Dieter nodded, carefully avoiding the subject of children as they set their empty glasses by the wash basin.

That night, Oscar held Greta in his arms and thought about his conversation with Dieter. He loved Greta deeply and instinctively knew that the subject of children would only cause her more pain. This was why he had become silent on the issue of late.

Oscar turned so he could see the outline of Greta's peaceful face in the moonlight. It was Greta's loyalty and honesty that had attracted Oscar to her in the first place. Planting a soft kiss on Greta's forehead, Oscar knew he would put those qualities above all else, even the possibility of creating a family. If having children was not likely with Greta, he rationalized, that was God's will. Holding his dear wife, he breathed in her familiar smell and soon fell fast asleep.

2
The Prediction
(Die Vorhersage)

The next day, as the three enjoyed a sumptuous breakfast of weisswurst[2], blood sausage, fried eggs, apple pancakes, and rye bread with strawberry preserves, Dieter announced that he had to go to a nearby town to complete a stonemason job. Around the trio, the home seemed a bit brighter thanks to the cornflowers Greta had placed in glasses around the main room.

"My journeyman, Rudolph, and I will be traveling to the worksite within the next hour," he said after swallowing a bite of blood sausage, so dark it was nearly black. "I promise to be home by supper, and I will leave the surrey and mare in case you two would like to travel to the forest to hunt steinpilz."

Greta's eyes began to widen at the mention of the small, thick, white fungi with toasted-brown caps. Oscar glanced at her and smiled.

---

2   Bavarian veal and bacon sausage named for its white color

"Yes, I think we will do that, Uncle," he said. "Steinplitz mushrooms are one of Greta's favorite delicacies."

"I will bring a paring knife and the wicker basket you have in the kitchen to cut and gather them," Greta said enthusiastically. She stood to refill Dieter's milk cup, already dreaming of the little mushrooms that nestled in the forest leaves starting in late spring, though they were often difficult to see. The steinpilz were delicious when brewed in stews or soups, but Greta's favorite preparation was sautéing them in butter and wild garlic. Just the thought of finding a basket made her giddy.

Soon, the journeyman pulled up in his wagon. Around Oscar and Greta's age, he had a round face and a thick black full beard. He waved as Dieter climbed aboard the wagon, the couple and Isaiah trailing behind him.

Greta pulled her shawl around herself against the morning chill; the air was cold and straightforward, but there were few clouds in the sky, and she thought they would enjoy a beautiful Lord's Day. She had donned a one-piece dress and apron that would do nicely for the mushroom-hunting excursion.

"Rudolph, this is my nephew Oscar and his wife Greta," Dieter said. "They are going mushroom hunting today."

"Ah, the steinpilz!" Rudolph said. "I hope you find plenty."

"We will set some aside for you," Greta said.

"That's very kind," Rudolph replied.

"We must be off. Have a day of merriment, you two!" Dieter said. He started to turn, then reversed his course and looked at Oscar.

"Oscar, you've been here before, so you'll remember that the woods are generally safe," he said. "Only small herds of red deer wander the forest. Wolf sightings are rare since farmers have killed off most. Nevertheless, a fox or two might be about. They seem to enjoy eating my chickens as much as I do," he said. "Though I never seem to have the heart to shoot them."

"We will be careful," Oscar said. "God bless you, Uncle!"

Rudolph tipped his hat and was about to pull away when Dieter turned again.

"Oh, by the way, it is best to keep an eye out for Jenische!" he said. "They're harmless enough, but they are just not a very principled lot."

"What do you mean?" Greta asked.

"They are tired of being maligned," Dieter said, "and now they seem to be attempting to blend into the German landscape. Most of the families still travel in their wooden wagons and have some dealings with locals. They earn a living by telling fortunes, tinkering, and blacksmithing." Dieter nodded to himself. "There are those that believe they are descendants of the Romani, though the Romani are much more aloof."

"Those vermin all have mixed Yekke blood and speak a secret language," Rudolph said. Dieter gave him a disapproving glance before turning back to his nephew and niece.

"Anyway, as I was saying," Dieter said, "the Jenische seem to have conflicts with the Romani, and they keep their distance. The Jenische aren't usually a threat to anyone . . . they are like scattered stars in the sky. You can find them everywhere in Europe, living as they may." Rudolph grunted derisively, but Dieter ignored him, his eyes determinedly fixed on his relatives.

"They are probably not so different from us," Oscar said, peering curiously at Rudolph. "I'm sure they love their families and do what they feel is necessary for survival."

"Precisely," Dieter said. "And now, we really must be off. I shall see you both later!"

Greta and Oscar waved as Rudolph and Dieter rode away, Isaiah briefly giving chase as Rudolph drove the wagon down the road. When the wagon was out of sight, Oscar and Greta looked at each other.

"What is so wrong with Jenische blending in with the locals because they feel it is the best way to avoid conflict?" Greta asked.

"I am not sure," Oscar said. "Rudolph seemed to find it objectionable. Truly, Greta, I have a feeling most people around here would agree with him."

"Our local church is willing to welcome Jenische people to share meals and fellowship when they pass by. I've seen that before," Greta said. "We can certainly sympathize with societal bias because of our passive nonpolitical beliefs."

"That is true, but the Jenische are still outsiders to our faith," Oscar pointed out. Greta knew this was true. The Jenische usually practiced the local religion wherever they chose to settle, and in the German Republic's Prussia, the dominant religion happened to be Protestant Christianity. The Jenische, therefore, attempted to placate the local parishioners by following the same direction of faith.

"Yes, but we can identify with the Gypsies' struggles," she insisted. "It makes sense that the church brethren generally trust Gypsies. After all, we must welcome all strangers."

"Greta, you have a good heart," said Oscar, placing a hand on Greta's shoulder. "I agree with you, and clearly, Uncle Dieter does also. However, we must be cautious. Gypsies are known for practices that run contrary to our church beliefs. You know they practice divination, which is a blasphemous practice enabled by Satan."

"Of course," Greta said. "We will be cautious." She did not mention that she had always been curious about clairvoyance. In passing, she had once mentioned her interest to Oscar before they were married, but he seemed to have selectively forgotten her statement. It was also possible that he had decided the less said on the subject, the better, she mused.

Eager for their excursion, Oscar and Greta loaded their surrey with a blanket, an axe, friction matches, and a large cloth sack containing a simple lunch of cheese, rye bread, cured ham, and hard-boiled eggs. There were a few bottles of Federweisser[3] in the cellar; Greta thought this was likely kept for guests, as Dieter didn't seem to indulge in alcohol himself. In adherence with the avoidance of all fermented drinks or stimulants in German Baptist culture, Oscar avoided the wine and chose a bottle of unfermented sweet grape juice instead. A small sack of oats for the mare rounded out the tightly loaded carriage.

"You'll have to stay here, boy," Greta said to Isaiah, who looked at her reproachfully. "I don't think you'll do well in the surrey, and you might trample the mushrooms."

The couple followed the road on the edge of the dark Tarnow forest, pursued briefly by Isaiah, who quickly gave up and stood in the road, tail between his legs, as the carriage disappeared. It was now half past nine, and the sun was creeping higher in the sky, revealing a landscape of forests and wetlands dotted with patches of vibrant green. As the mare ambled forward, the surrey rhythmically lurched eastward along the sandy dirt road rutted by wagon tracks.

---

3   A type of carbonated alcoholic beverage made from freshly pressed grape juice

Just ahead to the left, Greta saw smoke from a campfire. Craning her neck, she saw that it was rising from the small chimney stack of a brightly painted and carved round-roofed Gypsy wagon nestled within the forest.

"Jenische, just as your uncle said," Greta said quietly, nudging Oscar. Neither Oscar nor Greta felt fearful as the surrey slowly passed by. The sweet scent of goulash wafted from the camp.

"There is no large caravan, only one lone wagon," said Oscar.

Greta carefully examined the scene, trying to appear nonchalant. Two draft horses grazed on the sweet grass by the roadside. A dark-skinned, middle-aged man dressed in peasant's clothing, with his pant legs tucked into his high black boots, knelt and oiled the tack for the two horses. An older woman with snow-white hair tended the campfire kettle from which the smell of garlic emanated. She wore a loose, dark headscarf and black calico dress, and a short clay pipe protruded from between her withered lips.

Looking up from the kettle, the woman gave a slight smile and raised her chin, staring at Greta as the couple passed by. Greta greeted her with a friendly wave.

The mare tugged the couple's small coach around a bend and up the meandering road into the forest. The breeze carried the earthy smell of the woodland, and the foliage of pine and hardwood trees closed in around the couple as they traveled deeper into the forest. At last, Oscar stopped beside a small brook at the base of a wooded hill.

"This will do," he said.

"We should search the area on the hillside," Greta said. "It's a good place to begin." As Greta took the blanket, food sack, and basket from the wagon, Oscar unhitched the mare and loosely tethered her near the brook. He measured a ration of oats for the horse to supplement the Dutch clover covering the ground.

"Shall we begin?" Oscar asked. Greta nodded, her eyes shining with anticipation. Since both she and Oscar had grown up in the country, they were quite aware of which mushrooms were edible and which were not, and there was no danger of accidentally selecting a poison specimen.

The couple had only gone a few steps when Greta called out, "Here! I've found one!" There, hiding in dead leaves, stood a mushroom nearly three inches high. The fungi had a few minor marks on its cap where a critter had nibbled at it, but it was otherwise perfect.

Greta knelt and carefully cut the stock of the mushroom at its base, then covered the stem with leaves so it would regrow. Oscar, encouraged by Greta's find, climbed higher up the hill, poking through leaf piles around the trees with a short walking stick.

The couple searched for an hour, wandering further into the forest and discovering dozens of undisturbed mushrooms. The breeze was gentle and warm, and the tall trees creaked and twisted in the wind as the pair searched, feeling peaceful and far from the drudgery of working on the government farm. Greta's basket was nearly complete when they both decided to stop for lunch.

"Dieter's home and the surrounding area are very quaint," Greta said as she spread out their picnic. "It has been nice visiting him and getting to know him better."

"He is special to me," Oscar said. "It was good that we could visit him before we voyaged to America. I think he likes you, Greta."

"I have a feeling he likes most people," Greta said teasingly.

The couple fell into an easy banter, and though they discussed much, they automatically avoided the subject of beginning a family. Finally, Greta shook out and folded the blanket; then, the companions took a short jaunt a little further into the woods to fill the rest of the basket.

Greta's eye was fixed on the ground as she searched for mushrooms, but some instinct suddenly prompted her to look up. She was surprised to find she was inches away from a crumbling stone wall. Peering around it, she gasped and rushed forward, momentarily forgetting all about the steinpilz.

"I've kept sight of the way back to the surrey," she heard Oscar call. "It will soon be time to return to Dieter's farm."

"Oscar, never mind that for now. Come look at what I've found!" Greta cried.

Oscar found Greta standing in the center of a circle of six megaliths, some over shoulder high. The spotted dolerite rocks, covered by lichens and moss, were unlike anything either of them had seen before. The green velvet grass inside the stone circle was compressed and flattened; it appeared that deer or something larger had bedded there overnight.

"Early people built such circles for spiritual purposes, to honor their dead," Oscar said, loitering at the edge of the stones. "The church bids us hold sacred and honor those who have lived before us. We mustn't desecrate this place."

Greta, however, didn't seem to be listening. She turned in circular patterns around the stones, examining and touching each one. Her fingers tingled as she ran them over the ancient rocks while detecting a whiff of cinnamon in the air.

Feeling strangely energized, Greta was overcome by a sudden urge. She unfolded the blanket and spread it on the ground in the center of the circle. Turning toward Oscar, Greta outstretched her arms to him. Her gaze followed Oscar as he stepped into the stone ring, his expression shifting from reluctance to desire. Oscar gently took Greta's hand, then enfolded her in his arms.

Greta looked deeply into Oscar's eyes as if to reassure him. Slowly, they tumbled to the ground, entwined in love's embrace. Laying upon the blanket, the couple soon found themselves staring at the tree branches rhythmically swaying above them as they pulled each other closer.

Time and space seemed suspended by the power within the circle's flow. Within the heartbeat of a sparrow, an hour had passed. Oscar slowly stood and straightened his clothing.

"I will walk down the hill to bridle and hitch the mare for the trip back to Uncle Dieter's house," he said. His voice sounded strange after the mesmerizing silence.

"I will join you soon, my husband," Greta said. She watched Oscar carefully pick his way down the hill through the woodland toward the brook, soon disappearing. Slowly, she stood to brush the grass from her dress and fold the blanket.

The strange euphoria of the circle began to give way to the uncomfortable sensation of being watched. A red squirrel in a nearby tree began to chatter nervously as Greta glanced to her left, wary. Standing by a tall oak tree, the largest she-wolf Greta had ever seen stood watching her.

Greta froze. Her mind flashed to her childhood when she and her parents had visited the zoological gardens in Hamburg. There, she saw a wolf for the first time. This creature, however, was much, much larger than any zoo animal. With its gray coat flecked with black, the beast held Greta in its all-consuming gaze. It slowly lowered its shoulders and began moving forward.

Greta stood still, her heart pounding inside her chest. Her terror increased when she saw the smaller tan and gray male flanked the she-wolf. Both animals stared intently at her.

Greta knew she should not run. She knew also she would not be able to fend off the wolves alone. So, instead of running, she turned and faced them. She felt almost as if she could have reached out and touched their coarse, bristling fur. The beasts' eyes remained fixed on Greta's face, and with a strong sense of disorientation, Greta wondered if this would be her last moment on Earth.

A breeze rustled the tree leaves, and the she-wolf tilted her head, rolling her stare downward at Greta's belly. The large wolf remained still for what seemed an eternity as Greta's heart thundered. The stones stood as silent witnesses to the impasse.

Finally, the canine pivoted her ears and cocked her head, taking a glance toward the smaller wolf at her side. She then took a final step forward and stood upright on her back legs, her face level with Greta's. For a moment, Greta's breath stopped as she looked deep into the enormous wolf's amber eyes. A warm, sweet smell enveloped her, and air whooshed out of her lungs. All the fear that had overwhelmed her flowed away.

As quickly as it had reared, the animal silently returned to its natural four-legged stance. Without pausing, the she-wolf turned and retreated into the deep woods, her companion following closely behind.

Greta, now shaking with adrenaline and lack of air, left the stone circle. She stumbled down the hill to where Oscar had just finished hitching the mare, and when he turned and looked at Greta's face, his expression clouded with worry.

"Are you alright?" Oscar asked. Greta closed her eyes.

"Yes," she said, "Maybe just tired from the hike." For some reason, she could not find the words to explain what had just occurred.

Oscar moved toward Greta and held her in his arms. "You tremble," he said. When Greta didn't reply, Oscar helped her into the wagon and steered the horse back to the road without pressing the issue further.

After the couple had ridden on in silence for a few minutes, Greta touched Oscar's hand.

"Please stop at the Gypsy camp," she said.

"The church elders frown on such fraternization, especially if it involves fortune-telling," Oscar warned.

"I know," Greta said, her eyes hazy. Oscar looked at her expression and said no more.

Though the old Jenische woman was nowhere to be seen when the couple approached the lone wagon, the embers of the campfire still glowed. In the distance, Greta could hear someone chopping wood in the forest. She helped herself down from the surrey, her long skirts swishing around her ankles.

"I'll not be long," she said. Oscar nodded, a tiny wrinkle appearing between his brows. She touched his cheek before turning and approaching the painted trailer.

The late afternoon wind began to kick dust about as Greta stepped up the wooden stairs and lightly knocked on the wagon door. Moments passed, and then slowly, the door opened, the pungent smell of burning oud wafting out to meet Greta. The older woman, still in her long black calico dress and headscarf, nodded at Greta as if she'd been waiting for her. Up close, Greta saw a myriad of wrinkles in the Gypsy's brown face. An ancient-looking bronze Celtic cross dangled on a small chain around the woman's neck.

"Welcome," she said, her words carrying a Yiddish lilt. She beckoned Greta into the small, neatly arranged quarters. Candles flickered as Greta's eyes adjusted and surveyed the unfamiliar surroundings.

Red tapestry blanketed the inside of the vardo. Handmade pans, pots, and wicker baskets hung on the walls, and a thick, red, handwoven Persian rug covered the floor. A small cooking stove occupied one end of the trailer, with curtained bunk beds at the other. A small round table covered by draped black linen dominated the center of the living space.

"I am Tshura," the old woman said. "Come sit." She pointed toward one of two wooden chairs on the left side of the table. Greta slid into one.

"You visited the Geisterkreis[4] in the forest?" the old woman asked. Greta's eyebrows shot up.

"Yes," she told Tshura. "We found a place where large stones were placed in a circle."

"A passageway, built long ago, for spirits to travel from one realm to the next," the Jenische woman said flatly. "There are those who say if you enter the ring and a schutzengel judges you to be worthy, that guardian angel will follow and protect you."

Greta thought immediately of the amber eyes of the she-wolf. She swallowed hard.

"Brethren precept indicates something similar," she told Tshura. "It says God often sends angels to guide and protect the faithful, as written in the book of Psalms." A shiver ran down her

---

4   German for "ghost circle"

spine, and Tshura looked hard at Greta's face, nodding as if she understood.

"Give me your hand, child," Tshura said, holding out her own. Greta automatically proffered her hand, and the Gypsy studied Greta's palm intently, tracing the lines below Greta's little finger. She glanced up at Greta, her wizened face crinkled into a smile.

"You will bear two children," she said, stretching her free hand across the table and pointing at Greta's stomach. "Even now, you carry a new life inside you, a boy child perhaps."

Greta's heart began to beat rapidly, and she felt her face flush. Tshura touched each line of Greta's open palm as if sensing a coded message.

"You have found your true love, and I see a long journey for you both," the Gypsy whispered hoarsely. "Your life in this new place will not be easy, however. There is hard work and struggle ahead. It seems death will try to make its claim before your time on Earth is complete. But do not fear, for around you is a strong force that will protect and guide you."

Tshura then reached for Greta's other hand. She looked hard at Greta's palm while Greta's mind raced. Was she truly with child?

"You have a good sense about you, and it will keep you safe," Tshura finally said. "However, you must not only rely on yourself. God will send you friends who will try to guide you, but always first do what your heart commands."

Tshura released Greta's hand. Shaking her head as if waking from a trance, Greta reached into her dress pocket, took out two copper pfennigs, and held them in her palm to the Gypsy. Tshura took Greta's fingers and gently folded them over the pennies.

"Save your coins, child," she said, "for your life only now begins." Greta smiled.

"Thank you," she said. Tshura ushered her to the door and, thanking the Gypsy again, Greta stepped into the blinding light of day.

Oscar had nodded off in the buggy; he was slumped into an uncomfortable position in the seat as the mare grazed. Greta looked at him fondly for a moment, smiling to herself before gently touching his hand. Oscar's eyes fluttered open, unfocused for a moment before fixing on Greta.

"You look better," he said.

"Yes, somewhat," she said. "Let's go back to Uncle Dieter's now."

Greta took her seat in the surrey, and in just a few moments, the small Jenische camp was out of sight.

"Dieter will be pleased with the mushrooms," Oscar said as they traversed the bumpy road.

"Oh, certainly. We have plenty for Rudolph also," Greta said. She paused, then added, "I saw various cooking pans for sale in the vardo, but I decided against buying one."

"I am sure Dieter has an appropriate pan for the steinpilz," Oscar said. The pair fell into an easy conversation about how to prepare the delicacy. Oscar did not ask Greta anything else about her visit to the Jenische camp, and Greta did not volunteer the information. She knew Oscar would worry about what would happen if the church found out she had visited a seer.

The whole way back to Dieter's, Greta sat unusually close to Oscar. Oscar leaned over to place his head atop hers a few times. The couple did not mention their intimacy at the stone circle aloud; such things were to be held close, internally cherished, but never openly discussed. It was, however, clear to Greta that something had changed. She felt even more connected with Oscar as they completed the journey back to Dieter's farm, laden with steinpilz and perhaps something that meant even much more.

3
The Journey
(Die Reise)
July 1895

G reta and Oscar stood with their heads bowed, standing in a circle with three bearded church elders. Around them, the seaport of Bremerhaven in the city of Bremen, Germany, bustled with activity. The gray iron-wheeled cargo wagon creaked and rocked nearby as draft horses pulled it along the dock to the massive, moored ship. There, officials would register and offload Oscar and Greta's trunk and belongings for passage to America.

"Dear Lord, we ask that you grant Sister Greta and Brother Oscar your mercy and protection as they begin their voyage," Brother Franz prayed in his soothing, familiar voice. "We ask that you guide their new life so they are worthy of the mercy and love you send the world. In the name of our Lord and Savior Jesus Christ, we ask all these things. Amen."

As the prayer ended, all six German Baptists looked up once again in wonder at the SS Saale, a massive iron-hulled steamship with two large funnels and four masts. Greta took in a deep breath of salty air. She felt blessed that on this day, July 27, 1895, the embarkation had finally arrived.

"I have never seen such a sight outside of pictures," Greta said. She and Oscar reflexively took each other's hands, admiringly studying the magnificent sea vessel. "It's no wonder so many passengers fit inside."

"I wish we had the chance to tour the ship," Brother Franz said as they gazed upward, his long beard fluttering in the breeze. He and the other elders, dressed in white linen shirts and leather-suspendered black trousers, looked distinguished among the harried and disarrayed city folk. "It has a good reputation and history."

Greta's gaze wandered to the hull of the ship. She knew, once inside, they would be housed below. The SS Saale was capable of holding 1,000 people in steerage, and Greta instinctively knew it would be a cramped and challenging voyage. Steerage travel was widely known to be the most dangerous for passengers, as criminal predators were always about. Such third-class travel was crowded and unsanitary, offering very little modesty, but it was also the least costly.

Greta knew that had they taken Uncle Fredrick up on his offer to arrange steamship travel, they would likely have had their cabin. However, paying for this portion of the journey themselves had been the right thing to do. They did not, after all, want to take undue advantage of Uncle Fredrick.

"We will write to you about all our experience on the ship," Oscar told Brother Franz.

"Yes, please do," Brother Gunter said. He was the oldest of the elders present and seemed to forget things often these days, but his hoary eyes were kind as he looked upon the young couple. "We will pray for your safe arrival each day."

"Well, with that, we will be off," said Brother Hamm, looking distrustfully around at the hubbub of the port. "We would stay longer if we could wave at you from the shore, but since you won't be on deck, that seems futile."

"Oh," said Brother Gunter. "That's too bad."

"Yes," Oscar said. "We are not allowed, as third class, on the top deck unless invited. The first-class passengers wouldn't want us occupying their areas of the ship."

"It would be nice to see the ocean at night, though," Greta said with a sigh.

"Perhaps you will," Brother Fisher said with a small smile. "May God watch over you on your journey."

In typical German Baptist Brethren fashion, the group said their goodbyes without undue emotion. However, Greta felt a pang as she watched the four men retreat. She had known them ever since she was fourteen when she had moved in with her grandmother. Now, she suspected she would never see them again.

"Come," Oscar said, taking her hand. Together, the couple turned and walked toward the looming SS Saale.

Steerage proved squalid and poorly ventilated, as suspected. The damp, foul air, already smelling of vomit and rat urine, formed a haze in the light of the kerosene lamps. Greta and Oscar were assigned to family berthing; in addition to couples and families trying desperately to maintain some semblance of privacy, the confined space held freight boxes, mailbags, and luggage.

Oscar and Greta took their place on makeshift wooden cots near a bulkhead. Positioned by the stairwell in the starboard hull of the ship, they hoped to catch a breath of fresh air now and again.

"Our home for the next ten days," Greta said, looking forlornly around.

Oscar patted her knee. "In favorable weather, possibly as little as eight. It shouldn't be too bad. Besides, I overheard one of the other steerage passengers saying we may be allowed to look at the Liberty Statue from the deck once we reach the New York harbor."

Greta perked up. Despite feeling more tired than usual, she knew she could tolerate anything for a week or two.

"A new, safe home with economic opportunities is well worth a short stretch of discomfort," she said.

After a few hours, their first meal was announced. The group made their way up to a contained galley above the sleeping area for their supper. Long, gray wooden tables and benches stretched in rows across the room. Each person made their way through a line to receive tea, water, potatoes, white bread, and vegetable and boiled beef soup. Greta and Oscar found a space on the cramped benches, but Greta found she could only stomach the bread and a bit of the broth.

"I must be a bit seasick already," she said, offering the rest of her food to Oscar. He frowned, then tucked his uneaten bread into his pocket.

"You can eat it later," he said at Greta's questioning look, pulling her soup toward him. "We must keep our strength up."

Keeping their strength up proved difficult. Five and a half days into the trip, Greta and Oscar found themselves having trouble sleeping. Far past midnight, Oscar stared resignedly at the ceiling, contemplating the journey so far as nearby a baby began to scream. The ship had made a brief stop in Southampton, England, to pick up more cargo crates, laborers, passengers, and security personnel before making way for America. This made the already cramped steerage even more crowded, but everyone did their best to stay agreeable.

Meals had varied little. They usually had a gruel made of oats, rye, and wheat thinned into a watery base for breakfast. Dinners sometimes included salted pork or fish instead of beef, as well as pickles. The nearly inedible mush that the ship's staff insisted was some vegetable or fruit was everyone's least favorite item. Greta's appetite had waned as periodic bouts of nausea overtook her, and Oscar had continued to secret away as much bread as he could for her to munch on in their bunk.

On the fourth day, a somber-looking health inspector had made his way through the crudely partitioned third-class quarters accompanied by a burly man with a cauliflower ear, a scarred crooked nose, and a large walrus mustache. The unlikely pair caused a lot of nervousness among the passengers. Oscar had watched warily as Greta did her best to appear in good health during her inspection; she stood tall and pleasantly smiled as the inspecting officer looked her up and down and checked her throat and eyes. Both she and Oscar knew the health inspector would separate anyone sickly from the rest of the group, and a quarantine was the last thing the couple wanted. At last, the health inspector and his mustachioed bodyguard had moved on.

Now, Oscar felt Greta turn over yet again, breathing heavily. The ventilation of their berthing area was better than most due to the nearby stairwell. Still, the late July temperatures intensified the heat of the ship's lower quarters, already heightened by proximity to the boiler room. Oscar's shirt seemed permanently stuck to his person. Nearby, the howling baby's voice was accompanied by the loud snores of another passenger.

Oscar felt Greta rise. He turned to see her staring at the stairwell, and following her gaze, he saw the brilliant silver of moonlight flooding down. They could not see the sky or even the door, but the intense white glow had clearly been enough to draw her to do the unthinkable.

Greta looked over at Oscar and held her finger to her lips. On silent feet, she approached the stairs. Stifling a groan, Oscar rose and followed.

"There may be consequences if we go to the first-class area," Oscar whispered urgently in Greta's ear. Greta took no heed, slipping up the steep and narrow metal steps. Ahead, the bulkhead door hung slightly ajar. Oscar followed closely, tightly gripping her hand.

Like two curious children approaching forbidden sweets, Greta and Oscar poked their heads out the door. No attendant stopped them. In the briny ocean breeze, the temperature felt many degrees cooler. Looking at each other in silent confirmation, the pair swung the door open and stepped onto the top wooden deck.

Above, the sky shimmered with countless stars and a luminous moon. Oscar had never seen the sky this intense or the moon so close in Germany. At intervals, shooting stars streaked across the scene.

"Look," Greta said, his eyes downcast to the lunar reflection on the rolling sea. The couple walked to the rail, looking out at the horizon. With relief, Oscar felt his sweat-soaked garments drying in the cool breeze. Occasional flying fish below in the moonlight only added to the excitement as the large ship smoothly cut through the water and the salt breeze rushed past.

"I have never seen anything so beautiful," Greta softly whispered at length.

"God's power is great," Oscar said, drawing Greta close to him and holding her in his arms. The private moment washed away their wariness and modesty. Tenderly kissing and gazing into each other's eyes, Oscar and Greta bathed in the moonlight that shone so brightly, burning every detail of the upper deck and ocean into their memory.

Greta and Oscar were not alone, however. Their innocuous climb to the starboard deck had attracted a dark-cloaked stranger who followed at a distance until he was sure no one was watching.

"Who the bloody hell do you think you two are?" the stranger said in a brusque voice with a thick cockney accent. Neither Oscar nor Greta spoke English, and they were startled to find someone so unkempt had followed them. The man, sporting oily hair and a four-day growth of beard, stood a mere two meters behind the couple.

The man approached, pulling a sharp utility knife with a four-inch blade from his grimy coat pocket. He stared at Greta, who was clad in her usual German Baptist garb and white bonnet.

"Now I wonder, you little tart, what milk and honey you've got hiding under all that rig-out[5]," the intruder mockingly cooed, moving the knife from one hand to the other.

This man may only mean to steal from us, but there is also a chance he is desperate enough to inflict injury, Oscar thought. He was all too aware that the Anabaptist faith forbade violence of any

---

5   Antiquated term for a bizarre costume

kind, even in self-defense. The German Baptists took "turning the other cheek," as biblically stated, literally.

Oscar watched the man intently as he swiped the knife back and forth through the air, moving closer and closer. Greta stood passively, looking remarkably calm, her back to the rail and the sea.

Oscar knew the time for action had come. Gritting his teeth, he stepped swiftly in front of Greta. The blade of the knife came close enough to tear the material of his coat. Oscar felt the blade's force against his jacket, and then he heard the sound of a hollow, ringing thump. His assailant crumpled to the wooden deck.

Standing where the thief had stood seconds before was a mustached, hulking man weighing at least 240 pounds. His small police badge gleamed in the moonlight, half hidden by his green tweed overcoat. A spark of recognition flared; this was the health inspector's companion from yesterday.

A pugilist, thought Oscar, looking at the marks of battle the prominent officer wore on his face. This man was very different from the pacifist church folk he was used to.

The officer stood staring downward at the crumpled figure on deck like a lion admiring its prey. He gently tapped his foot-long billy club into the palm of his hand.

"I've been watching this lad for a time now," the man said in a low, parched Irish brogue. He fumbled in his coat pocket, pulling out a pair of nickel-plated handcuffs.

"I'll be putting ya in the gyves fer yer own protection, sawn," the large policeman said in a taunting manner to the man. The only response he received was a groan. Oscar and Greta both stood motionless, clutching each other as the officer cuffed the collapsed criminal's hands behind his back.

The constable then stood up and pulled at Oscar's coat.

"Alright, are ya?" the Irishman asked. Though Oscar could not understand a word the man was saying, the man's intent was clear. With a trembling hand, Oscar pointed out the small cut the thief's sharp knife had left in the fabric of Oscar's coat. Miraculously, the blade had not broken his skin.

"Lucky lad," said the deck cop as Greta ran her hand over the tear, making sure he was not injured.

"I can repair this," she said in German, her voice uncharacteristically shaky.

There came a scraping sound from behind them. Everyone turned as the fallen criminal struggled to pull himself forward, but the large policeman grasped the nape of his coat with one hand and quickly pulled the man to his feet. The policeman turned the thief and faced him eye to eye, grabbing him by the throat and slamming his back into the bulkhead of the ship. Oscar and Greta jumped simultaneously.

The cop stared deep into the criminal's eyes. The man made eye contact for a few seconds before looking down and away.

"I own ya now, lad, don't I?" the policeman whispered into the broken man's face before leading the would-be thief toward an ascending stairwell. The large constable turned as he was leaving and pointed with his nightstick to the lower stairwell that Oscar and Greta had ascended.

"Best ya boa' be getting back down da stair, where you belong, afore the ship's purser starts chargin' ya first-class fare," he said. He chuckled loudly before striding away with his unfortunate companion. His meaning was clear to Oscar and Greta, who slowly went back down to steerage, returning to their wooden bunks.

"You were willing to risk your life for me," Greta said, laying her head on Oscar's chest. Oscar softly placed his arm around Greta's shoulder.

"It is God's word that I should always do so, Greta," he said. As they held each other and drew closer, Greta whispered, "Did you see his eyes?"

"Whose?" Oscar said sleepily.

"The policeman. They were deep amber . . . almost gold. Strange . . ."

"Hmm," Oscar said, and he fell promptly asleep.

* * *

Five days later, Oscar and Greta's voyage ended at last. The Brethren couple anxiously sat in vigil over their steamer trunk and bags, finally ashore in their new country. They'd thought the worst was over when they'd left steerage behind, but two days at the immigration center at Castle Garden had been chaotic. In the large round-stone immigration building, they had proceeded through the required health inspections and paperwork, along with a short quarantine. The herding and examination had left the couple feeling overwhelmed, and they had clung tightly to each other during the slow and degrading processing procedure.

When the couple had emerged, the haphazardly organized, row-by-row, trial-and-error search for luggage and trunks had taken several hours. Now, Oscar kept his watchful eyes on the petty thieves, swindlers, and lookers-on who strolled the areas where hordes of immigrants gathered, waiting to assimilate into America. When Oscar took Greta's hand, he found it was as cold as stone. They had been waiting a good while, and the harbor breeze had begun to chill as evening closed in.

Nearby, some immigrants attempted, through mixed languages, to barter with the horse cab and wagon drivers and determine the locations of nearby boarding houses. Oscar watched them with pity. For those with little or no money, finding labor opportunities and cheap shelter was a pressing task.

The sun cast an orange glow across Greta's pale face. She looked exhausted, with blue bags under her eyes and a layer of dirt on her cheeks. Both she and Oscar were in desperate need of a good meal, a bath, a change of clothing, and sleep.

Oscar looked around for what felt like the thousandth time. He was beginning to worry, though he did not say so aloud. German Baptist clergy from the East 14th Street church in New York were supposed to meet them here; Uncle Fredrick had contacted them through the Indiana district. The coordination process had taken several months of planning due to the plodding pace of mail delivery, but all was reportedly in order. However, Oscar had only the assurance of Fredrick's letter he had received months before. What if there had been some miscommunication?

Greta leaned on Oscar's shoulder. Oscar saw a few vagabonds scooting closer to their suitcases, and he tried to look stern. Despite his concerns, he attempted to maintain the German Baptist tradition of never allowing oneself to become ill-humored or gloomy.

"We must be careful and take turns if we sleep," Oscar said. "Otherwise, our belongings will soon be stolen from under our noses. However, I'm sure the brothers will be here soon." Just as the words left his mouth, he spotted a small horse-drawn wagon coming down the street among the chaos. The three bearded men decked in black broad-brimmed hats and dark collarless suits sitting on the wagon were a piece of home, clearly demarcated from others on the busy streets.

"Greta!" Oscar said, pointing. He felt the muscles in her hand relax as she saw the familiar-looking men approaching. They had located Oscar and Greta easily, thanks to their garb, and in a few seconds, the wagon pulled up in front of the travel-worn couple.

"Hallo, Freunde," a man called to them in German.

Oscar and Greta enthusiastically greeted their American church brothers and quickly loaded up their few belongings. As they rode across town toward the German Baptist Brethren Church, Oscar finally felt like he could relax. He looked around at the sights and sounds of the city surrounding them. The day was winding down, and fruit and vegetable cart owners packed up their wares for the evening. Children played stickball in the streets, hanging onto the last moments of sunlight and fun before they had to go inside for the night. Laughter and singing, drinking, and arguing poured from the brightly lit taverns. Many immigrants walked about, sidestepping new street repairs and building construction—the smells of ethnic foods hung in the warm air.

"There is nothing serene or traditional here like in the cities in Germany," Greta said. When Oscar glanced at her, he saw that her eyes were alight with curiosity about the new adventure. The noise and gaiety excited her, her fatigue momentarily forgotten.

"Our Lord tells us not to imitate abominable practices of foreign lands," Oscar quietly reminded Greta so the Brethren in the front of the wagon couldn't hear.

"Of course, I will maintain spiritual focus," Greta said.

After an hour's ride through the busy streets and tall buildings, the wagon pulled in front of the large stone East Street German church, with its towering spires pointing to heaven and glorifying God.[6]

6   This is the real First Baptist East Church at 336 E. 14th Street near First Avenue in New York City. The building is now a designated historic site and the home of Town and Village Synagogue: Town & Village Synagogue (tandv.org)

"Our church was built shortly following the Civil War," Brother Wagner, the eldest of their companions, said, looking up at the church. "It has been an inspiration for those of the faith."

"It is indeed a welcome sight," Oscar said.

The elders settled Oscar and Greta into a temporary rooming area, where they had time to wash, change, and have a bite to eat before going into the central part of the church for fellowship and prayer.

"We know you must be starving, but try not to overeat just yet," Brother Wagner said before excusing himself. "We have prepared a traditional German meal for after the service."

"Greta, are you feeling alright?" Oscar said as soon as Brother Wagner closed the door. Greta had slumped down on the bed and closed her eyes. "I can tell them you need to sleep."

"I am fine, Oscar," Greta said. "I don't want to be rude to our hosts."

Indeed, both Greta and Oscar felt somewhat refreshed once they had washed away the dirt of the road and enjoyed the bread, cheese, and sausage the brothers had provided. Upon entering the magnificent sanctuary, they found that the inside the house of God was, as expected, quite plain so as to not distract from the purpose of consecrated worship. Rows of wooden benches with no pretense or ornamentation provided seating, and only a few religious paintings hung on the walls. Gas lights and candles provided illumination for the evening prayers.

Though the German Baptist Church was segregated by gender, with women and girls on one side of the church aisle and men and boys on the other, Oscar and Greta always tried to sit in an aisle seat so they were as near to each other as they could manage. They did this now, and they tried hard to understand the English prayers.

"We thank you, God, for the safe arrival of our brother and sister from Germany," the pastor said at the end of the usual prayer. A few heads turned to look at the young couple, who smiled pleasantly.

During the meal, which indeed included many favorites from home, Oscar and Greta sat with the elders and discussed the coming journey west. True to his word, Uncle Fredrick had arranged connections between train and wagon to the last detail.

"You will both travel to Indiana by way of Pennsylvania and Ohio," a tall, serious-looking clergyman named Wolfgang Mahler told Oscar, lancing a piece of knockwurst.[7] "You are expected to arrive sometime in late August or early September. Once you arrive, you will take your place in the small Brethren community near Peru."

"How many are in the congregation there?" Oscar asked, hungrily swallowing a large bite of braised cabbage.

"About forty families, I believe. Meetings took place in barns and homes there until a few years ago, when a small church also was built on a church brother's farmland in Washington township."

"God provides," said Oscar.

"Yes, the Lord knows what we need," Brother Mahler said. "And His people do what they can to provide for others in His name. Many of the Indiana Brethren assisted in the underground railway movement before the great Civil War. They helped many enslaved people from the South travel to Canada and Michigan."[8]

---

7   A pork and veal sausage from northern Germany. It sometimes also contains beef.
8   El Wardani, Sheilah Rana. "Accepting the Cost: German Baptist Brethren, Faith, and the American Civil War." Dissertation, Scholars Crossing, 2022. Accessed 1/15/22 at https://digitalcommons.liberty.edu/cgi/viewcontent.cgi?article=4900&context=doctoral

"Doing the Lord's work," said Greta, looking tired but still interested as she ate her way through a roll dipped in gravy. Oscar was relieved to see her clearing her plate.

"Indeed. Slavery has long been considered an act of evil," said Brother Honneck, who was younger than Brother Mahler and had a large, brown mole in the center of his forehead. "The Brethren congregants here have strongly condemned it." Oscar nodded in agreement, and there was a monetary silence as everyone enjoyed their food.

"It is apparent, Brother Beck, just how much your Uncle Fredrick has done in arranging and financially assuring your lives here," Brother Mahler remarked. Oscar and Greta shared a look. They knew their journey, though not easy, was still much better than what most new immigrants experienced.

"We are very grateful," Greta said.

"Who is this man?" Brother Mahler asked, reaching for his glass of water. "I understand he is not a direct member of the church."

"He is, I believe, a good person nevertheless," Oscar said after swallowing his bite of mashed turnip. "Not always walking in the way of our Lord, perhaps, but he tries to do what is right. From his letters over the years, it seems he's become in many ways invested in the Baptist Brethren cause. Maybe it's because of our family's church affiliation in Germany and his belief in abolishing slavery."

"Oh!" said Greta. "I did not know he had interests in that cause also."

Oscar nodded. "He arranged many slave escapes, travel routes, and hiding places for the underground railway. He used German Baptist farms in Ohio and along the Wabash River in Indiana as he bought farm commodities for the government,"

Oscar explained. "He arranged communication and travel through his acquaintances in the North and even in the South."

"He was no doubt chosen by our Lord to conduct good works," Brother Honneck said. Oscar smiled.

After dinner, as Greta and Oscar went back to their quarters feeling wonderfully full, Oscar looked sidelong at his wife.

"I may have left a few things out of our conversation with Brother Mahler," he said. Greta looked at him questioningly. Her face had a pink glow that Oscar had not seen for some time, though she still looked fatigued.

"Uncle Fredrick is not completely altruistic," Oscar said. "He always seems to ensure some profit for his efforts. Nonetheless, he is still considered to be a bit of a champion among the German Baptists, even though he isn't really a part of the church anymore."

"You did mention that. What happened?"

"After the church was divided in 1881, the conservatives kept our manner, dress, and customs. Politics and the military had no place in our order of things, as you know," said Oscar, opening the door of their small room. "Holding to tradition, our brothers and sisters watched the Brethren Church go its separate way. For Uncle Fredrick, business dealings and affiliation with the Old Order Church seem to have appealed to him, as that was how he was raised as a child in Germany. He never really felt much of a connection with the Brethren except perhaps some nostalgia, from what I can surmise."

"Ah," said Greta, stepping into the room. Oscar closed the door behind them.

"It's a bit of a paradox, though. He related and understood the religious beliefs of our brethren, yet he used politics and circumstances of war to build a large amount of wealth."

"He seems to be quite complicated," said Greta. "Too complicated for my tired mind." Oscar laughed.

"Yes, I think we could both use a good night's sleep."

The next morning, after many hours of deep slumber, Greta awoke early. She was feeling nauseated once again.

This seems to be happening to me each day, she said to herself as she quietly rose from the bed. *I thought it was just seasickness, but I prayed it was the old Gypsy's vision coming true.*

Greta had still not told Oscar about the Gypsy's prophecy or even of her encounter with the wolves in the German forest. It was not her intention to be deceitful but only to avoid disappointing Oscar. She had missed her menstruation, but it had been late before. She and Oscar had had their hopes dashed so often that she wanted to be sure before sharing her news.

Greta walked slowly towards the entrance of the sleeping quarters. *Maybe some fresh air will help,* she reasoned.

Slipping outside into the hallway, Greta walked toward an east-facing window and leaned her back against the cool stone church wall. She closed her eyes and pressed her hands to her stomach, fighting the nausea. Even though she felt ill, she couldn't suppress a smile.

Greta had always believed Oscar would make a good father. He was a person of character and took the duty of marriage seriously. She had noticed how gentle he had been with the children in the Hannover parish back home in Germany, and his seriousness and dedication to the faith were admirable.

The nausea subsided a bit, and Greta opened her eyes. The sounds of the city were muffled by the thick walls and tall towers of the church, and the sunlight streaming in the window warmed her face and arms. She soaked in the peace of the moment, thinking of her husband and this new stage of their lives. As the sun bathed her in light, Greta felt God's guidance and protection surrounding her and Oscar. Deep within her heart, she knew the decision to come to America had been the right one.

4
New Brethren
(Neue Brüder)
August 1895

L ong train and wagon rides through Pennsylvania, and Ohio filled Oscar and Greta's days for the subsequent six weeks. They made periodic stops at German Baptist parishes for fellowship, rest, and meals as planned by the elders of the church. Finally, after a journey of over 4,000 miles, the small river town of Peru, in Miami County, came into view with its railroad, rich farmland, and rigs for newly discovered oil. Oscar and Greta looked out over the fields and forest where Native Americans had once lived, listening as their escorting brother from the area told them about his home.

"The territory had a history of havin' been considered the 'consecrated huntin' ground' of the Miami Indian Nation," Ezekiel Wagoner said as they plodded ahead in their wagon, his high-pitched voice competing with the squeaking wheels that pierced the humid August air. "About half the Miami Indians relocated thirty years ago to Oklahoma territory, so there are still many Indian descendants hereabouts. Those who stayed mostly inter-married with white folks that reside in town."

"How did they avoid being relocated?" Oscar asked.

"A government judge granted them an exception from the reservations due to a white blood connection, even if it wasn't always true," said Ezekiel. "There are many descendants of German and Irish settlers livin' here, too. Most of their kin helped build the railroad and the Wabash Canal."

"Indiana has many different kinds of people, it seems," Greta said. She felt excitement bubbling inside her as they drew closer to their destination, though the journey had been draining. She now fatigued quickly, and her body felt dramatically changed by the day. When she and Oscar reached their destination, she knew it would be time to ask for a doctor.

"Do all those souls commune well?" Oscar was asking. "Germany has some large class divisions, as you know, but they are not always harmonious."

"Folks with the same kinship in Peru, for the most part, are clannish and stick together," said Ezekiel, brushing a mosquito from his wrist. "Most of the Europeans who built their churches in Indiana keep to their old ways and their family trade. They just sort of blend in. Colored folk mostly keep to themselves in their section of town. Often, they and other communities confuse us with the Amish or Mennonites who also reside in these parts."

"Do all those groups all speak English?" Oscar asked. "There's still a language barrier for us, after all."

Ezekiel smiled as he steered the horses down a bumpy stretch of road. "Our people do speak English when we go out, but don't worry too much. As you can see, we are very comfortable speakin' our mother tongue. Ours are the same traditions we practiced in Germany, and you'll be spendin' most of your time within the Brethren fold anyhow."

"I am glad there are many different types of people here, even if we will not associate with them every day," Greta said, carefully wiping a drop of sweat from her brow. "It is our Lord's will that we find a commonality with all people."

"We are all created in God's image and worthy of His grace," Oscar said, looking at her strangely. "We must live the Bible in a literal fashion, and we must do so without succumbing to outside influences."

"Indeed," Greta said. "But, life is too hard and busy to dwell upon religion or the color of people's skin, or even if they're rich or poor." Her mind flashed back to Tshura and her fragrant, smoke-filled wagon.

"Now, since we are all doing so much speakin', let's work on your English," Ezekiel said, clearly not noticing the strangeness of the exchange as he switched smoothly from German. "You need practice!"

"Ja, we practice," Greta said, smiling. She and Oscar were already feeling more comfortable speaking English thanks to the patient assistance of many church members throughout their journey. Their latest practice session, with Greta and Oscar haltingly speaking along, ended when they finally arrived at their destination.

As the wagon pulled up to a large white farmhouse, an older couple in their early 60s, wearing traditional Brethren garb, came out onto the porch and waved. It was late afternoon now, though the sun still hung high and hot in the sky. Chickens fled from the wagon's path, clucking in alarm, and a Border collie barked joyfully at the wagon. Greta smiled as the collie's tongue dangled from its mouth. The brethren kept dogs and cats for the service they provided for each farm—cats caught rats and mice, dogs herded livestock and hunted game—and Greta had always had a soft spot for them.

"This will be your home for a little while," Ezekiel said. "And this is the church couple who have volunteered to sponsor you: Brother and Sister Fisher."

"Welcome!" the man said, approaching as the wagon came to a stop. He had a round, kind face and skin darkened and weathered by a lifetime spent in the fields. "I'm Bauer Fisher, and this is my wife, Sarah," he said. The slightly plump, pink-cheeked woman next to him nodded, her eyes crinkling at the edges.

Bauer helped Oscar and Ezekiel take the couple's belongings to the guest bedroom of the large farmhouse. The modestly furnished home smelled sweetly of baking cinnamon apple pies, and a bevy of open windows provided a welcome breeze.

"Please make yourselves at home," Sarah said.

"You must come with me, Oscar, to see the barn and livestock," Bauer said. "Sarah, will you help Greta settle in and show her the kitchen and washhouse? And don't forget the cellar!" He looked at Greta with a proud smile. "Sarah has plenty of vegetables and fruit preserved from the garden there. That's also where we will go in case of tornados."

"The weather seems similar to Germany. Is it so all year?" Oscar asked, gesturing at the farm as he and Bauer reached the barn. The pink-nosed collie, whose name he'd learned was Rosa, flopped over and scratched her black-and-white back on the grass.

Bauer nodded, looking out at his verdant farm. "Quite similar, yes, though we have more windstorms here. Summer is our busiest season, of course, as winter survival takes hard work. Each day is preparation for winter. The women harvest large amounts of potatoes, canned fruits, and vegetables for storage in the root cellars. When a late autumn frost brings an end to the growing season, we bring the cattle in from pasture to hay and grain feed over the winter. We hang butchered beef and pork in the smoke-house, and the women render lard for soap on Saturdays."

Oscar nodded. "Yes, it is similar in Germany. We must rely on our labor and God's grace to carry us through the leaner months."

"In all our works, the act of first praising the Lord gives us strength," Brother Bauer said.

The couple's first few days at the farm flew by. Greta and Oscar instantly found the Fisher's farm relatively easy to manage, as it was similar to the farm where they had lived in Germany. The Fisher's children had all grown and farmed near the Zion Church, and they got to meet them and the rest of the community at an evening prayer meeting. The community of Brethren congre-gants was small, comprising only forty families, but they believed strongly in the Word of God.

On their second morning, when chores were finished, Greta sat next to Oscar on the Fisher's wide porch.

"I've been shooed out of the kitchen by Sarah," she said with a rueful smile. "She said I look tired."

"You do," said Oscar, glancing at her. "How are you feeling?"

"Just fine," Greta said breezily. "My dear, we have met so many people recently, but your Uncle Fredrick has yet to make an appearance," she said. "How much longer until we can meet him?"

"I'm not sure," answered Oscar. "Uncle Fredrick is busy, but I know he planned to meet us soon after our arrival."

"I am eager to meet this man who has made such a difference in our lives," Greta said.

"As am I," Oscar said. "I have never really seen Uncle Fredrick in person, after all. I'll be meeting him for the first time, too."

The screen door of the farmhouse opened, and Bauer came out holding two fresh cups of buttermilk.

"I couldn't help but overhear," he said, handing the mugs to his guests. "Fredrick contacted the church elders and is planning to arrive by train in two days. Sarah is just finishing up breakfast."

"Do you know Fredrick well?" Greta asked.

"Somewhat. Our congregation welcomes Fredrick's visits," answered Bauer. "He helped negotiate early land settlements here twenty-some years ago."

"Do you see him often?"

"Not exactly," Bauer admitted, stroking his beard, which was primarily white. "Fredrick travels between our community and the locals, doing what he can to make Brethren folks' lives easier."

"He sounds like a diplomat," commented Greta.

"And sometimes a peacemaker," Bauer said. "Though there are those that see Fredrick as a Yankee profiteer who made his fortune, he is still respected by the Brethren folks for the many good deeds he has done along the way. His heart seems in the right place, though he does have a love of money, some declare."

"Breakfast!" came the cheery call from the kitchen, and the group set aside their conversation for the time being.

The next few days sped by in a happy blur of labor, company, and conversation, though Greta still often had to hide her malaise. At sunrise two days later, Greta heard a noise as she stood behind the farmhouse, trying to fight a fresh wave of nausea. A black horse-drawn carriage with fringe surrounding the roof of the cab was pulling up to the farmhouse. The reins slapped the large bay mare's back as she plodded up the drive, ranging poultry scurrying out of the way.

Greta watched from her covert viewing spot as Uncle Fredrick stepped down from the buggy and tied the mare to the post by the side of the house. Even if she had not known who he was, Greta immediately recognized the visitor due to his resemblance to his brothers. The family similarities were evident in his considerable height and the set of his jaw, though his thick gray hair and bushy eyebrows were unique to him. In his plain white muslin shirt, tan leather suspenders, and blue military-grade trousers, Fredrick looked rather imposing as he put his hands over his head and stretched his back, looking around the farm. Greta knew he was well past middle age, but he moved like a much younger man.

Fredrick stepped to the screen door and loudly knocked, reaching down to pat Rosa as he waited. Greta heard the door creak open, and then a few murmured words were uttered before Sarah's voice rang out:

"Bauer, Oscar, Greta! Fredrick is here!"

Deciding there was nothing for her vertigo, Greta sucked down a big gulp of air, straightened her skirt, and walked purposefully around the side of the house, hoping she didn't look too peaked. Bauer and Fredrick were shaking hands like old friends, greeting each other as Oscar slipped out of the house and stared at his uncle for the first time. Greta sidled up beside him, and Fredrick's eyes shifted to the young couple. When he smiled warmly at them, Greta was startled to see Carl's blue eyes once more.

"You must be Oscar and Greta!" Fredrick said enthusiastically.

"We are so happy and honored to meet you finally," Greta said.

"I am so glad to finally meet Carl's son and daughter-in-law," Fredrick said as he shook Oscar's hand, patted him on the shoulder, and smiled at Greta. "Goodness, Oscar, you look just like your father!"

"I was just thinking that you look a lot like him," Oscar said with a grin. Greta smiled, trying to breathe through her nose to fight the queasy feeling in her stomach. Fredrick's eyes shifted to her pallid face.

"Are you feeling alright, Greta?" he asked.

"I believe so. I'm just a little tired," she said. Why hadn't she been able to hide her condition more effectively?

"I will have Dr. Miller stop by for a visit just to make sure neither of you caught the consumption on the trip over," Fredrick said, narrowing his gaze. "After all, the medical screening at the entry port in New York can be slipshod."

Greta smiled through her discomfort, knowing she needed to see a doctor posthaste, though not for consumption. "Yes," she said, "that would be appreciated and welcomed."

Fredrick stayed in town a few days, taking up his usual room in a hotel in the city and visiting other Brethren congregants. There was much talk about the weather, crops, Fredrick's business dealings, and the Becks' long journey. On the third day of his visit, as promised, Dr. Miller's buggy came to the house.

"The doctor only charges what he feels his patients can reasonably afford," Sarah shared with Greta and Oscar as they watched the buggy trundle up the drive. "Sometimes he gets paid in eggs, chickens, clothing, or something for his wife. This time, though, your uncle has paid in advance."

"But—" Greta started to protest.

"It's done, and that is that," Sarah said crisply. "Now, here he comes."

Dr. Miller turned out to be a thin, middle-aged man with large, warm brown eyes. He quickly introduced himself to the new couple.

"Sarah, I'd like to use the spare guest room to talk with Oscar and Greta," the doctor said in English.

"Of course," Sarah replied in the same tongue. "I also believe an interpreter may be in order."

"I will go with Oscar," Bauer immediately offered. He, Oscar, and the doctor filed into the guest room, leaving Sarah and Greta to sit in the kitchen and sip buttermilk for a few minutes.

"Oscar had rarely ever encountered health problems," Greta told Sarah, smiling. "Even while in school, Oscar's teachers seemed amazed at how resistant he was to illness."

"What a blessing," said Sarah. "Now, can you say that in English?"

Greta tripped through her sentences with Sarah's help and patient encouragement. Soon enough, Bauer and Oscar emerged.

"The doctor says all is well," Oscar said.

"I am so glad to hear it," Greta said as Sarah ushered her into the spare bedroom.

"Well, dear, how are you feeling?" Dr. Miller asked Greta.

"Doctor . . ." Greta looked helplessly at Sarah. "The truth is," she said in German, "I don't want to get my hopes up, but after many years, I believe I may finally be with child."

Sarah immediately teared up, her pink cheeks growing even pinker.

"Dear, I didn't want to say anything, but I've noticed you looking unwell in the mornings. I was beginning to wonder," she said breathlessly. Sarah then relayed the information to Dr. Miller.

"Let's take a look, then, and I'll ask you some routine questions," said the doctor. "Have you been experiencing morning sickness?"

Greta, with Sarah's help, answered Dr. Miller's questions as he checked her pulse and, with permission, conducted a brief pelvic exam.

"Well, you certainly have all the signs," he said finally, straightening up. "I do have one last question. I know you mentioned you have not had your menses in some time. Do you remember approximately when your last cycle started?"

Greta carefully calculated and relayed the information.

"Ah. In that case, I would like to stop by in a week or so," the doctor said. "At that point, if you have not started your monthly cycle, we can be sure. It does look very positive as of now, however."

"I look forward to that," Greta said, trying to hold in her excitement. Sarah held Greta's hand and gently squeezed as the doctor packed up his things.

"My instinct tells me you are with child, and if it happens, I am right. I believe you will make a good mother," she said.

"My life was meant to be devoted to my husband and the bearing of his children," Greta told Sarah. "That is our Lord's plan for me."

As the trio left the room, they said nothing to Oscar and Bauer about the news other than that Greta was healthy. Greta beamed at Oscar, trying to stay composed. Her hopes would have to be suppressed for another week before her expectant status could be absolutely confirmed; she could not allow herself the luxury of celebration for fear of another disappointment. As with all things, she knew God would reveal the outcome in His time.

5
Great News
(Gute Neuigkeiten)
August 1895

Greta couldn't help but feel optimistic all through the next week, especially when her monthly courses failed to arrive. She was especially excited when seven days passed and when Fredrick appeared at the Fisher farm early in the morning. Not only was this the day the doctor would likely return, but she and Oscar were to see a promising piece of property for sale nearby—the potential home for their new family.

Greta and Oscar, already dressed in their traditional clothing, left the comforting clatter of the kitchen as soon as they heard Fredrick's carriage approaching. It had rained the night before, and the wet ground reinvigorated the late corn in the fields. New-mown hay waited for tedding to dry away the moisture from the night drizzle. Harvest was not so long away, and the feel of summer's end could also be detected in the air.

"Who is that?" Greta quietly asked as the carriage came to a halt. A stranger sat next to Uncle Fredrick.

"I am not sure," Oscar said, smiling and waving as the two men disembarked the carriage and strode forth.

"Good morning," said Fredrick to the young couple. "I brought along a longtime friend of mine, Colonel Benjamin Tillett, for our excursion. The colonel is a fine fellow and a bit of an expert when it comes to land appraisal." He clapped Colonel Tillett on the back.

Colonel Tillett's expression did not change as he nodded sternly at both Oscar and Greta, his cold steel-blue eyes glinting. Oscar couldn't help but watch the newcomer warily. Colonel Tillett's thick salt-and-pepper hair was closely clipped on the sides, offsetting his dark felt campaign hat. He wore a bushy white field mustache, which he kept neatly trimmed above his top lip, underscoring his military bearing. A forty-five-caliber Army revolver sat reversed, holstered on his right hip, barely hidden under his brown frock coat.

As Oscar examined the colonel, he could practically hear his father reading words from the book of Matthew: "He who liveth by the sword shall perish by the sword." Most German Brethren would avoid a man who appeared to have dedicated his life to war. But, of course, Uncle Fredrick was not German Baptist and did things his way. Oscar knew very well that they could not afford to insult a friend of Uncle Fredrick's.

"Sarah has prepared breakfast for all of us," Greta said. "Please come inside and eat."

"That'll do just fine, thank you," Uncle Fredrick said. The group had just begun walking toward the house, Rosa trotting after them, when the colonel stopped in his tracks.

"Wait a moment," Uncle Fredrick said as the colonel strode back to the buggy. "Musta forgotten something."

Fredrick turned back toward Greta and Oscar with a bright smile. "I think you will like this property," he told them. "It is only a few miles north of the Fisher home, nearer to the small town of Deer Creek. There is a large congregation of Old German Baptist Brethren there."

"That sounds very nice," Greta said politely. "It would be good to be near Bauer and Sarah."

"Indeed. God-fearing folks," Fredrick agreed.

"Do you happen to know who is selling the property?" Oscar asked.

"An elderly widow," Fredrick said. "She owned the farm and had refused to sell the property for undisclosed reasons. It even stood vacant for a few years. But now, here you are, and here it is!"

The squelching sound of boots on mud announced Colonel Tillett's return. Giving the strange man a sidelong glance, Oscar immediately noted that the pistol had disappeared. As Uncle Fredrick and Colonel Tillett walked ahead, Oscar wondered if perhaps he had been too hasty in judging the man. After all, the colonel had chosen unprompted to leave his service pistol in the buggy so as not to bring conflict of belief into the Fisher home.

Oscar felt a light tap on his arm and turned to see Greta leaning in close.

"I smelled whiskey and cigar smoke coming from the colonel's direction," Greta whispered.

"Come now," Oscar said, giving his wife an encouraging smile. "Nothing we can do about that."

Once they were all seated and enjoying Sarah's breakfast spread, Uncle Fredrick began talking about his friend, who had yet to utter a word. Between bites, Oscar couldn't help noticing the colonel looking about, seeming to analyze everything around him as Uncle Fredrick talked. To Oscar, the man seemed perfectly functional; he was perhaps overly alert but not drunk.

"Now, how did the two of you meet?" asked Bauer, spreading raspberry jam onto a slice of bread.

"I've known Ben since before the Civil War when he was just a young Union lieutenant and still arranging civilian contracts," said Fredrick, patting his old friend's shoulder. "The colonel has led quite an interesting life!"

"Have you, now?" Bauer asked, setting down the jam knife. "Please tell us."

"He's a descendant of pioneers," Fredrick continued as the colonel glowered and sipped water. "French and English on his papa's side, Scotch and Huron Indian from his mama's. He grew up in the east and graduated from West Point. Decorated for bravery and wounded at the First Battle of Bull Run, early on in the war."

Fredrick looked proud as he took a large bite of eggs. The pacifist German Brethren group nodded and smiled politely. Colonel Tillett munched his bacon, his eyes still darting to and fro.

"Not that he's been off warring lately," Fredrick continued, seemingly unconcerned for the brethren's unenthusiastic response. "The last action he saw was with the Fifth Cavalry during the Apache wars out in the Arizona territory. He retired after twenty-eight years, finally serving as the post commander of the quartermaster depot at Jeffersonville. After that, I helped him purchase a tract of oil land near Peru, and the rest is history."

To Oscar's surprise, Colonel Tillett, who was now finishing his eggs, had a slight smile pulling at the corners of his mouth under the umbrella of his mustache. He swallowed, then opened his mouth to reveal a complete set of surprisingly white teeth. "You could talk the hind legs off a donkey, Fredrick," he said gruffly. His voice was low and gravelly, as though it was not often used. "I'm old and boring. Let's talk about young Oscar and Greta here instead."

Everyone around the table chuckled, and the tension seemed to dissipate. Their banter grew more effortless, and by the end of the meal, Oscar felt much more optimistic about the strange colonel.

"God works in ways of mystery," Oscar said quietly to Greta as Sarah packed a hamper with their lunch. "Perhaps it is God's will we accept this man's help. He is certainly open to doing favors for Uncle Fredrick, and he seems well-intentioned."

Greta gazed out the window, where the colonel and Uncle Fredrick were standing in front of the house, talking.

"You are right, of course," she said finally. "It is not for us to judge anyone."

As the group traveled to the site with Colonel Tillett behind the reins, the Army veteran began speaking in earnest. Occasionally, Fredrick translated unfamiliar words related to real estate and history.

"The ground was purchased from what was left of the Miami tribe in 1849 by the government," Colonel Tillett explained, "and President Zachary Taylor signed the contract. To the Miamis, the land was considered sacred."

"Why did the Indians sell the land if they considered it sacred?" Greta asked.

"The Injuns were persuaded, so to speak, to sell the land when the tribe was strong-armed and resettled to Oklahoma," Colonel

Tillett said, a hard note in his voice. "But what's done is done. The farm includes about seventy-five acres of land and is near Bunker Hill and Deer Creek, so shopping and medical treatment are not too far away. It's a typical Indiana farm with plenty of game."

"Sacred . . . our Lord blesses the land," said Greta as she looked out at the passing landscape. The day was growing warmer, though a slight breeze ruffled the edges of her bonnet. "We will tithe our earnings from the farm for the church, of course."

"The community will have another brother and sister in the flock," Oscar said, reaching for his wife's hand as the colonel pulled the buggy to a stop. Everyone gazed at the small brick farmhouse, framed barn, spring cellar, smokehouse, and chicken coop.

The party filed out of the buggy, and Greta slowly walked around the abandoned home. Watching her lithe form move around the building, deftly avoiding puddles and wet spots left by the previous night's rain, Oscar began envisioning their life here. Days spent working the fields, summer evenings sitting on the small front porch, winters curled up by the fireplace. Smiling, he looked out on the land and small barn.

"This will be where I raise beef and dairy cattle in time," Oscar said.

Colonel Tillett and Fredrick began pacing around and talking about details of the property and sale. When they were a short distance away, Oscar and Greta ducked behind the farmhouse, where they held each other close.

"This will be a good home for us," he said. Greta gazed up at him and kissed him softly on the chin above the line of his strap beard.

"A good home for our children, too," she whispered. Oscar

smiled; this was the first time Greta had mentioned children to Oscar since long before visiting Dieter.

"The price is right on this property," Colonel Tillett said from close by, causing the couple to leap apart in surprise. "It's an affable deal and a good piece of ground." They came around the side of the building, and Fredrick smirked at the guilty expression on his nephew's face.

"The buildings are in disrepair, but they'll be no match for my carpentry," Uncle Fredrick said, his eyes twinkling. "The Baptist Brethren has also pledged to lend tools, horses, and labor to settle their newest members once a location is set. Bauer was telling me about it. Plenty of hands will make short work."

"Well, I think we've settled," Oscar said, looking at Greta. She nodded back, beaming.

"Ja, good!" Fredrick exclaimed, slapping his hand on the side of his leg. "I'll notify the elders of the church, who will want to conduct a prayer vigil, I imagine. Then it'll all be finalized."

Oscar stooped down to grasp a handful of moist earth.

"The soil is good," Oscar smiled, "and with God's help, I will make it better."

Colonel Tillett smiled at Oscar. "Let's get back into the carriage. I can drive back to take a look at the woods."

"Lots of native hardwood to be cut out of there," said Fredrick.

After a quick walk about the forest that sat on the north edge of the property, the company turned back toward the Fisher home in high spirits. On the carriage ride back, under a cornflower-blue sky dapped with thin clouds, Oscar and Greta could not contain their excitement. The young couple chattered about all they planned to do with the new farm. At the same time, Colonel

Tillett discussed step-by-step details for bidding on the land with Fredrick, occasionally raising their eyebrows as giggling emanated from the back seat.

"Now, children, I have something to say to you," Uncle Fredrick said when they were nearly at their destination, craning to look back at his nephew. Greta and Oscar instantly went silent, listening intently. "The owner is anxious to sell now, but she has not been given any reasonable offers thus far. I am willing to loan you the money for the purchase, though I must wait until the church elders approve the arrangement."

"That is kind of you, Uncle, especially after all you've done for us already," Oscar said, his face flushing. Fredrick waved a hand.

"Anything to help my family," he said modestly.

As Fredrick's carriage approached Sarah and Bauer's farm, Greta spotted Dr. Miller's buggy tied at the house.

"The doctor is here," she said. Her heart beat rapidly, and she reflexively grabbed Oscar's hand.

"Why is he back so soon?" Fredrick asked, a note of concern in his voice.

"Just to conduct a follow-up appointment," Greta said, trying to sound steady. "There is nothing to worry about." Oscar looked at her curiously, saying nothing.

As Fredrick tied the horse to the rail, still discussing the land with Colonel Tillett, Greta cautiously stepped from the carriage and opened the front door. Sarah greeted her with a holy kiss on her left cheek.

"Ah, Greta! There you are. Let's get started," Dr. Miller said, standing from a plate full of biscuit crumbs and motioning the two women toward the guest room. He again asked questions and performed a few routine pregnancy examinations, and Sarah stayed by Greta's side for moral support and translation.

"Child," Dr. Miller said at last, "I do not want you to be taking any more long carriage rides like you did today, especially on those bumpy roads. Is that clear?" He looked sternly at Greta.

As she realized the implication of the doctor's order, a broad smile overtook Greta's face. She squeezed Sarah's hand as she excitedly repeated, "Danke, danke," to the physician. Tears filled her eyes.

"Perhaps by mid-February, you'll meet the new addition to your family," the doctor said, his round face breaking into a smile at Greta's delight. "My sincerest congratulations. In the meantime, I want you to take one drop of this before meals when you feel you need it." He handed a small dropper bottle labeled "Cocaine Solution" to Greta. "It will help ease the morning nausea if any remains."

Greta, still emotional from the news of her pregnancy, impulsively stood. Handing Sarah the bottle, she walked to the door.

"Thank you very much. Now, I am telling Oscar the good news," she said before striding out, leaving Dr. Miller and Sarah grinning behind her.

As though by prearrangement, Oscar walked into the house and saw Greta. Greta approached him, holding out her hand.

"Oscar Beck, you are soon to be a papa," she said, trying to stem her tears of happiness.

Oscar closed the distance between them in a few swift strides. Weeping openly, Greta nuzzled her nose against his neck.

"I love you so, my Greta," Oscar whispered. "The Lord has surely blessed us this day. There is much to be thankful for."

6

Our New Home
(Unser neues Zuhause)
October 1895

Meine hoffnung stehet feste,
Auf den ewig treuen Gott,
Er ist mir der allerbeste,
Der mir beisteht in der Noth;
Er allein,
Soll es sein,
Den ich nur von Herzen mein'.[9]

The cool breeze played across Oscar's face, carrying with it the a cappella singing of the Zion German Baptist Brethren Church. The familiar melody mingled with the rustling of leaves and the gurgling of Pipe Creek. Next to him, Greta stood in her white baptismal gown, which matched his own. Pastor Yoder, his back slightly bent with age, smiled knowingly at them both.

---

9   German version of the hymn "All My Hope on God Is Founded." Text from https://hymnary.
     org/text/meine_hoffnung_stehet_feste

Taking in the loving scene around him, Oscar knew that he and Greta had made the right choice in undergoing this "believer's baptism" ceremony. They had, of course, been baptized in Germany, but they felt this symbolic gesture was meaningful. It not only affirmed their commitment to God; it also showed solidarity with their new American church.

The hymn concluded, and Pastor Yoder gestured for the couple to kneel. Oscar glanced at Greta in concern, but she quickly got down on her knees unaided. Oscar knew that soon, her belly would grow so large that tasks like this would be impossible.

Pastor Yoder prayed over the couple in a resonant voice, asking God to bless them. Oscar already felt blessed beyond measure. This was a time of rebirth and new beginnings for their whole family, with the land purchase approved and a new baby on the way.

"Sister Greta, please rise," Pastor Yoder said, "and follow."

Oscar watched his wife follow the old pastor into the waist-high water where the ritual of "trine immersion" would be consecrated. She shivered and put a hand to her belly; Oscar wondered if she could feel their child move inside her. *Only five months to go before our little family welcomes a new member,* he thought.

Pastor Yoder then held a hand out to Oscar. Quietly, Oscar moved into the creek, his skin tightening with goosebumps from the cold water. The white baptismal robes billowed around them in the moving stream.

Pastor Yoder gently guided Greta under the water, placing a hand on the top of her head.

"I baptize thee, Greta Alsa Beck, in the name of the Father, and of the Son, and the Holy Spirit," he said, immersing Greta three times. Greta blinked her deep blue eyes open after the third immersion, immediately meeting Oscar's gaze. They stared at each other for a moment, feeling the weight of the symbolic rebirth. Then, it was Oscar's turn.

"I baptize thee, Oscar Carl Beck, in the name of the Father, and of the Son, and the Holy Spirit," Pastor Yoder recited. Oscar held his breath during each immersion, and when he opened his eyes, creek water streaming from his hair and robe, the first face he saw was Greta's. Their sins were now washed away, and Oscar felt renewed in his earthly union to serve and honor the will of the Lord at Zion. The Brethren standing on the shoreline greeted the couple with smiles and towels as they walked from the slow-flowing water.

"We have heard the good news about your new farm," Ruth Bowman, the woman seated next to Greta, said an hour later. To Greta's ears, after the long silence, Ruth's voice sounded strange. After the baptism and a hasty change of clothing, the congregation had partaken of a simple evening meal of beef and water in silence. During that contemplative time, the Brethren had reverently thanked God for the new souls who were welcomed into the flock. Now, following the meal, they could uplift each other with a believer's fellowship.

Greta blinked at the younger woman, trying to think of the right English words. Ruth was every inch as tall as Greta, and sharp cheekbones accented her dark eyes and eyebrows.

"Congratulations to both of you," Ruth said with an encouraging smile. "How many acres is it?"

"Seventy-five," Greta answered carefully in English.

"The elders and deacons approved the purchase without hesitation," Bauer, who was seated next to Oscar, said as he touched the younger man on the shoulder. Though he spoke in English,

Bauer took care to slow his speech down somewhat. "Of course, there's a lot to do yet. The local bank of Bunker Hill is handling the land purchase. You'll need to get an appraisal and go into the bank to sign documents and pay taxes."

Bauer paused for a moment. "As there's also a tract of forest on the property, you need to discuss its management and not allow vagabonds or Gypsies to park there. Sister Bowman, you and your husband will know all about this, I suppose."

"It all sounds very familiar," Ruth said. Her husband, Hans, nodded ruefully, shrugging his shoulders as he looked around the church.

"We just went through the process last year," he said. "It was a lot of work, but, of course, it was well worth it."

"Land buying is hard in Europe," Oscar said in English. He did not understand all the English terms Bauer used, but he could already tell this was a much better system than the one-sided governmental arrangement he and Greta had left far behind in Germany.

"Indeed," Hans said. "Is your uncle helping you?"

"Yes, very much," Oscar replied.

As the Bowmans began an avid conversation with the Fishers about their farm, Greta leaned over to Oscar.

"If our child does turn out to be a boy," Greta said, "Fredrick will make a good Christian name for him."

"Yes," Oscar said, touching her hand. Just as he said it, however, Greta's expression lifted, and she turned to Sarah.

"Gypsies? Did you say there were Gypsies around here?"

"Yes," Sarah said, looking surprised. "Most Gypsies here are from the old country. A few are from Bulgaria and Romania, though I don't think they are really Romanian. Other folks think Gypsies might even come from India."

Oscar watched as Greta leaned forward. "Do they speak English?"

"Some speak in their own Gypsy talk, some speak in mixed-up German English or just whatever they feel like at the time," Bauer said with a shrug. "I never talk with them, so it's hard to say."

"I met some Jenische Gypsies in Germany," Greta said. "They seemed sincere." Oscar patted Greta's elbow under the table in a slight warning.

"Gypsies do seem nice," Bauer said. "But that's what they want you to think. They know how to seem that way."

"They've even been known to train and use their children as a distraction while an adult Gypsy slips into your chicken coop to grab up a few hens or sneak in through the back door of your house," Ruth said, eyes narrowed.

Greta turned back to Oscar. "Maybe they are hungry."

"As Pastor Yoder reminds us often, the book of Leviticus says, 'thou shalt not interpret omens or tell fortunes,'" Sarah said, turning to stare hard at Greta. "God reminds us that such things are blasphemous and forbidden. Fraternizing with such people can only compromise our souls and bring about damnation."

Greta smiled politely and said nothing, nodding.

"The local government doesn't always agree with our community on many things," Hans said, "but it does agree with this. The sheriff even addressed this issue during a recent council meeting; I overheard some men talking about it in town last time I was there."

"Is that so?" Bauer asked.

"Oh, yes," Hans said. "The sheriff strongly warned that Gypsies are not what they seem. Apparently, he shared the sentiment that they are grifters who scam and deceive people they consider to be 'outsiders.'"

"Mmm," said Greta noncommittally. Oscar suspected she was preventing herself from arguing by quietly praying.

"Gypsies, for the most part, have a low opinion of people in our community, too," Sarah said. "'Gadjos,' they call us,"

"Now, Sister Fisher," Hans said. "Gypsies sell us metalware and do lots of repairs on German Baptist farms. It's not all bad blood between us."

"They know to choose us because the Amish, German Baptists, and Mennonite people generally are less hostile toward them due to our Christian generosity," Sarah said, her naturally pink face flushing. "They choose to journey through Anabaptist territory whenever they can, it seems."

"In Germany, there is an . . ." Greta threw up her hands and switched to German. ". . . unspoken understanding between most Anabaptists and the Gypsy people. They know we will be, as the book of Hebrews says, hospitable to strangers who may be angels disguised in human form . . ."

"Hans," Oscar said in German, smiling broadly and turning to the large man, "How have the first few years of starting a farm been for you? I believe we may be facing many of the same challenges soon." He nudged Greta's foot under the table with his own, and the whole table dropped the subject of Gypsies.

* * *

Oscar and Bauer hurried onto the porch, sopping wet after the morning's chores. Cold rain spattered across the farm, but on the porch, it was warmer and mercifully dry. Rosa greeted them as they stepped onto the worn wood; she, too, seemed grateful for the shelter of the porch.

"With the last of the hay in the mow this morning, there's nothing left to do now but bring in the cattle from pasture," Oscar said, sitting down next to Bauer in the front porch swing. Both men began tugging off their sodden boots.

"Still a few apples yet to pick when it dries off," Bauer commented, shielding his eyes as he looked out at the orchard.

"Sarah and Greta plan to start husking walnuts tomorrow if it's still raining," Oscar said, letting his second boot hit the planks with a clatter. The two men shared a comfortable silence, sitting on the porch swing, taking in the cold, damp fall air and letting their toes dry. Rosa curled up next to the swing, occasionally lifting her head to sniff the air.

"Shucked a few ears of corn yesterday, and it looks 'bout ready," Bauer said in a monotone, mostly to himself. "Expect we can start picking in the next couple of days as soon as this rain front passes. We ought to start getting the wagons and harnesses ready tomorrow. It may be an early winter; cattle's coats are heavier, I've seen. We'll have to move them out of the pasture later today."

Oscar, whose mind had wandered as the older man pondered the autumn tasks, looked at his companion. "Brother Bauer, may I change the subject?"

Bauer glanced over. "Of course, Brother Beck. Speak your mind."

"How did you stay calm when Sarah was giving birth? Childbirth is a blessing, but it's not without risk." Oscar plucked up one of his socks and began wringing water out of it. "This weighs heavily on my mind. We're all familiar with childbed fever." It was no secret that childbirth was one of the most common causes of death for German Baptist women.

"I did not stay calm," Bauer admitted, smiling ruefully. "I was agitated the whole time. All I could do was pray."

Bauer laid a hand on Oscar's shoulder, giving it a comforting pat. "Dr. Miller is competent. He has delivered many children, and with the Lord's guidance, he will successfully deliver yours."

Oscar opened his mouth but snapped it shut again as Greta walked out on the porch. Clutching a black woolen shawl tightly around her shoulders, Greta looked out at the rain, her pregnant belly protruding slightly.

"Brr! It's getting chilly," she said. Oscar refocused his thoughts, smiled, and reached for Greta's hand.

"Come on in," Greta said. "Breakfast is ready, and you'll need to change before Uncle Fredrick gets here."

"Go back inside, and quickly now," Oscar said. "There's no use catching a chill before I have to leave for town. I'll be worried sick the whole time."

By the time they finished breakfast, the drizzle had subsided, and the sun had begun to warm the Earth. Fredrick's carriage, right on schedule, trundled up the pathway of Bauer and Sarah's home. Colonel Tillett's military hat bobbed next to Uncle Fredrick's Stetson as they pulled up to the house. While the mare sauntered reflexively to the hitching rail, Rosa ran to greet the buggy, her great, long-furred tail wagging frantically. Alerted by Rosa's yips, Oscar, Greta, Sarah, and Bauer were already filing out.

"Would you come in and have something to eat?" Sarah asked.

"Thank you, but no time today, Sister," Fredrick replied as Oscar, freshly scrubbed and wearing his hat, clambered into the carriage. "We'd best be going while the weather is clear. We'll have something to eat in town."

"Do be careful," Greta said, looking up at the three men.

"There's nothing to worry about," Oscar reassured her. "We'll be back before you know it."

The countryside, with its turning leaves and sweet autumn air, made Oscar smile as the carriage pulled out into the road. Everything seemed so peaceful and serene here, with each day predictable, quiet, and stable despite his current errand.

"All the necessary paperwork is in here," Uncle Fredrick said, patting a pouch at his side. "Everything is taken care of. The land will be purchased in your name, Oscar, and I will co-sign as we discussed. Greta will inherit the farm if the worst should happen."

"Thank you, Uncle," Oscar said. "I cannot find the words to convey . . ."

Fredrick waved a hand. "Just helping out my family. This will solidify your place in the church as well."

"I believe Greta and I made the right decision to leave the old country behind," Oscar said. "God has blessed this land and the journey we made from Europe." Though there was much he missed about Germany, Oscar's experience thus far in Indiana had been more than he could have hoped for.

"Fifteen minutes yet, I reckon," Colonel Tillett said, looking at his pocket watch.

The trio passed the short journey to town with a bit of conversation about Uncle Fredrick's business dealings and the baby, with a few interjections from the stoic Colonel Tillett, who looked as stern as ever in the autumn sun. The town was quiet and nearly deserted when the three arrived at the bank.

"Slow Wednesday morning," the colonel said in his gravelly voice, glancing around.

"Lucky for us," Fredrick said, sliding out of the carriage.

The three men entered the red-brick bank building to find themselves in a close foyer separating the outside and inside doors. Oscar started when he realized they were not alone in the small space. A tall, thin, unshaven man wearing a long dark woolen coat sat alone on a bench along the short expanse of wall, his neck craned stiffly toward the main room.

"Looks like someone is expecting an early winter," the colonel commented as he eyed the man up and down, opening the second door to the bank lobby. The man did not budge.

Inside, a few bank patrons stood lined up in front of the single teller. Fredrick and the colonel took their places in line, with Oscar sandwiched between them. Peering ahead, Oscar saw two people waiting in front of them: a young man in a loose, knit sweater and dirty tweed cap and a wizened older gentleman whose wheezy breaths could be heard throughout the room.

"Not too much of a wait," Oscar said. "Good thing, too. You two must be hungry, having turned down Sarah's offer for breakfast and all."

"There's a good restaurant nearby," Fredrick said as the lone clerk, an older man wearing a visor cap and thin wire-rimmed glasses, counted out cash for a tall, thin man in a suit. "We can go there afterward. I know you're partial to their steak and eggs, eh, Colonel?"

The colonel said nothing, instead whipping his head around as the door to the bank opened. A middle-aged, modestly dressed couple walked in, giving him a startled look. Oscar looked sidelong at Colonel Tillett, who seemed to be even more on edge than usual.

"At ease, friend," Fredrick said with a laugh. "You do seem in need of a meal. Luckily, this won't take long. We'll need to let the teller know we're here to finalize. Then we can go to an office to finish the transaction."

As the man in the suit strode out of the bank, the teller gestured for the young man to come forward. Then, the teller's eyes widened behind his glasses.

"Just do what I tell you. This will all be over soon," Oscar heard a voice say. All the little hairs on the back of Oscar's neck stood to attention.

Slowly, Oscar turned. Both Colonel Tillett and Fredrick stood alert, but the couple behind them seemed utterly unaware of what was going on. Behind them, however, Oscar saw the man with the long coat slip through the doors holding a sawed-off, twelve-gauge, double-barreled shotgun. Oscar's heart hammered as the man turned to lock the deadbolt on the door behind him, then stood and peered nervously at the street outside from the small glass portal of the door.

"So that's what he had under that coat," Uncle Fredrick muttered.

"Put every damn dollar you can muster up in this sack, and be quick about it!" the crook at the bank window shouted, no longer trying to be subtle. Turning again, Oscar saw the man shoving a brown burlap bag through the bars that separated the teller from clients. The teller took the bag with trembling hands.

"Be damn quick!" the man demanded, his impatient voice getting louder and higher. By now, everyone in the room knew what was happening, and panic was setting in. The older man standing directly behind the robber held his forehead and began staggering backward.

"Oh, my stars and garters!" the old man cried in a hoarse voice as he lost his balance. "My stars!"

Fredrick quickly stepped to the side, hooking an arm under each of the man's skinny armpits to stop the fall. The couple that had been last in line fled to hide under a nearby table; Oscar glanced over to see the woman hyperventilating as her husband prayed loudly and clutched his wife. He was instantly grateful that Greta, due to her pregnancy, could no longer go for long carriage rides and, therefore, was safe at home.

"Don't nobody move," the criminal in front said in a shrill voice, turning and waving a thirty-two-caliber pistol at the patrons behind him. The man had pulled a red handkerchief over his nose and mouth, though his wild eyes were visible in the crack between bandana and hat. Dull brown hair stuck untidily out from underneath the tweed cap that rested low on his forehead.

As the man turned back to focus on the badly shaken bank teller, Oscar was alarmed to see that Colonel Tillett had stepped out of line, silently eased his revolver from his side holster, and sidled six feet away from the gunman. The gunman, who was busy watching the bank clerk fumble to stuff cash into the gunny sack, remained oblivious. However, that changed when the colonel's locking pistol hammer slid into place with a quiet click.

"Drop your piece, son," the colonel said in a low, commanding voice. The outlaw, keeping his gun trained on the terrified clerk's chest, turned his head and looked into the colonel's fixed stare. Oscar looked around; to his relief, the man in the long coat remained focused on the door, looking away from his accomplice. Although they had no idea, the panicking bank patrons were providing a valuable distraction from the scene unfolding before the counter by creating such a racket.

"You're makin' a big mistake, Grandpa. I ain't a-foolin'," the thief said in a low and threatening voice, turning entirely away from the clerk and aiming his pistol at his challenger.

Crack! Oscar winced, then opened his eyes as a cloud of pink mist formed around the young gangster. The would-be thief's head slumped forward, and he slid into a collapsed sitting position, leaving a streak of blood smeared on the front of the teller's cage.

Sucking in a deep breath, Oscar fought back nausea. His head swam, and his ears rang as he looked away from the gore and focused on the robber.

The colonel held his firing position momentarily, then moved into a side stance facing the bank's front door. Turning his handgun, he aimed for the shotgun-wielding accomplice. The man, of course, had heard the shot and now stood facing Colonel Tillett, fumbling to cock his weapon. The bank was dead silent.

"Disarm yourself, sir," the colonel demanded.

A metallic sound rang out as the shotgun blast reverberated through the room. The couple under the table screamed as shards of wood splinters and dust flew into the air. The panicking crime partner had inadvertently discharged his weapon into the floor. He glanced up at the colonel, who was slowly advancing, pistol held at arm's length.

"Shit! shit!" the bandit stammered as he finally managed to lock the second hammer of his scattergun with shaking fingers.

Coldly, the colonel stared into the eyes of his intended target,

now at point-blank range. Time passed by in slow motion. The hap-
less thief began to raise his shotgun, and Oscar clapped his hands
over his mouth to stifle a scream as the colonel fired one shot.

Crack! This time, Oscar hadn't closed his eyes fast enough.
He watched in frozen horror as the criminal's brain tissue and
skull fragments splattered the entryway door. The man collapsed
face down, his body involuntarily twitching on the floor.

Backing up until his back hit something cool and solid,
Oscar slid to the floor, panting. The colonel, meanwhile, relaxed
the grip of his revolver. Surveying his work, he swiveled his pistol
to a reversed position, holstering his weapon. A smoky haze and
the smell of burnt gunpowder filled the bank building.

As if a switch had been disengaged, Colonel Tillett moved to
assist Fredrick, who had carried the older man to a bench and was
now patting the retching man's back. The bank environment had
grown chaotic; employees had come out of the back of the building and were weeping or hiding behind furniture as they surveyed
the scene. Oscar gulped down unclean breaths of air, trying and
failing to think of a comforting scripture. He had never seen or
even imagined something this gruesome happening in America.

"Son, come along," a voice said. Oscar tried not to cower
when he looked up and saw the colonel standing there. Without
another word, the colonel took Oscar's arm and helped him up,
leading him to a nearby bench. Oscar sank into the seat just as the
door to the bank banged open.

"Everyone, stay where you are! No one leaves this room!"

Oscar looked wearily up to see the town constable and a
young deputy looking wide-eyed at the scene. The marshal, carrying a weathered-looking Winchester rifle, anxiously scanned

the bank floor. The colonel sat down beside Oscar and waited as spectators and curiosity seekers filtered in the door after the police, peering through the windows and gawking at the corpses of the two lawbreakers.

The marshal set about sweeping the building and speaking to patrons as the deputy hurriedly collected the weapons strewn on the floor.

"That man is a hero," the woman who had been under the table said, pointing at Colonel Tillett. "He saved us all! He deserves a reward at the very least."

"I beg to disagree, madam!" the clerk, who had somewhat recovered and was leaning on a worried bank colleague, said. "That robber had that gun aimed right at me, I tell ya! What if he hadn't been killed? That old man there endangered all our lives!"

As people began moving freely around, Fredrick sat down on the bench next to Colonel Tillett.

"Maybe we should settle our business another day," he said quietly.

"That is my proposal also," the colonel said. "I suggest you take Oscar home as soon as the marshal allows it. I'll stay back. I've got errands I need to do in town, and I'm sure the lawman will have questions for me."

Oscar could hardly remember speaking to the marshal or leaving the bank. The next thing he knew, he was seated next to Uncle Fredrick in the carriage, trying to keep his teeth from chattering with adrenaline.

"Now, Oscar," Fredrick said in a deceptively casual tone, "I'm sure this goes without saying, but the German Baptist Brethren elders might not well receive Colonel Tillett's actions today."

Oscar nodded stiffly.

"Keeping a distance from him would now be for the best," Fredrick said.

Oscar cleared his throat. "Will . . . will he be arrested?"

"Doubt it," Uncle Fredrick said, guiding the horse around a turn. "Knowing him, he's probably given a statement already and is enjoying a lunch of steak and eggs at a nearby tavern before heading back to his hotel room."

"He can eat after doing something like that?" Oscar asked, feeling the blood drain from his face.

"Trust me, Colonel Tillett has seen and done far worse," Fredrick said darkly.

When the pair arrived at the Fisher farm, Greta and Sarah were finishing hanging the wash on the clothesline. Oscar slid off the carriage and walked straight into the house, where he sat at the kitchen table, staring out the window at the pasture. Greta entered the kitchen a few minutes later, her belly looking larger than ever, her face flushed with life.

"Uncle Fredrick told me what happened," she said in a soft voice.

"Such violence goes against all that we have been taught and believe," Oscar said, fidgeting with a small red tin of baking powder on the table. "1 point no blame toward the colonel, but the brothers and sisters of our church will feel differently about us now for our association with him."

Greta stood close behind Oscar, placing her arms around him. "Uncle Fredrick told me he would talk with all the elders and deacons. From now on, he says, he will be careful not to include the colonel in future business where the church is involved." Greta rubbed Oscar's shoulders comfortingly. With a sigh of relief, he felt the warmth of her hands, restoring his equilibrium.

"We must pray for the souls of those who were killed," she said.

"Yes," Oscar said. "Greta, I thank God you did not come with us."

7
Namesake of Our Brother
(Namensvetter unseres Bruders)
November 1895–February 1896

"Well, after a short delay, it's finally official," Uncle Fredrick said. He spoke clearly in English, a bit faster than he would have a few months earlier. "Oscar and Greta, you are now the owners of your farm."

The young couple bowed their heads in thanks. Earlier that day, after a month's respite, Fredrick, Oscar, and two church elders had returned to the bank to activate the purchase of the land and homestead. This time, everything had proceeded according to plan, and Uncle Fredrick had consented to sup at the Fisher home.

"We are so grateful," Greta said, setting glasses of milk on the table. "The farm is perfect for our family." Her English was already quite good.

"Now comes the task of readying the property for living and farming," Fredrick said, accepting a glass of buttermilk.

"You must continue to stay with us for a while during this

time of transition," Bauer said to Oscar as Sarah passed around a bowl of fried chicken. "It will be safer for Greta to wait until after the delivery."

"It will take some time for the new house to be livable," Sarah agreed, unfolding the top of the breadbasket and passing it along. "You're welcome as long as you like."

"Thank you," Oscar said. "I don't want to . . . *Eine Belastung sein?*"

"Be a burden?" Bauer offered.

"Yes, be a burden," Oscar said, "but you are right. We need to stay longer."

"You have the support of the congregation, as you know," Bauer said. Oscar smiled and nodded, thinking back to when the property acquisition became public knowledge in the church. In the evening worship service, the congregation said prayers for the land to be prosperous and to provide a good home for Oscar, Greta, and their soon-to-arrive child. Oscar knew he could count on his brethren for assistance in fixing up the property.

"Not to mention the support of your favorite uncle," Uncle Fredrick said, piercing a chicken breast with his fork.

"Of course," Greta said.

After the meal, Oscar offered to walk Fredrick back to his carriage. It was the first time they had been alone that day, as the village elders had met them at the Fishers' property earlier for the ride to town.

"Have you heard from Colonel Tillett?" Oscar asked quietly as they approached the carriage, Rosa trotting at their heels. The men's breath rose in front of them in a hazy mist; winter was nearly upon them now.

"We agreed it was best that he take the train back to New

York," Fredrick said. "He'll be busy managing his oil leases or depleting the trout population of Ninemile Creek with his fly rod, I reckon."

"I'm sorry he had to leave," Oscar said. Within a few days of the incident, news had quickly traveled across the county. Gossips whispered of an alcohol-fueled ex-soldier indulging in a mid-morning slaughter, and the city council had been deeply concerned for the reputation of the town. Uncle Fredrick was correct in that no charges were leveled at the colonel; as a veteran, he was legally allowed to carry a sidearm for self-defense.

"Yes, well, I'm sure he's having a fine time," Fredrick said with a shrug. "After the Bunker Hill Women's Christian Temperance League started petitioning to prevent the carrying of firearms, he knew he had to go. Anyway, we keep in touch through occasional letters. I am sure I will see him again soon enough."

"He seems like a good friend to you, although he is certainly eccentric," Oscar said as Fredrick placed a foot on the carriage step.

"That he is," Fredrick said, the corner of his mouth twitching. "We have one of those friendships; we can go a long spell without seeing each other, but every time we do, it feels like no time has passed at all."

* * *

Greta straightened, wincing as her lower back gave a painful spasm. It was shortly after five on a cold mid-February afternoon, and she and Sarah were washing clothes in the wash house connected to the kitchen as new snow blew across the dormant fields. The baby was due any day now, and everyone, especially Greta, was ready for that time to come.

Greta put her hands on her lower back and stretched, a smile playing across her face despite her soreness. The new home, on the cusp of readiness, would not be finished in time for the baby to be born there. However, it was coming along rapidly, and she and Oscar had spent joyful days and evenings preparing the baby's room. The barn took much labor to complete, as did the new home. However, carpenters from the congregation appeared daily to assist Oscar during the renovation, just as he would for others in the years to come. Skilled hands had crafted simple furniture and painted the inside of the home a plain, clean white. Church sisters sewed curtains, clothing, and bedding. All was nearing completion.

"I think Oscar and I should be moving to our house by the time spring planting arrives," Greta said. Sarah looked up, her round, pink face glowing.

"You and Oscar have accomplished much in five months," Sarah said, but Greta did not hear. Something shifted inside her, and a torrent of liquid gushed from her body and splattered on the floor.

"My water has broken!" she shouted in surprise.

Sarah sprang into action. Urging Greta to sit down, she quickly fetched a pan and towel to wipe up the liquid on the floor.

"This signals the first stage of labor," Sarah said. "The time is nearing."

Alerted by Sarah's cry for help, the men, who had been washing eggs in the cellar, rushed up the stairs. Gently weaving his arm around Greta, Oscar helped her through the kitchen and into the guest bedroom where the birth would take place. Greta sat on the edge of the bed, panting.

"The contractions are starting already," she said, her face crumpling in pain.

"I will drive the wagon to town and bring Dr. Miller immediately," Oscar said.

"You don't have to rush. There is still much time," Sarah said, coming in with a cup of broth. "Since this is your first child, it's hard to estimate how quickly the birth will come about, but I think there is considerable time to go."

"Just the same," Oscar said, wringing his hands, "I will go now to find the doctor."

Oscar knelt by Greta, holding her hand. He looked into her eyes. "I'll be back soon, Greta," he said. "Please stay in bed." Greta nodded.

Over the next few hours, the slow process of labor continued. Greta gritted her teeth, drank the broth Sarah brought her, and tried to bear the pain gracefully. Oscar returned, announcing that the doctor had been informed.

"I saw some of the church members when I was looking for Dr. Miller," Oscar said, his hat slightly askew, his voice higher than usual. "They said they would inform Pastor Yoder."

"Excellent. Now, dear, I think I hear someone at the door," Sarah said to Oscar. "Please go get it, and then try to find Bauer and help him with the farm chores. You're doing no good here."

Oscar left in a fluster. A few minutes later, two sisters from the church knocked to enter Greta's room. Greta recognized Ruth, the taller of the two.

"We rushed over to help with the birth," Ruth said. "Greta, this is Sister Kunkle."

"Hello, Sister," Greta said, grateful she was between contractions. She recognized the slender woman with her pale skin, dark brown hair, and penetrating eyes. "Thank you so much for coming to help."

"Yes, so pleased to see you, sisters," Sarah said, mopping the sweat from her brow. "Would one of you mind getting a cloth and more hot water?"

The sun made its way ponderously across the sky. As night approached, Sarah, Ruth, and Dorcas lit kerosene lamps and readied linen and basins of clean water, working as an experienced team. Bauer convinced Oscar to help with evening chores so he would stop pacing and mumbling.

Greta's contractions and pain grew more intense as dilation progressed; she tried to breathe and pray, squeezing her eyes shut and picturing waving boughs and the green-filtered light of early summer. Telling her to drink, Sarah handed her a large cup of water, but Greta could only manage a few sips. Ruth fed the small woodstove in the corner, and Dorcas threw an extra blanket over Greta as she convulsed.

"Sister," Dorcas said, her large, dark eyes full of pity, "we are with you. The Lord will see you through."

It was nine o'clock at night when Dr. Miller finally arrived. Greta shivered slightly as he entered.

"I am sorry it took so long for me to get here," he said, shrugging off his coat and handing it to Sarah, who held out a hand. "There were a few emergencies I needed to handle before I came out. How is the pain now, my girl?"

All Greta could manage was a nod. She grimaced as a new wave of contractions engulfed her.

"Take some long, deep breaths," the doctor said, unpacking his things. After the wave had subsided and Greta had collapsed, exhausted, against the pillows, the doctor proceeded with his examination and asked questions. Sarah translated the physician's more technical words.

The door creaked, and Oscar poked his head in the door, eyes wide.

"Greta," he said weakly. Greta looked at him wearily and tried unsuccessfully to smile.

"A couple more hours," the doctor said. Sarah, rising, patted Oscar's shoulder and gently pushed him out.

The next few hours were excruciating for Greta. The contractions were a rhythmic torture of stretching and tearing tissue. Though Greta tried hard to hold the pain, a shriek eventually ripped from her throat. Her vision wavered, and her breath caught.

"Oscar," she said. "Please, Doctor. Oscar."

"Hand me a wet cloth, please," Dr. Miller said to someone out of Greta's view. Greta closed her eyes, unable to stop the tears from mingling with the sweat on her face.

When Greta began seeing spots, she heard Sarah say as though through a blanket, "Doctor, I think she's going to faint!"

Greta opened her mouth to pant and gasped as something bitter and sharp dripped onto her tongue.

"The laudanum will help," he said. "Drink it, please." Greta obediently swallowed, and the spots eased a little. A few minutes later, she was able to sit up and drink some water before the next contraction hit.

It was four o'clock in the morning when Oscar finally heard the sound he had been waiting for. Unable to sleep but continuously shooed away from the labor room, he had been pacing downstairs all night, praying and wincing with each scream of pain. As soon as the first tiny, unfamiliar cry reverberated through the house, Oscar threw off the wool blanket he had wrapped himself in and raced to the top of the stairs. When he knocked at Greta's door, a tired-looking Dr. Miller emerged and smiled. The doctor put his arm around Oscar's shoulder.

"Congratulations, Oscar. You have a strong son."

"May I see Greta now?" Oscar asked in a weak voice. He did not think he could wait any longer.

"In a bit," answered the doctor. "Sarah and the sisters are with her. Perhaps you have some chores to do first."

Oscar moaned, and the doctor smiled at him sympathetically.

"I'll need my horse soon," Dr. Miller said, fumbling for his pocket watch. "Why don't you go get her ready? By the time you get back, it should be time for you to meet your new son."

Oscar hastily rushed outside to get the doctor's horse and buggy, only to be greeted by a hollow-eyed Bauer.

"Let's get the chores done, son," Bauer said. "Sarah is making up some sausage knipp for the doctor and sisters."

"But—" protested Oscar.

"They sent me out here to keep you occupied," Bauer said, raising his eyebrows. "Don't make this harder than it has to be, Brother Oscar."

Bauer insisted on inspecting Dr. Miller's mare, which had cracked a shoe Oscar hadn't noticed. By the time Oscar and Bauer had replaced the shoe, finished the chores, washed their faces and hands at the pump in the attached washhouse, and entered the kitchen, it was five o'clock in the morning. Everyone except Greta and the new baby was downstairs. Oscar looked to Dr. Miller hopefully.

"Yes," the doctor said with a big smile. "You may now go see them." Oscar took off at a run.

"Don't stay too long!" Dr. Miller called. "They both need their rest."

Oscar slowly opened the bedroom door. Greta looked pale and exhausted, but she was also clean and well cared for. In her arms lay the new baby.

Oscar sat down on the side of the bed and gently touched Greta's forehead.

"You did well, my Greta," he said. Greta smiled faintly.

"*We* did well," she replied, looking down at the child in her arms. Oscar followed her gaze down to see a round-faced, pale, sleeping baby boy. A wisp of blonde hair protruded from the swaddling cloth.

Oscar felt his breath catch as he held out a trembling hand and stroked the infant's cheek. He and Greta had waited long for this moment. This child was the fruition of so many dreams over so many years.

"Oscar," Greta said, her dark blue eyes full of joy, "At last, God has given us our son."

8
Familiar Patterns
(Vertraute Muster)
May 1896

Greta jumped as something soft hit her in the face, blown there by the warm southerly breeze. Standing upright and brushing her forehead with a muddy hand, she watched a pale pink dogwood flower flutter into the soil of her garden. She smiled down at it, then looked around her, breathing in the scent of freshly tilled soil.

Dogwood trees flowered in the nearby woods, and the winds spread their sweet fragrance over the countryside. Greta had already prepared a stew for lunch, and little Fredrick was taking his usual morning nap. Nearby, she could hear ratcheting sounds as Oscar skillfully spliced fences around the north field while he waited for Bauer to deliver more posts from the town sawmill lumber yard.

Greta's heart fairly glowed as she thought of her son, reminiscing about the conversation she and Oscar had had with Uncle Fredrick about the baby's name.

"We've decided to name our son in your honor, Uncle Fredrick," Oscar had told Uncle Fredrick when he came to visit the newborn at the Fisher residence. Uncle Fredrick's eyes gleamed as he looked at the child in his arms. Young Fredrick had looked peaceful as he napped, his blonde hair shimmering in the afternoon light filtered by the windowpanes. Sharing a loving glance, Bauer and Sarah looked on.

"It is an honor," Uncle Fredrick had said, his expression soft. That moment, Greta had known instantly, would become a special memory of carrying on the childless Uncle Fredrick's legacy.

"You have done so much to help us, Uncle Fredrick. So have both of you," Greta had said, turning to Bauer and Sarah. "It is our wish that you become Fredrick Jurgen Beck's godparents." Sarah and Bauer had smiled, tearfully welcoming the responsibility.

Thinking, Greta briefly stopped her work and looked up at the window of the room where Fredrick slept. At first, she indulged her son day and night, ignoring fatigue and loss of sleep. Now, Fredrick slept off and on nine hours per night and took daily naps. He was alert and fascinated with the world he saw around him, and he waved his arms and legs to greet Greta when she entered his room each morning, lifting his head to look at her with large, sparkly blue eyes when she peered over the top of the crib.

The German Baptist Brethren community had rallied to move the new family into the new property once Fredrick was born, leaving Greta and Oscar deeply grateful. Uncle Fredrick had also been an enormous help, bringing provisions and paying and transporting Brethren Church brothers to help work and plant the ground. Greta felt a profound sense of thankfulness and love as she knelt back down and began to work in the soil of her little garden, her contribution. She'd planted the little vegetable plot and was now fertilizing with horse dung and compost, evenly measuring and marking row by row. In addition to working on the garden and the interior of the house, Greta and Sarah had taken turns watching the new baby and carrying water from the stream that ran in a north-to-south direction through the farm to nourish the garden Oscar had tilled.

Over the past months, Oscar had worked tirelessly to finish the interiors of the barn, sheds, and new home. The church brothers had constructed furniture and designed and built cabinets to match the handmade dining table and chairs. The previous family had left behind an old wood-burning stove, but Greta had already made plans to replace it with an enameled range as soon as it was financially possible. The house was plain, simple, and without frills, Greta thought with satisfaction as she spread fertilizer over the fertile garden. No graven images or adornments that could distract from the singular purpose of keeping God foremost in mind hung on the walls or sat on the shelves. The home was designed purely for function, and for her and Oscar, it represented a realized dream.

Meanwhile, Oscar and Bauer's spring labors commenced on both farms by planting the fallow fields. Bauer was scaling down his operations, preferring to help his children along with Oscar and Greta as he grew older. Oscar helped Bauer move the cattle to their spring pasture on his farm; working soil, sowing, and seed consumed most of their days as the sun slowly warmed the ground. The seasoned sows, bred in January, began farrowing, and new chickens began to hatch.

Smiling to herself, Greta glanced back at the shirts waving on the clothesline, blowing gently in the warm breeze. A faint clanging sound caught her attention, and she looked past the house to the dirt road. There, a brightly painted vardo with colorful designs rattled and clanked as it rolled along the path. Copper pots and pans attached to the outside of the trailer struck the penny boards as the wagon traversed the bumpy road. A large piebald Vanner horse pulled the clattering caisson, its distinctive black-and-white pattern making the vardo stand out even more.

Greta straightened as the wagon approached, and the clanging grew louder. When the wagon finally came to a halt in front of Greta's garden gate, Greta smiled at the short, dark man of slight build in the driver's seat. Now that she could see the wagon and the driver clearly, she could guess who these people were: the "Black Dutch," or Gypsy transplants from Germany, that the German Baptists had seemed so wary of.

When the driver smiled down at Greta, his drooping mustache twitched over his two-day beard growth. He wore a gray felt fedora, a baggy white shirt with rolled-up sleeves, and a black leather vest adorned with petite, tarnished silver buttons. Two ragamuffin children—a boy and a girl around ten years old—sat beside the driver on the wagon seat, chattering quietly to one another in a language Greta didn't recognize.

"Guten Morgen," Greta said, walking forward. The small and well-curried black pony behind the wagon whinnied in a friendly way at her approach, its majestic tail sweeping the ground.

"Sastipe,"[10] the man said, then hastily added a heavily accented greeting in German. "Can my children have a drink of water?"

Greta nodded. "Come down," she said, reaching up a hand to help the children off the caisson. "Your children look hungry. Perhaps you would like to go to my henhouse and take two of the meat roosters for butchering."

---

10   Romani greeting

The man's eyes widened in puzzlement, and he tipped his hat. "You are kind, madam," he said.

"Not at all," Greta said. "All German Baptists believe in charity." As she pointed to the henhouse, a long-haired, dark-skinned woman stepped out of the back of the wagon. She looked to be in her thirties, with striking amber-colored eyes, bronze skin, and a bright cloth scarf cap pulled over her forehead.

"I am Greta Beck," Greta said to the family, smiling broadly. "Welcome to my home."

"My name is Kezia Ivailo," the Gypsy woman said, looking baffled by Greta's warm greeting. "I am called Kezi. My husband is Manfri, and my children are Mahai and Anca."

Greta reached out and took Anca's hand, feeling the little fingers close around her thumb. "Come with me, little ones, and we'll see if we can find a cookie or two while your father fetches the roosters," Greta said, leading Kezi and her children to the house. She turned for one last look at Manfri, who was standing sheepishly in front of his caisson. With one hand, she gestured for him to make his way to the henhouse before going inside.

Soon, everyone was seated and enjoying freshly baked biscuits dipped into a tin of Sarah's delicious strawberry preserves.

"When did you come to America?" Greta asked, passing out glasses of cool buttermilk she had brought from the spring cellar.

"We are the second generation," Kezi said. "We came from Europe, and both our parents immigrated to Canada."

"And now you live in Indiana?"

"We move around often," Kezi explained. "My family and I travel in Illinois, Kentucky, and Indiana during the summer months."

"What do you do for a living?"

"We sell at fairs and towns we pass when we're allowed. We hunt and dig the white ginseng to sell the Chinamen in the late summer and fall." Kezi looked at her children, who were quietly eating as many biscuits as possible from the large basket, before turning back to Greta.

"I am not afraid of admitting we are not allowed in certain communities. I am sure you are aware of that." Greta nodded, and Kezi smiled wanly.

"I see it only as part of the fate life has chosen for us. I must admit, however, that your kindness is a nice change. It speaks well of you and your faith."

"'Whoever brings blessings will be enriched, and one who waters will himself be watered,'" Greta said, smiling at Kezi. "Aside from that, however, a Gypsy in my homeland helped me before I sailed here. I am only passing along her kindness."

Soon, their trepidation was forgotten, and Kezi and her children began telling Greta all about their lives. Greta laughed and exclaimed as Anca and Mahai told her tales of their travels and adventures, admiring the proud look on Kezi's face as she watched her children, noting the way the two youngsters seemed to look up to their mother. *I would like to know this family better,* she thought.

Outside, Oscar looked up from his work on the fence and noticed the parked Gypsy wagon. He walked from his field to the farmhouse to further investigate, and he found Manfri brushing his heavy piebald's thick mane by the wagon.

After exchanging greetings in German, Manfri briefly explained his directions from Greta.

"I decided to wait until she came back outside before entering your henhouse, however," he told Oscar, glancing at Oscar's face, then to the henhouse, then down at his feet.

"Is something the matter?" Oscar asked.

"The local sheriff warned us earlier in the week to stay only on the roadways and off private property unless we get invited," Manfri said quietly. "I don't want to cause problems."

"Why did he say that to you?" Oscar asked. Manfri shrugged, setting his grooming brush on the ledge of the caisson.

"I suppose the sheriff simply didn't care for the looks of me. I was on public property at the time, giving my horse and pony a drink."

The men heard the swinging of a door and the sound of voices. The children ran to Manfri, grinning and wiping biscuit crumbs from their shirts, speaking in a language Oscar couldn't understand.

"Did you find the roosters?" Greta asked Manfri, walking up with Kezi.

"No," Manfri said. "I thought it best to wait until you showed me the ones we could take."

"I told Manfri he could have two birds," Greta said. "Perhaps two of those older red roosters we got from the Bontragers."

"Yes, we can spare them," Oscar said. "One of them has been limping anyway. Wait here."

When Oscar returned a few minutes later, a gunny sack containing two squawking chickens was slung over his shoulder. The group was talking like old friends. Oscar smiled as he watched Greta ruffle the little boy's hair. He handed the bag to Manfri, who thanked him profusely.

Tugging Kezi's sleeve, Anca said something in their peculiar language, pointing to the sack. Kezi smiled at Anca and then reached for the bag, which Manfri opened slightly.

"What are you doing?" Oscar asked.

"You will see," Kezi said with a smile. She hoisted a protesting rooster from the sack and held him with both hands high above her head as Greta and Oscar starred. She then repeated magic in her foreign tongue.

Holding the squawking rooster tightly in both hands, Kezi lowered the bird to her waist, gently tucking his head under his wing. She began to slowly swing the chicken from side to side in a rhythmic motion while repeating words Oscar couldn't follow. The squawking sounds subsided.

The rooster's head was still hidden under his wing as Kezi carefully laid the chicken on the ground. She placed her hand above the bird and said, "Close your eyes now and sleep."

Oscar and Greta quietly stepped over to look. The bird remained motionless, drawing long, slow, pulsing breaths. He appeared to be in a state of deep slumber, his head still under his wing.

Nearly a minute passed as Greta and Oscar stood watching in amazement.

"Is he . . . alright?" Greta finally asked. But just as the words left her mouth, the chicken sprang up from the ground, clearly disoriented. He staggered in circles for a moment before Manfri seized him and returned him to the sack.

"Even the least of God's creatures can pass through the veil and return," Manfri said, smiling at his children.

As if on cue, the Gypsy family climbed back aboard the Vardo wagon, thanking Greta and Oscar for their kindness. Greta followed Kezi to the back door of the wagon, patting the black pony as she went. From the house, she could hear a cranky wail from the open nursery window as Fredrick awoke from his nap.

As Kezi was about to close the door, Greta leaned in, catching a hint of oud wafting from inside the wagon. Goosebumps rose on her arms.

"I want to talk more with you," she said quietly. Kezi smiled.

"Yes, soon, my friend," the Gypsy answered. "Blessings upon you and your family." She gently closed the vardo door behind her.

That night, as the couple enjoyed a meal of ham, fried potatoes, and Sarah's canned green beans cooked in chicken broth, Oscar cleared his throat. Nearby, Fredrick played on a blanket on the floor, seeming very interested in his toes.

"Greta," Oscar said, cutting his ham absentmindedly, "I've been meaning to ask you something for quite some time."

"And I've been meaning to tell you something for quite some time," Greta said.

"About the Gypsies? About your interest in them?" Oscar said.

"Yes," Greta said. As they ate, Greta finally told Oscar about her experiences in Germany while visiting Dieter's farm before leaving for America. She described in detail her encounter with the two wolves at the stone circle she and Oscar had discovered in the forest. She revealed the calm she had felt since leaving the ring of stones in Germany and chronicled most of what the Jenische woman had told her. However, she did not mention that the circle in the forest supposedly served as a harbor for angelic spirits; she suspected this would be too far a stretch for Oscar, whose face was already creased with worry. When she got to the part about Tshura, she also failed to tell him the prophecy about two children, only revealing the prediction of a son. *Just in case,* she told herself.

Oscar patiently listened, eating quietly with his eyes fixed on Greta's face. Greta felt a strong sense of relief now that the tale was out in the open.

"Greta, you should have spoken of these things before," he said at last. "The wolves might have killed you! Why didn't you call out to me?"

Greta sat rocking Fredrick, who was now asleep. She and Oscar were both done eating, and he began to clear the plates.

"At first, I was frightened," she said, her eyes unfocused. "But then I felt as if something or someone was protecting me from harm. It was as if the wolves sensed it too and then let me pass."

Oscar stopped, holding the dirty plates, to look quizzically at Greta.

"I had the same feeling that night onboard the ship when the thief threatened us," she said. "It was as if a powerful force was standing by my side to eliminate any fear."

Oscar took the plates into the kitchen, then came back and slid his chair over beside Greta's. Greta leaned her head over slightly to rest on his shoulder.

"There was another reason also," Greta said. "I did not want to distract you with things I was not sure of. Not while we had so much to do. Now, though, we are in our own home, and we have seen the unfolding prophecy that the old Gypsy spoke of."

Oscar reached out to stroke his son's soft cheek with a farm-roughened finger. "There are many in the church who believe Gypsies only pretend to be kind, as you know," he said in a measured tone. "They say Gypsies simply want to swindle those who believe they can tell the future or reveal secret passageways to hidden realms."

Greta sat upright and looked into Oscar's worried eyes as he continued to speak, her expression unreadable. "'I will set my face against those who turn to soothsayers, saith the Lord.' You must be careful, Greta."

"I must put our baby to bed," Greta said, trying to keep the chill from her tone. As she walked up the stairs to the nursery, she frowned. Oscar only had her best interest in mind, and even if somehow he was intrigued by the Jenische predictions or by Kezi's performance that afternoon, he would never openly admit it. Such a fascination would serve to validate Gypsy practices, and Oscar was not capable of that. Heavily, Greta reiterated to herself that such talk could never leave the safety of their home.

9
The Ultimatum
(Das Ultimatum)
June 1896

A month or so passed before Greta saw Kezi again. It was June, and Greta was once again in the garden, pulling the weeds that persistently tried to drown out her potatoes and turnips. Fredrick, nearing four months of age, lay in his baby basket nearby, and Abraham, a large tabby cat who had decided to join the family a few weeks before, was purring and nudging the sides of the basket. Fredrick giggled as the bushy tail waved in the air just out of reach.

"It was nice of Sister Sarah to visit yesterday, wasn't it, Fredrick?" Greta asked as she threw another handful of weeds onto her growing pile. Fredrick responded with a laugh. Sarah stopped once a week to take Greta and Fredrick to Bunker Hill for groceries and hardware or to mail correspondence to Germany—usually to Dieter, relatives, or members of the old congregation. Sarah was as fond of Fredrick as any godmother could be, and to Greta, it seemed that little Fredrick was constantly the center of attention when she took him to church or town.

Greta brushed the dirt from her hands and walked over to the basket.

"Why are you cooing, little one?" she asked. Fredrick had turned over from back to stomach and was waving his arms and legs, while Abraham had lain down next to the basket, alert and protective, ears twitching.

"What a strong boy," Greta said affectionately. Watching young Fredrick grow each day was her greatest fulfillment. As she patted Fredrick's small back, she silently thanked God for her happiness. Being a mother was more than she had ever hoped for.

"Now, what are you looking at, Abraham?" Greta asked the cat. Following his stare, she saw a black pony outfitted with a bright red saddle and bridle tied to the post in front of her house.

Strange, she thought. She hadn't seen the pony approach on the road.

Greta gently picked up the baby basket and walked to the house, tailed by Abraham. There on the front porch swing sat Kezi, slowly moving forward and back with her eyes closed, the ropes of the swing rhythmically creaking.

"Kezi," Greta said, mounting the steps. "I am happy to see you again." Kezi opened her eyes, green flecked with gold, and reached out her arms in greeting.

"Hello, my friend."

After Kezi fussed over Fredrick, Greta welcomed the Gypsy into her house.

"Sit at the kitchen table, Kezi," Greta said, placing Fredrick's basket carefully down on the floor. "I have freshly baked mulberry pie; I found a tree at the edge of our woods on the other side of the cornfield. I'll get us some milk from the cooling tank." She soon returned and bustled around the room, collecting plates and seizing glasses, pleased when Kezi lifted Fredrick out of his basket and spoke softly to him in what she now surmised was Romani.

Soon, enjoying their pie and milk, the women fell into an easy conversation as Fredrick entertained himself by sucking on his fists in his basket.

"Kezi, where is your camp at the moment?" Greta asked, savoring a bite of the pie. It was the perfect amount of tart and sweet, with a beautiful flaky crust thanks to the freshly churned butter she'd used.

"The caravan is at the north edge of Bunker Hill," Kezi said. She took a bite of pie and moaned. "Oh, Greta, this is a pie from heaven." Greta smiled, and both women took a moment to relish the flavors.

"My family connected with other travelers there," Kezi said, swallowing.

"Will you be here for long?" Greta asked.

"I believe we will stay until late summer," Kezi said, heaping her fork with more pie. "The fair season has now begun, and we are busy working the circuit."

"And then? Where will you go in the fall?"

"Northern Indiana for blueberry season," Kezi said, "where we will pick, and Manfri will do farrier work for the northern Amish. There are lots of pie fixings up there, but I don't think any are better than yours," she said, smiling before taking a bite.

Fredrick made a few coughing, cranky baby sounds from his basket. Greta picked him up, wiped his wet fists off with a cloth, and held him to her breast, covering herself with Fredrick's blanket. He quietened instantly.

"Somebody was hungry too," Greta said, smoothing his fair hair. She looked back up at Kezi. "What is it like for you to move among all these religious groups?"

"I respect it," Kezi told Greta. "I have been baptized as a Catholic myself."

"Really? You are Catholic?"

"I wouldn't say that exactly in the purest sense," Kezi said. "Although I certainly believe in God."

Greta looked at her friend, pondering, her heart beating a little faster in her chest.

"Kezi, I'd like to tell you a story," she said.

"I'd like to listen to a story," Kezi countered. She patiently sat at attention as Greta disclosed her odd experiences in the German forest. When Greta described the standing stones, Kezi's amber eyes shone with a strange light.

"I know the forest of which you speak," she said. "My mother's family was from Bulgaria, but they traveled through Germany when I was very young. They told me about a site in the Northern German woods that sounds very similar to what you are describing."

"That's quite a coincidence," Greta said, laying a slumbering Fredrick in his basket.

"It is a strange place," Kezi said. "My mother often spoke of that spot as having supernatural power. 'Immortals dwell there,' she told me, 'intuitively guarded by forest creatures.'" Kezi pitched her voice down, clearly quoting her mother. "'When a person pure of heart enters the circle, a heavenly spirit might choose to follow and keep them from harm.'"

"Well, then, let me tell you the rest of the tale," Greta said, smiling. She told Kezi of the wolves and her sense of serenity.

Kezi reached out and touched her fingertips lightly to the back of Greta's hand.

"I knew there was something special about you," she said quietly.

"Was your mother chosen like this?" Greta asked. Kezi shook her head.

"My mother would have told me if she had an angel at her side."

Greta swirled the last bit of milk around in the bottom of her cup, pondering. The soft sound of Fredrick's breathing and the chirping of birds filled the kitchen.

"I believe your mother's story to be true, Kezi," Greta said. "I felt as if one of God's angels had been specifically directed to protect me."

Kezi nodded. "My mother used to say, 'Guardian angels lead you to places where they can also be near to God in order to renew themselves.'"

"Now, there is one more part of the story," Greta said. She told Kezi the only other part of the story she'd withheld from her husband: the part about Tshura's prediction that Greta would birth a daughter in addition to a son.

"Well then, it must be so." Kezi reached for Greta's hand, and Greta automatically extended her arm. Kezi flipped the hand over and traced Greta's right palm with her index finger.

"You will have a daughter; it's true," Kezi said, "but it will not be soon. At least three seasons will pass before you will bear another child. If you wish, I could read the cards for you and look deeper into your future."

Greta glanced at the road, where a wagon carrying a German Baptist family was traveling by. "I would like that, but I will come to you at your camp," she said. "I also want to see your children again."

As Greta bid Kezi goodbye, she felt a pang in her chest. She hated not knowing when she would see the woman again. Kezi climbed quickly upon the pony's gullet saddle.

"I hope soon to see you, my friend," Kezi said. She smiled, and with a wave, she turned her pony down the road.

Greta waved and watched as the pony, quickly becoming a black streak on the road, passed a buggy approaching the farm. As the buggy drew closer, Greta saw that it was Pastor Yoder. An unpleasant fear gripped her, but Greta smiled and waved as the buggy pulled up.

"Hello, Sister Greta," Pastor Yoder said, pulling the horse's reins toward him and setting the carriage brake.

"Welcome, Pastor. Please, come inside," Greta said. "I will get you some refreshments and then go and find my husband."

When Greta ushered Pastor Yoder in, she heard him let out a sigh as he looked at the pie plates and empty cups on the table.

"I see you have had company before I arrived," the minister said.

"Yes," Greta replied, keeping her voice bright. "Just being a good neighbor as the Bible instructs."

The pastor sat down on a chair at the table while Greta cleared the dirty dishes away.

"Would you like some mulberry pie and milk?" she asked.

"Yes, but I can only stay for a short time," the clergyman said. "I simply wanted to see that you and the baby were all well and visit your new farm." Greta nodded and peeked around the corner into the front room, where she had placed the baby basket.

She beckoned Pastor Yoder to follow, and the two looked down at Fredrick, who was still fast asleep.

"Such a sweet child," Pastor Yoder said quietly as he watched Fredrick's eyelids flutter. "It won't be long now before he'll be ready to be baptized."

Hearing voices, Greta and the pastor looked out the front room window. Oscar was with three other church brothers who, having finished mowing hay, were approaching the house.

"Pastor, I am going to move Fredrick upstairs where this clamor won't wake him," Greta said, gently lifting the basket. Pastor Yoder nodded.

"Of course," he said. He watched from the windows as the men, their work shirts and suspenders soaked with sweat, took off their hats and wiped their sticky faces.

Thanking the men for their help, Oscar came into the house, where he saw the pastor sitting at the table.

"Welcome, Brother Yoder," he said. The two men greeted each other with a holy kiss on the cheek and a shaking of hands. Outside, the three church brothers approached the barn to get their horses for their short journeys home.

"A strong son you have, Brother Beck," the pastor said. "Greta just took him upstairs." Oscar grinned.

"Thank you, Pastor," he said as Greta hastened down the stairs and began serving milk and pie. The trio spent a pleasant twenty minutes speaking about crops, the church, and plans for an upcoming barn raising until Fredrick awoke. Greta, excusing herself, slipped upstairs to breastfeed.

As the two men heard the door closing upstairs, Pastor Yoder leaned forward toward Oscar, who was pinching a few stray pie crumbs from his plate.

"I noticed as I approached your farm that a Gypsy woman was riding away," Pastor Yoder said in a low voice. Oscar abruptly looked up, pie crumbs forgotten.

"Yes," Oscar said. "She is a Gypsy. We met by chance when she and her family were passing by. We gave her family some food at that time. I saw her leaving as we were cutting the hay."

Pastor Yoder paused for a moment, his sun-weathered face serious behind his bushy beard. "It is good to welcome strangers into our homes, Brother Beck, in order to talk of God and to help them find salvation. It is good to assist them if they are unsaved and truly are seeking God's Word."

"Yes, of course, Pastor."

The minister then pitched his voice even lower. "However, one must take caution that strangers do not lead our brothers and sisters in Christ onto a path of deception. First Corinthians 15:33 tells us that bad company ruins good morals."

Oscar swallowed. "I am sure Greta has not intentionally chosen a wrong path by inviting the Gypsy in," he said. "She was simply trying to be polite, knowing her." The pastor brought his wiry eyebrows together.

"I recognized the woman you have welcomed; her black pony is very distinct," he said. "She is known for practicing divination and selling potions, among other things." The pastor sighed and steepled his fingers together, placing his elbows on the table. "I am sorry to say this, but perhaps you should speak with Greta about this tonight, Oscar. As Saint Peter has warned us: 'Be watchful, for the devil prowls like a roaring lion seeking someone to devour.'"

"Yes, of course, Pastor." Oscar felt sick, the pie heavy in his stomach, as Pastor Yoder stood and adjusted his collarless suit coat, then gathered his hat and Bible.

"Thank you, Oscar, for your hospitality," Pastor Yoder said. "Please, thank Greta."

"Any time, Brother Yoder," Oscar said. "Let me walk you out."

As he climbed up into his carriage, the pastor turned back to Oscar.

"Think upon what we have spoken, Brother Beck. Perhaps you could talk to other brothers of our church familiar with the Gypsies and their deceptive ways." Oscar squinted against the dust as Pastor Yoder's horse and buggy went off down the road.

Sitting down on the porch steps, Oscar put his head in his hands. Abraham burst silently from the garden and sidled, purring loudly, into his lap.

"What am I supposed to do?" Oscar asked the cat. Abraham blinked up at him with large yellow eyes.

Stroking the tabby cat absentmindedly, Oscar pondered the situation. He was hesitant to speak of Pastor Yoder's conversation with Greta, who had plenty on her hands between Fredrick and chores. Perhaps he would give it more time and slowly bring up the subject when Greta was feeling particularly rested, he thought to himself.

Four nights later, Oscar decided it was time to speak of the minister's concerns. Fredrick was fed and sleeping soundly, and the evening had turned refreshingly cool. Oscar started a small fire in the front room fireplace to take the evening chill from the house and provide some light. Lit by the flickering firelight, Greta sat patching Oscar's shirt with needle and thread.

"Greta, what is it that you and Kezi talked of when she visited last?" Oscar asked, working to make his voice sound light.

"Oh!" Greta said, her eyes shining happily. She enthusiastically told Oscar of their conversation about children, God, and the traveling the Gypsies had planned.

"Yes, I saw the caravan yesterday as I went to town," Oscar said. He paused, twisting the hem of his shirt in his hands. "Do you talk of other things, such as the telling of fortunes or seeing the future?"

Greta looked up, her expression guileless. "I told her about my experiences when we visited Uncle Dieter's home," she said. "She only gave me her thoughts about that."

"Greta," Oscar said, deciding he had to be somewhat direct. "There is no good way to tell you this, but Pastor Yoder fears for your soul. He made it quite clear on his last visit here. He fears that though you may only want a friendship, you might also become seduced by the dark forces that follow Gypsies."

Oscar got up and began to pace, his worries pouring out and poisoning the easy air between them. "These 'Black Dutch Gypsies' may be intermarried with Germans, but Lord only knows what else they are. There are now so many more of them, it seems, coming from Europe and moving to Chicago and Gary. Everyone in the congregation says Gypsies only pretend to be kind and wise in order to fool people into paying money for card readings, charms, spells, and potions. They lie about their abilities to heal the sick, knowing the future, or hidden portals."

Oscar stopped, still twisting the bottom of his shirt, staring out the darkened window. "Most are not even true Christians, according to some I have spoken with. Pastor Yoder says that 'the only work they do is hawking cooking pans from their wagons and selling wild sang root to the Chinee in town.' There are even stories of kidnappings and the selling of white children."

"I do not believe that," Greta said simply. Oscar shook his head.

"I know you welcome Kezi in, but Pastor Yoder knows her to practice sorcery, which the scriptures strongly forbid," he said, struggling to keep his voice level. "Since he said that, I have asked around. There are Brethren in the church I have talked with who have seen her at the fairs."

"I like Kezi. You also liked her when you met her."

Oscar felt desperation welling up inside him. "She may seem nice, but Kezi performs occult acts and lures people to have their fortunes told," he said. "There are rumors that he bites the heads off of chickens and drinks the blood during rituals they perform!"

When Greta still said nothing, Oscar pressed on.

"Greta, there have also been many rumors about this woman you have befriended. It is whispered that for a price, she will perform prostitution."

The air in the room seemed to grow cold despite the fire, and Oscar turned to look at Greta. Her face had gone hard and pale. With a quiet snap, she broke her thread, having finished patching the work shirt.

"Kezi told me she believes in Christ and God's angels," Greta said resolutely. "She also believes that God enables her to heal people. And, Oscar, do you honestly believe that the nice man we met bites the heads of chickens and drinks their blood? Or that Kezi sells her body for money?" Greta scoffed, a sound unfamiliar to Oscar's ears. "As Proverbs says, 'With their mouths the godless destroy their neighbors, but through knowledge the righteous escape.'"

Oscar walked behind Greta's chair and reached down to put

an arm around her. "Greta, I am afraid," he said finally, his voice shaking slightly. "The church will not hesitate to banish us. It has happened here before."

Greta stood stiffly, wending her way from Oscar's embrace.

"I think what really needs to be happening here is less gossip and casting of stones," Greta said, her voice trembling with anger. "I must attend Fredrick now." She strode from the room, and Oscar, well aware Fredrick hadn't made a sound, stared into the fire.

Upstairs, Greta entered her bedroom rather than Fredrick's and threw herself onto the bed. She knew in her heart that there may be truth to the rumors; perhaps Kezi was practicing sorcery or something worse. Yet Greta felt Kezi would never intentionally harm anyone. As a wife and mother, Kezi did only what she needed to do for the survival of her family.

Greta grabbed one of the feather pillows from the head of the bed and buried her face in it. Without the support of the church, she knew existing in this community would be all but impossible. The brethren had done so much to help them, moving mountains to start their lives here. The church had also banned congregants before for even lesser things; Sarah had told her tales of families who had been banished for consistently performing labor on the Sabbath or failing to dress modestly.

Leaving the pillow on the bed, Greta slid off the side of the berth and knelt. Tears pricked her eyes. She didn't have the heart to end her friendship with Kezi outright, but she knew more brazen visits were out of the question. She would have to relegate interactions to the written word and the occasional passing meeting to protect her family.

"God, forgive me for being so willful," she quietly prayed.

"I ask for deliverance from all that conflicts with your Word. I was hoping you could help me to be a good wife and mother and protect my family from harm. Allow me to do thy will and only that which honors thee."

10
The Struggle for Life
(Der Kampf ums Leben)
April 1899

"Pa, you're sweaty," little Fredrick said. Brandishing a stick, he whacked the log in front of him enthusiastically, mimicking Oscar's sledgehammer swings.

"It's hard work surviving the winter," Oscar replied in accented English, wiping sweat from his brow and smiling down at his four-year-old son. "Farmers can only plan for spring and wait out the cold."

Oscar glanced at the sizable pile of wood he'd split with the wedge. The freezing temperatures and record snowfall of 1899 had lasted through the beginning of April, and splitting wood to heat the house was hard work. That particular winter, Indiana, had turned extremely cold; Oscar wasn't surprised when, in later years, that winter became known as the "Great Winter of '99."

"That's enough wood, I think. Come now, Fredrick, let us go check the animals."

Fredrick, who followed Oscar whenever possible, hurried over and took Oscar's hand. Oscar felt the weight of the little glove in his larger one, and warmth seemed to spread from within him. Bundled up in a woolen winter jacket and gloves lovingly crafted by his mother, the boy seemed to be wrapped in love. Looking at Fredrick's rosy cheeks, Oscar felt a pang of regret that his father had not lived to meet his grandson, the heir to the family name, as he had so wished.

In the barn, father and son gathered dry corn cobs and wood kindling, then fed it into the burn boxes that heated the water troughs. The animals seemed happy to see them, grunted and surged forward, staring at them with large, dark eyes, their earthy breath fogging the air. Fredrick handed Oscar oil-soaked cobs to feed into the tank heaters, keeping up a steady stream of questions as he went.

"Pa, why can't the horses just break the ice and drink?" he asked, peering at the trough. Nearby, Abraham napped in the hay, occasionally looking at them with narrowed, glinting eyes.

"I told you why yesterday and the day before," Oscar said, laughing. "Do you remember?"

Fredrick wrinkled his little forehead as he thought. "The trough might freeze all the way," he said, watching Oscar stand up and move to the calf pen. "Then the animals won't be able to drink."

"That's right," Oscar said. "Fredrick, we must always treat our animals with kindness."

"Why, Papa?"

"God has put them on this Earth to provide food and labor for us. We must help them survive the winter and make them comfortable."

Fredrick nodded and reached out a tiny hand to touch a calf's velvety nose. "Look, Papa, I'm being kind," he said. Oscar laughed, looking at the calf, which had been born in late winter. He then thought of Greta, once again great with child, and he closed his eyes with worry.

Initially, this pregnancy had seemed more relaxed than the first. However, in mid-March, Greta had begun to experience increased discomfort. The new baby was actively moving and kicking, and sometimes Greta suffered from pain and pressure under her ribs. The pressure seemed to increase gradually as the birth date neared. Dr. Miller's exam in late March confirmed Oscar's concerns.

"I believe the baby is in a frank breech position," Dr. Miller had informed the concerned couple. "I can attempt to manually turn and guide the baby's head downward when the time comes, but there is always the possibility that surgery might be necessary." The baby was due any day now, and trepidation had been preventing both Greta and Oscar from getting much sleep.

Oscar felt a tap on his thigh. Looking down, he saw that Fredrick was trying to hand him a corncob. Clearing his expression, Oscar stooped down, opened the burn box, and took the corncob from his son. As he did so, he heard barking and footsteps slapping the ground.

Oscar and Fredrick both straightened and turned to see Dorcas charging toward them, bonnet strings flying, with no hint of a shawl in sight. Cheese, the one-year-old hound that Greta had unfortunately promised Fredrick Jr. he could name, ran excited circles around her, yipping. Behind her, the sun was already getting low. Dorcas reached the barn and gasped, grasping the wall to steady herself as Cheese leaped about obliviously.

"I just came by with Lena when it happened," she panted. "Greta's water has broken. It's time." Oscar felt his insides tighten.

"I'll go for the doctor," Oscar replied. Reaching out, he took Fredrick's hand. "You will soon be a big brother," Oscar told his son. Fredrick blinked up at him and smiled, calm and trusting as only a child can be.

Due to the possibility of complications, the doctor quickly rearranged his schedule upon hearing the news. Dorcas had brought along her two-year-old daughter, Lena, to see Fredrick. The two church friends were playing with some wooden horses on the floor, supervised by Oscar, who struggled not to display the extent of his worry to the contented children.

Upstairs, Dr. Miller strode to Greta, whose face was white with anguish. Near the disarrayed bed, the crib sat awaiting its new occupant.

"I'll need to give you a small amount of laudanum, Greta. Just enough to reduce your pain and help you relax," he said immediately. "Though some may argue biblically that women are meant to suffer during childbirth," he muttered as though to himself, "I can't support such archaic convictions."

"I am grateful for that," said Greta, her hand trembling as the doctor held out the dropper full of reddish-brown liquid. Dorcas smoothed Greta's sticky hair back from her forehead.

Even with the laudanum, however, Greta's pain increased to alarming degrees. She labored to breathe through the increasing contractions.

Sigrid, she thought. *Sigrid, we will get through this together.*

Although she never mentioned the gender of the baby to anyone, Greta was certain, as Kezi had envisioned, that she was carrying a girl. Greta had already chosen the name "Sigrid" in honor of her Swedish maternal grandmother, who had taken Greta in after her parents' accident.

"You are brave like a Viking girl," Greta remembered Momor Sigrid saying. "You will sail to distant shores one day."

I will be brave like a Viking for you, little Sigrid.

Greta groaned in pain as another contraction swelled. Trying to distract herself, she thought back to last August when she began to feel profound nausea after rising from bed. She had missed her period twice, which had not been of concern to her. Dr. Miller had told her often that she was "physically overworking, and such stress often caused irregular cycles." But by November, it had become clear to Greta and Oscar that another child was on the way.

"Greta, my dear sister in Christ, how are you?" Greta opened her eyes briefly to see Ruth taking off her bonnet, leaving only her prayer covering. "We are here to help again however we can."

Ruth took Greta's hand comfortingly. Greta tried to thank her, but instead, she locked Ruth's hand in a vice-like grip as the spasm intensified. Even though she couldn't express it at the moment, Greta was genuinely grateful for the Brethren sisters of the church, especially Ruth and Dorcas. They had periodically visited to assist Greta as a sign of support and love throughout this pregnancy.

"It's almost time," said Dr. Miller. "Ladies, please go and fetch some linens and boil water." When Greta's eyes fluttered open, she saw him ready the instruments and chloroform on a cleared dresser.

I don't remember those from the last time, she thought, trying not to panic. *What are those for?*

She heard quiet voices and then felt Dr. Miller gently palpating her abdomen.

"Greta, I am going to attempt an external cephalic version to turn the child," the doctor said finally. "Frankly, this will not be comfortable. Please do your best." Greta nodded, bracing herself.

Dr. Miller applied mineral oil to Greta's protruding abdomen to reduce the friction, and then he slowly began applying counterclockwise pressure in an attempt to reverse the baby's birth position. At the midpoint of the turn, Greta screamed in pain, and Ruth and Dorcas held both her hands and steadied her.

At last, the pressure ebbed for a moment. Greta opened her eyes to see, through her tears, that Dr. Miller was frowning. She wanted to ask what was happening, but before she could attempt to speak, a soft knock on the door came. Turning her head, Greta watched as Sarah entered the room, accompanied by another church sister cloaked in a white shawl and the white bonnet of a married woman. Greta did not recognize the sister, as everything seemed blurred with pain, yet she felt comforted by her appearance and added support. She watched out of the corner of her eye as Sarah hurried to her side. Seemingly unnoticed, the unnamed sister knelt and began to pray at the foot of the bed.

A deep sense of calm washed over Greta as Dr. Miller continued the turning procedure. Finally, to everyone's relief, the baby's head turned to a downward position. Significant contractions followed, and with a final excruciating push, little Sigrid entered the world.

"You have a daughter," Dr. Miller declared as Sigrid's tiny, forceful voice reverberated throughout the room. Dr. Miller tied off the cord, then wrapped and placed the baby on Greta's stomach as he waited for the placenta to be dispelled.

"Thank the Lord the baby is a bit on the small side," Dr. Miller said, patting Sigrid on the back and looking at her eyes and ears. Greta's body felt raw, but she felt a deep psychological relief to know the nearly seven-hour labor process had finally ended and her child had arrived safely.

Meanwhile, Oscar stood at the stairway, one eye on the children now sleeping side by side on a blanket in front of the fireplace, glancing often upward at the bedroom door. Bauer and Sarah had arrived halfway through the night with a large pot of soup and a basket of biscuits, but even Bauer's company and a home-cooked meal could not make Oscar forget what was happening upstairs. Hearing Greta cry in pain had shattered Oscar, especially with all he knew about her strength and character, but Fredrick and Lena's distressed, sleepy questions about the noise had been a good distraction. When the door of the bedroom opened, and Oscar heard tiny Sigrid's faint rhythmic cries, he bowed his head and thanked God.

Thirty minutes later, Dr. Miller allowed Oscar to visit Greta and Sigrid briefly. Dorcas, Ruth, and Sarah slipped downstairs to check on the children and fix something to eat while Oscar, tears in his eyes, came to his wife's side. Greta, cradling the sleeping baby, beamed.

"We now have a daughter," she said. Oscar gently touched Sigrid's head. Glancing around, he tried not to be alarmed by the amount of blood on the heap of towels and sheets in the corner of the room. Had it been like that last time? He couldn't remember.

The pair heard a soft knock at the door before Sarah stepped in.

"Greta, would you like me to take the baby so you can sleep?" she asked gently. Greta gratefully handed Sigrid over.

"Thank you, Sarah," Greta said. "Please thank Dorcas, Ruth, and the other dear sister who visited me. I don't know her name, but I took much comfort from her prayers." Sarah looked curiously at Greta.

"Only Dorcas, Ruth, and I assisted Dr. Miller," Sarah said. Oscar looked at his wife and saw a look of pure confusion pass over her features, though it was quickly overtaken by fatigue. Oscar touched her cheek, watching as Greta fell asleep.

Silently, Sarah and Oscar took a sleeping Sigrid to the next room before tiptoeing downstairs. The morning sun had now risen in the east, and the doctor was finishing an early breakfast in the kitchen. Oscar gratefully sat down as Ruth brought him a plate of eggs, bacon, potato pancakes, and canned tomatoes.

Dorcas carried the older children upstairs to Fredrick's room as Ruth, sitting down with a cup of warm milk, smiled at Oscar. Oscar grinned gratefully back.

"Sisters, thank you for all you have done. And thank you, doctor."

"I am glad it went as well as it did," Dr. Miller replied. "I'll be back in a day or two to attend to Greta and the new baby. My wife just gave birth last week, as you probably already heard."

"Yes, I heard it was a boy," Oscar said. "Congratulations to you and Mrs. Miller."

"It must be something in the water," the doctor chuckled. "By the way, my wife thanks you for the eggs and apple pie."

"Thank you, doctor, for taking them as part of your bill." Oscar finished his eggs, feeling as though his heart would burst with happiness.

* * *

Nearly a month later, Bauer and Oscar stood surveying the area of Oscar's farm near the woods, absorbing the welcome feel of the sun on their faces. The view was serene and beautiful as the Indiana hardwoods began to bud and leaf. The wood itself was on a ridgeline, which provided an overview of the valley through which Pipe Creek ran.

"Seen any young sassafras trees?" Bauer asked. "Always good to make some bark tonic to help thin the blood after such a long, hard winter."

"I do not know if thinner blood would help my Greta right now," Oscar said quietly. Sigrid's birth had not come without cost. Greta had lost much blood, and Dr. Miller insisted upon bed rest and minimal activity while Greta fought to heal and regain her strength.

To everyone's dismay, Greta's health was not returning as quickly as it had following Fredrick's delivery. She still became fatigued quickly, and feeding her newborn daughter seemed to exhaust her.

"Brother Oscar, there is much to be grateful for," Bauer said encouragingly. "As I look around, I think this would be a good place for your son's home someday."

Tearing his thoughts away from Greta, Oscar sought to survey the scene with fresh eyes. Baptist Brethren children tended to stay near their parents, either by building extensions onto their parents' homes or constructing a new one nearby. Would this be a good place to build a home?

Oscar glanced around. It was lovely here this time of year. Nearby, he could see some of the oversized rocks that had emerged as he'd plowed and harrowed his fields; Bauer had helped him move them to the field's edge with the horse-drawn stone boat. Perhaps, he thought, they should have moved them to a different location.

"Such a home would require even more help from a congregation that has already given us much," Oscar said.

"In time, it will be what is best for the church, too," Bauer said. "And, Oscar, don't forget that you have been helping with lots of various construction on other farms, part of the weekly rotation. We all help each other."

The two men walked around the location of Bauer's proposed site. Bauer immediately busied himself with sketching outbuildings on a crumpled notebook he pulled from a pocket, already excited about the future project. Oscar, however, felt a deep weight on his heart.

"You'll have plenty of room for the cattle and hog barns and a granary, too," Bauer said, closing the notebook. "It will work out for the good, Brother Oscar. Perhaps we could get your Uncle Fredrick out here next time he calls on Greta."

"Yes, that's a good idea," Oscar said. "I believe he is coming later this week with Dr. Miller." Much like Oscar, Fredrick was concerned for Greta's health. However, he would also be a valuable resource for planning the new home. "Your uncle has been given many gifts," Bauer ruminated, "but his gift of knowing what hides below the soil truly comes from God." He tapped his temple. "Fredrick has found water when other so-called 'experts' have failed."

Oscar turned to Bauer. "Is that so?" Oscar knew Fredrick had learned the art of water dowsing from his father while in Germany, as was usual for those who possessed the skill. He took great pride in sensing and interpreting the Earth's vibrations to find water, and his ability had only been sharpened by his more recent experiences with stem auger drilling. Unlike the Gypsies' uncanny psychic powers, however, dowsing (or "witching," as some called it) wasn't thought to be based on superstition or the occult. It was considered a sort of intuitive practice, and the brethren, therefore, did not frown upon it.

"During the war, your uncle used his talents for the Army," Bauer said. "He found everything from water, oil, ore deposits, and even human remains. Some may scoff at it, but your Uncle Fredrick's skill seems to defy logic."

"Uncle Fredrick is full of surprises," Oscar mused.

As expected, Oscar and Bauer were working in the field a few days later when Uncle Fredrick found them. Bauer, knowing Fredrick was coming that day, had made a point to come to the Beck residence once again.

"Dr. Miller is seeing to Greta," Fredrick said by way of greeting. "He has decided to spend time with Greta and possibly consult the hospital in Peru later in the day. Greta suggested you might want to see me out here." Fredrick nodded to Bauer, who smiled.

"Yes, we'd like to get your thoughts on a potential building site for little Fredrick's future home," Bauer said.

"Now, that's an interesting notion," Fredrick said. "Show me the way, would you?"

As the men walked to the site, Oscar looked with gratitude at the man who had done so much for his little family. Uncle Fredrick, who had now become more involved in crude oil development north of Peru along with government railroad contracts, had increasingly made time to stop by to play with his grandniece and nephew. His occasional secreted envelopes containing cash, though never solicited, greatly assisted Oscar's family.

Uncle Fredrick surveyed the ridgeline that extended into the woods.

"I was thinking the house could be here and the barn there," said Bauer, gesturing. "That's the highest area, but still far enough away from the creek just in case of floods."

"Yes," said Fredrick, nodding. "We could put the front door facing this way . . ." Fredrick, always analytical, immediately began picturing the layout with Bauer, who excitedly showed Fredrick his sketch. Oscar let the two men methodically debate the configurations of the future farm. He had difficulty focusing on anything these days.

After a few minutes, all three men stood, looking out at the space and imagining the house and farm that would someday stand there. Oscar tried not to wonder if Greta would even step foot in that house.

"Brother Oscar," said Bauer, "the book of Proverbs says, 'A good man leaves an inheritance to his children and children's children.' It is right that you build this farm for your son and perhaps your grandsons."

Fredrick nodded. "You will leave a legacy to your future kindred."

Oscar swallowed. "Such a project will take patient and gradual work," he said. "This farm will be a lifelong investment."

"Before we get ahead of ourselves," Fredrick said, "let us make sure we can secure water here. That's the most important consideration before driving the first nail or laying the first brick." His gaze sharpened; he was on a mission.

Fredrick walked to a willow tree growing by Pipe Creek.

Pulling out his pocket knife, he cut a forked stick that was in the shape of a letter Y. Reversing his palms and grasping the two ends of the Y, both palms facing upward and fists clenching the willow branches, he pulled both elbows to his rib cage and began to walk forward. Silently, Bauer and Oscar followed.

Fredrick approached a thirty-by-thirty-foot slight depression in the earth, where the long end of the Y-shaped branch began to move downward.

"I've never felt such a strong presence before," Fredrick said. "The energy is of such strength I can scarcely hold the rod." He shook his head and turned around, wonder written on his features. Bauer's eyes sparkled, but Oscar felt only bewilderment.

"We must mark this spot so as not to forget where to begin the drilling when the time comes," he said. Though he was baffled and sure the future house would not be constructed for a long time, Oscar nodded.

"Yes, alright, Uncle," he said. In his mind, unbidden, swam the circular configuration of the six stones he and Greta had found in the German forest. "I have an idea."

After Bauer and Uncle Fredrick had said their goodbyes, Oscar went to the wagon for a pointed digging shovel. He dug six holes around the sides of the ground depression Fredrick Sr. had proposed as a well site.

When the holes sat ready, Oscar chose one of the large waist-high fieldstones he'd dug up during ground clearing. He and Bauer had to leverage the boulders onto the stone boat with jacks and lumber slabs to move them; now, Oscar would hitch chains to the double trees of his four large draft horses connected to the stone boat. The heavy, meter-high stone slowly moved forward as Oscar worked the reins of his horses in measured thirty-foot distances. Finally, they reached the edge of one of the freshly dug holes. Leveraging the stone with a pry bar, Oscar worked the rock until it was standing on end, then slid it into one of the holes. He was sweating and caught up in the work, his mind mercifully clear.

"Five to go, boys," he told his draft horses.

One by one, he and the horses filled all six holes with the prominent upright stones, which stood as if at attention surrounding the ground depression. When the last stone slid into place, Oscar felt more peaceful than he had in a month. Getting down on his knees, he tamped down the soil around each stone to secure them into place. The stone circle, a ripple of another ocean away, now marked the spot Uncle Fredrick had declared extraordinary.

11
The Brink
(Der Rand)
June 1899

"It might be best for you and the children if I were not such a burden to everyone," Greta said in a thin voice that seemed not to be her own. She watched as both Dr. Miller and Oscar's faces paled.

"My Greta," Oscar said, seizing her hand. "Don't say that. You'll get better. God will see to it."

Greta looked at her beloved husband's face as though through a veil. Despite his protests, she knew her words to be true. Six weeks had passed since Sigrid's birth, yet Greta's physical condition had improved very little. She felt herself wasting away, both physically through weight loss and emotionally through a great, gaping sadness that seemed to swallow her very soul.

Squeezing her eyes shut, Greta tried to block out the sorrow on her beloved's face. She hated how hard everyone toiled to try to save her when it was so clearly futile. Oscar prayed daily with the elders and Pastor Yoder, who visited regularly to anoint and lay hands on her. The women of the church rotated duties, caring for the children she could not bear to see and the household tasks she was too frail to perform. Dr. Miller visited several times a week, charging a reduced rate they could only afford because of Uncle Fredrick's generosity. But even the love of her community could not save her.

As Dr. Miller got up to leave, Oscar pulled an envelope from his pocket.

"Perhaps this will cheer you up," he said, placing it on the bedspread. The door creaked, and Sarah slipped into the room, holding a tray laden with a knitting project and a bowl of steaming bone broth. "It's a letter from Dieter. Arrived this morning. Sarah could help you write back, I'm sure."

Greta, not even glancing at the letter, rolled over without responding. Oscar rubbed her shoulder and stood.

I should have died in the birthing bed, Greta thought as the men exited the room.

"You must make sure you never leave Greta unattended or alone," Dr. Miller told Oscar grimly in the kitchen. "I fear she may harm herself if her health does not improve soon." Oscar immediately felt grateful for Sarah, who camped out in Greta's room for much of the day, knitting and watching his wife sleep fitfully.

Dr. Miller's face looked ashen as he stared at Oscar. "Our town hospital offers little in the way of assistance. I do not know what more I can do for her, and she is too weak to make a long journey to another hospital."

Oscar looked into the main room, where Fredrick was focused on a children's book, his little face scrunched in concentration as he attempted to make out the letters. Next to him,

Sigrid was lying on her back on a blanket, flailing her arms and murmuring. Oscar felt his heart breaking. If he were to lose Greta, he knew he would never recover.

Oscar felt his throat close as he fought back tears. The thought of his children growing up without their mother was more than he could abide. Raising two children, even with the help of the church, would be incredibly difficult, and the church allowed only one spouse per lifetime. Even if he could remarry, Oscar knew Greta was his true life partner and could not be replaced.

Dr. Miller, seeing the look on Oscar's face, seemed to wilt further.

"The truth is, Oscar," he said, "Greta and Sigrid never should have survived that birth. It was a true miracle. I was sure we were going to lose them both, but then a calm seemed to come over Greta, and by the grace of God, that child turned in her womb. Perhaps the miracle of Sigrid's health is all God could provide this time."

After Dr. Miller said goodbye, Oscar went into the living room with his children. Greta's room was, unfortunately, no place for children at the moment.

"Would you like to come outside with me and play in the stone circle?" he asked.

"Yes!" cried Fredrick, bouncing up. He carefully placed his book on a low table.

"Sigrid, what about you?" Oscar asked. Sigrid looked up, her mouth in a perfect little O. Dr. Miller had brought a large can of powdered baby formula, and Oscar had mixed it up for bottle-feeding the hungry little girl as Greta's milk waned.

Oscar, with a bag slung over his shoulder and tiny Sigrid in his arms, walked to the stone circle. Fredrick ran ahead, laughing and breathing in the fresh May air, his hair shining bright gold in the sun.

"Wow!" cried Fredrick as they reached the circle. Swarms of barn swallows furiously pursued dragonflies over the ring of standing stones, and pine squirrels from the surrounding woods scampered from one rock to the next.

"Shhh," Oscar said, hurrying up behind Fredrick. "Look!" He pointed at a large fox squirrel lurking next to one of the stones. Fredrick's big eyes sparkled, and he looked so much like Greta that Oscar felt tears come to his eyes.

"It seems animals are drawn to this circle," Oscar said. He remembered what Uncle Fredrick had said about the energy here and wondered if the wildlife could, too, sense the power of this place.

The squirrel scampered away as Fredrick rushed into the circle, shrieking with laughter, and threw himself tumbling into the green grass within. Also laughing, Oscar followed him down, placing Sigrid carefully on a soft mound of grass. She stared up wide-eyed at the glittering dragonflies and butterflies, reaching up with a small hand. Oscar caressed her velvety-soft head and looked at her sparkling blue eyes.

Sigrid was blessed. Fredrick was blessed. This afternoon would be even more joyful if only Greta were there with them. Closing his eyes, Oscar said a silent prayer, begging God not to take his life partner from him before either of them even reached the age of thirty.

On the way back, filled with biscuits and cold buttermilk from Oscar's bag, Fredrick took Oscar's hand.

"Papa, Mama going to die?" he asked in an uncertain voice. "Auntie Sarah and Auntie Ruth say it."

Oscar, looking off towards the road, saw a familiar wagon on the roadway with a black pony trotting along behind its left rear wheel.

"God won't let that happen, son," he said with conviction. "Hurry along, now."

A few minutes later, breathing heavily, Oscar pulled his horse to a stop next to the wagon. He'd dropped his children off with Sarah and pelted down the road to catch up with the vardo. He waved and nodded to Manfri and Mahai, who were sitting on the front seat board of the wagon.

Manfri's eyes widened, and he pulled the vardo to a stop. Mahai, now nearing twelve years old, smiled in recognition.

"Good afternoon, Manfri," Oscar said.

"I did not recognize you at first glance, old friend," Manfri said. "You have grown thinner." Manfri didn't mention that Oscar's beard had grown longer over the winter months, nor that his eyes were darkened and his face appeared gaunt, but he didn't need to. Oscar knew these things.

"It is good to see you," Oscar said. "I need to talk with Kezi for a moment if it is agreeable with you." In response, Manfri set the brake of his wagon, came down, and walked around to the back door of the trailer.

"Kezi, you have a visitor," he said, knocking. Manfri then went to the middle of the wagon, where he pulled out a wagon jack and pry bar. He set them alongside the road, adding skid pans and brake blocks.

"This way, it will appear to anyone passing by that we have

merely stopped to repair the wheel," he told a curious Oscar. "Just in case the county sheriff or deputy are about. This is why we haven't stopped to see you—we don't want to get you into any trouble. When Greta did not come to see Kezi in the camp, we suspected she must have run into conflicts with your church. Then her letters confirmed it."

"I appreciate your concern," Oscar said as the back door opened, and Kezi slowly emerged wearing a golden calico dress. She squinted her eyes in the sunlight. Anca, now nearly as tall as her mother, peered out in a matching outfit and offered a soft smile.

"Good morning," Kezi said. "Has the new baby been born?"

"Greta had a little girl," Oscar replied. Kezi smiled tightly.

"Congratulations to you both," Kezi said. "But I can see this is not a happy visit."

"Kezi, I will get to the point," Oscar said. "I fear for Greta's life."

Kezi's face hardened. "Tell me what has happened." Oscar, beginning to pace, started with the traumatic birth and then described the decline in Greta's health and will to live. Kezi stood silently, listening.

"She trusts you and believes you to have the gift of healing," Oscar said, finally stopping right in front of the Gypsy. Kezi thought for a moment, and then she looked up at the sun, her strange eyes glowing green and gold.

"I should not visit your home," she said cautiously, "for fear of being seen and causing problems. And yet, I need to see her. We can meet somewhere other than your home if she is well enough."

Oscar stared at the sky, thinking. "There is a place with six large fieldstones placed in a circle near the woods behind our farm," he said finally. "Follow the wagon tracks along the side of the cornfield road to the woods, and I will bring Greta. You will see the wagon there."

Kezi nodded. "I will be there in two hours," she said. "I must gather some supplies. I am glad you came for me, Oscar."

Thanking her earnestly, Oscar said his goodbyes, climbed back onto his wagon and headed south toward his farm. When he arrived home, Oscar waved at Sarah and Fredrick in the family room and climbed the stairs to Greta's sickbed. The beef broth sat abandoned on the side table.

"Greta," Oscar said, lowering himself onto the bed and stroking his wife's cheek. Greta's eyes fluttered open. Once the indigo of deep water, they were now almost gray and rimmed with tiny, angry veins.

"Oscar?" she asked in a tiny, unfamiliar voice.

"Greta, I met with Kezi on the road today," Oscar said, taking Greta's frail hand. "She wants to meet with you by our woods. Will you come with me?" Greta weakly nodded and closed her eyes again.

Sarah and Fredrick asked no questions, instead watching solemnly as Oscar carried Greta, clad in a simple nightdress, to the wagon. He was alarmed at how light she was—so light she felt like she would float away at any moment. He placed her on a blanket where she could lay between the soft sacks of ground cornmeal in the wagon.

Greta breathed heavily as Oscar drove the horses slowly down the narrow wagon tracks north to the woods. Once there, Oscar prepared a blanket inside the stone circle, then gently placed Greta in a sitting position against one of the large stones.

Greta, who had been outside only once to sit on the porch since Sigrid's birth, let out a sigh.

"Greta," Oscar said. "Do you see where we are?" Greta's eyes opened, then fluttered closed again. Oscar scooted in next to her and held her emaciated body, his heart pounding under the swirling dragonflies overhead.

Kezi appeared at last, weaving between the ruts and carrying a small red carpet bag. An aura seemed to surround her as she entered the circle.

"Dearest Greta," Kezi said. The Gypsy knelt, her golden skirts spreading on the grass, and gently took Greta's hand. Greta's eyes opened blearily.

"Kezi," she said.

"My dear friend," Kezi said, smiling warmly. "All will be well."

Oscar stood and stepped back as Kezi withdrew a small blue glass bottle from her bag and uncorked it. Rubbing some of the liquid between her hands, she began to massage the back of Greta's neck slowly. Oscar caught the sweet scent of lavender as Kezi gently placed her hands on both sides of Greta's head and closed her eyes.

"You are in danger, Greta," Kezi said. "We must make you strong again."

Standing politely by, Oscar watched Kezi fish through her bag. This time, she removed a large, dark brown bottle and a handmade copper spoon. Uncorking the bottle, she poured an amber liquid into the spoon. This time, the breeze carried a scent of potent blended herbs to Oscar.

"Drink, Greta," she said. Greta, who had been watching with

a glazed expression, swallowed the thick, bitter, earthy concoction without comment.

Placing the spoon aside, Kezi closed her eyes and began chanting a rhythmic incantation, placing her right hand over Greta's head.

"*Khamlea Devla, sastar Greta thaj bichal kire angelonen te garaven la.*"[11]

Kezi repeated the chant over and over. Greta closed her eyes, and eventually, Oscar did as well.

Oscar had lost all concept of time when the conjuration stopped. He opened his eyes to find that the sun had moved but a little towards the west and that the dragonflies had gone. Kezi looked up at Oscar, her eyes lit by the evening sun.

"Take Greta home," Kezi said. "Let her sleep, and give her small drinks of potion four times each day." She withdrew a cloth sack from her carpetbag, placed the elixir and lavender oil in it, and handed it to Oscar. "Rub Greta's shoulders and neck with the oil once a day, and give her some of the tea each day also." Oscar peered inside the bag to see there were two jars of tea within.

"Thank you," Oscar said. He looked at this woman, her complexion dark, her eyes full of kindness, and he felt a surety fill him. "Kezi, despite what the church may say, I believe it was God's will that you were passing by today."

"As do I," Kezi said.

The breeze was growing cooler as Oscar carried Greta to bed. She faintly smiled, looking up at Oscar, and then closed her eyes once again. Placing her in bed, freshened with clean sheets from Sarah, Oscar dared to hope.

Over the next few days, Greta periodically awakened and

---

11   "Dear God, heal Greta and send your angels to protect her" in Romani

sipped Sarah's chicken broth before falling back into a prolonged deep sleep, taking heavy, rhythmic breaths. Oscar awoke her to take the potion four times a day, rubbed the sweet-smelling oil into her cool skin, and brought her herbal tea in the morning and evening. Although Greta didn't say much, there was no more talk of giving up, and her eyes seemed to hold just a little bluer than before.

On the third day, after morning chores, Oscar entered Greta's room with a cup of Kezi's herbal tea. Dorcas had taken Fredrick and Sigrid to her home the night before to give Sarah and Oscar a rest, and Oscar was looking forward to being able to focus on his wife this morning. As he swung the door open, he nearly spilled the tea when he saw Greta sitting on the edge of the bed, darning one of his hole-worn socks.

"I am very hungry," Greta said. "Have the eggs been gathered yet?" Oscar stared in amazement.

"Yes, Greta," he replied. "I will make you breakfast."

"I must nurse Sigrid," Greta said. "What day is it?"

"The Sabbath," Oscar answered in a choked voice. "It's . . . it's the Sabbath." Tears welled as he turned away, hastening down-stairs to cook an enormous meal.

Each day following, Greta became stronger and more like her old self. Sarah was soon able to stop coming as often as Greta developed a routine of caring for Sigrid, Fredrick, and their home.

For the rest of the summer and into the fall, and indeed for as long as Kezi and Manfred came to camp there, Oscar left sweet corn, tomatoes, milk, chickens, and cornmeal at the Gypsy campsite. He smiled and nodded to Kezi and Manfri when he saw them, even as his church brothers blanched. Although Oscar knew some church elders would have considered Oscar's acts to be the enabling of sacrilege and Kezi's rituals as sorcery, he knew better. The Gypsy had invoked God's will in an unfamiliar and mystical way to save Greta's life, and his family would be forever in Kezi's debt.

Part Two

The Great War (Der große Krieg)
1915–1918

12
Children's Providence
(Vorsehung der Kinder)
June 1915

Oscar rose one Sunday morning to the sounds of his family already busy downstairs. He went to the washbasin and splashed water on his face. Looking into the small mirror above the basin, he saw skin cragged with lines and sagging with time. Where had the years gone?

Hearing the front door slam, Oscar went to the window. Fredrick was off to do the morning chores, his shadow long in the dew-covered greenery, Sammuel, the small herding dog running alongside him.

My son has grown into a young man, Oscar thought. In Oscar's head, he still sometimes thought of twenty-one-year-old Fredrick as the intelligent boy who had made so many friends and quickly learned to read, write, and cipher. He could picture little Fredrick chattering away in German at home and English with his friends. But Fredrick wasn't that little boy anymore. He worked on the farm with Oscar, and for the past three years, he has also worked a part-time job at the sawmill. His diligent nature and love of the Lord made Oscar proud to have him as a son.

As Oscar watched, a more petite figure streaked out from the house toward Fredrick. Barefoot sixteen-year-old Sigrid was never far behind her brother. "Sigi," as she was lovingly called, looked very much like Greta, Oscar thought with a smile as the young woman caught up to her brother. She was tall, strong, and capable, just like her mama.

Giving the pair one last affectionate look, Oscar went down the stairs to find Greta in the kitchen, frying eggs on the stove.

"Good morning, Oscar," she said, leaning in for a kiss. Greta was aging gracefully, and Oscar thought she was as beautiful as the day they'd first met.

"Sorry for sleeping so late," Oscar said, pouring himself a cup of buttermilk. "It wasn't like me." The mantle clock read 6:47 a.m.

Greta sliced some bread and put it in a pan to brown. "Well, while you're waking, let me tell you the latest news about our son," she said.

"Hmm?"

"Dorcas has noticed that Fredrick and Lena have been spending more than a peck of time together. She is quite excited."

Oscar smiled. "Yes, it is hard not to notice that at this point."

"There is a good balance between the two," Greta agreed. "They both take comfort in the Lord and each other's company."

"Fredrick is calm and patient," Oscar mused. "He is reserved, never calling attention to himself unnecessarily, respects his elders, and is God fearing. He will make a good husband for Lena, who seems more spirited and enthusiastic."

"Lena is very inquisitive but also hardworking and loyal," Greta said. "I believe they are well matched."

Greta took her seat at the table, and for a minute, the couple ate breakfast in companionable silence.

"What about Sigi? She makes quite a contrast to Fredrick in a way," Oscar said after swallowing a bite of toast.

Greta tilted her head. "Sigi is young but obedient," she said. "She has such maturity, and others often tell me she has the abilities of someone beyond her years."

"And yet, she always seems to celebrate life to the fullest extent God provides," Oscar said, smiling. "God has truly blessed us with her."

Greta picked up her cup of milk, a small smile playing on her lips. "I still remember when her schoolmarm told me Sigi would watch the older children and absorb everything that was being taught to them in addition to doing her lessons. The teacher admitted to me that Sigi was one of her favorites."

"Yes, she's always been a quick study."

Greta took a sip of milk. "I am glad Sigi always finds lots of folks to socialize with," she said, wiping her mouth. "The church has grown so much larger since the time we first arrived here. So many new families are coming to our community now. It makes for so many opportunities for new friends to be made and new knowledge to be learned."

"Indeed! Eighty people in our parish now," Oscar replied, scooping up his scrambled eggs with his fork. "It is nearly doubled from where it first began. I believe Pastor Yoder and the elders are right to contemplate building an addition to the church. I must admit I do not like having to divide into two separate services due to space."

"Perhaps if meetings and meals were held in our brothers' and sisters' homes instead, it could unite us closer to practice the Word of God," Greta suggested.

"Yes, that's an idea. Whatever happens, though, I have much gratitude for the support the church has shown us and our children," Oscar said, eating his last bite of toast. It was true that parishioners had closely watched over children to ensure the security of their souls. The elders called such for their years of loyal dedication and service to the German Baptist Brethren community, and they took a personal obligation to mentor young ones like Sigrid and Fredrick.

After everyone had completed their chores and eaten, the family cleaned themselves up and climbed into the wagon for the ride to Sunday service. It was cloudy, but the air was pleasantly warm and smelled of summer rain. The farm-studded landscape was now dotted with modern farming equipment, including occasional tractors poking up above healthy summer foliage. Oscar saw Sigi looking curiously at a tractor sitting in a barn lot as they passed by in their buggy.

"The old methods have served us well for generations," Oscar reminded her. "The good book teaches us to 'walk in the paths of the old ways.' No matter what name our church calls itself, there is no reason to change or weaken traditions."

"Papa, I heard the Wagners recently got a tractor," Sigrid said with a slight smile. Oscar frowned.

"There is no need for such changes," Oscar insisted. "Each season, our farm yields have progressed. The crops have been good, and our numbers of hogs and cattle grow greater each year. They have allowed a better life for your mama and me and a better life for your children, too."

Oscar's brow furrowed as he remembered the day in 1908, now seven years ago, when Pastor Yoder had begrudgingly announced the proposed renaming of the German Baptist Church as the Church of the Brethren. A move toward more liberal ideas had begun to influence personal dress and behavior within the church, forcing the proposal. The Zion German Baptist loyalists had ultimately rejected this change and chosen to remain part of the distinct German Baptist Brethren sect, continuing to abide by the old ways. However, the Church of the Brethren had formed and separated from their congregation, taking with them many younger members.

Oscar and Greta had decided to stay with Pastor Yoder and the old-order church, where they continued to practice traditional farming and dress. The schism hardly depleted their congregation; even after the split, their congregation was so large that they were outgrowing their current accommodations. But now, some of the German Baptist Brethren wanted the freedom to use farm machinery and tractors in their labor, and a few were even making purchases without church blessing. This insistence swayed the church leadership to edge toward a more progressive direction and yet another inevitable division in philosophy.

"Our tithing has also increased, of course," Greta said. "We must always give thanks for the life we have in America."

"I was just telling you," said Sigi with a little pout. She turned toward Greta, and Greta put an arm around her, then looked over at her son.

"Fredrick, were you reading late into the night again?" she asked. Fredrick snapped his eyes open guiltily.

"Ah, er, not that late," he said. Greta shook her head, but she was smiling. Indeed, Fredrick, analytic and studious, often read well into the night by candlelight. Oscar often had to ask him a few times to go to sleep.

Soon, the little wooden church, with dozens of buggies and horses lining the field, came into sight. Many people could be seen approaching on foot as Oscar pulled his carriage up. His family descended into the sea of familiar faces and chatter. Ruth and Dorcas, who were standing nearby with their children and husbands, waved Oscar and Greta over. Their children, most of whom were between the ages of Sigrid and Fredrick, lived within easy walking distance of Oscar's farm and were all fast friends.

Seeing the family nearing, Otto and Elija walked over first. Otto was tall for his age, with deep blue eyes, sandy brown hair, and an easy smile. Elija, smaller and thinner, shared Dorcas' darker coloring.

"Good morning," he politely said to Oscar and Greta.

"How are you on this day the Lord has blessed?" Elija asked.

"Very well, thank you," Greta said. Otto quickly turned toward Fredrick and Sigrid, Elija following suit. Greta and Oscar, after glancing at their children affectionately, closed the distance between themselves and their friends.

Greta couldn't help but smile at the group of excited young people. "Now that all of the children are out of school, they look forward to their visiting with friends at church even more than ever," she said, shielding her eyes from the intense morning sun with one hand.

"Yes, they certainly do," Dorcas said. Her frame had gotten a bit wider over the past decades, but her eyes were as sharp as ever. "Looks like Lena has already run off to see some of her other friends."

"I think these young people would like it even more if

Sunday school classes were not always divided between boys and girls," Oscar said. He was looking, eyebrows raised, at the pink flush that was creeping up his daughter's cheeks as Otto talked with her.

"Things may be shifting, it's true," Hans, Ruth's husband, said. "But I don't see that changing any time soon at the German Baptist Church."

"The children seem to have plenty of time to form mixed friendships outside those constraints," Dorcas said, narrowing her eyes. Following her gaze, Oscar saw that she was looking at her son Elija, who was glancing furtively at Sigrid. *Oh dear*, Oscar thought.

"The members of the Church of the Brethren are encouraging higher education for children as part of a more progressive direction," Amos, Dorcas' husband, said in his deep voice. "It seems the young people will have plenty of time to mingle under those conditions."

"Our children have voiced no complaints about forgoing higher schooling," Ruth said. Indeed, Fredrick, Elija, and Otto had all finished their education and begun helping their fathers on the farm and serving their church.

Greta looked over at the children. "I do think Fredrick would have . . ."

"Excuse me," said an angry voice. The group looked over to see Max Bontrager, Dorcas's and Amos's neighbor, scowling at them.

"Brother Bontrager, how are you on this Lord's day?" Dorcas asked politely.

"Not good, Sister Kunkle," the man said, crossing his broad arms. "Early this morning, it seems the rains caused a washout near the creek bank in my pasture. One of my cow's distress calls garnered my attention."

"I am sorry to hear that," Amos said.

"So was I," Brother Bontrager huffed. "When I went to check on the sound, I found a prized steer had fallen into the gully and lay helpless on its back! I hitched my team and was headed back to the pasture to rope drag the beast from the ditch when your son, Elija, happened to pass by on the roadway in his buggy."

"Oh, yes," Dorcas said. "I asked Elija to take the Baumanns some blackberry jam before church. Mrs. Baumann has been ill, and I didn't think they would make it here this morning. He didn't mention seeing you, however."

"Well," Brother Bontrager said, waving his hand as though to brush the kindness away, "I think I know why that is. When Elija stopped his carriage, I supposed he meant to lend a hand of assistance and waved him over. But instead of helping, he began to chastise me for 'disobeying the Word of God by toiling on the Sabbath.'" Max looked sullen over at Elija, who now had his back to the older group, his attention fixed on Sigrid as she told a story of some kind.

"I have just spoken to Pastor Yoder concerning the matter," Brother Bontrager said, squaring his shoulders and facing the Kunkles. "He believed my intent was rightful to have saved the steer, which would have ne'er survived the day had I not pulled him from that pit. Even our Savior rebuked the Pharisees for castigating brethren who performed such necessary labors on the Sabbath!" Brother Bontrager sniffed, his wide nostrils flaring. "It was not right for young Elija to have accused me of a violation of the Lord's day and disrespected his elders in such a way."

Dorcas sighed. "I'm very sorry you're upset," she told Brother

Bontrager. "Elija is quite serious about becoming a servant of God. He tends to be very questioning of secular things, especially if he feels it doesn't conform to the ideals of God's teachings. I have no doubt he believed he was doing the right thing."

"Well, he was not!" said Brother Bontrager, raising his voice. "In fact, were I not a patient and temperate man, I would lend him a piece of my mind!" Amos opened his mouth to protest, but Brother Bontrager turned and stormed away.

"Patient and temperate indeed," said Amos under his breath.

"Oh dear," said Greta. "I hope this doesn't lead to another argument."

"Elija is often quick to jump into debates over religious topics of right and wrong," Amos said, shaking his head. "During discussions with his church brothers and neighbors, he often renders admonition to those he feels do not conform to strict biblical standards."

"My stars," said Greta. "I wonder where he gets that from."

"We aren't sure," Dorcas admitted, her face hard to decipher as she stood with her back to the sun. "Amos often tries gently to discourage Elija's overzealousness, but such occurrences seemed to underscore Elija's steadfast determination in interpreting the Word of God, or at least how he believes it's meant to be interpreted."

"His sister Lena doesn't seem to share that proclivity," said Ruth thoughtfully.

"Lena sometimes joins her brother's arguments," Dorcas said. "However, she seems more comfortable in staying out of his battles to remain at home, tending her own business and helping me mind the house."

"And he certainly has a good friend and a tempering influence from Otto," Oscar said. "Otto is no doubt the more level-headed of the two."

Ruth laughed. "He is that, but he can be quite a daredevil. Otto often showed undaunted courage when it came to exploring the woods or tracking game animals. The way he would stand up to school bullies whenever tested makes me nervous."

"Bravery is an admirable trait," Greta said. "Both Fredrick and Sigi admire that about him, I know."

Soon, the first wave of the congregation entered the building that had once so adequately held everyone. Pastor Yoder, now bent with age and as wrinkled as a walnut, shuffled to the pulpit to begin the service. Oscar was always filled with gratitude and thanks when he saw the old pastor. Of late, Pastor Yoder's visits to Oscar and Greta had become less frequent due to the influx of newly arrived immigrants who needed his more immediate attention. The old pastor also was forced to deal with the political infighting that had separated the two individual parishes. However, despite his weakening body, Pastor Yoder was as staunch as ever when it came to traditional Old German Baptist ways. As he took his place at the front of the church, the congregation hushed, and the familiar service began.

Sunday passed quickly by in a blur of worship, fellowship, and family. Bright and early on Monday, Uncle Fredrick's carriage pulled up in front of the family farm. Oscar went out to greet him, watching as Uncle Fredrick seized the handrail and carefully put a foot down on the ground. With a pang, Oscar remembered that Uncle Fredrick, too, was getting older. However, though Uncle Fredrick's energy levels were not as they once were, he still seemed to have a knack for accomplishing much. The man's enthusiasm for his family had never wavered.

"Nephew! I've purchased eight thousand bricks from the Peru pug mill," he said to Oscar without preamble as he approached.

"Uncle Fredrick!" Oscar exclaimed.

"They'll be transported to the site for the future farm home the day after tomorrow," Uncle Fredrick said, his snow-white hair just visible under his broad-brimmed hat. "I'm sure glad the county graveled the wagon path along your wood and made it an access road. That will make transporting the bricks much easier, not to mention finishing the new house and barn."

"I can't thank—"

"—oh, Oscar, you don't need to," Fredrick said with a grin. "You should know that by now."

The pair wandered into the field where Fredrick Jr. was working, his light brown hair hidden by a wide-brimmed hat.

"Fredrick will soon need a place to live and start a family," Uncle Fredrick roared when they were within earshot of the young man. "Time is of the essence!" He turned to Fredrick Jr. "Hello, my boy. How is your friend Lena these days? Your father mentioned you've been seeing a lot of each other."

Fredrick Jr.'s blush was bright enough to see even under the shade of the hat. "Ah, she is doing just fine, I suppose. I sometimes go with Ma and see her and Sister Kunkle."

"And does Greta go see Sister Kunkle often?" Uncle Fredrick asked in a casual tone.

"Ma has been visiting Sister Kunkle a lot the past few years," Fredrick admitted. "Pa and I also look in on my godparents, Brother and Sister Fisher, and help with their chores . . ." Fredrick trailed off, blushing harder than ever, as the older men chuckled.

"I'm going to go get a drink of water," the young man said.

"I'll keep an eye out for arrowheads on the way back. I found two of them yesterday in that spot we just tilled."

"Lena and Fredrick blend well," Oscar told Uncle Fredrick as they watched Fredrick lope back to the house, eyes on the ground. "Both were raised in the faith and have a clear understanding of what God expects of them."

"I remember her as a child, accompanying Dorcas here and there along with her brother," Uncle Fredrick said, bending down to pick a blade of sweet summer grass. "She was a good child. As a woman, is she worthy of my namesake?"

"Lena is dedicated to being a good steward of the Lord," Oscar said. "She works hard at her folks' farm, particularly where homemaking is concerned. Elija, her brother, has directed himself to the Lord's work and now serves Pastor Yoder as an assistant when he's not helping his pa on the farm."

"They sound to be an upstanding pair, I reckon," said Uncle Fredrick, chewing on the grass. The two men watched young Fredrick, who was now walking back from the house and visually scouring the newly harrowed soil.

"Our two families have become closer and have an understanding, or so it now seems," Oscar said. "Fredrick's admiration for Lena has grown over time. Our families' mutual prayers for Lena and Fredrick's happiness will begin now in earnest."

"In what sorts of endeavors do they engage?" Uncle Fredrick inquired. "Surely Fredrick isn't calling on her yet."

Oscar smiled and shook his head. "Their courting mostly centers on family fellowship. They meet with friends at church, picnics, or sheave gatherings."

"Hmm," Uncle Fredrick said, flicking his blade of grass into the soil. "No doubt they may be requiring this homestead sooner than I thought. They would like some privacy before much time has passed, I should think."

"Got one!" Fredrick Jr. said, stepping close to show them the gray flint arrowhead in his large, earth-stained hand.

Later that evening, the arrowhead lay freshly washed on the banister of the front porch, forming a line with the others Fredrick had found over the past few days. Lena and Fredrick perched on the porch swing nearby, talking to Lena's cousins Paul and Conrad. The sun had just set, and the first of the lightning bugs glowed softly in the sweet clover-scented air. Lena felt Fredrick's presence acutely even as she chatted with her cousins.

"The older folks are in there gossiping about you, Paul," Conrad teased.

Paul, still sporting a baby face at seventeen, put a hand to his chest and widened his blue eyes so that nearly the whole iris was visible.

"About me? With my unsullied reputation?"

Lena laughed softly. "Oh, Paul. We all know your heart is in the right place, even if your reputation is just a tad smudged."

"Why, thank you for your support, cousin," said Paul with a mock affront.

"You just like to take shortcuts when it suits you," Lena said. "It's understandable. Practical, even."

"I will carry your comforting words with me when I go on my mission trip to Europe," Paul said with a lopsided, sarcastic grin. "They will keep me going in times of trouble."

"Paul!" Lena chided. "You know we believe in you." Next to her, Fredrick laughed softly, and she felt a blush creep up her cheeks.

Paul put his nose in the air. "I indeed choose to rub elbows with people that most churchgoing folks would try to avoid—"

"Like that livestock dealer from Logansport," said Conrad, cocking his head and looking slightly down at Paul, who was a few inches shorter. "That man had a covenant with people of ill repute."

"—and I guide work in the direction that best suits my interests, as any good businessman would—"

"As any good hornswoggler would, you mean," Conrad muttered, then winced as Paul slapped him on the back. "Ouch, my back is sore."

"—but people can scratch their heads all they like," Paul shouted over him. "I might bend the rules, but I'm bending them in order to follow the Lord's direction better."

"Why is your back sore, Conrad?" Lena asked politely.

"I got roped into helping the Sommers with their hay mowing," Conrad said, arching and cracking his back with a loud pop. "Not used to that kind of work with my soft academic pursuits." Everyone chuckled, knowing Conrad's pain. Twenty-six-year-old Conrad had just graduated with an advanced degree in sociology, and the summer mowing was strenuous work that tired even the most well-toned bodies. Members of Zion made weekly rounds to lend assistance to congregants who needed help with the task. Summer harvesting and storing crops was critical for survival; if one of the congregants struggled, then it was the duty and commitment of the church to come to assist. Wheat and oats were cut, tied into sheaves, and shocked[12] to dry in an enormous outpouring of prayerful labor until all the church farm harvests were accomplished.

"You don't need to convince us of your goodness," said Fredrick, continuing the conversation with Paul. "You need to convince

---

12   Stacking bundled grain to dry

those people in the house. In fact, if you can convince Uncle Fredrick, I'd bet he'd finance some of your missionary plans."

"You don't say," Paul said. He straightened his shirt and brushed his brown hair back, then puffed out his chest and stood proudly. "How do I look?"

"Like a rooster," laughed Lena.

"Perfect," said Paul, and he strode into the house. Conrad trailed after, chuckling.

"Is all that really true?" Fredrick asked, turning to Lena. "I don't know Paul well."

Lena nodded and turned to Fredrick, her heart pounding with his nearness. "Whether he is buying livestock or selling merchandise, there always seems to be a cloud that hangs over Paul's dealings. He regularly makes people scratch their heads with suspicion," she explained. "There had indeed been doubts about Paul's ability to become an effective missionary, not because of his lack of love for the Lord, but because of his unorthodox methods." Lena cracked a smile. "However, It was seen as a positive thing when Paul voiced an interest in missionary work overseas. His family deemed it a true 'calling by the Lord.'"

"He's a charmer," Fredrick remarked. "I'm sure he'll be very good at it one day."

"I'm sure. In any case, he won't be going for a few years yet. He is young, and it takes a while to fund and plan such an undertaking."

A breeze, warm and heavy with the smell of new-mown sweet clover, played across their faces. Around them, small golden lights began to flicker and float through the air.

"Should we catch lightning bugs?" Lena asked.

"Yes, that sounds fun," Fredrick said. "I'll fetch two jars." He disappeared into the house and soon returned holding two Ball mason jars with tiny air holes punched through the lids. Conrad, Paul, and Uncle Fredrick followed.

"We're headed out after a pleasant evening of food and company," Conrad said, tipping his cap as the Fredricks said their goodbyes. Lena turned immediately to Paul and leaned in.

"How did the conversation with Fredrick Sr. go?" she asked quietly. Paul grinned.

"I think it went well," he said.

Lena and Fredrick watched and waved as the carriages trundled away. Streaming silver moonlight and twinkling stars filled the cloudless sky along with the lightning bugs. Fredrick and Lena walked down the front porch stairs into the yard and across the road to the hay field, which was alive with hundreds of fireflies sending glowing signals in the darkness.

While the moon shone brightly over the small farm, the couple set about carefully catching lightning bugs and placing them inside the jars, giggling and whispering. When the jars were filled with enough bugs to give off a radiance, they took the jars inside the house.

"I'll turn down the lamps and blow out the candles," Lena whispered, trying not to disturb Oscar, Greta, and Sigrid, who had already gone to bed upstairs. She and Fredrick sat and watched the insects sending out their ethereal light through the darkness in the living room.

"Reminds me of the light God sends across the world," Lena said reverently.

Fredrick nodded, then gently took the jars. He and Lena went back outside, where they released the glow worms back into the night.

"It is late," Fredrick said, taking Lena's hand. "I should take you home."

"I hope my parents aren't worried," she said.

As the couple drove along the winding gravel road, the night music of crickets and cicadas surrounded them. The full moon shone above, and sweet clover perfume filled the air. Lena moved close to Fredrick as he drove and took his arm, her heart glowing brighter than a hundred jars of fireflies.

Fredrick pulled the buggy to a halt on the side of the deserted road, turning to face Lena. Engulfed in the sweet summer breeze, he opened his arms, and Lena stepped into them without hesitation. Their lips met. Lena ran her hands across Fredrick's strong back, and her breath caught in her throat.

Fredrick pulled away first with a frustrated sigh. "Our Lord instructed us to 'watch and pray so as not to enter into temptation,'" he said. "My spirit is willing, but my flesh is weak." Lena closed her eyes, listening to Fredrick's ragged breathing and her own.

"Our Lord is testing us to resist temptation," she said. "We must stay strong. I know we must. But when we are apart, I ache for you, Fredrick," she said.

"As do I."

At Lena's home, Fredrick helped her down from the buggy and walked her to her front door. Coal oil lights flickered inside the house; Fredrick could see Lena's parents had waited up for her. Fredrick held Lena's hands and gently kissed her lips, their noses pressed together under the large full moon.

"Were it winter and Pa was of a mind, he would be obliged to allow you to stay the night in our spare room or between a separation board," Lena said, her eyes silver in the moonlight. "We could lay and speak to one another and the Lord of our plans and love."

"I'm not sure a bundling board would be adequate to hold my love from you, sweet Lena girl," Fredrick said. "But I reckon since it's summer and your pa's been a bit on the grumpity side of late, I'll best be traveling home. I'll still hold out hope for a blizzard, however."

Lena laughed, feeling flighty and alive with this new feeling.

"I love you, Lena," he said.

"I love you too, Fredrick," she replied. Reluctantly pulling herself away, Lena walked inside the house, waving at Fredrick through the window as he drove the carriage down the road and out of sight.

13
The Past and the Present
(Vergangenheit und Gegenwart)
June 1915

Clad in their dark dresses and head coverings, the women rode in their buggy across the rural dirt and gravel roads to Kokomo. Greta looked around at the small, bustling community, which had already changed much since she and Oscar had moved to the area. The interurban electric railway train rattled across town to scheduled passenger stops, and the sputtering engine noise of T-model Fords and Chevy 490s circling the downtown square reverberated through the cool air.

"I hope we find a material you like, Lena," Sigrid said. She held her shawl around her shoulders to keep out the morning chill.

"I am sure we will," Lena said. Sigrid looked wistfully out at the changing foliage, and Dorcas and Greta exchanged a knowing glance. Both women could tell Sigrid might just be imagining herself in a wedding dress and cape similar to the one Lena would be picking fabric for today.

The Union Dry Goods store was their first stop once they arrived at the downtown square. Inside, groups of people shopped and gossiped loudly. There was a strange tension in the air, and Greta listened carefully as they walked.

"Did you hear Jennings Bryan is resigning?" a red-faced young man was saying to a friend standing by a barrel of dry beans.

"Thank God that anti-American coward is out of office," his friend replied as the women walked by. "Some Secretary of State."

"The Huns[13] are to blame for the war. Just look at their aggression and crimes in Belgium," another man said irritably to his wife as the women passed behind them. "Bryan is a damn German-loving traitor."

"Bob, goodness, keep your voice down," the man's wife said. Greta winced as she guided her little party towards the baking supplies.

"Mama, what's going on?" Sigrid asked quietly as she helped Greta take a sack of sugar from the shelf.

"Nothing for us, sweet girl," said Greta. "Just politics."

Greta didn't see why she should worry anyone else, but when Lena, Sigrid, and Dorcas were safely absorbed in the fabrics section, she had to assuage her curiosity. She seized a discarded copy of the local paper. She scanned the news, quickly finding the source of the trouble: a German U-boat had sunk the English Lusitania, and Secretary Bryan's subsequent clash with President Wilson over the possibility of war had ignited debate and anger across America.

"The German sinking of the British liner drowned 2,000 innocent civilians, including 128 American souls," Greta read, her lips moving along with the horrifying words. "In the European

---

13   Derogatory wartime slang for Germans

war," the next page declared, "French casualties are mounting, and the recent British failure to capture the city of Baghdad during their expeditionary campaign has added to the many reasons anti-war supporters want to stay out of the European quagmire."

Greta quietly placed the paper back where she found it and went to join the women, pasting a delighted smile on her face when she saw the crisp white cotton Lena had selected, trying not to imagine the devastating last moments of all those passengers.

When the woman exited the shop, Lena clutched her precious package of fabric. An angry local merchant stood near the door, waving *The Sentinel* and talking loudly to a few colleagues. When one of them gestured to the Brethren women in their distinctive outfits, the whole group fell silent, staring. Greta resolutely walked on, her jaw set. It was clear that anti-German sentiment in Indiana was rapidly growing.

"Mama, are you sure it's nothing?" Sigrid asked in a hushed voice. Greta sighed and looked at her daughter. She was not a child anymore. She had the right to know.

"Sigi, do you remember what Pastor Yoder told us about the war on Sunday?" she asked. She saw that Lena and Dorcas were listening intently.

"'Blessed are the peacemakers, for they will be called the children of God,'" Sigi recited.

"He said that because of some recent events," said Greta, stopping near a stone wall to rearrange the contents of her heavy shopping basket. The women gathered around while Greta explained what she had gleaned.

"The paper I saw seemed to lean in a pro-war direction," Greta said finally. "But it's clear from what people are saying that they aren't particularly partial to German immigrants."

"People are angry," Dorcas said, nodding. Greta locked eyes with her friend. This was no time for a lighthearted shopping trip.

"Hold hands, girls," Greta directed Lena and Sigi. "Our Brethren communities vow never to interfere in politics or wars in any manner regardless of the circumstances, but Dorcas is right. People are angry, and we must try to block out all such hatred."

The women hastily concluded their trip, visiting a few more shops for items on their list. Baskets full, Sigrid and Lena went to ready their horse for the trip home while Dorcas and Greta stopped at the local apothecary for Greta's rheumatism medicine. The women had left the mare tied at the water trough by the courthouse square.

Small children sang and pointed their fingers; Sigrid smiled until she made out the words, "Have you ever seen a Dutchman go this way and that way?" Trying to ignore it, she walked faster, glancing at Lena. As they approached the buggy, Sigrid noticed two arguing men hovering nearby.

"Walk quickly," Lena said under her breath. The two women began untethering the horse, and the male voices became louder. Dismayed, Sigrid looked over her shoulder and saw that one of the men was approaching, his glassy eyes locked on Lena.

"If'n we all go ta war, which side you people gonna support?" the man asked Lena. "America or the krauts?" Sigrid could smell the stench of his sour alcohol breath from where she stood. Lena did not speak, her young, smooth face set in a severe expression.

The other man approached the two women and stood staring at Sigrid. Sigrid gave a start; she recognized the distinctive birthmark on his forehead. She'd seen this man and his port wine stain mark years before.

"Do any of you plan to stand with America to fight the damn

Boche,[14] or are you with them?" the man with the birthmark asked Sigrid.

Lena and Sigrid moved close to each other. They silently endured the jeers and accusations as they untied the horse and readied the buggy. Finally, Sigrid looked up to see Greta and Dorcas hastening over with their packages. Their eyes were wide as they joined their daughters. The men were drawing closer, and a small crowd had begun to gather around, watching, waiting.

"You're nothing but traitors!"

"Cowards and traitors!"

"We oughta lock you all up!"

Greta reached them and took Sigrid's hand tightly. Sigrid felt her heart leaping in her chest as her mother, eyes now closed, began to sing in her warm, comforting voice.

Come Brethren, ye that love the Lord,
And walk according to His Word,
Let true humility abound,
And in His footsteps too be found.

Dorcas and Lena joined hands as well, and Lena clasped Sigrid's free hand. They closed their eyes and sang the familiar hymn along with Greta. Sigrid found her high, clear voice joining in automatically, trembling slightly. The momentum of the verbal attacks began to wane, and several of the onlookers even joined in the hymn. The two men stood uncomfortably, petering into silence as the women, still singing, opened their eyes, released their hands, and climbed into the buggy.

Greta took the reins and guided the horse onto the brick street. Turning around, Sigrid watched the two men blend into the crowd as the buggy rolled down the brick city streets and

---

14   A rude term for Germans

eventually to the county road to home. Sigrid's heart rate gradually slowed.

"We are united in our faith," Dorcas said after a few minutes of reflective silence. "God protects us and never places before us more burdens than we can handle."

"Well said," Greta stated, her chin high.

Sigrid couldn't help herself. "Mama, why do those men hate us so much?"

Greta's strong profile was outlined by the waning sun. To Sigrid, her mother looked immutable, solid, and sure. "He who saith that he walks in the light yet hates his brother and sister so liveth in darkness," Greta recited. "Those men do not know God, Sigi. It is the distance from God in which they have placed themselves that causes their hatred."

"We must pray for those men and America," said Dorcas. "Remember, God tests our faith on occasion. Remaining committed to God and His church is the most important response we can make to such hatred."

Sigrid looked at Lena, whose face was pale and severe, eyes downcast. Turning away, Sigrid stared out the window into an open pasture field, watching the cattle meander about, battling back her worry.

Upon their return to the Beck house, the women busied themselves with putting away Greta and Sigrid's dry goods and preparing the evening meal. Amos had joined Oscar to help him with fencing while Fredrick Jr. and Elija moved the stock to the small pasture near the barn. Everyone would eat together on that brisk, late spring evening.

Greta focused on making the meal of hocks, beans, cornbread, and dandelion greens with vinegar—a meal that Sarah had once taught her how to make. The other women seemed lost in their thoughts. During dinner, nobody said anything about their trip to town except that they'd purchased the clothes and prescriptions along with some other necessities. Enjoying the company and the positive atmosphere of the evening, it was easy to forget the unpleasantness of the afternoon.

Later, after Lena, Dorcas, and Amos had departed and Oscar had added the cost of the purchases into his budgeting record book, Greta and Oscar retired to bed for the night. Then, finally, Greta confided in Oscar about what had happened that afternoon in town.

"Was anyone hurt?" Oscar asked, his eyes full of concern.

"No," Greta replied. She slid an incomplete letter to Dieter to the corner of her nightstand and turned down the kerosene lamp. "I was worried for Sigi and Lena, though. They do not understand why we should be blamed for what takes place in Europe."

"I cannot give a clear answer for that either," Oscar said. "Such troubles seem so far away, and yet they are so connected to people living in America."

"We are all Americans here," Greta puzzled. "We should not be indicted for what people in Germany, people we don't even know, are doing."

"It is a way that God tests us," Oscar answered. Closing his eyes to sleep, he held Greta's hand.

"God is faithful and only allows such troubles to measure the genuineness of our faith," he said.

Greta said a silent prayer for those lost in the naval disaster while, on the other side of the wall, Sigrid lay wide awake in bed. She could not stop thinking about the man with the port-wine stain birthmark. Her mind wandered back to the afternoon when she'd first seen him, which had been one of the strangest of her childhood.

* * *

"The Lord has given us such a nice spring day," Oscar said to Greta that Saturday morning. Nine-year-old Sigi slurped her breakfast porridge at the kitchen table, and Greta gently nudged her.

"Mind your manners, sweet girl," she said with a smile. "Now, I hear the neighbor children very much want to go mushroom hunting in the woods by Pipe Creek today."

"Oh, please," Sigi cried as Fredrick stopped on his way to place his dish in the washbasin. Thirteen and full of energy to explore, he nodded enthusiastically.

"I do love mushrooms," he said.

"Rumor has it people are starting to find the yellow sponges," Oscar said. "Today may be a good day to try our luck."

"Thank the Lord!" Sigi exclaimed to general chuckles.

"Do you know another name for 'yellow sponge mushrooms'?" Oscar asked his children.

"Morels," Fredrick said, carrying a tin cup of water back to the table and sitting down. "The Indians thought morels had special powers."

"That's right," Oscar said. "They are much like finding the steinpilz in Germany."

"And they'll need to be expertly prepared," Greta said, her eyes shining. "I'll have to soak them in salt water to rid them of insects. Then I'll split them in two, batter them in egg white, add butter and flour, and fry them in my skillet."

"Mama!" Sigrid said, holding her stomach in an exaggerated fashion.

"My mouth is watering too," Fredrick admitted sheepishly. Oscar also nodded.

"That makes four of us," Greta said wistfully. "I can't wait. Hunting mushrooms reminds me of Germany and the forest searches we went on as children."

"And as adults," Oscar said with a meaningful look.

"And as adults," Greta agreed with a smile, "The Indiana mushrooms are more difficult to find than the steinpilz, though."

"I want to go to Germany someday!" Sigrid said.

"Perhaps one day you will, sweet girl," Greta said, patting Sigrid's cheek.

As the early afternoon began to warm, Greta, Oscar, Fredrick, and Sigrid were joined by several other churchgoers for the excursion, including Otto (Ruth Bowman's son). Dorcas brought Lena and Elija along with their cousin Paul. The children bantered and played, glad to be in each other's company, as Greta handed out white hand-sewn cheesecloth bags. Elija clasped his hands nervously, and Paul poked him in the ribs.

"Where are we going exactly, ma'am?" Elija asked Greta. Sigrid had looked sidelong at the nervous little boy. He was not a risk-taker or one for adventure, seeming more content to stay indoors and read than work on the farm or explore the woods. On the other hand, Sigrid, who could outrun all the boys her age, was practically bouncing with anticipation.

"Don't worry, dear, we aren't going far," said Greta. "Besides, don't you like mushrooms?"

"Yes," admitted Elija, looking down at his feet. Otto slung an arm around Elija's shoulders.

"Come on! We'll have fun!" Otto said with an easy, confident smile. Paul, with an equally confident smile, slung an arm over

Elija's other shoulder. Elija looked miserable and scrawny, braced between the two grinning boys, and Sigrid stifled a laugh.

"We can use the walking sticks to part the underbrush when we hunt," Greta said, handing out a set of sturdy wooden canes. Dorcas and Greta then paired up the mushroom hunters: Fredrick and Elija, Sigrid and Otto, and Paul and Lena. Sigrid skipped happily to Otto's side.

"Now, we will need to search in opposite directions and meet back at the farmhouse in two hours," Dorcas said.

"Lena and I are going that way," Paul said immediately, pointing. "There's a great spot for mushrooms over there. Billy Earl told me about it."

"Paul!" Dorcas said, dismayed. All the children closed their mouths and stared at the exchange, wary of trouble. "Why are you talking with Billy Earl? His family does not follow our Lord's commandments!"

Paul shrugged his shoulders. "We've all fallen short, Aunt Dorcas," he said. "Anyway, he's a useful person to know."

"I forbid you from consorting with that boy again," Dorcas said firmly.

"We'll see, Aunt Dorcas," Paul muttered under his breath so that the adults couldn't hear. Lena shot him a warning glance.

"You will need to focus," Greta said. "This will be an afternoon spent scouring the woods, but it will be well worth the effort if we find enough morels for a meal."

"I can smell them frying in the butter already," Sigrid sighed.

"All right now," Greta said, laughing. "Off with you, or there will be nothing to fry!" Paul and Lena ran forward first, whooping and swinging their sticks.

"Ah, one second, Sigi," Otto said as he bent down to tie his boot.

"Hurry!" Sigrid complained.

"Can't I go with Lena?" Fredrick asked Greta forlornly, watching Paul and Lena run off. Otto and Sigrid raised their eyebrows at each other.

"Son, I think you make Lena feel a bit shy as of late," said Greta. "Perhaps in a few years, she will want to go mushroom hunting with you." Fredrick frowned, and Sigrid stuck her tongue out at him behind his back, making Otto snort with laughter. Then, all the children were hustling away with their cheesecloth bags.

"I'm a better mushroom hunter than Lena anyway," Elija could be heard grumbling. The women stood for a moment, watching the children go.

"Let's go in this direction," Greta said, gesturing. She and Dorcas walked towards the woods at a leisurely pace.

"I am sorry about Paul," Greta said.

"Never mind about that for now," said Dorcas. "Greta, we pulled in right when the mail carrier was passing. I placed your mail on your kitchen counter for you."

"Thank you," Greta said, glancing sidelong at her friend.

"There were some unexpected pieces of mail in there, I must say."

Greta said nothing, staring ahead, waiting.

"There was a letter addressed to you from someone with a Gypsy-sounding name . . . careful of that one. It might be some tinker scam."

Greta rolled her shoulders back. "Dorcas, I'm going to have

to ask you to trust me where that is concerned. It's a long and complicated story, but I believe I owe the woman who wrote me that letter my life."

Dorcas' dark eyes widened. Greta nodded, knowing her friend likely remembered those tenuous weeks after Sigrid's birth. Although she and Kezi could not see each other in person due to the risk of ostracization by the congregation, they continued to write to each other when possible, and Oscar still sometimes snuck supplies to a location where Kezi's family knew to pick them up. They may not be able to meet, but Kezi was as close to Greta's heart as ever. However, the less Dorcas knew of this, the better.

"I promise I am not doing anything our Lord would not approve of," Greta said when Dorcas remained silent. "Please put the matter out of your mind if you can."

Dorcas looked hard into Greta's face, then nodded. "I trust your judgment and your love of our God."

"Thank you, Sister."

Dorcas cleared her throat. "Now, the other item I wanted to mention was the Sears catalog."

"Yes," Greta answered, somewhat relieved after the previously loaded exchange. "Oscar is simply curious about the farming equipment others use."

Dorcas raised an eyebrow. "I wonder what Pastor Yoder would think of that."

Greta looked at her friend. "He's only looking, Dorcas. Besides, don't tell me your husband isn't interested." Dorcas pursed her lips in explicit consent, and the two women started after the children.

Dutifully, the pairs of mushroom hunters had split up, going their separate ways in search of the elusive morels.

"Paul, why do you like to make friends with such odd fellows?" Lena asked as she and Paul headed off in the direction of Billy Earl's recommended spot.

"Odd fellows know odd things," Paul said with a crooked, charming smile. "They can be helpful."

"But Paul, what if it angers God?"

"It's got nothing to do with God!" Paul said defensively. "It's just that sometimes it's good to know different types of folks. You never know when you might need different kinds of help, y'know? C'mon, that looks like a good spot over there."

"Fine," grumbled Lena, and the two strolled deep into the woods.

Meanwhile, Fredrick and Elija walked over the ridgeline downward toward Pipe Creek. The woods were still damp from a recent morning rain, and they headed toward a patch of May apples growing near the creek. Jack-in-the-pulpits, Dutchman's breeches, Indian turnips, and other spring plants were in full bloom, and their sweet fragrance filled the woodland. Small pine squirrels scampered about on the ground, searching for food.

The children had been taught that silence was the first rule of mushroom hunting, as if somehow the fungi would conceal themselves when alerted by the human voice. Therefore, the boys mainly looked in silence once they reached a likely spot. While Fredrick busily scoured the underbrush for mushrooms, Elija seemed more concerned with the nettles and cockleburs that stuck to his clothing.

"I found one!" Fredrick announced as he knelt to pick his first yellow sponge mushroom of the season.

"Where?" Elija said, hurrying over to watch as Fredrick

gently broke the three-inch mushroom off at its base and placed it into his cloth sack.

When Fredrick and Elija began collecting mushrooms, Otto and Sigrid had already filled the bottoms of their sacks. Though Otto was only twelve and Sigrid nine, they were skilled hunters, working as a team to outperform everyone else.

"Let's climb to the top of the ridge," Sigrid whispered to Otto. "It's sunnier there, and the ground may be warmer."

The pair scrambled up the slope, which overlooked the six large stones that Oscar had placed years before. There, panting, the two children sat down to rest for a moment.

"My father will build a house down there," Sigrid said, pointing down to the stones.

"For Fredrick?" Otto asked.

"Yes. For when he is grown and married."

Just then, forty yards below, a small red fox with a white-tipped tail appeared. Panicked, the fox quickly glanced back at the thicket from where it had come. Otto and Sigi froze, suddenly alert. They could hear barking and footsteps shuffling through the dried leaves that clung to the ground from the past winter.

The fox, without hesitation, ran into the stone circle and crouched near one of the larger rocks. It lowered itself into the tall orchard and rye grass just as a beagle hound bounded out of the thicket, baying and sniffing.

Sigrid and Otto quietly concealed themselves on the ridge, peering from behind a giant ash tree. They held their breath, watching the scene. The hound, though quite near the fox, appeared confused and unable to locate a scent. It furiously ran in circles outside the stones, sniffing for the trail. The fox had somehow become undetectable to its expert pursuer.

Thirty seconds later, two disheveled and unshaven men carrying long guns emerged from the brush. Sigrid, seeing the guns, felt her stomach lurch. She grabbed Otto's hand and held it tightly.

"Coulda swore I seen'd him a runnin' from tha' crick up this way," the larger of the two men, who had a deep red wine mark on his brow, said in a Southern drawl. The smaller man, who was wearing a floppy brown felt hat, walked around the outside of the stone circle, poking at the grass with his rifle. Otto and Sigrid could clearly see the fox crouched in the tall grass from their high vantage point, but to the dog and two men below, the fox seemed to have mysteriously vanished.

"Who owns this damn wood?" the man in the floppy hat asked, straightening up and holding his gun limply at his side.

"Not sure," said the other man, "but I reckon it's one of them yella go' damn German Bible thumpers. They tha nigga lovas my Kintucky grandpap told me wouldn't fight tha' Civil War."

Sigrid's mind raced as she watched the men and the hound search. Mama had told her many times about the Jenische stone circle in Germany and what the old Gypsy woman had told her about it.

"Spirits rest within the circle," she could practically hear her mother say. "If you are pure-hearted, an angel will follow and protect you."

Is the fox pure-hearted? she thought. *Is there an angel in the circle here, too?*

After wandering the area around the stones for a minute or two, the hound ran in a confused zigzag pattern back toward the creek with the two men trailing behind. Sigrid and Otto stayed where they were, their hands clenched together in a white-knuckled grip, scarcely breathing.

Finally, the fox soon stood up with its ears perked. It briefly surveyed the area, then darted out of the circle and up the ridge within ten yards of Otto and Sigrid. The two children stared as the red blur disappeared into the thick underbrush.

"Who were those men?" Otto asked, breaking the tense silence. He let go of Sigrid's hand, and she found herself wishing he hadn't.

"I don't know, but they were trespassing just the same," Sigrid said.

"Look, we've already found plenty of mushrooms," Otto said, his voice higher than usual. "Let's just go back up toward the farm."

"Good idea," Sigrid said. "I don't want anyone to think we're foxes. Luckily, I don't think anyone else came this way."

"The hunters seem to be on their way off your property," Otto said.

With some trepidation, the children hurried back to their meeting point. They saw that Dorcas and Greta were already there, with morels spread on an old quilt on the ground before them. Greta had begun slicing the fungi in half, preparing them to soak.

Otto and Sigrid, happy to be back, poured their mushrooms onto the growing pile and sat, peeling off their socks and feeling the spring grass between their toes.

"We have a story to tell you," Otto said.

"Why don't you wait until everyone is together?" Dorcas said. "Here, make yourselves useful and help slice. I brought an extra paring knife."

Fredrick, Elija, Lena, and Paul followed soon after, pooling their afternoon finds for what would be the highlight of their evening meal. In the excitement of preparing and devouring the mushrooms, there wasn't a good time to share the story, though Sigrid was dying to do so. Finally, after the supper of roast potatoes and beef, stewed greens, and all the yellow sponge mushrooms they could eat, the family and the guests sat in the living room lit by the flickering light of the coal oil lamp.

"Is it time for our story now?" Otto asked, looking at Sigrid.

"Yes," Sigrid said. "The fox and the hunters."

Everyone was mesmerized by the astounding tale.

"It was as if the hunters couldn't see the fox that was right there in front of them," Otto said, arms spread wide.

"Yes," Sigi said. "The hound wasn't able to pick up the scent once the fox was inside the circle." The children broke into a chorus of exclamations, sensing the tale was over.

"That's impossible!" Lena said.

"I wish I had been there too," Paul said, his eyes gleaming dangerously.

"God has told us that 'every beast of the forest is mine, and mercy extends to all creatures,'" Greta said, and the children fell silent. "So it is then that in times of danger, 'God will make you invisible to your enemies and place you out of their reach,' just as God hid David from King Saul."

"All the same, it was wrong for those men to trespass on the property of others," Oscar said. "I hope they stay away from now on, and I am glad you two are safe."

The group continued to mull over the story as the evening progressed. The boys played checkers while Sigi and Greta parched corn over the stove. Oscar read his Bible and occasionally stoked the fireplace as the evening temperatures began to cool. Sigrid stared into the fire, lost in thoughts about the mystery of the invisible fox and the warm, unfamiliar feeling of Otto's hand in hers.

14
The Passing of Our Kindred
(Der Tod unserer Verwandten)
May–July 1916

O scar's boots thumped as he dropped them on the floor, weary from the evening chores. An unseasonably cool spring drizzle had left his thinning hair plastered uncomfortably to his head.

"Greta, would you bring me a hand cloth so I don't drip water everywhere?" he called. The clangor in the kitchen ceased, and a moment later, Greta hurried in with a towel. Her face changed when she saw Oscar alone.

"Where is Uncle Fredrick?" she asked, handing over the cloth.

"He's not in here?" Oscar asked. Greta shook her head, and the pair of them held each other's gaze for a moment, eyes widening. Uncle Fredrick was staying with Oscar and Greta; he and a few other church congregants had been helping Oscar put finishing trim into the new farm home. Nearing his seventy-fifth birthday, Uncle Fredrick had been visibly short of breath when helping with the finishing work on the new house.

"I must be getting old," he'd say, smiling sadly. "I just hope to live long enough to see the new place ready for young Fredrick and his bride."

"I'm going out again," Oscar said, running the cloth over his head quickly before handing it back to Greta. He pulled his sodden boots back on, trying to quell the sinking feeling in his stomach.

Rushing back out into the cold rain, Oscar jogged down the road to the new house and barn. The buildings stood proudly, the fruit of so many laborers. Church artisans had first completed a communal barn raising in early September 1915. Then, as soon as 1916 thawed, Oscar, Uncle Fredrick, and Fredrick Jr. began making progress on the new house by the woods. Lena and Greta had planted a garden and settled in the chicken flock. The farm was nearly ready for its new residents, but as Oscar hurried to the structures, he prayed the cost would not be Uncle Fredrick's health.

To his dismay, Oscar saw the outline of a man on the roof, hammering away through the cold rain.

"Uncle Fredrick!" Oscar called, cupping his hands around his mouth.

"Don't worry!" called down the old man. "I'm almost d—" his sentence dissolved into an ugly cough. Oscar grimaced.

Working late on that cool, wet evening to finish shingling his nephew's new home turned out to be a very bad decision for Uncle Fredrick. After three days of coughing and what he had called "only the croup," he developed a high fever and pneumonia.

"Oscar and I have decided it's time to send for the doctor,"

Greta told Uncle Fredrick sternly, sitting at his bedside. Uncle Fredrick waved a dismissive hand, sweat standing out in beads on his forehead. For days, the family had been trying to send for the doctor, but Uncle Fredrick remained stubbornly resistant. He had always believed in doctors for others but rarely saw one himself.

"Not necessary," he said in a weakened, hoarse voice. "Just keep me company. That's all I need."

Greta looked with concern at Uncle Fredrick's feverish face. He looked up at her, his gaze still radiating intellect despite his state. "Tell me what's going on in the world. Has America sent soldiers to Europe yet?"

"Uncle, you know we pay no mind to such things," said Greta. Uncle Fredrick snorted.

"Fine. I will ask young Fredrick next time he is here." Uncle Fredrick continued to stare, and Greta let out a resigned sigh.

"All I know is that America has yet to make a war commitment," she said begrudgingly. "We still send supplies to France and Britain's efforts, as we have for the past two years, but America is still resisting commitments to sending soldiers."

"Ah, so you do know," Uncle Fredrick said with a wink.

"Only because of town gossip," Greta said, "and because Dieter often writes about the war in Europe." In truth, though reluctant to discuss it openly, the Brethren community had become increasingly concerned in the face of the strong anti-German sentiment. If the U.S. were to join its allies against Germany, the enthusiasm toward German Americans could become even more extreme.

"But do not bother Fredrick Jr. with such things, Uncle," Greta continued, trying to distract herself. "Lena and Fredrick do not concern themselves with politics and the possibilities of war.

They are focused upon the planned declaration of their love for each other in holy matrimony."

One of Uncle Fredrick's bushy eyebrows shot up. "What do you mean? They haven't said a whit about it."

"As tradition dictates, they have kept their wedding secretive and not shared with the church until the last possible moment," Greta said, taking a wet cloth from the side table and dabbing the sweat from Uncle Fredrick's brow. "However, as you know, there is much to prepare for as the marriage approaches. We cannot keep arrangements entirely quiet."

"When will they stop being so . . ." Uncle Fredrick paused to cough, then cleared his throat, ". . . so sneaky?"

Greta replaced the cloth and patted Fredrick's arm. "They have asked for the wedding date to be announced at the beginning of July. The ceremony will take place three weeks after that."

"Seems a long time to keep a secret," Uncle Fredrick said, reaching for the water on the table. Greta handed it to him with a chuckle.

"The Brethren have all anticipated the union would 'happen soon enough,' but the gossip mill has settled correctly on a July date. It's hardly a secret anymore."

Uncle Fredrick sipped his water, then fixed a bleary eye on Greta. "Now, tell me what's going on with Sigi and that Otto boy," he croaked.

Greta blinked, then smiled. "Sigrid and Otto have become more serious over the past year about their marriage possibilities," she said, adjusting the blanket. "Watching Lena and Fredrick Jr. fall in love and plan for their future was an inspiration to them, I believe."

"He seems . . ." began Fredrick before dissolving into a fit of heaving, his water spilling across the blanket as he grabbed for a handkerchief. With horror, Greta saw traces of blood spattering the white cloth.

"That's enough," said Greta, standing abruptly. "Like it or not, I'm sending for Dr. Miller." Uncle Fredrick again waved a hand in protest, but the coughing continued as Greta swiftly left the room.

By the time the busy doctor made it to the house, another day had passed, and Uncle Fredrick was severely weakened. He coughed constantly, and despite Sigrid and Greta's constant ministrations, he only seemed to be declining.

"His advanced age and his current condition are not in his favor," young Dr. Miller confirmed as he prepared to leave, looking much like a younger version of his now-retired father. He looked grimly at the family who had assembled in the kitchen, clutching each other's hands. "I am so sorry to have to tell you this, but there is nothing much left for me to do. He could go any minute now."

Greta burst into tears. Sigrid clutched at her mother, and Fredrick Jr. looked stunned, frozen in place. Oscar, trying hard to hold in his emotions, stumbled into the room where Uncle Fredrick was sleeping. Oscar gazed in disbelief at his uncle, who had been so strong and independent up until so recently. This was the man who had changed the course of his family's life, the man who had brought Oscar and Greta to America, and he was now on death's door.

Collapsing into the chair next to the bed, Oscar gently placed a hand on Uncle Fredrick's shoulder. Uncle Fredrick opened one exhausted eye. Wordlessly, Oscar took his hand.

"You have become the son I never had," Uncle Fredrick gasped.

"And you are a second father to me," replied Oscar, tears sliding down his face. As Fredrick smiled up at his nephew and released his grip, Oscar felt the life leave Fredrick's body.

That evening, Pastor Yoder came to the Beck residence, summoned by Fredrick Jr. German Baptist Brethren had already started arriving with gifts of food and words of comfort. Fredrick Jr. and Sigrid spoke with the Bowmans and the Kunkles, who had just stepped in, as Oscar and Greta went off into a side room to speak with Pastor Yoder.

"Though not a true member of the German Baptist Brethren Church, your uncle has done much to provide solidarity for the church community," Pastor Yoder said gently, his own hands trembling with age.

"There will be a large funeral attendance," Greta added. "Uncle Fredrick helped . . . so many." Her eyes were bloodshot from weeping.

Pastor Yoder nodded. "We must meet and officially agree, but I have no doubt the elders will approve burying Fredrick Beck at the cemetery outside of the Zion Church meeting house following the viewing and ceremony."

Later that evening, when everyone had gone home and they were readying for sleep, Oscar sat down on the corner of his bed and wiped his face on his sleeve. Though no eulogy or flowers were part of the German Baptist ritual, the congregation would say many prayers and sing beautiful a cappella hymns for Uncle Fredrick as he departed his time on Earth. Oscar was glad that Uncle Fredrick would be afforded such a funeral by the people he loved. It would be a fitting end, Oscar thought, for a man who had changed many lives for the better.

Greta sat beside Oscar and gently wrapped her arms around his shoulders.

"Fredrick has gone on to be with our Lord, where he will be forever safe in His love and mercy," she whispered. Oscar silently rested his head on Greta's shoulder.

The church required that they wait three days after Uncle Fredrick's passing to hold the funeral. Oscar and Greta, grieving and hurrying to get everything done in time, were grateful for the help of their congregation. When Dorcas asked what she could do, Greta asked if she would be willing to travel to Peru the day before the funeral to purchase some provisions needed for the after-service meal.

"Sigrid would be pleased to accompany you," Greta added. "This is no time for any of us to be traveling alone. I hate to ask this of you, but for a large event like this, the trip cannot be avoided, and I have my hands more than full as it is."

"Anything for you," Dorcas said, clasping Greta's hand in hers. "Lena can come along too."

"Thank you, sister. May the Lord protect you."

Wearing mourning dresses, the three women made their way cautiously into town.

"The bias toward German Americans has grown to the point where it is somewhat dangerous to leave the seclusion of the farm," Dorcas told Lena and Sigrid as they made the journey. "We will need to be very swift."

"I understand, Ma," Lena said.

"Yes," Sigrid said. "We haven't forgotten our last trip. We won't dawdle."

Heads down, the women worked together to gather the

foodstuffs on their list without incident quickly. However, when they left the grocery store, they saw three men standing in front of the family buggy. The horse stood hitched at the rear of the general store across from Jacob Op's Tavern, and Dorcas immediately surmised that the men must have watched their arrival.

"Stay calm," Dorcas said, adjusting her heavy bag. "God will protect us." Holding her head high and trying to think of Greta's bravery during their previous trip, Dorcas approached the buggy.

"Huns," said one man. He took a swig from a brown glass bottle, displaying the confederate flag tattooed on his hand as the women approached their buggy. Stale cigar smoke from the nearby saloon permeated the air.

With a belligerent glance at the woman, the man walked up to the horse and raised his half-full bottle. Smirking, he poured beer onto the buggy horse's forelock. The mare shook her head, batting her eyes as the beer ran down her face.

"Jes coolin' her off fer ya," the man said, his speech slurred. His companions guffawed, and the three men began to crowd around the women. Shaking, Lena tried to glide past them to untie the mare, but the men would not let her pass.

"Where you goin', fraulein?" asked a man blocking Lena's path. Dorcas took a deep, shuddering breath, trying to steady herself. Then, from the corner of her eye, she spotted a thin, older man in a brown top coat approaching the buggy through the alleyway. The slight man came quite close, then stopped and stood staring brazenly at the three men, his wrinkled face alert.

"What's ailing you, grandpa?" one of the men said. The man only stood and watched, slowly unlatching the waist button of his coat. When he pushed the coat open to reveal a holstered sidearm, one of the men let out a loud jeer.

"How'd this codger get out of the county home? Just hand over that six-shooter, grandpa, so you don't hurt yourself?"

The elderly gentleman eased the Colt out of its holster and cocked back the hammer, still watching the men. He held the pistol lowered by his side, waiting. Dorcas instinctively sidled in front of the younger women, shielding them from the conflict.

One of the drunken men stepped toward the newcomer, grasping the neck of his beer bottle precariously between two fingers.

"Go back inside the saloon you came out of," the armed man said in a low, gravelly voice, tilting his head toward the tavern. The drunken men smirked as they began to walk forward.

"Reckon I could do with a pistola like that'n," one of the men said, eyeing the spotless blued revolver. As if in response, the old man raised his aim, and a loud "crack" abruptly split the air. The woman jumped, and Lena wrapped her arms around her mother's waist.

The heckler's beer bottle burst, and Dorcas watched as tiny spots of blood bloomed on the man's hand and wrist, maimed by shards of glass from the bottle.

"You crazy old son of a bitch!" the startled man screamed in a high-pitched voice, shaking the beer and glass from his hand and shirt sleeve. The old gunman raised his weapon higher, pointing it at the ringleader's face.

"I don't care to repeat myself, Johnny Reb," the gunman said. The three drunkards, now obviously much more sober, hastily retreated down the alley. The women turned and stared at the grizzled man as he holstered his pistol and calmly buttoned his coat.

"Ma'ams," he said, touching the brim of his felt hat, "judging by your manner of dress, I'd wager you'll be able to tell me when and where the funeral of Fredrick Beck is to be held."

"Tomorrow morning at ten o'clock at the Zion Church," Lena, still shaking, answered nervously.

"Well," said the pensioner, "Suppose I'll see you there." He again tipped his hat and walked off toward the livery's taxi building across the street.

"I know who that is!" Sigrid said in a shaky voice as the women hurried into the buggy. "I heard the story secondhand from my ma, but I think he may have killed some bank robbers a long time ago in Bunker Hill. He was Uncle Fredrick's close friend."

"Oh, yes, I remember that," Dorcas said, quickly grabbing the reins. "Your Uncle Fredrick certainly had some interesting friends."

"Mama, you said God would protect us, and He did," Lena said diplomatically. Dorcas was silent, her hands still trembling as she steered the buggy out of town.

Meanwhile, at home, Oscar had received an unexpected couriered telegram from a lawyer in Ohio responsible for Uncle Fredrick's estate. He quickly called Greta from the kitchen so they could look it over. Greta had been cooking frantically with many of the sisters for hours, filling the kitchen with the smell of pork stew and fresh bread, talking all the while.

"My goodness," Greta said as the couple, heads touching, scanned the page. Uncle Fredrick, it seemed, had left them a generous sum of money.

"My goodness indeed," murmured Oscar.

"Uncle Fredrick bequeathed young Fredrick and Sigrid a sizable amount also," Greta said after a moment, running her finger along the page. "'. . . to receive the funds upon their marriages, to be used at their sole discretion . . .'"

"That sounds like Uncle Fredrick," said Oscar.

"What should we do with what he has left us?" Greta asked, looking at Oscar. "We should set some money aside as a rainy day fund, I believe."

"Of course," Oscar said. "As for the bulk of the funds, however, let us pray about how best to use it. I'm sure God will direct us."

"Perhaps we could sit for a spell with the church elders to establish a plan as to how to share the inheritance for God's glory," Greta said. "That is, as soon as we talk with Fredrick's lawyer." Oscar nodded.

"As for now, there is much to be done," Greta said. "We must write Uncle Dieter. Of course, he will be unable to attend the funeral; the amount of travel time to America exceeds the Anabaptist time constraints for burial many times over."

"Even if that weren't the case, new travel restrictions in Germany also would not allow Dieter's trip," Oscar said. "Plus, Dieter himself is quite old. He is only one year Uncle Fredrick's junior, after all. It may not be safe for him to travel."

"In any case, he will want to know right away."

"Of course," Oscar said. "I think I will write him a letter tonight."

True to his word, Oscar sat down that evening and wrote a letter by the light of his oil lamp, trying not to damage the delicate paper with his tears.

May 27, 1916

Dearest Uncle Dieter,

It brings me such sorrow to share the news of your brother Fredrick's passing. He was called home to be with our Lord and Savior last evening on the eve of his seventy-fifth year of life on earth, surrounded by his family who loved and honored him as a good and faithful servant to our Lord Jesus Christ.

The funeral is to be conducted by Pastor Yoder at the Zion German Baptist Brethren Church of Peru, Indiana, on Tuesday at 2:00 on May 30th, 1916.

Uncle Fredrick has been a generous loyal friend and benefactor to me, Greta, and our family. We will always owe a debt of gratitude, one that can never be repaid. Even in death, he has entrusted us with a gift to sustain the work and word of our Heavenly Father with whom he now resides.

It is our sincere hope that you are well in Germany. We pray that God will give you his comfort and countenance in this moment of grief we all now bear.

Sincerely, from your obedient nephew,
Oscar Beck

15

An Ending and a New Beginning

(Ein Ende und ein neuer Anfang)

June 1917

As Greta had anticipated, the following day's funeral had a sizable turnout from the German Brethren. Parked horses and buggies lined the road in front of Zion Church. Oscar and Greta stuck together in the melee, but their children dispersed to find their friends and help with last-minute preparations.

"Oscar, look!" Greta said, gesturing to his right. Oscar turned and saw someone he hadn't seen in twenty years: Colonel Tillett, older but still recognizable, climbing out of a black Dodge taxi.

"Ah, so Sigrid was right after all about the identity of their protector yesterday," Oscar said, watching as Colonel Tillett helped a dark-skinned woman in her thirties exit the car. As soon as the pair looked up, Oscar waved, and Colonel Tillett ambled over, his eyes darting to and fro just as they had decades before.

"Mr. Beck," Colonel Tillett said stiffly. "Mrs. Beck. Sincere condolences for your loss."

"And for yours," Greta said.

"This is Rose," Colonel Tillett said. "We seem to get along well enough. As I'm part Injun myself, we tend to think a lot alike."

Rose smiled at the Becks. Up closer, it was clear by her features that she was of native Indian ethnicity. She was dressed in a black ankle-length dress and a plumed, Edwardian-era, broad-brimmed hat. Her coal-black hair was done up in a thick braid.

"Rosie is a full-blooded Sioux," said the colonel. "Ever met a real Injun before?"

"I don't believe so," Oscar replied. "Though Rose doesn't sound much like an Indian name."

"It's not," Rose said, smiling. "My mother named me Ojin-jintka, but most whiteskins can't say that, so I just go by Rose." She turned her palm face up, and Oscar could see a small red rose tattoo on the inside of her left wrist.

"Fine names, the both of them," Greta said.

"Colonel, we have already heard from our daughter what happened yesterday in town," Oscar said. "We appreciate your intent and are thankful no one was hurt."

The colonel nodded mechanically. "I thought one of the girls might have been your kin. Nevertheless, I know how you feel about violence."

"Things are troubled enough for our brethren because of the war in Europe," Greta acquiesced. "We have taken no side and wish harm on no one."

"No need to fret," Colonel Tillett said in his raspy voice. "I'm only here to bury my old friend. We'll be leaving on the train after he's in the ground—that is, if I can avoid the sheriff. I understand he has been floating questions around town," he said, grinning at Oscar.

"It does seem you get into a skirmish every time you come to these parts," Oscar said, unable to suppress a small smile.

Greta soon swept Rose away to talk with the women while the colonel came closer to Oscar. Oscar noticed a few church elders scowling from a distance at the sight of the military man and his dark-skinned companion, but in memory of Uncle Fredrick, Oscar chose to ignore this.

"Rose seems to be an intelligent young woman," Oscar said. "She has no accent of any kind from what I can tell."

"She was part of the Dakota tribes that were sent to White's Institute in Wabash," Colonel Tillett said.

"A school for manual arts, I recall," Oscar said. He reached down to grab a stem of early grass to chew on.

"I suppose they tried to 'wash the Injun out of her' there," the colonel laughed. "Didn't work. She was trained to be a seamstress at the school, but mostly she has just taken in laundry and worked the saloons ever since." He paused. "I gained an adversarial respect for Injun folks during my duty out west. They were put through a lot."

Oscar watched as Greta and Rose conversed nearby. He wondered about the multi-decade age gap between Colonel Tillett and his companion. Still, perhaps the hardened-looking young woman sought the colonel's financial security as a means of escape from her difficult life. And perhaps the colonel, for his part, was looking for companionship and solace in the autumn of his years.

"It is good to have a partner," Oscar said aloud. "I don't know what I would do without Greta."

"Affirmed," said the old colonel, looking at Rose with warmth instead of his usually rigid gaze.

"You seem happy," Oscar said presently. Colonel Tillett nodded his assent. People were naturally drifting toward the burial site, and Oscar and Colonel Tillett joined them, their boots squelching in the moist May earth.

"I met Fredrick in Ohio a few weeks before his death, working on oil leasing," Colonel Tillett said.

"Oh!" Oscar said. "I am so glad to hear it."

Colonel Tillett nodded. "I thought he looked somewhat frail, but I thought nothing of it. I was still there when I received a telegram from his lawyer about Fredrick's passing."

"It all happened so quickly," said Oscar, shaking his head. "At least you got to see him before he died."

"One last time," agreed the colonel. His steely eyes shifted, meeting Oscar's gaze, and he pitched his voice down. "From our conversation, it was my understanding that Fredrick was to leave you and Greta a sum of money."

Oscar nodded, still feeling overwhelmed by the suddenness of it all. "Greta and I prayed together last night. We plan to ask the elders to use the money to spread the gospel through mission work, helping the German Baptist Brethren Church to serve God more devoutly."

"Seems noble," Colonel Tillett said.

"We have several missions to support, including one in Africa and one in Denmark," Oscar said. "Our soon-to-be daughter-in-law's cousin Paul plans on starting a Scandinavian mission, perhaps even for the tribes in Lapland. Uncle Fredrick already lent some support to that trip, so it seems only fitting that we continue to do so now."

Colonel Tillett nodded. "That sounds like Fredrick. I think he would be pleased with your plan, but don't forget to keep something for yourself and your family. Above all, he would want you to be cared for."

Oscar, straining to keep his composure, managed to say, "I know."

Oscar and the colonel walked to the graveside, where Greta and Rose waited by the churchyard gate. The burial gatherers stood, and Fredrick and Sigrid came out of the crowd to take their places with her parents. Soon, Pastor Yoder began singing a cappella hymn, "Jerusalem, My Happy Home," in his warbling voice. The mourners joined in, singing the words they knew by heart.

Jerusalem, my happy home,
When shall I with you be?
When shall my sorrows have an end?
Your joys, when shall I see?

Four pallbearers carried Fredrick's casket to the gravesite to the solemn tune. Oscar bent his head, remembering.

The graveside funeral lasted an hour and a half, and the many gathered Brethren paid their respects to Fredrick Beck Sr. Oscar and Greta wept for the uncle that had given them so much and had saved them from strife in Germany. Many mourners came to greet the Becks and offer them their condolences, while others rushed off to make final preparations for the communal dinner.

As the crowd thinned, Brethren men began shoveling dirt into the grave as two others with long wooden poles tamped the loose soil around the casket. Congregates moved towards the church building where the after-service meal would soon take place, and Colonel Tillett and Rose approached Oscar.

"We'll be leaving now," said the colonel.

"Can't you stay for the meal?" Greta asked.

"No, unfortunately. We're going to catch the late eastbound train out of Peru."

Rose touched Greta's arm. "Life will, in time, return to what it was."

Greta smiled weakly. "Do you need a ride to the depot?" she asked.

"Our taxi is arranged, but thank you just the same," said the colonel. He slipped a folded paper from his pocket and handed it to Oscar. "I doubt I will see you again, but I'm a friend to anyone dear to Fredrick. If you need anything, write."

Overcome with emotion, Oscar merely nodded and cleared his throat as he shook the colonel's hand. Rose smiled sadly at the pair, and then she and the old soldier turned and walked away, arm in arm. That was, indeed, the last time Oscar and Greta saw Colonel Tillett.

Just a few months later, on July 22, the warm Indiana sun shone down upon Fredrick and Lena Beck's new farm. Greta and Oscar, having walked over early to make sure everything was prepared, surveyed the beautiful new structures. The red cattle barn stood forty yards from the brick farmhouse where Fredrick and Lena planned to raise their family. The house and land plot was Oscar and Greta's heartfelt gift to their son and his bride upon the day of their wedding, and Greta knew the young couple would soon fill the property with love and laughter.

"The red sky last night foretold a rainless wedding and surely a happy life to follow," she said, taking a breath of the fresh morning air. A constant clicking could be heard as the sails of the wooden windmill, circled by the six large stones, turned in the wind and drew water from the well drilled deep in the ground. Greta found the sound extremely comforting.

"God has provided for our family from the time we first arrived in Indiana for over twenty years now," Oscar said, reaching for Greta's hand. "I am grateful to our Lord to have such a lovely summer day for Fredrick and Lena's wedding."

Oscar and Greta stood silent for a moment in anticipation of the wedding day ahead. Nearby, the livestock Oscar and Fredrick had moved to the property were chewing sweet bluegrass. Greta knew they had been right to choose to have the wedding here, at the new couple's home, because of its larger guest capacity. For the past two months, she had walked the distance almost daily to ensure the house was immaculate inside and out.

In Lena's roadside garden, the gently swaying sunflowers gathered wild honeybees and waved a greeting. The ceremony itself would be conducted by the front yard's large maple tree with its rough barked branches. It stood twenty-five feet tall and shaded the freshly clipped lawn, casting a shadow in the morning light. Within view, the long pine tables that Oscar and Fredrick had built over the winter stood lined with benches, awaiting table-cloths and dishes and guests.

"Everything is ready," Greta said aloud.

"Are you ready?" Oscar asked.

"As ready as I can be to have to say goodbye to our firstborn," Greta said.

"Luckily, he isn't going far," Oscar said, putting an arm around his wife. Greta sniffed, and the couple shared a moment of thought.

"I do wish Uncle Fredrick was here," Oscar said presently.

"As do we all," Greta said, bringing a hand up to rest on Oscar's.

To Greta, it seemed but a moment later that the cooling late afternoon breeze, scented by newly mown hay, rustled the white linen tablecloths. Many of the brethren had arrived early and spent the morning assisting with preparations. Rounded plates and bowls of traditional German farm food weighed down the delicate tablecloths, displaying a veritable feast that had taken many hands many days to complete.

Greta's eyes skimmed over the various tables, ensuring everything was in order. The first was covered by overflowing plates of sweet baked ham, cabbage rolls, pork pudding, fried chicken, and roasted beef glazed in maple sugar. Platters of sour sausage, kraut, and gravy in porcelain bowls, knipp sausage, and chicken and noodles rounded out the second table, along with buttered roasting ears, green beans, mashed potatoes, and sliced tomatoes. Rye breads, pretzels, potato rolls, golden brown biscuits, honey, and pitchers of water and sweet milk pasteurized on Lena's wood stove rested on the third table.

Greta stepped forward as a gaggle of children got a little too close to the fourth table with its desserts: blackberry, molasses, apple, cherry, and rhubarb pies accompanied by cinnamon star cookies, bread pudding, sliced watermelon, applesauce, and homemade ice cream in a unique chest. The two families had also prepared a long white sheet cake that now sat alone on a unique table, lovingly made with churned butter, milk, stone-ground flour, and fresh eggs, but the children knew better than to try to creep too close to that. As the giggles of the fleeing group filled the air, Greta felt fortunate that the breeze, along with various covers and lids, kept the wedding banquet free of insects.

Feeling suddenly nervous beyond belief, Greta smoothed her freshly washed modest dress, made sure no flyaway strands poked out of her bonnet, and glanced over at the path. A procession of chestnut, white, and bay horses tugged the plain black buggies of arriving guests up the short lane to Fredrick and Lena's home. Greta saw Oscar leading the guests' lathered horses to the hitching rails by the barn, where they drank rationed cool water from the windmill's tank. Glancing up again, she confirmed there were no rain clouds that July afternoon. Nothing would dampen this happy day.

Soon, the whole congregation was there, the elderly finding their seats quickly while the young frolicked in the verdant grass. Lena's family was more established and quite large in Indiana. So Greta socialized with many soon-to-be relatives, taking delight in finding Lena's large, dark eyes and lustrous brown locks adorning many different people.

The next moments were a blur of happiness. Greta and Dorcas, sitting side by side, both smiled through tears as Fredrick and Lena took their places in front of Pastor Yoder. Fredrick's collarless black suit and Lena's white linen dress, carefully crafted from the fabric they'd purchased in town, lent balance to the occasion.

Pastor Yoder's white, coarse chin beard quivered as he raised his calloused hands.

"Please kneel," he said to the couple. All was quiet except the chirping of the birds as the ceremony began.

As Pastor Yoder directed the young couple to follow biblical commandments and speak vows to honor their passage into marriage, Fredrick and Lena glanced admiringly at each other, holding eye contact but for a moment before glancing downward.

Greta knew it would take time for them to learn comfort in total intimacy, even though the pair had known each other since childhood.

"Please rise," Pastor Yoder said, his voice carrying well over the assembled guests. "Fredrick Beck, will you take Lena Kunkle to be your wife? Will you love her, comfort and keep her, and forsaking all others, remain true to her as long as you both shall live?"

"I will," Fredrick said. Greta took a deep sip of air, trying not to make a sound as tears slid down her face.

"Lena Kunkle, will you take Fredrick Beck to be your husband? Will you love him, comfort and keep him, and forsake all others, remain true to him as long as you both shall live?"

"I will," Lena said. Dorcas let out an audible sob next to Greta, and Greta reached over to take her friend's hand in comfort. Then, Fredrick and Lena, pronounced man and wife, stood and turned to face the waiting church congregation.

The newlyweds were soon lost in a sea of congratulations. The women welcomed Lena with a holy kiss, as the men did the same with Fredrick. A few of the older congregants greeted the couple in German. Then, the eager celebrants turned their attention to the grand wedding meal.

"This wedding will always be a cherished memory in my heart," Greta said to Dorcas as she set her heavy-laden plate down.

"The marriage of a firstborn child is special," Dorcas agreed, smiling and spearing a piece of sausage with her fork. "I wonder if I will feel this way when Elija marries."

"I'm sure it will be just as joyful an occasion."

"Although these days, Elija keeps alluding to following his cousin Paul into missionary work in a few years," Dorcas said. "It may be a while before he finds the right woman, I think." She popped a piece of sausage into her mouth.

"Perhaps missionary work would help Elija widen his social circle and come into his own," Greta commented, slicing into a thick piece of scrapple. "He and Otto are so close, but I think sometimes Elija gets overshadowed by him."

"Perhaps," Dorcas said, thoughtfully sampling her chicken and noodles. A moment passed, and then she said, "I am so glad Lena and Fredrick have chosen to remain in the Zion congregation."

Greta nodded. Now that they were married, Lena and Fredrick were able to opt to continue in the church tradition or choose another path. They had been counseled in this choice by the parish elders beforehand, and out of a deep abiding love, both had elected to stay devoted to the faith of their parents.

Hearing laughter, Greta turned and saw Fredrick and Lena sharing a private joke nearby, positively glowing with happiness. Swallowing and dabbing her face with a napkin, Greta looked at her friend and leaned toward her.

"I know there are those in our church who will not agree, but I have arranged to have photographs taken of the couple later today," Greta confessed quietly. Photographs were still considered to be "graven images" by some in the parish.

Dorcas leaned forward, too, eyes sparkling. "The photos will be heirlooms for long generations," she said. "I understand. In fact, would you be able to have a copy made for me? Lena looks so beautiful on this blessed day."

16
Conflicts of Beliefs
(Glaubens Konflikte)
June 1917

"The Anabaptist churches were founded as churches of peace," Pastor Yoder declared from the pulpit. Elija sat rapt at attention, nodding his agreement. Next to him, Otto was staring absentmindedly into the pews on the other side of the aisle. Tracking his gaze, Elija saw Sigrid sitting there, her pink cheeks and long lashes perfectly highlighted by the morning sun streaming in the window.

Pursing his lips, Elija gave Otto a quick poke in the arm. Otto's eyes snapped back to Pastor Yoder.

"Serving directly or in support of killing, regardless of circumstances, is a sin against the Almighty God. 'Thou shalt not kill,'" Pastor Yoder said firmly. "The German Baptist and Brethren Church affiliate's stance is quite clear. The church will not be part of an engagement of war in any form."

Elija nodded along. He knew well the literal interpretation of the Bible that the Anabaptists practiced. He also knew it collided with what the majority of Americans saw as a clear and necessary action. On April 2, 1917, when President Wilson officially asked Congress for a declaration of war on Germany, the German Baptist stance became problematic overnight. According to most of the country, war was the only way to save Europe and, ultimately, the United States' independence.

Elija also knew all too well why Pastor Yoder had been emphasizing this specific belief as of late. There was a growing resentment of German Americans who, as conscientious objectors, shunned military service while prospering from America's freedoms and opportunities. The church community was indeed celebrating its harmonious increased tithing from land revenue. The shared tithing from grain and livestock sales may have helped the mission of the church, funding much-needed building projects and repairs as well as mission trips. Still, the surrounding communities had begun viewing the Church of Zion with resentment and cynicism.

As the service ended and people began reverently leaving their seats, Otto stretched.

"The good pastor has been giving that same sermon for as long as I can remember," he mumbled.

"Only for two years," said Elija. "That's when this all began. America is being pulled into this stupid war, after all."

That was the crux of the matter, and it had started keeping Elija up at night. He would stare at the slatted ceiling of his bedroom, listening to the mice scurrying and wondering what was going to happen. The anger toward the American Germans had come to a head when, in June, the national military draft began calling up Americans between the ages of twenty-one and thirty for national service. American troops were already being shipped to France with the expectation of being shuffled to the front lines in the fall. In the German Baptist and Brethren churches, "conscientious objector" status had not been generally publicized; instead, it had been taken for granted as a way to avoid military service. However, the draft laws made clear that unmarried males with no dependents were eligible for military service regardless of their religious beliefs.

This is what kept Elija up at night, but Otto didn't seem to share the concern. Rolling his eyes, Otto got up and cracked his back. "We will be alright. You'll see," he said.

"Sure," Elija said, scratching his arm nervously. Otto, who was again staring unabashedly at Sigrid, was tall and strapping thanks to good genetics and years of farmwork. Elija, on the other hand, was of slight build and small for his age. He had always preferred academic, indoor pursuits to the manual labor and sports Otto gravitated towards. Otto would fit well in the Army, Elija thought as he looked at his friend. But Elija himself? He wasn't so sure.

"Sigi. Sigi!" Otto said, and he left Elija sitting in the pew. Elija sighed. Just ahead, he spotted Lena, his sister, her belly already protruding with her first child.

Elija leaned against the pew in front, watching as Fredrick beamed at his sister. Lena and Fredrick's life at the new farm was uncomplicated and straightforward, and Elija was happy for them. They'd received an inheritance from Fredrick's uncle, and they'd used part of it to purchase adjoining tillable land and additional livestock, further adding value to the new farm. Fredrick had even been able to convince the local Peru draft board to grant him an exemption when the first wave of draftees from Miami

County was being called up. His family situation and religious beliefs helped, but his farm's food production for the war effort had sealed the exemption.

Idly, Elija couldn't help but wonder if there was something he could do to make himself draft-exempt also. He peered hopefully around the church, looking for any eligible young woman he'd missed whom he could quickly marry and start a family with. Unfortunately, no such woman was in sight. The only woman he was interested in was enamored with his best friend. In fact, the church was practically empty now.

Elija slumped back in his seat, lost in his thoughts. He had always loved his studies and his religion. He thought fleetingly of Paul, off on his mission trip overseas. But Paul was only nineteen, not yet in danger of being drafted. Elija then thought about joining the seminary—something he'd always thought of doing—. Still, he would have to seek approval for funding from the elders, and most seminaries didn't start until fall. Would that be too late?

Elija barely held in a surprised shriek when, with a thump, Otto landed on one side of him and Sigi on the other.

"Do you want to go into town tomorrow evening after chores?" Sigi asked him eagerly.

"We can't," Elija said, disguising his fright by sticking his nose in the air. "Unnecessary trips to town must be avoided. Sigrid, you, of all people, should know that after the harassment you've experienced firsthand. As Pastor Yoder has been saying, the danger just isn't worth the risk."

Sigi frowned at Elija, who blushed as he tried to maintain eye contact with her. Her indigo eyes, framed by long, blonde lashes, seemed blinding to him.

"I don't see what they have against us," she said. "What did we ever do to them? In any case, they don't intimidate me."

"Well, it's true that our habit of speaking German to each other no longer seems so quaint to outsiders in the community who overhear us," Otto said. "However, the hatred is not only directed at us. The locals' hatred is for any Anabaptist, Mennonite, Amish, or German Baptist. It's anyone who gets special draft status. The discrimination and property vandalizing hardly feels worth the exemption sometimes."

Elija groaned and covered his eyes with his forearm. "It doesn't matter anyway. I've heard there are no more exemptions for single boys like you and me, Otto."

"Yes, well, no use worrying about it then," said Otto flatly. "Come on, your ma has vittles waiting."

Out on the lawn in front of the church, Greta and Oscar were deep in a private conversation about the very same topic.

"We must not become distracted from God's purpose for us on Earth," Greta said. "Fredrick and Lena now have their own lives. God has blessed them. We must give God praise for the new life that is coming and carry on living God's will, though we may all soon be tested."

"If America is drawn into this unholy war, it will greatly offend our Lord," Oscar said, furrowing his brow. "Otto is interested in Sigi; that much is clear. I have no doubt the feelings are mutual. But he has only the argument that he helps out on his family's farm and belongs to an Anabaptist Church. That won't be enough, in the eyes of the draft board, to avoid military service."

Greta sighed and crossed her arms over her chest, saying nothing.

"I also can't help but notice that the sons of our local politicians, doctors, and lawyers seem somehow to avoid being conscripted," Oscar said darkly.

"Yes, well, the German Baptist community has no such political power or advocacy," Greta said. "Nor do we want it. Besides, those are all rumors."

"Some rumors are based in truth," said Oscar flatly. "And so our sons, predictably, will be picked off one by one."

"Oscar, I understand your fears," said Greta, taking his hand. "All we can do is pray and be grateful that neither of our children will suffer that fate. In any case, Germany's aggression is not simply going to go away because the Zion Church does not believe in taking up arms."

Greta looked up into Oscar's furrowed face. "It is a blessing that our first grandchild is coming soon," she said. "Now, I'm going to go find Dorcas. She told me she would give me her wonderful dumpling recipe." She hurried away, leaving Oscar standing alone in the sunshine.

Oscar thought that the past year had held both a wedding and a funeral. These events, which seemed so monumental, will be overshadowed if America is pulled into a world war.

Oscar's words came to fruition on a blazing midsummer afternoon just weeks later when the mail hack delivered a letter for Otto. Opening the letter, Otto felt his heart begin to race. He knew full well what it would say.

All brothers who fell into specific age ranges had begun to receive orders to report for military induction. At first, there was denial within the church that the government was really serious about young men having to report to the induction center in Indianapolis. Church elders believed there had been a mistake in paperwork since the German Baptist stance on war was well known, particularly by the local draft board. However, it soon became clear that the government was not mistaken, nor were they willing to look the other way for religious belief exemption. Under federal authority, those defying the draft would be prosecuted by law.

After scanning the letter, Otto quickly folded it and placed it in his pocket, feeling his stomach sinking. He saddled his corralled gelding to ride up the road to Fredrick's house.

Lena, Elija, and Fredrick were sitting at the kitchen table sharing fresh cornbread muffins and buttermilk as Otto entered the front door with a letter in hand, mopping sweat from his eyes.

"I see you got one, too," Elija said, holding up his draft letter. With that, Elija stood and walked out of the house, plopping dramatically into the porch swing outside the window. Otto, knowing his friend well, sat down at the kitchen table rather than following.

"Don't get me wrong; I'm relieved that Fredrick had been exempted," Lena said, taking Fredrick's hand. "But I fear greatly for my brother's welfare. He is not the type of person who will stay quiet and not question the purpose of being sent to war."

"I can't say I haven't thought about that," Otto said, reaching for a muffin. "I hope he doesn't get himself into trouble."

"Ma and Pa are very concerned," Lena said. "Pa had considered sending Elija away to Ohio to live with relatives to avoid this draft law. But as the whole world seems caught up in this war, it would be impossible to hide for very long. He would no doubt risk arrest."

"What about you, Otto?" asked Fredrick, dusting cornbread crumbs off his shirt. "I thought you and Sigrid were enjoying each other's company as of late. Would you consider marriage to avoid the draft?"

"Yes, well," Otto said, "I have always been fond of Sigi, even when we were just kids." He tried not to let color rise into his cheeks, fixing his eyes on the blue sky outside the open window instead. "We've been good friends and have always supported each other. But now, I suppose that any thoughts of marriage will have to wait. We cannot marry and start a family so swiftly as that."

Otto paused for a moment. "To be honest, it's Ma and Pa's worries that concern me most. Pa has not been in good health for some time. The fear of what our country might ask of me has left him riled inside. I don't know what I'm going to say to him about this."

"Well, at least you have certain advantages," Lena said, spreading her palms on the table to heave her growing body out of the chair. "Otto, unlike Elija, you seem to see bad situations as a challenge rather than a reason to balk." Otto shrugged.

"She's right," said Fredrick. "Otto, you were the first to leap off the high bridge at the Pipe Creek swimming hole—"

"Hmm. Guess I never gave it much thought," said Otto, taking another bite of muffin.

"—and once you even put yourself in front of that charging Hereford bull to divert it from your pa when he tripped and fell in the barn lot! Can you see Elija doing that?"

Otto shrugged again. The answer hung in the air, and Lena sighed. "Your personality is the opposite of Elija's. You will fare much better in the army, I have no doubt."

"Well," said Otto, gulping down the last bite of cornbread and enjoying a gust of a breeze from the window, "I'm still sincere in my faith. I believe that war and the taking of life is a grievous sin. I'm just not as loud about it as Elija."

"That may well make all the difference," Lena said quietly, her gaze on Elija's slim shoulders. Otto watched as his best friend swung slowly back and forth on the porch swing in the summer heat.

17

Reckoning

(Abrechnung)

October–December 1917

"Our pleas and petitions to the draft board seem to have fallen upon deaf ears," Pastor Yoder lamented. Otto looked around at Elija and the other three unhappy young men who had received orders to report for military induction. It was Friday, October 19, and the group of German Baptist Brethren stood clustered on the train platform, waiting to board the southbound train to Indianapolis to report for duty that day. The Zion Church had held a prayer vigil the day before, but only the families of the recruits, along with Pastor Yoder, came to the train station to send the men off.

"Seems the anti-German sentiment within the community has extended itself," Pastor Yoder said, his sagging skin nearly transparent in the bright daylight. Otto wondered how old Pastor Yoder was. "It has ensured that the draft board gives no special privileges for conscientious objectors. We have been placed in a difficult situation indeed."

"Don't worry," said Elija, stepping forward and meeting the old pastor's eye. "We will stand by our faith, Pastor Yoder." Otto, behind Elija, looked at his boots.

The little group disbanded, separating into families and saying tearful goodbyes.

"This draft transgresses our beliefs, as you well know," Dorcas told Elija as she wiped her large brown eyes. "Still, we hold fast to the hope that you will not have to fight in a war."

"Or perhaps God will just suddenly end the war due to the inhumanity of it all," Lena added. "The warring countries may still come to their senses and call an end to the fighting. We will pray this comes to pass."

Elija gazed at his family, his heart thumping wildly in his chest. "I . . . I will uphold our beliefs at all costs," he managed. "I will not let you or our Lord down."

"We have no doubt," Amos said, "but please take care of yourself. We will see you again soon enough, at Christmas."

"Yes, Pa," Elija said. "At Christmas."

Nearby, Sigrid held Otto's hand as they said farewell.

"Please stay safe and come back to me," she said in a trembling voice. Looking into Otto's eyes, she drew a small envelope from the folds of her dress and pressed it into his hand.

"I will write as much and as often as I can," Otto assured Sigi. "I won't forget my promise to come back after basic training. We will marry after the war and begin our lives anew." Sigi's eyes filled with tears, which she quickly dashed away.

Pulling themselves away, the recruits left their families and boarded the train. Otto, falling into line, turned and took one last longing look at Sigrid before stepping aboard. Then, the new passengers rushed to the windows, waving to their loved ones.

Around them, as the train pulled out, recruits already aboard the train began spontaneously singing a funny popular song. The German Baptist Brethren men exchanged looks; they didn't know any popular music.

Oh, they took me in to the army and handed me a pack,

They took away my nice new clothes and dolled me up in khak.

They marched me twenty miles a day to fit me for the war

I didn't mind the first nineteen, but the last one made me sore.

As the rhythm of the train's driving wheels clicked down the rails and away from the station, Otto and Elija found seats together. Otto opened the envelope Sigrid had given him to find a small lock of blonde hair tied in a blue ribbon. His throat constricted, and he ran his fingers along the soft, blonde curl. He'd never seen Sigrid's hair loose before.

Hearing a sound, Otto looked up. Elija shifted nervously in his seat. Sweat stains crept from under the arms of his dark suit, though the October weather was relatively mild.

"Are you afraid?" Otto asked. Elija did not speak, but his ashen complexion was telling. Otto waited, staring at his friend.

"I suppose it doesn't matter at this point," Elija said finally. "It doesn't matter if the war is right or wrong to those who want to sacrifice us for their political ambitions."

"That's the spirit," Otto said, trying to sound casual. Elija crossed his arms.

A few days later, in the oversized general-purpose tent near the Fort Harrison parade field, Elija's attitude had not improved.

Otto sat on the edge of his cot and leafed through his file, glancing up at Elija's back now and again. His friend was lying on his cot, silent, his back to Otto.

Otto was grateful that his and Elija's cots were next to each other, even if this was their last night together. The canvas tents on wooden platforms, with small wood-burning stoves warming the chilly autumn nights, had been their temporary home until the wooden barracks became available during the eight-week training cycle. Now, Otto and Elija were headed for different recruit companies, unsure of when they would see each other again due to the massive number of men being drafted.

"Oh, c'mon, it hasn't been so bad," Otto said, standing up and stretching. He sighed with relief as his shoulders popped.

"Felt like herded cattle during that induction exam," Elija said, still facing the tent wall. Otto thought back reluctantly to their first stop of the trip: a sprawling physical examination center that took up the entire fourth floor of a downtown Indianapolis building. Medical and dental examinations followed endless forms to fill out. It had been an all-day ordeal, with the recruits marching in their underwear through each exam station. Once officials determined them to be disease-free and mentally fit for service, it was time for vaccine injections and fingerprinting. Then, they'd been railed off to their current accommodations at Fort Harrison.

Otto grimaced. The truth was that the past few days had been an exhausting shock of reality even for him, but he wasn't about to say that aloud.

"Sure, that wasn't so agreeable," he admitted to Elija. "But it's over, and now we've got basic training to complete. Learning the drill and ceremony and how to wear the uniform properly seems pretty straightforward and reasonable. We have physical training, too." Otto couldn't help brightening at the thought of this. "It will feel good to get some exercise. There's been far too much sitting around so far."

"You are different from me, Otto," Elija said. He flopped over onto his back and looked at his friend. "You'll have no problem with physical drills. Your work habits will put you through recruit training, I expect."

Otto made a face. "You're a farmhand, too," he pointed out. Elija snorted, sitting up and making an attempt at organizing his footlocker.

"We both know you're much better suited for anything athletic," he said. "I should have joined the seminary as soon as I turned eighteen or become a missionary like Paul and avoided all this. Even if I was willing to try, I'm not a good shot. You're so good with a rifle with all the hunting you've done."

Otto looked a bit sheepish. "You're not a bad shot," he said.

"Otto. We both know I couldn't hit a horse from ten feet away."

"Fine, well, those claiming a valid religious belief were historically assigned a non-combat function," Otto reminded Elija, sitting back down on his cot. "German Baptist Brethren generally serve as medics or in transporting or caring for the wounded in hospitals, I've been told. We could work away from all the shooting. Sometimes, we're even put in food service. That wouldn't be so bad, would it?" Elija remained silent, shuffling his meager belongings.

"The path of least resistance is to just get through it all," Otto told Elija. "I will fight if necessary, but I'd rather save lives than take them." He hadn't even claimed CO status on his paperwork, knowing it wouldn't help.

Otto looked hard at Elija, who was still silent. His footlocker somehow looked more disheveled than before he'd tried to tidy it.

"Elija, what's clear to me is that those who absolutely refuse to serve in any capacity or claim that the aiding or abetting of war to be immoral, particularly those of German descent, seem to anger the cadre here," Otto said, forcing some sternness into his voice.

"What's clear to me is that you are putting your survival over your beliefs," Elija snapped. Otto was surprised to see his friend's green eyes burning with emotion. "You seem to have been built for war, Otto, and willing to go as well. I know you'll survive this and perhaps even thrive within this system. But as for me, I cannot do what I know is wrong. God does not want me to kill anyone, no matter what the reason."

Otto stared at Elija. "Be careful. I do not want you getting into any more trouble than you need to."

"And I hope that when you die at a ripe old age, you can face your judgment with a clean conscience," Elija said. He whipped around and stormed out of the tent. Otto slumped down onto his cot, holding his head in his hands.

The following day, Elija and Otto barely said a word to each other as they packed up their belongings to travel to their newly assigned companies.

"Brother Kunkle," Otto finally said before he left, hoisting his bag over his shoulder. Elija turned his face a mask of resignation.

"I will see you at Christmas," Otto said. His voice wavered, and he clapped a hand on Elija's shoulder. Elija gave a halfhearted smile.

"Goodbye, my friend," Otto said. "Do what is right by you, and may God protect you."

"May God protect us both," Elija replied.

There was a heavy feeling over both young men as they parted ways. Though Elija tried to convince himself he was grateful to get away from Otto's perpetual optimism and lackadaisical attitude about the war, he was not comforted when he met the leaders of his new company. His drill sergeant, Staff Sgt. O'Brian was a raw-boned man of six feet and nearly two hundred pounds. His drab brown campaign hat had been blocked, his field uniform starched and pressed. He was the very picture of military precision.

"He's a veteran of the Spanish-American War," Elija heard another recruit whispering as Sgt. O'Brian walked by in the distance. Elija turned to face the recruit.

"Have you heard anything about the company commanding officer?" he asked, hoping for an older leader gone soft. The recruit, who looked like he was sixteen years old, nodded feverishly.

"Major John Scot, yeah," he said, his eyes shining in his acne-covered face. "He was a first lieutenant when he served in Nicaragua. He just pinned on major[15], so he probably won't be here too much longer."

"What did you do, read a history book about him?" jeered another recruit.

"I'm interested in the military, that's all," said the first recruit, glancing around. Elija had heard a fellow recruit call the boy Stevenson. "My older cousin was in Scot's company not too long ago." He turned back to Elija. "Major Scot is hardcore, from what Jeremy told me. He's a committed officer, and he wants his soldiers capable of fighting in the most extreme situations. He'll shape us up. He's not going to put up with that, that's for sure," Jones said, pointing at Elija's wrinkled uniform.

---

15   Military speak for acquiring the rank of Major

Later, during the mess call, Elija slid into the empty seat next to the recruit with skin eruptions.

"I'm Elija Kunkle," he said, picking up a fork full of chipped beef on toast.

"Bill Stevenson," the boy said, scratching at his neck. Elija quickly looked back at his food.

"Tell me more about your cousin's experience with Major Scot," Elija said. He wanted to know exactly what he was up against.

"Well," said Private Stevenson, settling into his seat like a man about to tell a long tale, "there's this perception that the National Guard is less capable than the regular army. Major Scot isn't a believer of that conviction." Stevenson picked up half a piece of toast and gesticulated with it. "Jeremy says Major Scot wants to make his recruits not only relevant but high-performing soldiers too."

Setting his toast back down, Stevenson took a large bite of chipped beef, swallowed it alarmingly fast, and picked up his cup of milk. "Europeans seem to regard American military capability lightly, but officers like Major Scot and General Glenn have other beliefs about our capability." Stevenson's eyes shone with admiration.

"What are his thoughts on conscientious objectors?" Elija prodded, taking the slice of toast off the top of his tray and tearing it into tiny pieces. Stevenson scowled.

"Well, I'm not sure," he huffed. "But I'm willing to bet he's not a fan of them either. He wants to break down recruits and remodel them into disciplined soldiers who won't question orders. The American reputation is on the line, after all!"

"Ah," said Elija, looking down to discover that his tray was peppered with tiny bread crumbs. Stevenson's eyes followed Elija's gaze and then narrowed, focusing on Elija.

"You know, America might be making huge loans to France and England for the war, but we are only a 127,000-man army when it's all said and done," he said. "Every man counts in this war. You aren't a conscientious objector, are you?"

"Yes, I suppose I am," said Elija. "I'm of German Baptist faith."

Without a word, Stevenson gulped down the rest of his milk, picked up his tray, and moved away, leaving Elija to his shredded meal.

Over the next few weeks, while Elija was generally compliant, it did not take long for the drill sergeants to single him out for his rumpled appearance and lack of motivation. Elija, however, was determined not to fastidiously prepare his clothing and carefully follow instructions for a cause he did not support. After the third time, he was gigged for an unkempt uniform, and he was called in individually to the company commander.

As he awaited his fate, Elija sat in a chair outside of Major Scot's office, trying not to fidget.

Be like John the Baptist, he told himself. *Be like Moses. Have faith. Be not afraid.*

"Private Kunkle," Major Scot finally bellowed in his command voice, "get your ass in here."

Standing, Elija slowly opened the door, walked forward, and stood tensely at attention in front of the commander's desk. Major Scot, busy signing requisitions, looked up from his work with a glacial glare.

"Private, it has come to my attention that you aren't fully on board with the program here."

"No, sir," Elija replied truthfully. The major looked Elija up and down. Elija stood as tall as he could, though he was trembling.

"Your uniform looks like shit, and you smell even worse," the mayor said through clenched teeth. He rose and approached Elija. "My drills tell me you aren't willing to give your Uncle Sam his full ration, and that makes me angry. I don't like being angry."

The major stood nose to nose with Elija, staring directly into his eyes. Elija tried hard to stay stationary, but he was now trembling so much his teeth were audibly chattering.

"Explain the problem you have with this man's army," the major demanded, his coffee breath washing over Elija.

"I . . . I don't believe that we have a right to k . . . kill people or abide in enabling such things," Elija stammered.

"Are you a religious man, Private Kunkle?" Scot snarled.

"Sir, yes, sir. I'm a G . . . German Baptist."

"So, what makes you think the heinies[16] are gonna stop with merely sinking fuckin' cargo ships?" the major demanded, spraying Elija's face with spittle. "What makes you think if the jam eaters[17] beat the limeys[18] in France, they won't just polka their asses across our borders and take all your precious religious liberties?"

The major turned away, and Elija nearly collapsed with relief. "Private, ever heard of the Zimmerman Telegram?"

"No, sir," answered Elija.

"It was a secret communication between Mexico and Germany," the Major explained. "It was intercepted by British intelligence a while back, and it more than detailed the Krauts' plans for when they conquer America. That's right, Private. The krauts

---

16   Derogatory term for German soldiers
17   Slang for German soldiers derived from the jam in German military rations
18   Slang for British soldiers

figure to hand over Arizona and Texas to the bean bandits[19] in exchange for allowing them to invade our homeland through the Mexican border."

Major Scot whirled around and resumed his position inches away from Elija's face. "So, Private, it seems to me that if we don't beat the Germans in Europe, they'll be sittin' on your German Baptist Church front doorstep before we know what hit us. Do you want that to happen, Private?"

"No, sir," Elija said. He looked down at his shoes.

"What does your father do, Kunkle?" Major Scot snarled.

"Sir, he is a farmer, sir," Elija said. Major Scot smirked, slowly shaking his head.

"Son, he won't have a damn farm or anything else after the krauts get through here. You have no idea what's going on outside of your hick neck of the woods, do you?"

Major Scot turned again, walking back behind his desk. "Look, I just made rank, and I'm looking for my replacement to be here in three weeks. I'll be damned if I'll leave him with a pile of crap to clean up when I'm gone! I don't have the time to argue philosophy, so I'm going to simplify things for you."

Glowering, Major Scot placed both hands on his desk and leaned forward. Elija felt like a small animal caught in a trap. "You will become a soldier. You will do what your drill sergeants tell you to do, and you will defend your country. If your attitude does not improve, your ass will be sent to the monkey house.[20] Is that understood, Private? Do I make myself clear?"

"Sir, yes, sir," Elija replied.

"Go back to your company, Private Kunkle," Major Scot said,

---

19 Slur for Mexicans, Central Americans, and South Americans around the turn of the century
20 Slang for "prison"

pulling out his chair. "I'm going to be recommending that you serve two weeks in the disciplinary company starting next week if you don't start complying with standards." Before Elija could answer, Major Scot growled, "Dismissed." He slid into his seat and returned to his paperwork, no longer acknowledging Elija's presence in the room.

Elija left and was escorted back to his newly assigned wooden barracks. Feeling the adrenaline coursing through his veins from his confrontation, he wondered for a moment what he should do. Then, he remembered there was no choice in the matter at all.

I still believe my principles are from a higher authority, he reminded himself. *I am determined that nothing in my behavior will change if it means abetting the killing of men.* Kneeling by his cot, he prayed, feeling sure of his decision.

"That's it," Sgt. O'Brian said the next day during physical instruction. Elija had once again failed to perform up to par, displaying poor discipline and enthusiasm. "Soldiers, all of you will be doing a six-mile road march compliments of Private Kunkle's lackluster commitment to training," the sergeant bellowed. Elija looked around nervously as many pairs of eyes glared at him.

This was just the first time Sgt. O'Brian and the other drill sergeants disciplined Elija's entire company for Elija's poor performance. The extra duty, midnight locker inspections, and other punishments were all attributed to Elija. Even so, Elija did not waver, praying many times a day for the strength to carry on.

It was several nights later, at two o'clock in the morning, that members of his company awakened Elija. They wrestled him out of his bed and pulled him into the company latrine.

"What are you doing?" Elija wailed as he was held down.

Someone stuffed a rag in his mouth, and a torn sheet was tied over Elija's eyes.

"You're our company scrounge, and you're invited to a scrub party for all the shit you've put us through, kraut lover," a voice said. Gulping, Elija began to pray silently.

The vengeful team of recruits pinned Elija face down on the latrine floor and pulled his underwear off, pouring buckets of water over him. Members of the scrub party took turns scouring Elija's back and legs with Army-issued cane-bristle cleaning brushes and lye soap. Finally, Elija was left alone, lying on the wet latrine floor, writhing in pain. His skin was red and raw, blood seeping from the scrub wounds. It was then that four lingering recruits began a final assault. Kneeling on Elija's back, one of the assailants pointed at a toilet plunger sitting beside a nearby commode.

"Tonight you lose your virginity, kraut," one of the soldiers said as three recruits forcibly held Elija down while the fourth sodomized him with the handle of the plunger. Elija's cries were muffled by the jeers and laughter of the recruits as they left the latrine. Whimpering, Elija attempted to stand and wash himself off and then stumbled back to his barracks cot in the dark, suppressing his pain.

God's followers are often persecuted, he repeated to himself. *This is nothing compared to the pain Christ withstood for our sins.* He fell into a fitful doze, dreaming about home, his mother's chicken dumplings, and Sigrid's wide, blonde-lashed eyes.

As reveille was at five o'clock, Elija sat on the side of his bed staring into space. Dragging himself from his cot well before dawn, he slowly attempted to get dressed. None of the recruits spoke to him as they streamed out on the roadways in front of the barracks for morning formation. As the sun began to light the morning, Elija ignored the blood seeping through his tan khaki shirt and the seat of his trousers.

Sergeant O'Brian scowled as he walked down the rows of recruits, checking military uniform alignment, shaves, and boot shine. The drill stopped in front of Elija, who was trying to hold himself at attention despite the pain.

"What the hell is wrong with your uniform, Private?" the drill sergeant demanded. "Get your ass to the troop medical building now. Private Wilkins, escort Private Kunkle to the med clinic and report to me when you get back!" Without further comment on the matter, the drill sergeant finished his morning inspection, and Elija and his escort left the compound.

Later that morning, Elija returned to the barracks and was still in pain. The medics had cleansed his scrapes with saline and painted on iodine solution. They also gave him a tin of aspirin, a bottle of witch hazel, and some salve for rectal bleeding, which was medically recorded as "hemorrhoids." No one asked what had occurred.

Redressing in a clean uniform, Elija reluctantly rejoined the troops as they marched onto the parade field, where they drilled with their Springfield rifles. Trying to avoid further trouble for the time being, Elija attempted to execute the moves as best he could, his breath coming out in white gusts in the chilly November air. However, every gesture caused stabbing pain to ripple over his back and arms.

"Private Kunkle," the company drill sergeant said mockingly when Elija, yelping from pain, inadvertently dropped his rifle onto the soft grass. "You're to go with an escort to the disciplinary barracks, where you will be placed in company assignment."

Elija raised his watering eyes to meet the sergeant. "Sir, yes, sir," he said wearily.

"You will stay for two weeks, and if you complete the correctional training, you will be recycled into another training company to finish basic training." Elija walked away from his company, feeling numb. Perhaps the disciplinary barracks would contain some friendlier faces.

The afternoon sun had peeked out from behind the clouds when the disciplinary troops were told to fall into ranks. Elija stood in formation when the recruit next to him leaned over.

"You look familiar," he said quietly. "Do I know you?"

"Yes," said Elija, looking with dull eyes at the young man. "I am in the congregation near yours. I am Elija Kunkle," he said in a low, subdued, monotone voice.

The other recruit nodded. "There are two other German Baptist recruits from Indiana here in the barracks, too. We must stand strong for the commandments of our Lord, Brother Kunkle. Surely Daniel in the den of lions had doubts, too."

Elija nodded and stared straight ahead as the drill sergeant approached. He took solace from his church brother's words but could feel the creeping fear that his strength was dying inside.

The four Brethren, along with other "unmotivated" recruits, were made to drill for two hours, holding their rifles at arm's length for extended periods and duck-walking around the parade field with weapons held overhead. Those conscientious objectors who had come before Elija, those who refused to drill in any manner, were to be court-martialed and sent to the stockade. Elija knew this and did not want to wind up in a federal penitentiary, and so he held his gun aloft as best he could.

After about an hour and a half of this treatment, one of the other German Baptist recruits fell and lay on the ground, dehydrated and exhausted. He was taken to the post medical facility. Elija scraped by, but when he returned to his barracks, sweaty, in pain, and bloodstained from reopened scabs and skin tears, he found a nasty surprise: an empty pail, soap, and brush waiting on his cot.

"Private," the barracks' noncommissioned officer said, tapping a white nightstick against his palm, "I want the latrine spotless by morning. Is that understood?"

"Yes, sir," Elija said.

By three o'clock in the morning, Elija and another soldier—not a conscientious objector, but an obstinate sort who refused to say a word—had finished cleaning the latrine. The barrack commodes, sinks, and shower floor were spotless as the two men limped to their camp beds. Elija collapsed in sleep, wearing only his army-issued long underwear. The barracks windows always remained closed, and the heat from the barracks woodstove, along with the closeness of the sleeping quarters, forced most of the recruits to sleep on top of their blankets rather than under them. This also made for a quicker cot inspection in the morning.

Elija slept for two and a half hours and awoke with a slight cough and sore throat. Though his uniform was still damp, he put it on and buffed his brown Pershing boots. Reveille began with the drill sergeants overturning each recruit's footlocker early that morning. As Elija stepped outside, he shivered; the temperature had dipped to twenty-five degrees.

The pressure and harassment continued for the next several days. Elija was not allowed much sleep; he was assigned consecutive night watches that did not enable him to recover fully. He prayed constantly and even sang the familiar hymns in his head as he worked, feeling a sense of peace come over him as his body began to fail. He would not have to hurt anyone. The Lord would accept him with open arms. He only hoped his brother in spirit, Otto, would receive the same treatment.

During the third night, Elija developed a temperature and a deep cough. The following morning, he was cold, sweat-soaked, and unresponsive as he lay on top of his blanket on his cot.

"Private Kunkle isn't waking up, sir," said one frightened recruit. "There are several others in the barracks who are sick too, sir."

"What the hell is wrong with them?" barked the sergeant. Stepping into the stuffy, stale quarters, the sergeant peered at Elija's pale face. Elija's skin was almost blue, a small, tranquil smile frozen on his lips. Alarmed, the sergeant put a hand on Elija's chest. Though there was a heartbeat, it was weak and reluctant.

"Headaches and puking," explained the frightened soldier. "Neck pains and confusion." A groan emanated from a nearby bunk as if to confirm what the recruit was explaining.

The sergeant looked at the nervous man up and down. "Are you feeling normal, private?"

"Sir, yes, sir."

"Then get your ass over to camp medical. Tell the desk sergeant we need medical assistance over here now," commanded the sergeant, his eyes shifting back to Elija's unresponsive form. "Quickly, Private."

* * *

Many of the Zion congregants waited at the train station to support and silently pray with Dorcas, Lena, and Amos as the church brothers loaded the plain wooden casket onto a horse-drawn wagon. The two honor guard soldiers assigned to transport

Elija's body handed Amos some papers, which he took with trembling hands. Greta stood behind the family and watched Dorcas holding herself stiffly, trembling slightly in an effort not to break down. Amos had his arms around her and Lena, and Lena's face was buried in a handkerchief. Fredrick stood by, patting Lena's shoulder comfortingly.

"Dorcas and Amos were notified by telegram," Greta heard Ruth muttering to Hans behind her. "The Army coroner listed the cause of death as meningitis."

"Meningitis?"

"That's all. No further explanation or investigation."

"I believe the family was right to refuse a military burial," Hans said quietly. "That's hardly a satisfactory explanation for the death of a healthy young man."

After a brief viewing, the congregants moved to Zion Church cemetery for the burial. The weather had turned blustery, and snow flurries increased as Elija's coffin was placed in a hand-dug grave. The congregation sang, "Come Brethren, Ye Who Love the Lord," their breath clouding the cold air before Pastor Yoder stepped forward to offer one final prayer.

"Our Brethren hold no animosity, anger, or resentment toward the Army or the government," Pastor Yoder said, his eyes squinting against the cold. "We must find it in our hearts to forgive those who ignored the requests for Elija's exemption. We choose instead to occupy our time by giving supportive love to Brother Elija's family, who must face the reality of the loss of their only son."

Sigrid reached out and seized Greta's hand. Greta squeezed her daughter's hand back, glancing over to see tears sliding down Sigrid's cheeks.

"Elija stood by his beliefs and refused to harm another human being," Pastor Yoder proclaimed. "He has now joined our Lord in heavenly peace."

18
The Great War
(Der große War)
December 1917–April 1918

O tto peered out the train window as it slowed. There, waiting patiently at the station, were his parents, Lena and Sigrid. Otto couldn't help but break into a smile. His basic training had been difficult, but as had been expected, he had excelled. Now, on a one-week pass, Otto had returned home for Christmas before being shipped off to Camp Shelby. Since Otto was in the group of Indiana soldiers assigned to the Thirty-Eighth Infantry Division of the Army National Guard, he would do his advanced training in Mississippi.

As Otto seized his bag and joined the line of passengers waiting to disembark, the grin slid momentarily from his face. Otto had faithfully written Sigrid as often as possible describing what basic training was like. He had been crushed, though not altogether surprised, to learn of Elija's fate. By all rights, Elija should have been sitting with him on that train. Sigrid had already warned him about how badly Elija's parents were taking their son's death.

With a deep breath, Otto stepped off the train and strode as quickly as he could to his greeting party. He shook his father's hand and touched his mother's face. The little group smiled at each other and exchanged warm greetings.

As Hans and Ruth busied themselves with Otto's bags and Lena stood politely nearby, Otto took Sigrid's hand, standing in front of her in his uniform. Sigrid blushed as she looked at him, and Otto felt a bit overcome by Sigrid's innocent beauty. She was even more winsome than he'd remembered.

"Welcome home, Otto," she said. "I missed you."

"I missed you every day," Otto said quietly, leaning in. He then stepped over to Lena and gently placed his hand on her shoulder.

"I am very sorry about Elija," he said. Lena nodded her thanks. Otto noticed she looked thin and had dark circles under her eyes.

The week at home passed quickly for Otto, with many good meals, visits with friends, and opportunities for worship. However, a tinge of bitterness hung over the holiday, not just because of Otto's impending departure but because of the absence of Elija's constant scriptural anecdotes and complaints about the cold. Otto found that, at home, he felt his friend's absence much more acutely than he had at basic training. How could he ever get used to this?

On the final day of his leave, Otto and his family spent the evening at Greta and Oscar's home. Greta, Ruth, and Sigrid cooked a large Christmas dinner, including a fragrant roast turkey. The Beck house was cozy and warm, smelling of meat and gravy, with a fire crackling in the hearth.

"I am so glad to be home for Christmas," Otto told the family as they sat digesting after the heavy meal.

"Everyone enjoyed seeing you at church services," Hans said, wiping the corner of his mouth. Otto thought fondly of the German Baptist Christmas traditions. Though the church never celebrated with decorations or gift exchanges, solemn worship and prayers of thanksgiving commemorate the birth of the Savior. During the evening services at Zion this year, the congregation also sang songs and said prayers for Otto's safe travel and return.

"I am sorry Elija was not here to share it with us," Otto said, his heart giving a painful twinge. He had stopped by the cemetery to say goodbye at Elija's fresh gravesite and had made a stop at Amos and Dorcas' house to pay his respects. Elija's folks had not spoken much of the death to anyone and would only say, "it was God's will that Elija was taken."

"Otto, what happened to Elija?" Sigrid asked, leaning forward. "He was never prone to illness."

Oscar glanced at Sigrid. He had already decided not to mention Elija's struggles during the first few days in the Army, having heard Sigrid's pa often say, "it is best to let sleeping dogs lie." Otto felt that, in this case, that advice might be best for everyone. However, ignoring the situation didn't feel right either. Though he had not heard anything other than the Army autopsy report, Otto suspected that abuse had taken place. Elija had not been so frail as to keel over of his own accord simply.

Otto chose his words carefully before speaking again.

"Based on what I believe," Otto said, "Elija saw himself as a martyr. I hate to say it, and I don't want Amos and Dorcas to know this, but I think he knew his fate as soon as he was drafted."

"I have a feeling Dorcas knew too," Greta said, walking in

from the kitchen with a tray of walnut cookies. "All mothers of soldiers are worried, but she hasn't been the same since Elija left. It seemed to me she was in mourning as soon as he stepped on that train."

"Elija avoided ever having to hurt or kill anyone," Hans said, taking one of the cookies.

"Perhaps that was his plan," Otto said. He looked at his glass of buttermilk, trying not to think about his last night with Elija.

"Otto," Sigrid said, suddenly earnest, "don't you even think of trying that same sort of thing." Otto looked up in surprise.

"It never crossed my mind," he said, although Elija's burning, judgmental gaze had been haunting his dreams for weeks.

"There are other ways to uphold your faith," Sigrid said, pressing on, her cheeks flushed in the firelight. "Elija did what he thought best, but I don't believe God or anyone else will blame you for not laying down your life to resist."

"Sigrid," Otto said. "I will not do such a thing. I have too many reasons to live."

"Well said," Oscar said, brushing crumbs from his shirt. "I hope that you can find nonviolent labor to do in the Army. Perhaps you can save lives instead of taking them. Our Lord would certainly approve of such a course."

Otto nodded, his throat tight. "That is my hope."

The next day, at the rail station, Ruth, Hans, Greta, and Sigrid gathered to bid Otto farewell. Other soldiers were waiting at the station also, as families, holding small American flags, said their goodbyes to their sons. The day was frigid, and groups of people huddled together for warmth. Dressed in a thin woolen uniform, Otto shivered as Greta, her face so like her daughter's, gazed at him.

"May God make you invisible to your enemies and place you out of their reach," Greta said in a somber tone. Otto nodded gratefully.

Ruth, tears sliding down her face, gripped Otto's hands tightly.

"May our Lord protect and keep you," Hans said, looking hard into Otto's face.

"I love you both," Otto said. "I am determined to come back home. Please pray for me."

"Every day," Ruth whispered. "Every waking moment." Hans withdrew his handkerchief and brushed tears from her face, then surreptitiously wiped his own eyes.

Otto, trying to keep his composure, turned to Sigrid. He took Sigrid's hand as Oscar and Greta stood near. Otto felt he had fallen even more deeply in love with Sigrid over their two months apart. The pair gazed deeply at each other, memorizing each other's faces, knowing well that this might be the last time they would ever see one another.

Sigrid began to cry as she looked up at Otto softly. Her nose was red from the cold, and her eyes were red with tears, but she looked beautiful nevertheless.

"When you get to Mississippi, please write to me," she said. Otto gently wrapped his arms around Sigrid and held her, quickly kissing her.

Saying his final goodbyes to everyone, Otto adjusted his topcoat and stepped up onto the passenger car step. He turned, and Sigrid ran up, holding out her hand. The sun momentarily showed itself from behind the white winter sky, and Sigrid's eyes glowed the bright blue of cornflowers.

"I love you, Sigi," Otto said. Snow softly began falling as the train pulled from the railway station on its journey southward. The groups on the platform waved, calling their goodbyes and clutching each other in the cold.

Otto often reflected on that Christmas in the months to come, clinging to the memory through drills, uncertainty, discomfort, and weeks of travel. By late March of 1918, he was queasily disembarking after the trip across the choppy channel. As he set foot on the ground of Brest, France, he realized it was his first time on foreign soil.

"Oho, someone's got a delicate disposition," Otto heard one of his fellow stretcher-bearers, Private First Class Tom Purvis, say.

"Go away," Otto moaned. Tom's laughter filled his ears, but Otto knew his fellow soldiers were glad to be rid of the troopship USS Antigone as well. The Antigone had zigzagged across the Atlantic with a convoy of American destroyers and coastal air support. While many soldiers thought they had seen the ominous signs of German U-boats during the journey, none were conclusively documented. What had been conclusively documented was the frequent vomiting over the side rails.

"For someone who has never ventured more than twenty-five miles from his Indiana farm, this is going to be a shock, old boy," said Tom, clapping Otto on the back. Otto groaned, trying hard to regain his equilibrium and walk straight again. He saw in his peripheral vision that some other soldiers were suffering the same symptoms.

"Come off your high horse, Tom," Otto volleyed in between deep breaths. "What's your longest adventure been before this one? Going to visit your aunty in Ohio?" Tom snorted, and Otto knew he was right.

"At ease!" barked a commanding voice, and Otto and the

other seasick soldiers struggled to redirect their attention. "You four, over here."

Otto made his way over with the other members of his company, the medical team of the Thirty-Eighth Division. When his month-long Camp Shelby training concluded in late January 1918, Otto had been extremely relieved to be assigned duty as a "stretcher-bearer." Otto's battalion aid station would serve the Thirty-Eighth Division if and when they saw action.

This was the best assignment Otto could have received under the circumstances. Although Otto had never officially requested CO status, Otto's team sergeant was aware of his religious beliefs and appeared to have considered them. It was obvious to Otto that following Elija's death, strings had been pulled to grant Otto this medical assignment rather than that of an infantry soldier.

"Thank you, sir. This assignment suits me," Otto had told Sergeant Joe Campbell, a burly Scotsman from Glasgow, Kentucky, upon receiving the news.

The sergeant raised an eyebrow. "So that you know, you may still be on the battlefield. You might be put in a position where you have to fight for your life."

"Count on me, Sarge."

"Don't Anabaptist beliefs forbid the killing of all human beings?"

"I don't plan on taking lives," Otto said. "Only saving them."

"Well, Private, sometimes saving a life may involve taking a life," said the sergeant.

Otto had been trained in evacuation, first aid, and lifesaving along with the team that now surrounded him. Straightening up and taking a deep, steadying breath of the frigid air, he tried to focus on the Medical Corps Captain.

"You will be in echelon camp 'C' to train and await assignment to an ambulance company and an eventual infantry attachment," the man said. "You will be serving under General Pershing, commander of the American Expeditionary Forces. That's him over there." Otto turned to see a polished, stern-looking man rigidly walking towards the tactical operations tent.

Much to his dismay, Otto and his fellow soldiers were crammed aboard waiting trucks barely fifteen minutes after stepping ashore. They began the trip over rutted, muddy roads to their training and staging area, and Otto focused desperately on not throwing up.

"The French are still technically in charge here," a crusty-looking sergeant first class told the group as they rode. "The frogs[21] have stepped aside when it comes to policing American garrison activity, though. The tommies[22] call us 'doughboys.' It seems the limeys have their doubts that we have the stomach to fight this war. They don't expect much from us." The man smirked. "Reckon, they're in for a surprise."

Mercifully, the ride to the training area was relatively short. Otto leaned out the window, breathing deeply and gazing at the peaceful farmland that made his heart ache for home. Upon arrival, however, the sounds of shelling and small arms fire reverberated over the horizon. The ominous sound reminded Otto how far from home he really was as the men clambered out of the trucks.

Otto and the rest of his company were shown to their quarters: a pair of bare, general-purpose tents with cots and heating stoves. Still feeling queasy, Otto collapsed onto his new cot, nearly crushing the package and several letters that awaited him.

---

21   Slang for French soldiers
22   Slang for common British soldiers

"I can't believe my mail got here before I did," he said to a teammate as he looked at the deliveries.

"Since all the rear echelon letters travel by converted merchant ships for troops and cargo here in France, I didn't expect too much efficiency," remarked the fellow soldier. "Maybe it's our lucky day. Say, I thought your church was against war. Why all the packages?"

Otto smiled down at his parcels. The Zion Church regularly sent letters of encouragement and small gifts to Otto and other soldiers from sister churches, and the others had noticed.

"My church doesn't agree with the war," Otto admitted. "But on the other hand, they can't really fault those who got caught up in the draft. I expect I'll keep on getting plenty of mail."

Sitting on the bed, nausea forgotten, Otto leafed through the parcels until he found what he was looking for a letter from Sigrid. *Sigi touched this paper, and* Otto thought to himself as he gently ran his fingertips across the envelope. He remembered her beautiful blue eyes, wide and heavy with tears, when she'd sent him off after his Christmas leave. Her love and devotion had always been there in front of him, but when facing the reality of war, Otto truly understood how fortunate he was to have her love.

Unfolding the paper carefully, Otto slowly read Sigrid's letter, clinging to each word.

January 30, 1918

My Dearest Otto,

I am happy to learn your training is finally over. Inspections, training, and classes sound difficult, but I also know if anyone can handle it, it is you. I know you cannot tell me where you are going overseas, but I wish you a safe journey, and I hope and pray that you are well and safe, given the difficult circumstances.

I know you did not know them well, but Bauer and Sarah Fisher, my brother's godparents, passed away within weeks of each other recently. They were spared illness and seem to have died of old age. They hosted my folks when they first moved to America, and they were a huge help in helping our family get established on the farm and in building Fredrick's home.

My folks are both very sad at their passing. Both Bauer and Sarah were nearly ninety years old, and I have no doubt our Lord called them home so close to each other so they could be together.

Here in Indiana, the ground is frozen and we are all staying primarily busy inside work during the winter. The church has decided to start on a new building addition starting in the spring to be used for special occasions, weddings and such. I believe it should be finished by the time you come home. I am sure we will attend many blessed events there together.

I love and miss you so much, Otto. May our Lord bless and keep you safe.

Yours in Christ's love,

Sigrid

Otto reread the letter, then carefully refolded it and slipped it back into its envelope. It was always good to have news from home, even if it was sad news. For Otto, it could be more difficult to be candid or keep up with his movements in his letters. The stateside training for the members of the Indiana Thirty-Eighth Division had ended when they had begun advancing troops in October near Toul, France. Still, Otto wasn't able to include these details in his last letter due to the rapid deployment schedule. Sigrid didn't know the whole story of where he was and what he was doing, and he couldn't tell her all the details.

Around him, some of Otto's fellow soldiers were eagerly reading and writing letters. Many of them, like Otto, spent their free moment scribbling notes, attempting to maintain their anchor to home while providing some semblance of keeping loved ones informed. Letters from cherished friends and family had become a lifeline for Otto and the rest of his young division.

Otto dug around in his pack for a pencil and some paper. He planned to write to Sigrid daily while in the staging area. Sitting cross-legged on his cot, he smoothed a piece of paper atop a book cover and wrote, "My dearest Sigi," as he always began his letters. He looked up then, interrupted by the sound of distant but loud artillery rounds that shook the tent.

"Just a reminder of our future," a voice quipped.

Otto grimaced and turned back to his letter. He knew his communication would be slow to reach her, but just the act of writing helped blot out the distant battle sounds. Maintaining composure during the long winter months would be difficult, but the correspondence would help.

The days dragged by with a strange mixture of triage, training, boredom, and fearful anticipation. After several weeks of treating evacuated soldiers from the battlegrounds and honing skills that their division would depend upon when they entered the fray, company orders finally came to move forward.

"Pershing has made the decision to skeletonize the guard structure," a young second lieutenant ambulance commander informed his company stretcher-bearers. "He'll break the units up and assign them as fillers for the regular Yank divisions by the end of April. This strategy may change the momentum of the war." Otto had already seen French evacuees infected with lice and trench fever coming from the nearby battle, and he was becoming all too familiar with immersion foot and shell shock. He'd gotten his first glimpse of the war, but he knew it wouldn't be his last.

"I'll go through your assignments now," the lieutenant said. "Listen up."

"I heard that General Pershing earned the nickname 'Black Jack' during his time in the cavalry," Tom whispered to Otto. "He's supposedly a hard charger."

"Shh," Otto said, listening for his name to be called.

"Corporal Bowman," barked the company lieutenant. "You are assigned to the First Division, litter bearer. You'll be with the Twenty-Eighth Regiment and cover the Second Brigade as part of the Twelfth Company team."

The Black Lions, Otto thought. The Twenty-Eighth Infantry Regiment was known for its distinctive coat of arms.

After the announcements were over, the soldiers clustered around, discussing their assignments. Otto looked around at the team of medics, wide-eyed and untested, yet unafraid to do what was necessary to save lives and alleviate suffering.

"As if amputations and wounds aren't enough, we are gonna have to deal with blisters and chemical burns from the damn gas shells," Jim Travis, a tall, tousle-haired corporal from Tennessee and one of the company's litter team members said. "The situation is gonna be like one of them nightmares you can't wake up from."

Otto, whose nightmares were full of accusing green eyes, frowned. "At least as spring gets here, the warmer weather will give us easier movement toward the German command area and less time in the flooded trenches," he said. Indeed, the snow, rain, and dreary, foggy weather that hung over the French coast had made for an exceptionally cold and brutal winter, with the men relying on coal oil tent stoves as they waited for the weather to break.

"So we hope," Corporal Travis said flatly, though several others nodded.

At last, on April 28, the Twenty-Eighth Regiment of the First Infantry Division moved to Picardy, France. Otto wrote one final letter before his unit was sent forward.

April 28, 1918

My Dearest Sigrid,

I hope this letter finds you and your parents well. I want so much to be there at home with you.

I'm sorry to hear that the blizzard in Indiana was so bad. The heavy snows may mean lots of floods as it gets warmer. Hopefully, the spring stays warm enough for your pa to get the corn planted early.

France is a muddy place, as it rains a lot here too. The camp food is not nearly as good as yours or Ma's. I have gotten to try some French food, too, can't say I liked it much.

How is your brother? Have he and Lena picked out names for the baby yet? I hope Dorcas and Amos are also well. I think of Elija often and miss him very much. I hope he has found peace.

We receive some news from the States, but not too frequently nowadays. I hope the new time change in Indiana will be of benefit to the farmers.

I am sorry to hear of Pastor Yoder being ill. There are many here, too, that have come down with the grippe. All this wet weather doesn't help matters much.

We will soon be moving to the front, as the French Army needs our help. We have not yet heard how they are holding up under the German attacks, but I'm sure we will be a sight for sore eyes when we finally arrive. I have made the rank of corporal, and I guess that means I've got to keep my nose clean.

I am assigned to a brigade ambulance company and will work as a litter bearer when the time comes to move forward. One good thing for me, at least, is that we aren't required to carry guns.

I miss you, Sigi. I wish I could be with you and hold your hand. Please write when you can. I welcome your letters. May Christ bless and keep you always.

Sincerely yours in our Lord,
Otto
P.S. I love you very much.

19

The Dogs of War
(Die Hunde des Krieges)
May 28, 1918

A month later, Otto's moment of destiny at last arrived. At 06:42 (H hour), Colonel Ely called Company K, or Kilo Company, together for a final briefing. Otto glanced around at the three other medics, faces pale but determined and outward at the rest of the company. Their numbers had already dwindled somewhat. The First Infantry Division, pedantically called the Big Red One for the red "#1" worn on their left sleeves, had taken over 600 casualties merely waiting in what was referred to as the "Quiet Zone." German artillery and snipers had forced them to move into the trenches, but it looked like that was about to change.

"As you know, the German Army has taken Cantigny and has bunkers, sniper posts, and choke points throughout it," the Twenty-Eighth Regiment commander barked, his eyes wide and round like an owl's as he scanned his troops. "Over the past two weeks, our troops have moved forward by force into Cantigny with some help from the Eighteenth Regiment. We marched through those damn flooded trenches into position to support the French army. Now, we will add our ranks to theirs. We will attack the German Eighteenth Army."

The colonel's rough voice carried quickly over the attentive soldiers. "They've used the high ground at Cantigny for an artillery advantage. We will have to move across 'No Man's Land,' and we can expect to be under heavy fire. When we make it across, we'll be aiming to knock out the enemy pillboxes."

Otto winced. The "pillboxes" were small block houses from which German machine guns fired. They were strategically placed near heavy concentrations of barbed wire blockade, creating narrow corridors to maximize their kill zones.

"We will take the fight to the enemy," Colonel Hansen Ely declared, "and extinguish any doubts the Germans have regarding our American resolve."

When the colonel finished, Otto and the rest of the company medical team quickly united. They formed a tight-knit group, having worked closely together for months now.

"We'll move in to treat and evacuate Americans and French as our troops advance," Sergeant Campbell strategized. He looked at Otto. "If need be, Bowman, I expect ye may have to use the carts to assist in the evacuation of the dead and wounded. It's a bonney responsibility, but we may need to depend on horses if the vehicles break down a canna traverse."

"Understood, Sarge," Otto said mechanically. During training, Otto had demonstrated his skill with working horses, so it made sense that he'd be in charge of equine ambulance cart maintenance now. Masking the horses could prove critical to the mission because, despite French artillery and aerial strikes in the days before the advance, grazing German 08 machine guns had taken a toll upon the advancing Yanks on their way to Cantigny.

The motorized ambulance companies edged as close to the action as possible on the muddy access roadways. Otto sat in the back seat between Tom and Bill, who were both uncharacteristically quiet. They all looked out the windows at the countryside, lit by cheerful early morning sunshine. The artillery barrage had left the landscape pockmarked with craters, burning tank hulls, and collapsed buildings. Bloated rotting corpses of soldiers and animals, covered by trench rats, sullied the scene, and although the mud in the field was beginning to dry up thanks to the dryer weather, the terrain was not exactly smooth.

Otto closed his eyes against the horror that lay outside, thinking over the past few months. The German Army had launched its spring offensive with Paris as its goal, inflicting heavy casualties upon the British as they moved further east. The injection of fresh French troops had seemed to slow German progress toward the Marne, and the Americans, including Otto, had awaited their turn on the sidelines. Their turn was now at hand.

As soon as the vehicles stopped, the medical team poured out into the open air.

"At least the weather's agreeable," Bill quipped into the nervous silence, his freckled face alight in the sun. The medics all looked at each other while Sergeant Campbell appeared lost in thought, his thick, freckled arms crossed.

"That's true," Otto said. "The farming areas just a few miles away must be beautiful."

"Well, these farming areas sure aren't," Tom said, gesturing out over the horizon. "Some people are still living in that bullshit. What is wrong with them, anyhow?"

Otto followed Tom's gaze. Indeed, two children were playing in the yard of the bombed-out shell that had doubtless been a good home not so long ago. Those French civilians who had refused to leave the primarily demolished town were now forced to live like this.

"It's only going to look worse as we get closer, I suppose," Bill said.

"Aye, fookin Fritz[23] will ba waitin for us, lads," Sergeant Campbell said. "When we get ta Cantigny, we'll probably all be shot like bloody fish in a barrel. Rumor has it that krauts are getting fookin' crazy. They'll ba takin' no prisoners, lads. If you're captured, they'll just ba torturin' and killin' ye outright."

"No doubt about that," muttered Travis, the third member of their four-person medic team, who was easily spotted anywhere thanks to his shockingly red hair and eyebrows. "I heard the same damn thing." Otto haltingly agreed. The Germans were now in a position of defense and desperation, and they were indeed no stranger to committing atrocities. They were not about to easily allow the surrender of Cantigny or accept defeat, especially from an army they viewed as inferior. Otto steeled his mind, forcing himself not to think of the carnage and brutality sure to come.

By 13:00 hours, Otto would have done anything to go back to that moment of calm before the storm. The machine gun fire leveled at the advancing infantry proved unlike anything covered by advanced training. As Kilo Company left the trenches and entered the northwest edge of town, German sniper fire immediately dropped six of the advancing troops. Otto had watched with horror as soldiers' limbs and organs flew through the air, propelled by incoming German mortar and artillery rounds. Fallen soldiers

---

23   Slang for Germans in WWI

dotted the ground around the allied troops, and wisps of chlorine gas unleashed from cannon shells drifted through the trenches, hanging low to the ground.

"Be ready to don yer masks," yelled the ambulance commander.

"May God have mercy upon us," Otto swallowed, yanking his mask free of its pouch and inspecting it.

"Troops will ba getting dehydrated, just so ye know," Sergeant Campbell said in his mask-muffled voice as he peered up at the sun, which still hung high in the sky. "It's getting warmer, and no doubt there's plenty of adrenaline running through our boys. Just ba aware. Aye, there's the whistle now—move forward, lads."

Otto said a silent prayer as his four-person team began picking its way through the carnage. Any thoughts that the Red Cross armbands Otto and his teammates wore on their left sleeves made them invincible soon evaporated; the sounds of sniper rounds rattled across the terrain, and the men often had to take cover. A poisonous haze with a smell reminiscent of new-mown hay wafted from the western edge of town, where German artillery had no doubt dropped the phosgene and mustard gas.

The medic team was to approach and treat any living person they found, regardless of their uniform. The first man Otto found was a Frenchman. He looked like he had been lying injured awhile, and he was cradling his arm and moaning. Assessing the level of the damage, Otto decided time was of the essence. He seized the man in a fireman's lift, and using whatever he could find as cover, he dashed the man to a nearby transport vehicle, ignoring the feeble cries of protest. He then assisted Tom and Bill, who were struggling to lift another badly wounded soldier onto a stretcher nearby.

Throughout the afternoon, Otto cautiously removed the injured from the kill zone. He and the medic team used litter, horse carts, or their arms to carry the wounded to the sporadic-appearing transport vehicles. Exhaustion set in quickly, but Otto hardly noticed his fatigue as he looked at the twisted faces of the bleeding, dying men the team had collected.

As the sun neared the horizon once more, Otto stood and surveyed the battlefield, seeking out more injured men. Elements of the Twenty-Eighth Regiment had flanked the town; their attack on the enemy now commenced in full force. Gunfire filled the air as the Germans countered the Twenty-Eighth Regiment's northern elements with a heavy artillery barrage and troop surge. German mortars and the Mauser sniper rounds had caused havoc for the Yanks, and Otto tried not to despair as he saw the number of bodies piling up.

"Look," said Travis, breathlessly pointing in another direction. The medics turned to see a bank of liberty trucks screeching to a halt, soldiers streaming from the doors in full gear with their distinctive helmets and patches.

"The Twenty-Sixth Infantry," said Otto, chugging water from his canteen flask and wiping sweat and grime from his eyes.

"Headed in to shore up the Twenty-Eighth's assault," Tom agreed, paying no heed to the globs of blood that now coated his uniform. "That ought to change things. Maybe we'll at least finally secure the northern sector of Cantigny." A cry of pain rang through the air, and Tom, Bill, and Otto instantly turned toward the sound.

"Ready?"

"Ready."

Pinned down by gunfire, the medics crawled through the midtown rubble towards the cries.

"Jesus, have mercy on me," wailed the man when they came upon him. Otto looked down to see the soldier's eviscerated bowels. Tom stumbled a short distance and retched. Otto, holding his breath, grabbed for the man's emergency medical pack and loosened a battle dressing. He and Bill used it to bind and wet the gut wound, conserving their battle dressings and Zona's gauze.[24]

"There's a Frenchie with a chest wound over there," said Corporal Travis, stumbling back. "Gotta help him if I can."

One injured soldier at a time, Otto's comrades, worked their way to the southwest side of the village. Otto's uniform was covered from head to toe in gore, just like that of every other member of his team, but he was too busy to notice or care. They were treating a man whose arm had been blown apart when heavy gunfire started up again nearby.

"There!" said Otto, pointing to a large, crumbling Catholic church that stood at the town's edge. The French air strikes and artillery had left much destruction in the German stronghold, but a house of God could still protect them, Otto thought. Tom nodded, and the two men hoisted an injured soldier up toward the church. As they set the man down within the walls, an artillery shell whistled in.

Otto instinctively leaped into a nearby crater while Tom lunged for a ditch. The concussion wave rippled across the terrain, releasing its deadly contents. Otto heard a cry and saw Sergeant Campbell running toward them, skidding into the crater in his haste.

"Gas! Gas! Gas! Geh yer masks on now, lads!"

Otto scrambled for his mask, his hands slipping in the blood

---

24   A brand of gauze now under the Johnson & Johnson umbrella

of countless soldiers that now covered him. Gunfire rang through the air, and he heard a cry from nearby. Heart thundering, Otto managed to pull the cumbersome mask just as the sickly yellow gas reached his hiding place.

With his mask now securely affixed to his face, Otto looked frantically around for the rest of his team. The sun was beginning to set, and the hazy red glow lighted the whole setting. He could barely see through the gas and the clouded glass lens of the mask—finding the other medics was out of the question—but he could tell that their hiding place high in the cemetery was the result of an aerial bomb blast, undoubtedly French. The thirty-by-thirty-foot depression in the German-held territory had precisely excavated gravestones and crosses in its wake, leaving a perfectly circular crater surrounded by what were mostly intact granite monuments. The far east side of the church cemetery would be a good vantage point, Otto thought, relatively obscure to the enemy even when the gas cleared.

Nightfall left an uneasy quiet at the cemetery and the surrounding area. Unbeknownst to Otto, during the turmoil of the firefight, the U.S. forces had strategically withdrawn to regroup and hold overnight while waiting the morning to push forward again. Left on the battlefield, Otto tried calling softly for his teammates, but he heard no reply except the moans and cries of men wounded and exposed in the kill zone.

Otto became aware that he was beginning to regain some vision, even through the thick glass of the mask. A strong southerly wind was dispersing the gas, and he began to make out silhouettes of horses as they trekked across the battlefield. Deciding it was time, Otto slipped off his mask, said a silent prayer, and looked around the now-dark scene.

With the haze, there was not a single star visible in the sky. Even so, Otto could make out someone lying prone nearby. Otto crawled to the man on his hands and knees and cradled his fallen comrade in his arms, watching as Sergeant Campbell weakly gasped and clawed at his throat. His mask lay useless at his side, shredded by shrapnel.

Sergeant Campbell looked wildly into Otto's eyes. Otto could tell there was nothing he could do to help. Quickly saying the Lord's Prayer over Sergeant Campbell, Otto laid him down and made him as comfortable as he could before moving on in search of the rest of his team.

Otto made his way, slowly and carefully, to the spot where he had last seen Tom. There, he found both Tom and Travis still wearing their gas masks, lying in pools of blood, lifeless, mortally wounded by trench mortar fire. Bill was nowhere to be found, but Otto could only presume the worst.

Otto's mind desperately tried to rationalize all that he saw around him. Tearing his eyes away from his fallen friends, he steeled himself against the heaving, breaking feeling deep in his gut, the blood-curdling scream trying to exit his lungs. He knew now was not the time to mourn or even think about what had happened. Instead, it was up to him to do what he could.

Otto took a few deep breaths, breathing slowly in through his nose and out through his mouth. He imagined Sigrid's face, a stray thread of blonde hair escaping her bonnet, her beautiful eyes as deep and calm as the ocean.

Dear God, give me the strength to return to her.

20
The Mortal Sin
(Die Todsünde)
May 28–29, 1918

O tto crawled over the rough ground, searching for wounded soldiers. He quickly found two Americans propped up in a smoking truck, still wearing their masks. When Otto tried to pry one of the masks off, he was relieved to find that the soldier swatted him away.

"It's okay," Otto said. "The gas has gone. You can take them off."

When the two soldiers pulled their masks off, Otto saw that both their faces were contorted with pain.

"Got caught in the crossfire, transporting ammo," one of the men said in a high, hoarse voice. "Dave's been shot in the arm. A bullet grazed my side, but I'll live, I reckon."

"Come on," Otto said, "There's a safer spot over here. Can you both walk?"

Periodic artillery rounds whistled overhead as the three soldiers made their way back to the crater. Otto had to help Dave, who couldn't crawl because of his arm injury. Hobbling and slow, the trio somehow made it back to the crater unscathed as Otto muttered prayers under his breath. Otto treated both their wounds before heading back out, promising to be back.

Mauser rifle rounds buzzed past Otto's head as he stayed low to the ground, following the sound of moaning to a Frenchman being circled by two black dogs. Fur glistening with fresh blood, the dogs momentarily stood snarling at Otto.

"Git!" Otto said forcefully but in a muffled voice. The stray mongrels flinched, turned, and ran deeper into the battlefield. Otto tried not to think of what those dogs' lives may have been like just a short while ago as he pulled himself closer to the French soldier, whose head was oozing blood.

With the help of a blanket, Otto managed to half-drag the French soldier back to the crater. Dave was lying down, but his friend Steve, who had an arm injury, was sitting upright, looking alert in the darkness.

"We laid out your gear for you," Steve said, gesturing at the scattered blankets, collecting canteens and medical supplies from the medic team's packs.

"Thanks," Otto said as an overhead flare lit up his makeshift workspace. "Do you know where the bandages are?" He took a moment to try to flush the remnants of gas exposure away from his burning hands and neck with canteen water before binding the man's head.

With only the rising moon and occasional illumination flares for light, Otto treated wounds, stopped bleeding, and splinted fallen American and French soldiers in the war-torn rubble for hours. With some help from Dave and Steve, he managed to bring a total of twelve wounded soldiers to his makeshift triage in the cemetery circle. Otto treated and dragged the injured to the tombstone-encrusted crater, changing and packing wounds while periodically releasing pressure on tourniquets.

When the moon reached its zenith in the sky, Otto fell, exhausted, into the crater. He was cold, traumatized, and completely soaked in blood, vomit, and sweat. Dave and Steve had fallen asleep, and the rest of his wounded group were as comfortable as he could make them. He needed to get some rest.

A loud, short artillery shell fell and sounded to the south of the cemetery, but Otto hardly noticed as he propped himself into a sitting position on the edge of the bomb crater. However, when he heard a snuffling sound close by, Otto jerked his head to the right, afraid the black dogs had returned. Instead, a German shepherd looked up at Otto with bright amber eyes. Otto looked down at the dog's torso to see a red vest.

"So, you're a lost mercy dog, huh?" Otto said quietly, pouring a bit of water into his mess kit lid from his canteen for the tired animal to drink. "Parlez-vous Francais?" The dog licked Otto's face before drinking the proffered water.

"Good dog," Otto said, running his hands over the matted fur. After lapping up the water, the dog lay down beside Otto's feet. Soon, both dog and human were fast asleep.

Behind his eyelids, Otto's eyes darted as he had a dream he would never forget. An angel stood directly over the crater, standing seven feet tall. A glow emanated from the angel's porcelain skin, and those piercing, fiery eyes guarded the sacred cemetery site. Gazing at the formidable angel and his strong, sculpted wings, Otto felt no fear, instead enjoying a deep feeling of peace. The angel didn't speak, but Otto instinctively knew that he was there to comfort and guide both the living and the dead.

The heavy smell of burnt flesh and gunpowder permeated the air as the sun began to rise on May 29, but Otto awakened with a sense of calm and assurance that God would protect him through this ordeal. The fear he had felt during the night had left him completely. The shepherd dog awoke, stretched, and accompanied Otto on his rounds to check on each wounded soldier.

"Let's see to our patients, pup," Otto said, forcing his exhausted body to move. A few of Otto's collected wounded patients, delirious, moaned and cried out as he cleaned and rebounded their wounds. The dog comforted and lay beside each man for a brief time. As Otto finished his morning rounds, the dog disappeared, its wolflike silhouette fading into the early morning fog.

"Merci beaucoup," Otto whispered after the animal.

The morning haze had settled over the cemetery crater, partially concealing the wounded. The group of soldiers, groaning from pain and occasionally coughing from the residual chlorine gas still clinging near the ground, were momentarily safe. Steve, wincing a little as he moved, picked up a piece of Kraft cheese with his good arm and nibbled. Then, stuffing the rest of the cheese in his mouth, he reached over and picked up his forty-five-caliber revolver, holding it out to Otto. In the sunlight, Otto could see that the man looked to be little more than a teenager.

"You may be needing this soon enough, Corporal," Steve said. He then tossed a canvas sack of loaded half-moon clips and a trench knife toward Otto as well.

"I'm not sure I'll need to use it," Otto said, looking reluctantly at the weapons. "We are out of sight. The enemy won't be able to see us till we can get everyone evacuated."

"Just check it," said Dave, reaching over for a piece of the cheese. "You never know. Quiet down, you; your yowling isn't going to help," he added, chucking a pebble at a French soldier with a head wound who seemed to cry out every thirty seconds or so, sending eddies of fog rippling around them.

"Don't throw rocks at the wounded," Otto said, reluctantly checking to make sure the revolver cylinder was full. He knew though he was a pacifist, he might still be tested against his will.

The sun began to burn off some of the mist, and the sounds of random gunfire and screams began peppering the air.

"Morning Doc," muttered Dave.

"It's okay," Otto said, trying to sound confident. "The battlefield is practically deserted. With any luck, our company will come and find us in short order. Maybe they're already on their way."

Poking his head carefully out of the crater, Otto spotted a German soldier kicking at dead bodies, reaching down to go through their pockets, ripping chains from their necks and jewelry from their fingers. A group of four of his teammates was nearby, shooting wounded French and Americans and then burning them alive with a flamethrower. The smell of seared flesh coated the air. The cries of the dying made Otto feel ill, but he quickly batted that feeling away. *I'll deal with that later*, he told himself. *I'll deal with it all later, assuming I make it out of here alive.*

Crouching back down, Otto put his finger in front of his mouth. Steve, Dave, and a few other lucid patients nodded, but some of the soldiers were beyond such warnings. The sounds of some of Otto's more grievously wounded patients, though distinct, didn't seem to attract the German soldiers' attention at first. However, one of the German soldiers eventually began to wander in the direction of the distress sounds. He slowly stepped over the remains of the cemetery fence and strode toward the direction of the gravestone circle, which was still shrouded in the morning fog.

Otto's eyes fixed on the German soldier, who, clad in trench armor and carrying a Mauser rifle in his right hand, moved closer to the crater. He occasionally stopped to collect souvenirs or poke at the dead bodies littered across the cemetery grounds with his rifle.

God, please turn his course away from here. Please deliver me from this decision. Please.

Behind him, Steve, Dave, and a French soldier with leg injuries were attempting to muffle the sound of the moaning wounded with little to no success. The German soldier was within sixty feet of the crater when the soldier with the head wound, like clockwork, let out a loud yelp. Otto knew he had no choice but to act if the enemy came any closer.

Elija's angry face flashed before his eyes. "What's clear to me is that you are putting your survival over your beliefs."

This is not about my survival, Otto told Elija. *It's about protecting the wounded. It's about saving God's children.*

Because random gunshots were now frequently occurring across the open battle space, Otto knew that the noise of one more shot wouldn't draw the attention of the other roaming enemy soldiers. Easing himself forward, he put his back against a stone, crossing and cocking the hammer of his pistol to the rear. Holding his arms outstretched, handgun cocked and ready to fire at the standing enemy soldier, Otto waited and prayed that the man would turn away.

"You seem to have been built for war, Otto. . . . But as for me, I cannot do what I know is wrong," rang Elijah's words. "God does not want me to kill anyone, no matter what the reason."

I am protecting twelve injured people, Otto said. *Please, Elija, give me some peace.*

One of the severely wounded men within the circle unleashed a high-pitched cry of pain. Otto braced himself, but the German soldier seemed to have difficulty pinpointing the direction of the sound. He looked away to his left and then back toward his companions outside the cemetery fence. The soldier then walked forward, standing at the edge of the gravestone circle, peering straight ahead. He looked puzzled by the seemingly directionless moans of the men, oblivious to the danger directly in front of him. Otto, remembering the angel from his dream, felt prickles run down his scalp.

The German stared into the open circle of gravestones for a moment more, still appearing to see nothing. As the soldier turned his body to the right, glancing back at his comrades, he exposed his unprotected side to Otto. Otto could not risk waiting to see what the German soldier would do next. Bracing himself against the stone cross, he exhaled and fired.

In a detached mental state, Otto watched as the soldier collapsed in slow motion to the ground. The deadly round had gone straight into the side of the German's chest between his body armor. Refusing to think about what he had just done, Otto crawled forward, pushing and rolling the dead German soldier against a tombstone a few yards away. He returned to his post against the tombstone just as the four scavenging enemy troops began strolling toward the cemetery, pilfering fallen bodies and shouting their friend's name.

Otto stiffened as the marauding band moved inside the graveyard fence, coming closer to Otto and the wounded. Peering behind him, he saw Dave, Steve, and the French soldier still trying to silently stop the wounded men from moaning.

"Rutger!"

"Wo sind Sie?"

The soldiers were too close. Otto decided he must act. With nothing to lose, he replied loudly in perfect German.

"Ich nehme einen Scheiß. Geht weg!"

The marauding German soldiers began laughing upon hearing their friend was having a bowel movement. One of them, a sly look on his young face, began nonchalantly approaching the crater where Otto stood guard. Otto, crawling away from the gravestone circle, tried to suppress a cough as he passed through a pocket of chlorine gas near the ground. Positioning himself behind a headstone that flanked the German infantryman, he watched as the soldier looked directly at Rutger's lifeless body, which lay prone by a gravestone.

The enemy soldier's expression changed in an instant. He quickly raised his eyes, oblivious to Otto's wounded men within the stone circle twelve feet ahead of him. However, as the German scanned the cemetery, Otto could no longer hold in choking. A pair of sharp eyes snapped to his gravestone hiding place.

Pulling the cord of a stick grenade, the German soldier drew back his arm. He was caught mid-throw by Otto's pistol round, striking his jaw. Falling short of its target, the German's "potato masher" exploded five meters away from Otto.

Otto's world shattered. The grenade concussion propelled him sideways, bashing his left arm against a headstone. He tumbled, then lay still, disoriented. His hand felt limp, and a deep burning sensation engulfed his arm and wrist. A horrible ringing engulfed his head.

Alerted by the grenade blast, the two German soldiers to Otto's southwest position began firing toward the sound of the explosion. The flamethrower operator prepared to advance as, wincing, Otto slowly pulled himself up and back inside the crater circle. He lay wounded and dazed, wishing the high-pitched ringing would stop.

Suddenly, the sound of machine gunfire reverberated through the air, and then silence reigned. Sticking his head cautiously out of the crater, Steve let out a yell.

"Gun crew from the Eighteenth Infantry!" he said, using his good arm to help him scramble out of the crater. "That's our ticket out of here!"

Otto hadn't heard Steve's happy declaration over the ringing in his ears. Blindly fumbling, he located the trench knife and clutched it tightly in his right hand, standing guard over his patients. Dave came over and tried to look at Otto's bleeding foot, but Otto batted him away.

Looking up from the crater, Otto suddenly saw a baby-faced American second lieutenant staring down at him. The platoon leader surveyed the collection of wounded men and the dead German soldiers around the crater. Eyes widening, he looked back at Otto.

"Corporal, you are one heroic son of a bitch," the young lieutenant quipped. Otto shook his head and pointed to his right ear, which was still loudly ringing from the blast. The lieutenant, looking at Otto and his bleeding foot, instantly understood. He gave a thumbs up.

Otto was relieved to relinquish his responsibility. He thumped to the ground as, in an efficient military manner, the lieutenant assigned two soldiers to guard the twelve wounded men and dispatched a runner to bring up a litter team. Automatic weapons fire soon began to ring out west of the church, and the lieutenant rallied his platoon to respond.

"Corporal," the lieutenant shouted directly into Otto's face, "sorry we can't stay longer, but we gotta go send some more of the cabbage heads to hell," He pointed west, then gestured at the men in the crater. "Sit tight; there'll be someone here to help you in short order."

Turning, the lieutenant motioned his men toward the German gunfire. The two soldiers handed Otto and the lucid survivors fresh canteens to share while waiting for evacuation.

"I hope that when you die at a ripe old age, you can face your judgment with a clean conscience," Elija's voice said in his head.

I am sorry if I let you down, Brother Elija.

Otto used one hand to eat his rations, gingerly peeling off pieces of his decimated boot between bites. The blast from the German's grenade had ripped Otto's pistol from his hand, and it now felt limp and useless.

A French soldier let out a string of obscenities as Otto's right foot was finally revealed. The fourth and fifth toes looked like ground beef. Biting his sleeve, Otto poured canteen water over the toes and dabbed the wounds with iodine swabs from his medical kit just as the evacuation team arrived.

Nobody could explain how all twelve of the wounded had survived the night and why the enemy soldiers had been unable to see them. As Otto sat silently in the evacuation vehicle, he remembered Greta's solemn face on the train platform after Christmas, recalling her words.

"May God make you invisible to your enemies and place you out of their reach."

Otto shivered, his mind wandering to a spring day long ago when he'd watched a trembling little fox concealed improbably by nothing but a circle of stones.

21
The Spanish Lady
(Die Spanische Dame)
November 1918

On a chilly Friday morning of November 29, Kezi wrapped a wool shawl around herself and eased the door of her trailer open. Shuffling out, she looked at the waking camp. Her fellow travelers were building fires, boiling water, and doing laundry in the foggy air. Nearby, a child wailed between hacking coughs.

Kezi's Gypsy band was camped in the countryside outside of the small town of Wabash near the river, on an area of land frontage near a grove of catalpa trees adjoining a narrow county river road. Kezi glanced down the road, where she could barely make out the little house belonging to the elderly farmer and property owner. He only used the land to graze goats and sheep in the warmer months, and he had agreed to allow the Gypsies to camp there for a fee for the season. Now, smoke rose from the chimney of the little house into the cold November air, and Kezi knew her band had stayed long past their usual seasonal pattern.

The local community was no doubt suspicious. How long until the farmer asks them to leave?

Kezi felt a hand on her shoulder and turned to see Manfri smiling down at her, his dark eyes sparkling in his wrinkled face. It's hard to believe they were both now in their late fifties. Manfri eased past Kezi and out the door, and she watched him walk toward the nearby stream. Due to age and fears of disease, the pair now rarely traveled outside the camp, instead staying behind making copper cooking wares, leathercraft, and baskets. Younger members of the band sold the items in towns or found work on local farms, everyone doing what they had to in order to survive day to day.

Kezi looked forlornly back at her now-empty wagon. Mahai and Anca had both grown and married non-Gypsies, leaving the fold years earlier. Mahai had married a girl he had met in Kokomo, where he was also able to find factory work despite the limited jobs due to the flu outbreak. Anca's new husband's family was from Tennessee; she now lived there, where they focused on raising their own family.

Manfri came back with water, and soon, he and Kezi were sipping cups of strong, sweet black coffee by the fire. Around them, other Gypsies were doing the same. One of their neighbors was coughing ominously, her eyes bloodshot; Kezi noticed that the woman's husband didn't seem to have come out of their vardo. It was, no doubt, the blight that weighed on them all.

It was well known that the first case of "La Grippe," as the French called it, had come to the United States in March at a post in Fort Riley, Kansas. Troops returning from war in Europe had brought it home, an unwelcome parting gift. From there, the virus had rapidly traveled across the country. Now, it was devastating Indiana, including the Gypsy caravan.

Kezi shuddered as she thought back over the past several months. October had claimed 195,000 lives across the United States.[25] The local communities also had lost hundreds; Indiana death tolls surpassed 3,000 by late November of 1918.[26] Fort Harrison in Indiana became overrun with cases and deaths. Local churches, including Zion, had curtailed worship services. Disinfecting and quarantines, cures and treatments—nothing seemed to work. Masks were mandated at schools and all social gatherings, but the pandemic raged on.

Kezi sneezed, then wrapped her hands around the hot mug of coffee, taking comfort in the warmth and familiar scent. Wanting to stay in an isolated area and limiting travel to avoid the flu seemed reasonable to the Gypsies. The caravan had decided to stay, make wares, and do farm chores locally until the fears of the Spanish flu calmed in the local towns. However, many county residents felt differently. Kezi knew of the townspeople gossiping about Gypsies carrying the virus and intentionally staying in the county to spread it vengefully. The influenza had taken too many lives in the community, and any possibility of preventing further loss became a public health priority, even if that possibility was fueled by misguided fear.

"Wonder if Oscar and Greta are well," said Manfri, staring in the direction of Peru. His breath clouded the morning air.

"I wrote a letter to Greta this month telling her about our caravan base here," said Kezi, sniffling. Kezi had also mentioned

---

25 https://www.cdc.gov/flu/pandemic-resources/1918-pandemic-h1n1.html#:~:text=It%20is%20 estimated%20that%20about,occurring%20in%20the%20United%20States

26 https://www.in.gov/library/collections-and-services/indiana/subject-guides-to-indiana-collection-materials/1918-influenza-epidemic-in-indiana/

that signs of the disease were showing up in the camp, as they had all known would happen eventually. It seemed nothing could prevent the scourge.

Glancing back, Kezi saw that a wagon belonging to a young mother was still closed tight, though the other wagons all showed signs of life.

"I'm going to take Rada a cup of coffee," Kezi announced.

"I think she may need a lot more than a cup of coffee," Manfri said. "She and her children have been ill for a week now. No signs of recovery."

"Might as well try," Kezi said, pouring black liquid into an earthen mug. She carried the steaming cup to the vardo and knocked. When there was no response, she gently eased the door open and let herself in.

The young woman with her three children lay on the bed. The mother was struggling to breathe. Her and the children's faces and exposed arms were covered with dark mahogany-colored marks, and one of the children had pink, frothy foam seeping from her mouth as she labored for breath.

Silently, Kezi set the coffee cup down. She lit two coal oil lanterns, then cracked a window and filled cups of water from a pitcher on the table.

"Try to have some water," she said to Rada, placing the cups on the bedside table. "I will be back soon with some soup." Rada groaned.

Seizing the mug of coffee, Kezi hastened back to her encampment. Manfri had pulled a week-old newspaper he'd borrowed from a neighbor from the inside of his coat and begun to read. The pair of them had picked up this new skill in the last ten years as empty nesters, and now they read everything they could get their hands on.

"I'm going to finish my coffee," Kezi said, sitting down and grabbing her mug. "Then I'm going to make Rada's family some soup and also pray over them."

"I hope it does them some good," Manfri said. He handed Kezi an inside page of the newspaper. Kezi scanned the paper, then set it down and wiped her nose on her kerchief. So-called experts were trying all kinds of experimental approaches to combat the flu, but nothing proved effective. U.S. Military installations seemed to be bearing the brunt of the pandemic, and out of desperation, Army and Navy physicians were trying endless experiments to contain the virus. In nearby Illinois, according to the paper, one-half of the Navy corpsmen at the Great Lakes Naval Hospital wore masks to work daily while the other half of the medics did not in order to test the effectiveness of face covering. By the end of the six-month experiment, those who had worn masks mystifyingly contracted the flu more often than those who were unmasked.[27] The Gypsies had their remedies of herbs, medicines, and intuition, but like everyone else, they were not immune.

Even without the plague, the caravan was shrinking. Kezi's eyes wandered over the dozen or so wagons that remained. There was only minimal security now in staying in a caravan, and most Gypsies had long since begun building permanence in the local communities whenever possible. Working in construction trades or agriculture carried much less consternation than traveling about selling potions or telling fortunes. Some Gypsies still traveled with carnivals, but most were tired of the daily uncertainty of such a life with the flu restrictions.

---

27 https://circulatingnow.nlm.nih.gov/2021/04/22/probably-of-great-value-potentially-masks-in-the-us-military-during-the-1918-pandemic/

"Damn," said Manfri. Kezi looked up from her empty cup to see a county sheriff's black Model T police car trundling up the road. She swore under her breath.

"It seems the public scrutiny has come for an early morning visit," she said.

The car parked along the partially frozen washboard road in front of the Gypsy's camp. A tall, red-faced county sheriff stepped from his Ford police vehicle and walked toward Manfri, who had dropped his newspaper and busied himself with a metal pot near his trailer.

"What is your name?" the sheriff asked.

"Good morning," Manfri said, straightening. "I'm Manfri. Can I help you, sir?" Manfri asked. Kezi seized a pot and started some water over the fire. She only glanced up briefly, avoiding eye contact with the unfriendly sheriff.

"You need to answer some questions for me," the sheriff said to Manfri. "How many people are livin' at this camp?"

Kezi listened nervously as the sheriff tried to clarify the demographics of the camp and the nature of the Gypsies' business in the county. He began asking for details concerning the proximity of the community living quarters. Manfri did the best he could to answer as the rest of the camp darted into their wagons or slipped into the woods, wanting to avoid confrontation.

The crunching of gravel alerted Kezi to another county vehicle pulling up near the sheriff's vehicle. She turned just as a middle-aged man wearing a black wool coat and a bowler hat stepped from the car, closely followed by a nurse, whose blue starched uniform was just visible under her open dark trench coat. The officials stood side by side by the vehicle, donning face masks and gloves. Kezi watched as the young nurse affectionately touched the inspector's gloved hand, and then the couple turned and approached the sheriff, who was still busy interrogating Manfri.

"Good morning, Sheriff," said the man.

"Good morning, Inspector," the sheriff replied. *Public health inspector*, Kezi realized, turning abruptly back to her pot and stifling another sneeze. She continued to watch the newcomers out of the corner of her eye as she crumbled herbs into the boiling water.

"We need to see anyone here who is ill," said the public health inspector, showing the sheriff a document on his clipboard. The sheriff again turned to Manfri.

"You need to show these health department folks to anyone who may have the flu," he said.

Manfri hesitantly pointed to a trailer. "Our king lives there," he said. "You must talk to him first."

Kezi smiled into her fragrant pot of herbs. The "king," whose name was Florin, was a low-status Gypsy designated to intercede between Gypsies and the non-Gypsies. He drew attention away from others in the caravan and was skilled in hawking wares and delivering diplomatic diversion. The slight, dark, balding man was sitting in the open threshold of his wagon, smoking a pipe. Seeing Manfri pointing, he bounced up and walked to the sheriff.

"How may I be of service to you, officer?"

The sheriff grasped the man's upper arm and pulled him aside as Kezi ducked into her caravan for soup ingredients. When she came out a minute later, the sheriff was still arguing quietly but threateningly with the Gypsy. Finally, the sheriff pointed a finger at Rada's vardo.

"He says they've taken ill," he said to the two officials, who walked toward the wagon. Kezi turned unabashedly, watching the nurse swing her small black leather medical bag and adjust the black, wide-brimmed felt hat so it was centered squarely on her head. A knock and then a creak resounded as the officials entered Rada's vardo.

"Jesus, Mary, and Joseph," Kezi heard the health inspector yelp.

"How many others are there like these?" the nurse called across the camp. Reluctantly, Florin walked over.

After visiting two more wagons, the two health officials took off their gloves and walked to the road. The sheriff motioned them over to his Model T. Kezi, on the pretense of looking for a flat surface on which to chop ingredients, wandered closer.

"This place needs to be quarantined immediately," the now-agitated health official was saying as he lit a cigarette. "The pikeys[28] are not to leave this camp, and the ones who are out and about in the county need to be rounded up, brought back, and kept here."

"It'll take a while with what short amount of help I got," the sheriff replied. Kezi heard a clunking noise and glanced over; she saw that he had attached a cooking implement to his intake manifold and was using it to warm something in a pot.

"Is what you're asking even legal?"

"Legal or not, the community's lives depend on it," the nurse said. "I'll stop by next Monday to check on the families." There was a snap as the woman closed her medical bag.

"Some of the tinkers are asking for our help," the sheriff said. Kezi turned briefly and saw that he had poured something into blue tin cups for the health workers.

---

28 Derogatory slang for Gypsy or vagrant

"Ah, Postum,"[29] the health inspector said. "Thanks."

"Welcome," said the sheriff, then jerked his head toward Rara's vardo. "Those children look poorly. Perhaps we could lend a hand. The Gypsy woman cooking over there is trying to care for the others, it seems." Kezi swiftly chopped a carrot when she saw him gesturing to her, wiping her drippy nose covertly with her sleeve.

"That little chippy has quite the reputation around town," Kezi heard the nurse say. She stiffened but tried not to show she had heard as she propped her cutting board more securely over the flat rock.

"She and her companion have trundled their whoopie wagon around the entire county," the health official said. "In any case, there is nothing we can do for them; we can only offer comfort measures. We've dispensed a little medicine for fever, and they need to make some masks to wear. One thing for sure is we don't want these people coming into town, under any circumstances, especially to our hospital. In fact," he said quietly, forcing Kezi to focus intently to hear, "once the stragglers return to camp, it would be in everyone's best interest if all these transients were escorted out of the county."

The trio sat for a moment, sipping Postum, while Kezi busied herself with cooking.

"If it's what has to be done," the sheriff said, "under the circumstances, I suppose we'll do the best we can to round the Gypsies up."

"When you do, it also might be for the best if you wore a mask yourself, Sheriff," the health inspector said diplomatically. The sheriff chuckled.

"I suppose you're right."

29   A grain-based drink made by the Post company.

* * *

A few weeks later, Greta sat at her kitchen table examining the wax seal on a letter from Kezi. It had been broken, and someone had crudely attempted to reseal it.

"Nosy postal workers," Greta muttered, undoing the flimsy seal. It hadn't been the first time a curious worker had opened a piece of mail that looked interesting to them, and she was sure it wouldn't be the last.

Greta read the letter once, then twice more in quick succession. The news in the letter was not good, confirming her fears. The Gypsy camp had been placed in quarantine, and the caravan members who canvassed and worked in the rural area had been ordered back to the camp. Many of Kezi's group were ill, and now Kezi herself was becoming seriously impaired.

Greta set the letter down and pressed a hand to her face. The Church of Zion, despite precautions such as holding services in small groups and in homes and barns where ventilation and space could be optimized, had lost eleven of its members to the disease. Greta couldn't imagine how devastating the disease would be in a community like Kezi's.

"Hello, Greta?" a voice called from the door. Greta got up, the letter still clutched in one hand, and saw Lena standing there. Rachel, just a few months old, was asleep in her arms, and by her side stood Conrad, Lena's older cousin. Nearly thirty now, Conrad was an assistant professor at Manchester College, which had closed shortly before Thanksgiving due to a spike in flu cases there. He had been invited to stay with Fredrick and Lena until school reopened.

"We've brought you some pumpkin bread," Lena said, smiling. "Still warm from the oven." Conrad, his blonde hair shining in the winter sun and his casual clothing looking a little strange next to Lena's German Baptist garb, held out a basket. Glancing around the trio, Greta saw Conrad's polished black 1915 Overland in her driveway.

"That was very Christian of you, Conrad," Greta said, her hands shaking as she held out the letter. Behind her, Sigrid trotted down the stairs and appeared at her side. "God has sent you to me now. I need to ask for your help."

"Ma, I'd like to come too," Sigrid offered when Greta explained the situation.

"No, sweet girl," said Greta to her daughter as she packed some chicken soup, frozen from its stay on the back porch, and some fresh eggs into a basket. "I'm sorry, but you know it's not safe. The fewer of us who go, the better." Indeed, the family had done their best to stay isolated whenever possible, rarely traveling to town for provisions or hardware these days.

Grabbing her heavy coat, Greta turned. "Stay to help your pa with the livestock," she instructed Sigrid. "Please finish cooking the evening meal as well. We won't be long." Sigrid nodded.

Conrad walked back to his car, holding a blanket for Greta as she gingerly set foot into the vehicle Conrad had traveled to Indianapolis to purchase. She would have usually seen such an auto as the biblical definition of "prideful," yet she willingly climbed inside. She had not visited Kezi openly for many years, afraid that her family would lose the favor of the church. But now, in this moment and with her children grown, she had to act.

Within half an hour, Conrad and Greta had dropped Lena and Rachel back home and were en route to the Gypsy encampment. Greta had the letter in her pocket, and she traced the simple map as light flurries hit the windshield. She fidgeted, feeling uneasy in this modern mode of transportation.

"Thank you for doing this, Conrad," Greta said. "I felt an urgency reading my friend's letter."

"It's no inconvenience, Sister Beck," insisted Conrad.

"Have you heard from your brother lately?" Greta asked.

"Yes, actually," said Conrad, his eyes not straying from the road. "Paul sent a letter last week from Copenhagen. He says the mission there is all well."

"Praise God, that's wonderful news," said Greta. "I do wonder when we will get to see him again."

"Our Lord only knows such things," Conrad said with a laugh. "He has always been a free spirit."

"Do you enjoy your teaching at the College? Greta asked.

"I was enjoying it," he said. "Who knows when schools will open again? Everyone is constantly bickering, which only makes things worse."

"About what?"

"Public frustration about safety measures is growing. People are angry about being forced to wear masks." Conrad shook his head. "It is coming to a boiling point."

"Oh dear. I'm glad Oscar and I don't need to be in public much," Greta said.

"Most folks seem to view 'flu fences,' as they've been called, as pointless," Conrad said. "Additionally, the government's insistence upon restricting all gatherings is upsetting people."

"Pastor Yoder believes God is punishing the world for the abomination of the Great War," Greta said. "'Such a wanton taking of human life,' as the good pastor would say, 'has not gone unanswered by God's anger.'" She clutched the letter tighter in her pocket. "I am grateful, though, that the churches have been able to sponsor some orphans who have lost their parents to the pandemic."

"Oh, yes. It feels good to take some action." Conrad glanced sidelong at Greta. "Did I tell you I joined a Brethren anti-military movement at the college at the beginning of the war?"

"No! I was not aware," Greta said. "That sounds like a worthwhile calling." Greta knew that although Conrad had left the German Baptist Brethren Church for the more progressive Church of the Brethren, even choosing to eschew traditional clothing, he was still very much a pacifist.

"Yes. We were ultimately threatened with charges of sedition by the government for circulating anti-war documents."

"My goodness!"

"After that, I became more focused on my teaching career. These days, I'm more about pontificating academics and less on politics," he laughed. "However, I think it was a just pursuit. I would probably do it again, and I am glad to have avoided the draft thanks to my career."

"Look! I think that's the camp," said Greta, pointing past a copse of barren trees. The circled wagons, some hitched to small farm trucks, came into focus. A few tents and grazing horses filled out the camp, and cooking fire, smoke, and steam could be seen coming from near the trailers.

"This must be it," Conrad said as they drove closer. Greta pursed her lips at the public health quarantine signs clearly visible from the road.

"Greta, you can't go in there," Conrad said, looking from the signs to his passenger. "It is not safe. They are all infected."

Greta lowered her window from the passenger side as the car rolled to a halt. She could see Manfri, older but still very recognizable, stacking wood by his wagon. She waved to get his attention, and he cautiously approached the vehicle.

Manfri stood fifteen feet from the car, his face wary until his eyes found Greta's. Then his expression softened.

"Welcome, Greta," he said.

"I am happy to see you again, Manfri," Greta replied. "May I see Kezi?" Manfri's eyes began to tear as he pointed to his wagon.

"She is not well. She has no appetite. She has insisted I stay away so I do not catch the illness."

"I must see her," Greta said. She stepped out of the vehicle.

"Greta," Conrad said behind her. "This is a bad idea, and I beg you to stay. But if you must go, take this." Greta turned and accepted the cloth face mask from Conrad.

"Park your car out of sight behind those trees," Manfri said to Conrad as Greta closed her door.

"Wait for me here," Greta said, handing the basket of food to Manfri and tying her cloth mask around her nose and mouth.

Manfri led Greta to the wagon and slowly opened the door for her. As Greta passed the threshold, she felt a strange change come over her, as though she had been bathed in golden light. The air seemed to shift in quality and tranquility filled her as she breathed in the strong oud fragrance of the vardo.

Kezi was lying on a small pallet on the floor, shivering near the small woodstove. Her face had a bluish tinge, and coming closer, Greta could see the round mahogany-colored spots on Kezi's cheeks by the lamplight. Kezi's eyes blinked open, bleary and bloodshot.

"Welcome, my friend," she hoarsely whispered, struggling to turn and lift her hand toward Greta.

Greta knelt, feeling God's presence firmly around and within her. Trusting completely, she untied and removed her mask and, kneeling by Kezi, she took her friend's hand.

Kezi smiled. "Your angel is shielding you."

"I know," Greta said, her voice breaking with emotion. "I wish I could share it." Tears filled her eyes as she kissed Kezi's frail hand. Kezi looked at Greta's face and weakly smiled.

Greta's tears fell onto Kezi's blanket. "I will stay by you, Kezi."

Kezi blinked. "My time has come," she said. "I am not afraid. God sent you here to see me off, I think."

Reaching under her blanket, Kezi withdrew a worn wooden rosary and placed it gently in Greta's palm. Her hand trembled, and the skin blanched.

"You must tell Manfri goodbye for me."

"I will."

Neither woman spoke further. Kezi closed her eyes and labored for breath. Greta stayed for twenty more minutes, holding Kezi's hand and gently stroking her head. Then, Kezi's loving spirit passed from this world.

22

The Homecoming
(Die Heimkehr)
November–December 1918

"Your toe amputations are well healed," the physician told Otto. "Your lungs have also recovered well enough from the effects of the gas exposure, for the most part."

"My breathing does feel some better," Otto said.

"Your hand is another matter," the doctor said, furrowing his already wrinkled brow. "Despite having full active range, you only have a poor to a fair level of strength in your left hand and wrist."

"I see," Otto said.

"We'll do some dexterity tests today," the doctor said, "and then we'll decide on a course of action."

As Otto sat patiently through a myriad of function tests, he felt uneasy. He'd learned just after the battle that the grenade blast had severely damaged his radial nerve, causing palsy along with a fractured wrist. It had taken nearly six months of casting and splinting for sensation and use of Otto's left hand to begin returning. His toes had healed and desensitized, allowing him to wear shoes and resume walking. Despite the improvements, his injuries had made him unfit to return to duty.

"Very well," the doctor finally said. "We'll get you started with reconstruction training tomorrow afternoon. Nurse?"

A kind, middle-aged woman wearing a white face mask and dressed in a nurse's uniform strode forward and helped Otto into a high-backed wicker wheelchair. Otto stared out the window into the slate-gray November sky, then at the large room in which groups of convalescing soldiers chatted and played cards. Otto recognized a few faces from the Battle of Cantigny.

In the end, the allies had taken Cantigny in three days. Eleven of the twelve soldiers Otto had rescued and protected survived, moving along with Otto and the other wounded troops to a mobile British hospital. Shell-shocked and plagued with guilt, Otto had been stoic when at the hospital; word quickly spread through the hospital of the "German Baptist conscientious objector" who had single-handedly rescued a squad of Americans and four wounded Frenchmen. Though Otto was decorated, he took no pleasure from the praise or recognition.

Otto shifted in his wheelchair, trying to wiggle his toes as he looked out at the surprisingly barren Manhattan street around Rockefeller Hospital. Though anxious to get back home, Otto was aware of the upsurge in Spanish flu at the Fort Harrison post. He knew this was a big reason why Otto's physician in France had recommended he be rehabilitated at the New York facility rather than closer to home. Thus, he was stuck here until such time that he was functional enough to be sent back to Fort Harrison for final military discharge.

The nurse was wheeling Otto past a group of fellow patients in the hallway when havoc descended.

Bang!

Otto shot out of his chair. As Injured soldiers threw themselves to the ground, some ducking behind one another, Otto stumbled to a nearby table and crouched behind it. His knees buckled, and his pulse raced as he assessed the situation.

For a moment, no one moved. Then, nearby, someone let out a halfhearted chuckle. Others followed suit, and all gave up their defensive stances.

"Truck backfired outside," someone said. There were more mutters and chuckles and, nearby, a gasping sound. Otto looked around and saw that one man hadn't moved. His face was beet red, and he seemed to be in a panic-induced paralysis, unable to draw breath.

"Need help here," Otto called out. The nurse who had been wheeling his chair saw where he was looking and, ceasing to tug at Otto's arm, rushed over to the man.

"Hey, what's wrong with Georgie?" another man shouted.

"Shell-shocked, the limeys call it," one of the convalescing soldiers whispered as a team of medics loaded the hyperventilating man onto a stretcher.

"If his neurasthenia doesn't resolve soon, the white coats will be shipping his ass off to a locked ward," mumbled another observing medical sergeant.

"Sure," said Otto nonchalantly. He looked up at the speaker, who had a thick crop of chestnut hair and wore a black patch over his left eye.

"I'm serious," the worried-looking sergeant said. "They'll put him away in the sanitarium, commit him as a dingbat."

"Never gonna happen to me, I'll tell you that," Otto responded.

"Let's get you back in here, Sergeant," the nurse said, wheeling his chair directly behind him. With a small smile, Otto took her hand and lowered himself back to his wheelchair. The truth was that he had given up hope that any treatment would counter his persistent startle responses and nightmares. Though it had been six months since the Battle of Cantigny, he remained in a hyper-vigilant state, especially at night. The attempts at hypnosis and therapy had done nothing.

"Sergeant Bowman, how are you doing today?" asked an attending physician in the hall as the nurse propelled Otto forward.

"Feeling much better," Otto replied blandly. This is what he always said when asked about his "emotional hygiene" by the staff. The young doctor smiled reassuringly as Otto passed.

"You'll have a bit of downtime before lunch, Sergeant," the nurse said, wheeling Otto into the room he shared with a few other men. "Would you like a book?"

"No, thank you," he said. The nurse smiled and left, and Otto looked ruefully at his neatly made bed. He would never admit it to the doctors or nurses, but he had the same recurring terror night after night. He saw the faces of the men he'd killed, sometimes with Elija standing over them, praying. Otto shook his head, trying to rid himself of the images.

No matter what, I can't lose control and risk ending up in an asylum, he thought. *If I can get back home to Sigrid, everything will go back to normal.*

With some difficulty, Otto lowered himself onto the bed and removed a stack of letters from his bedside table. Shuffling through them, he chose a letter that he'd received while in France, recovering at American Base Hospital 17, which the French Auxiliary ran. The 800-bed facility, primarily for minor surgeries and recovery, was set up inside an old French seminary. That was when an attending French psychiatrist diagnosed Otto with "war neurosis" and prescribed a course of rest, massage, and hypnosis.

June 27th, 1918

My Dear Otto,

I learned from your ma and pa that you were hurt during a battle in France. They said the Red Cross also informed them that you were alive and moved to a hospital for treatment. We are all so apprehensive for you, and we pray every day for your healing and return home.

Lena had her baby on May 5th. She is a sweet little girl. Fredrick and Lena have named her Rachel.

The corn is near waist-high now. The weather has been quite warm, with a good amount of rain too. Your pa says, "it should be a good year for the crops." It sure looks like it.

Pa had six Hereford calves born this past spring. We named one heifer Daisy because she seems to love eating Ma's flowers every chance she gets.

We love and miss you, Otto. Please come home soon. May our Lord protect and keep you safe until I see you soon again.

Yours in Christ,

Sigi

P.S. I love you and miss you very much.

Otto smoothed his hand over the words Sigi had so carefully written. He remembered exactly when he'd received this letter: it had been Monday fore-noon of November 11th, and he'd been reading the letter for the fourth time when a young intelligence officer arrived at the hospital and Otto's ward.

"A cease-fire agreement has been signed in Compiègne," he'd declared. The hospital ward Victrola speakers filled the room with George Roby singing "If You Were the Only Girl in the World," but the cheers had been deafening, drowning out the song. Outside, the seminary bells rang out as though with relief.

By then, everyone had known the war seemed to be grinding to a conclusion. The German Army, overextended and deteriorating at home due to blockade food shortages, had sustained undeniable significant battle losses on the western front, not to mention the mounting numbers of seriously ill. However, the news of the official end of the war had been most welcome. Otto and the rest of the American troops were finally headed home.

Otto, smiling a little, carefully folded the letter and put it back on his nightstand. He desperately missed receiving letters from Sigi. However, his stay at the hospital would, with any luck, be too short for any correspondence.

The next afternoon, Otto sat at a table dressed in hospital pajamas and a robe, awaiting his rehabilitation assignment. Several other wounded soldiers sat around the small basement gym, many in wheelchairs spaced a measured distance from one another for flu precaution. A few wore cloth masks, and all were dressed in hospital garb. Looking around, Otto saw supplies for loom weaving, leather crafts, and woodworking. He wondered how these activities could be considered rehabilitation.

"So, what's your tale, buddy boy? How'd you get here?"

Otto turned to see the same one-eyed soldier who had told him about the sanitarium the day before.

"By ship," he said. "From Paris. You?"

"Same," said the man. "USS Mercy." Otto nodded. With the signing of the armistice at Le Francport, France, massive numbers of soldiers had begun the ship transport back to the United States. Those service members still hospitalized were transferred stateside as soon as they were able to travel. The USS Mercy made many trips returning the Yanks to the states between France and New York, and for Otto and many others returning from overseas, a stint at Rockefeller seemed the most logical.

"When did you get here?" the man inquired, picking something from his teeth.

"November 29. You?"

"Just a few days ago," said the man. "I imagine I'll be here for a while, but at least I'm back on home soil." He gestured down with a grin, and Otto looked down and realized the man was missing his left leg below the knee. Otto looked up, surprised, and the man blinked.

"That was meant to be a wink, but it's hard to wink with one eye."

Otto laughed aloud despite himself. He'd noticed most of the soldiers here, despite having severe amputations, lung damage, open wounds, and fractures, had a positive outlook about the end of the war and were simply happy to be alive. The fact that they had survived seemed enough for the majority to feel optimistic about their futures. This trooper, Otto thought, was a good example.

"What's your name?" Otto asked the soldier.

"William, but you just call me Bill," he said. "You?"

"Otto," he replied. He tried not to think of his medic teammate Bill, who had fallen in the line of duty.

Just then, a tall, well-groomed woman entered the ward. She wore a uniform resembling that of a nurse, and three other women followed her in similar garb.

"Morning, gentlemen," she said in a measured voice. "The reconstruction aides, and I will take care of you."

In under a minute, the woman had organized her helpers—the aides—and begun assigning patients to occupational projects. A few of the patients sat at small wooden tables, each working on individual projects. One of the women wheeled Otto in his chair to a small individual table with woodworking supplies.

"Please wait a moment," she said, and she disappeared. Otto's left arm lay motionless in his lap as he waited his turn. He glanced to his left, where Bill was fiddling with a loom.

"Yes, hold it like that," Otto heard a young woman tell Bill. "Then weave this part through here, and . . ."

"Ma'am," he heard the man say, "You and I both know a six-year-old could do better." He heard the woman laugh.

"Can I do woodworking instead?" Bill pleaded. The woman shook her head.

"This is designed to work on specific weaknesses," she said. "A means of restoring strength."

Within a few minutes, one of the reconstruction aides pulled a chair up on the other side of his table and sat down in front of Otto. She looked to be in her early to mid-twenties, with a rosy complexion and hazel eyes. The starched white uniform contrasted with her dark brown hair as she sat staring at Otto.

Otto felt his face redden; he had rarely ever talked with someone of the opposite sex his age outside of Sigrid. He shied as he looked across the table where the aide sat smiling at him, emitting the faint, sweet smell of Lily of the Valley perfume. He wondered what she saw in his face. Dark circles, thanks to his recurring nightmares? Premature wrinkles from his guilt-ridden heart?

"What's yer name?" she asked with a slight Irish brogue. Otto hesitated.

"Sergeant Bowman," he answered in a semi-military fashion.

"Do ya have a first name, Sergeant Bowman?" she asked.

"Otto," he replied.

"So, yer the hero, am I right about it?" she said with a smile. Otto shrugged his shoulders and stared down at the table.

"I'm Katherine O'Mara, but ya can call me Kate," she said. "So, where ya from, and what did ya do before the Army got hold of ya?"

"From Indiana. I'm just a farmer," Otto cautiously answered.

"I see," she said. "It's yer left hand's not workin' so well now?" Otto shook his hand.

"Well, let's see if we can't get ya back to milking yer Guernseys soon enough." Kate smiled as she moved her chair to Otto's left side and gently placed his left arm on the table, then slowly rolled Otto's oversized robe sleeve up past his elbow. Otto looked away from his arm, which had paled and withered from the casting, splinting, and six months of relative inactivity.

Humming quietly, Kate applied a small amount of castor oil to Otto's wrist and forearm and slowly began massaging and kneading the underused muscles. Around the pair of them, reconstruction aides moved from table to table, methodically encouraging each soldier's effort or assisting them with injuries.

"Pain?" she asked. Otto shook his head.

"Ya don't say too much, do ya now, Otto-mobile?" Kate said.

"Guess not," Otto replied.

"I suppose I will talk, then," said Kate. "I can tell ya about the great beyond."

"The what?"

"Life outside of this hospital." Kate ran her palm over a tender spot in Otto's arm. "Despite the flu, there's been a good mood now that the Great War has finally ended. As the newspaper puts it, "The nation has taken a sigh of relief.'"

"That's good," Otto said, trying not to grimace as Kate worked his muscles. "Wilson still hasn't publicly addressed the pandemic," Kate said, "but he did proclaim for the nation to be 'thankful' for the end of the war. And we are, certainly. The nation is proud of how you lads have performed in what was the most terrible war the mortal world has yet to see."

Otto was silent as, finishing the massage, Kate placed her index and middle fingers crosswise in Otto's left palm.

"Squeeze as hard as ya can," she instructed. Otto obliged, but he found he barely achieved a full closed grip around Kate's fingers.

"Hmmm. My granny in Kerry is stronger." Kate grinned encouragingly at Otto. "Try again, this time like ya mean it." Otto bore down and closed his left palm as tightly as he could, gritting his teeth.

"That's better," she said. "Your hand looks frail, but it seems there's some wick yet." She began to fish out some supplies off her cart.

"Do ya have a girl waiting at home, Otto-mobile?"

"Yes, we plan to marry when I return," Otto replied. Turning, Kate handed Otto a three-by-six-inch piece of cedar wood and a small square of sandpaper.

"I want ya to evenly sand this wood as smooth as glass," she told him. "Yer gonna make a gift for yer back-home girlfriend. Make sure ya use yer left hand only, now."

Otto seemed puzzled by the request, but he complied for the

remaining ten minutes of the session, clumsily trying to use his fingers to move the sandpaper back and forth over the wood. Bill wheeled up beside Otto as Kate walked away.

"If she doesn't motivate you, brother, then nothin' will," he said, watching Kate crouch to assist another patient. "Even with only one good eye, I can see that."

"How's your loom project going?" Otto said sarcastically, accidentally dropping his sandpaper.

"Looks like shit," Bill said with a grin before making his way back to his table.

At last, the session was over, and the transport orderly returned to take Otto to the ward. As Otto left the room, Kate gently patted him on the shoulder.

"We'll get ya back home soon," she said. Otto hoped she was right.

Over the next three weeks, Otto attended therapy every morning and afternoon for each hourly session. Kate presented new challenges for Otto's weakened left arm, massaging it and helping him perform strengthening exercises and woodworking. Though Otto's dexterity improved, he continued to jump at every noise and violently jerk awake in the middle of each night, trembling and profusely sweating. He still kept his lips sealed about this, although the other soldiers in his ward certainly knew and often exhibited the same issues.

During each session, Kate attempted to draw Otto out concerning his experience in the war. Each time, he was moot on the subject.

"I've been doing some asking around about ya," Kate said one day. Otto shrugged, gripping and releasing the ball in his left hand as instructed.

"I heard a famous American general presented ya with an Army Cross for bein' brave." Otto shrugged.

"And after that, ya received another War Cross from a French general for saving twelve soldiers."

Otto sighed, concentrating on squeezing a bean bag. His fingers were white with the effort.

"Medals were a cheap price to pay for your soul," Elija said in his head. He grimaced, and Kate seemed to think he was in pain from the exercise.

"Otto-mobile, we can move on for now," Kate said, laying her small hand over his white fingers. "But know this. Yer not just here to rehabilitate yer arm, and I fear that yer body is progressing faster than yer mind. I know you are a conscientious objector, but please understand that you are not to blame for what happened on the battlefield. Forgive yerself and get on with yer life."

Otto looked away, feeling slightly nauseous. "Can we please do some woodworking now?" he asked. Shaking her head, Kate picked up the supplies.

A few days later, a group of soldiers sat with Otto at a large table in the gym, working on their projects. Otto, feeling the hairs on the back of his neck rise, looked up to find Kate staring him down, her pretty face as stern as he'd ever seen it.

"Sergeant Bowman, today is yer last day here, and I have to ask ya," she said. "What do ya think would have happened to all those wounded, desperate souls ya dragged to safety in France if ya hadn't defended them, too?"

Otto, taken by surprise at Kate's question, only shook his head in response. The table around them grew quiet as each soldier waited for him to speak. He swallowed.

"There might have been a better way," he answered, his face beginning to redden. "I might not have had to kill anyone."

"Do ya really think those peace-loving German bastards would have just surrendered to ya or politely left ya alone because ya 'didn't want to fight no one?'" Kate asked. When Otto shrugged again, Bill, who was working across from Otto on a reasonably intricate weaving pattern, pounded a fist on the table.

"Look, boy, wonder," he said, "those krauts would have killed your ass and all the damn wounded you saved the first chance they got!" He leaned back and crossed his arms, glaring at Otto with his single eye. "Like it or not, you did right by killin' those sons o' bitches when you got the chance."

"Let's keep the language civil over there," a bored-looking top sergeant said from a nearby table. "There are ladies present."

"Killing those squareheads was probably the only thing that saved your troops from being butchered. I heard of a whole Belgium city the Huns raped and slaughtered once," a sergeant who had been seriously wounded at the Battle of the Marne quipped.

"I saw that shit at Ypres in 1915, eh," chimed in another Sergeant that had once served with the Canadian Army chimed in.

"The bosch be some cold-blooded ol' boys," a soldier with a thick Southern accent added. Soon, everyone at the table had insisted that if Otto had not taken the action he did, it indeed would have cost the lives of all those he'd saved.

Head down, Otto tried to concentrate on his work. His face felt hot, and his left hand shook. Kate stood by the chair next to him.

"My priest says that God sends angels to guide those on Earth to do his will," she said, touching Otto's shoulder. "From all I've heard, the Germans ya killed were the devil's spawn. God acted through ya to stop them from doing even more harm." Otto, thinking back to the angel he had seen in his dream that night in the Cantigny cemetery, said nothing.

As Kate walked away and the normal flow of conversation resumed, Otto's mind raced. Killing was wrong; he knew that. However, the arguments of his peers were persuasive, and even his best alternative scenarios seemed unrealistic. Had God purposely placed him in that specific battle for a reason—to save the soldiers entrusted to him?

Otto sanded stubbornly at a dull spot on his project. Unbidden and unwelcome, the face of his best friend swam up again before his eyes.

You and the wounded men in the cemetery circle were rendered invisible by God, Elija said in his head, green eyes aflame with judgment. *Perhaps if you'd only shown deeper faith in the Lord, the enemy soldiers would have gone away.*

Perhaps not, Otto said, scowling, shaking his head to rid himself of the apparition. He was well aware that verbalizing such peculiar admissions or having mental conversations with Elija would be equivalent to an expression of mental instability, and that wasn't a chance he could afford to take.

Otto held up the project, its surface now gleaming like a mirror.

Elija chose his path, and I chose another, he told himself, looking at his warped reflection in the wood. *I must accept and own my guilt as God's plan for testing my inner strength and faith.*

The following day, with orders back to his home of record and a train ticket tucked into his pocket, Otto stopped by a local jewelry shop near the hospital. It felt strange to be back out and about in public.

"How much for the cross in the window?" he asked, pointing to a tiny crucifix and chain. His left hand was still weak, but it was improving daily with functional use, and he had no issues now closing most of his fist and pointing at the piece of jewelry.

"Is it for you?" the balding middle-aged clerk asked in a thick Brooklyn accent.

"For a friend," answered Otto.

"Is your Catholic friend a mick or dago?" the man asked.[30]

"Irish, I think," Otto said somewhat forcefully.

"Well then," the clerk said in a fake brogue, clearly not catching Otto's tone, "this'll be a fine piece any self-respectin' mackerel snapper would be pleased tah wear." He smirked, amused with himself. "Want that I should wrap it for ya?"

"Please," Otto said sternly. "But there's something else I'd like to purchase. Can you do engravings?"

Leaving with packages in hand, Otto stopped by the hospital to say a final goodbye. He found Kate in the hospital gym, as she usually was at that time of day. With a smile, he handed her the small, wrapped crucifix.

"Thank you for all you've done for me," he said, looking affectionately at her now-familiar face. Even though they were of an age, he found himself thinking of her as an older sister. "You were right, you know. I forgot to rehabilitate my mind."

Kate smiled appreciatively, then strode to the other side of the room. She returned presently with the small finished wooden jewelry box Otto had labored over for the last three weeks.

---

30   Antiquated, pejorative terms for the Irish and Italians respectively

"Don't forget the present for the future, Mrs. Otto-mobile," she said.

"Thank you, Kate," Otto said. "I won't forget you."

23
Adjusting the Mind
(Den Verstand anpassen)
December 1918

Sigrid held her dark coat closely around her. A year ago, at Christmas, she'd said goodbye to Otto. Here she was again with her parents, Fredrick and Lena, and Ruth and Hans, all waiting patiently for the train's arrival. They weren't the only ones; the town of Peru had arranged to have the mayor, local civic leaders, and even carolers present when Otto and two other hometown soldiers, now considered war heroes, stepped from the train.

Sigrid glanced at the mayor, who had wrapped a thick scarf around nearly his entire bald head. She couldn't blame him. Pulling her bonnet farther over her ears, Sigrid thought about how much the world had changed since Otto had left Indiana. The Germans and French wrangled over the armistice. President Wilson was on an excursion in Paris, where he had contracted the Spanish flu. Meanwhile, con artists around the nation hawked various tonics to those recovering from the "grippe."

So far, Sigrid and her family have remained safe. She believed, from their correspondence, that Otto had, too.

In the distance, a train whistle blew.

"There they are!" someone cried.

Sigrid's heart fluttered like a bird in a cage as the train drew nearer. Reaching out, she seized Lena's hand. Lena, her cheeks red, squeezed Sigrid's hand reassuringly.

The town officials and carolers scrambled to get in position, and someone cursed as a pitch pipe clattered to the frozen platform. Then, the hiss of the train as it came to a stop masked all other sounds.

The doors opened, and passengers began to trickle out. Sigrid squeezed Lena's hand as she saw a soldier exit two cars down, only to exhale and release Lena's beleaguered fingers upon seeing that it was not Otto.

Someone tugged at her bonnet, and Sigrid turned to see Rachel, now seven months old, reaching for it with her small, chubby hands. Sigrid giggled and had just leaned in toward Fredrick to plant a kiss on the baby's cheek when she felt a hand on her shoulder.

Sigrid turned to see a tall soldier standing directly in front of her, two combat decorations pinned to his uniform. Her eyes widened, and she reflexively turned and wrapped her arms tightly around Otto. Decorum forgotten, they embraced, reunited at last.

Otto felt someone rubbing his back and turned to his right, where he saw his mother standing beside him. Ruth unabashedly joined the hug and began to cry.

"Thank you for serving our country, young man," said a voice. Peru's mayor and police chief had come by, interrupting the family reunion.

As Otto accepted the official congratulations, Sigrid felt Lena nudge her arm. Lena subtly nodded her head toward three men standing by a depot luggage wagon, staring at Otto's uniform. With a start, Sigrid realized they were the same three that had harassed her and Lena before Uncle Fredrick's funeral and referred to German Baptists as "cowards."

Otto, managing to extricate himself from the officials, stepped over to Sigrid and took her hand. Sigrid turned and stared defiantly at the men, who stared back for a moment. Then, the trio turned and walked back across the street to the pool hall from where they'd come. Sigrid felt a surge of pride despite herself. Just as Germany and the Central Powers had underestimated America's will to fight, so had many in the community underestimated the inner strength of those with deep faith, conviction, and love of family.

Greta and Oscar also welcomed Otto home, helping him load his duffel bag and valise into Ruth's buggy. Sigrid begged off to ride with Otto, saying she would help Ruth with dinner preparations.

"We will see you there in a few hours," she told her parents, who would come to Otto's welcome meal as well. Greta and Oscar exchanged a knowing glance as they stepped away.

"How was your journey home, son?" Hans asked as everyone settled into the buggy and began the short journey to the Bowman residence.

"Fine," Otto said, glad to be out of the cold. "Just happy to be home."

"Did you go through Indianapolis?" Ruth asked.

"I did," Otto said. "I passed through Fort Harrison for an overnight stay at the transient barracks. I made a stop at the personnel center, but only long enough to out-process and receive my discharge paperwork. The influenza is in an upsurge at the hospital, so I'm glad, for the most part, I managed to avoid it."

"Indeed," Ruth said. "We are blessed that no one in this buggy has yet contracted the disease."

Sigrid subtly placed her hand on top of Otto's. He took it in his, and she looked into his face. Without words, their eyes drank each other in as the carriage rattled along over the icy road.

When they rolled to a stop, Otto helped Sigrid from her spot on the bench.

"Sigrid and I would like to take a walk," he said.

"Don't be too long," Ruth replied. "We have lots to catch up on, and the weather is getting colder." Sigrid nodded as Hans and Otto unloaded the duffle bags before he drove the carriage to the barn.

Holding hands, Otto and Sigrid strolled, their breath clouding the air as the frost bit at their faces.

"Is your hand feeling better?" Sigrid asked, gingerly touching Otto's left arm.

"Still a little clumsy, but getting stronger day by day," Otto replied, holding the hand in front of him and flexing his cold fingers.

Otto looked sidelong at Sigrid. His slight smile melted her heart.

"Sigrid, you are even more beautiful than I remembered," he said. "I missed you every day I was away."

Sigrid looked down at her coat; her face began to warm. "I missed you too, Otto. Every day, I prayed you would come home to me. And now here you are."

The wind began to gently whirl flakes of snow about them as they crossed toward a grove of pine trees near the barn. Reaching the trees, they stopped and faced each other. The sky had grown darker, and Sigrid's face was flushed from the cold. She wrapped her arms around Otto and snuggled close.

"This is for you, Sigi," Otto said. Sigrid pulled away and took the small, wrapped parcel. Trying to keep her hands from shaking, Sigrid carefully unwrapped the hand-polished wooden box.

"It's beautiful," she said. "Thank you, Otto."

"There is something inside," Otto said.

Sigrid slowly opened the latch. Within the box, wrapped in a small white handkerchief, she found a simple gold ring with the initials SB engraved upon it.

"Sigrid Bowman is a very fitting name, don't you think?" Otto said. When Sigi looked at him through her suddenly teary eyes, she saw that he was glowing with happiness.

Sigrid slipped the ring upon her finger to find that it fit perfectly. Holding it up, she examined it in the waning light. She knew any jewelry, even wedding bands, was seen as "worldly adornment" by German Baptist guidance. However, more liberal conversations in the church these days seemed less concerned over a simple ring that expressed a marriage commitment. Sigi surely didn't mind. The ring gleamed as she placed both her palms on Otto's chest and looked up at him.

"Will you marry me?" Otto asked.

"Yes, Otto," Sigrid said. Warmth bloomed in her chest, a fire in the dark and cold. "I love you, and I have always loved you."

Otto gently kissed Sigrid's forehead. After a few precious moments, she carefully took off the ring, wrapping it in the cloth and putting it in her coat pocket to later hide away in a safe place at home. Holding the empty wooden box in one hand to show the families, she took Otto's hand.

"There is much to prepare for supper," she said. The couple, filled with quiet joy, strolled back to the farmhouse.

At precisely six o'clock, Oscar and Greta arrived. They warmed themselves by the fire as Sigrid and Ruth finished placing a glistening roast, apple and sausage stuffing, canned green beans, and red cabbage and potato dumplings on the table. The savory smells made everyone's mouths water as the families stood in a circle in the living room, hand in hand, heads bowed. Otto couldn't help but crack open his eyes and look around the circle at his family and friends, hardly able to believe he was really here, as Hans said the prayer.

"Our heavenly Father," Hans said, "We come to you this evening with praise and thanksgiving for returning our son Otto to us. We thank you for the fellowship with our neighbors Oscar, Greta, and Sigrid. We humbly ask that you bless this food and guide our lives in order to honor your holy name. Forgive our trespasses and keep your countenance upon us. All these things we ask in the precious name of Jesus. Amen."

A happy clatter ensued as everyone took their seats, passing plates around the table and tucking into their meal. At first, everyone was too busy eating to talk, but soon the conversation began to flow.

"Pastor Fisher's sermon last Sunday was quite interesting," commented Greta, holding up a forkful of dumplings.

"Who is Pastor Fisher?" asked Otto. Everyone became quiet, forks and knives stilled.

"Oh, dear," said Sigi. "I didn't want to burden you by telling you in a letter, Otto."

"Telling me what?"

Sigi took Otto's hand. "Otto, Pastor Yoder has died," she said. Otto set down his fork.

"When? How?" Otto had known Pastor Yoder had been old, but somehow, the man had seemed eternal.

"The Spanish flu," said Ruth heavily. "The frequent exposure while ministering to the sick came at the greatest personal cost for him."

"He lived to be eighty-one years old, however," said Hans, smiling comfortingly, his gray eyes crinkling at the edges. "He is and will always be remembered as a true servant of God and a faithful church brother."

Otto shook his head. "The Spanish flu has taken one hundred million lives, I read," he flatly stated. "The world will never be the same because of it. Pastor Yoder is a great loss . . . I can't believe he's gone."

"We were all devastated to lose so many, and of course, Pastor Yoder was well loved," Ruth said. "In his passing, the church deacons have accepted Pastor Henry Fisher to take over for a time. He's a nephew of Bauer Fisher, you remember."

Otto took a deep breath, picked up his fork again, and nodded. Sigrid patted his arm reassuringly. The shock of Pastor Yoder's absence would have to sink in over time.

"Pastor Fisher was an assistant minister from Deer Creek," Ruth said, her voice a bit louder and more demanding than usual as she scooped a little more apple and sausage stuffing onto Hans' plate. "After seminary, he had served as a supply pastor to several local German Baptist churches." She finished dishing out the stuffing and put the spoon back on the serving platter with a clunk. "Eventually, he will be replaced by a permanent pastor."

"Why do I get the feeling you're looking forward to that day?" asked Otto carefully. Hans, Ruth, Greta, and Oscar all exchanged a look. Oscar, swallowing a mouthful of dumplings, cleared his throat.

"Frankly, over the last year, the transition has not been smooth," Oscar said. "We've all been forced to take sides."

Slowly, the story came out. Sigrid watched Otto as he learned about Pastor Fisher, who was the antithesis of Pastor Yoder. The new pastor rarely took a committed stand on any issue, mainly when it came to the debate of modernizing and farm mechanization. He dismissed subjects like automobiles and telephones with a "live and let live" attitude, as he called it.

This noncommittal position, the parents explained, did not mainly sit well with the more conservative church members. The liberal and younger congregants, however, seemed to be positively swayed by the more relaxed approach Pastor Fisher took. Sigrid, watching Otto's sharp eyes dart over Lena and Fredrick's evasive expressions, could tell he had a good idea of the situation.

"There is a strong divide splitting the direction and philosophy of the church," said Hans. "None of this would have been acceptable if Paster Yoder had still been alive."

Sigi cleared her throat. "Perhaps preaching hellfire and brimstone and condemning every modern improvement is not necessary," she said. Greta visibly flinched, and Sigi smiled apologetically at her before looking at her father.

"As a farmer, surely you can see the need to use some modern machines," she said. He frowned.

"Perhaps the use of tractors and machinery is not always the issue," he relented. "It's more about the worldly ownership of such contraptions, not to mention other changes."

"What other changes?" asked Otto, moving a pile of green beans to and fro on his plate.

"A substantial number of congregants believe our future survival depends upon the ability to use machine-driven vehicles and telephones, for one thing," said Greta. Sigrid, listening to the familiar argument, watched as Hans and Ruth's black-and-white cat strolled into the room. "And let's not forget the more worldly changes of dress."

"Did you see that some of the married men within the Brethren Church started shaving their beards or replacing them with mustaches?" Ruth asked. She reached down to stroke Willa's head.

"It's becoming more popular there," Hans said, using a piece of bread to mop up the juices on his plate. "How do you suppose I would look with a mustache?"

Ruth scowled at him. "Mustaches have always presented a connection to the military, of which we should distance ourselves," she said with a furtive glance at Otto.

"Ma, you know I would never do such a thing," Hans laughed, touching his wife's shoulder. Willa pawed at Ruth's leg, and sighing, Ruth got up.

"Excuse me for a moment," she said. "Willa has been helping catch mice in the house, but I do believe it's time for her to go hunting outside." She walked to the kitchen, the cat walking calmly behind her, its tail sticking straight up into the air.

"Brethren women have begun wearing patterned dresses rather than the plain attire we ascribed to at the Zion Church," added Oscar. Sigrid tried hard not to look guilty; her hidden ring seemed to burn a hole through her pocket. "Some of the women have even been 'forgetting' their head coverings and wearing rouge."

"Change is on the horizon," said Greta. "I believe—"

Before Greta could further express her beliefs, a loud bang rang out from the kitchen, followed immediately by a "Goodness!" from Ruth. Sigrid jumped, then started in horror as Otto leaped from his chair and crouched by the table, his blue eyes wild and searching, his dinner knife clenched tightly in one fist.

"So sorry," said Ruth, coming back into the room. "Before I could close the back door, a gust of wind slammed it shut." She looked around at the blanched faces. "Surely it wasn't that . . ." Then her eyes fell on Otto, and her mouth snapped shut.

Shaking, Sigrid stood, took Otto's hand, and gently guided him back to his chair. Otto sat and quietly sipped his water, looking at no one. The knife lay forlornly in his abandoned green beans.

Sigrid held Otto's hand under the table as Ruth, with false cheer, began refilling glasses of water. The meal ended with a closing prayer and promises to see one another at Christmas service. No one said anything about Otto's startled reaction to the slamming door. Sigrid, her heart sinking, could only guess why he reacted in such a way.

When it was time to leave, Sigrid followed Otto to the barn to help fetch her parents' mare and buggy to the house.

"I'm sorry, Sigi," Otto said as he took the blanket from the mare's back. "I didn't mean to make such a scene."

"You and I will get through it, Otto," Sigrid reassuringly said to him. "There is nothing to be sorry for." She had known he wouldn't come back to her the same man, and she was prepared to help him, whatever it took. She felt a strong sense of resolve and protectiveness as, together, they brought the horse and buggy to the house.

24
The Twenties Roar
(Die wilden Zwanziger)
November–December 1921

"**M**y dear brothers and sisters," said Pastor Fisher to the congregation. Otto still wasn't used to seeing the dark-haired pastor, who couldn't have been older than thirty-five, at the front of the room. "It is after much prayer and contemplation that today, I announce the creation of a new congregation: the Peru Church of the Brethren."

Rustlings and mutters filled the room. Pastor Fisher lifted a hand, and they instantly stopped. Otto and Sigrid glanced nervously at each other.

"A group of Zion parishioners have pooled their money and, with the assistance of the district, purchased the vacated Methodist Episcopal Church building in Peru," he announced, a slight smile on his face. "I have agreed to serve as an interim clergyman in performing the services. I have already approached the Church

331

of the Brethren about taking a different approach and life direction in following the Word of God."

Sigrid took Otto's hand surreptitiously in the pew and squeezed for a moment. Since he'd gotten back from the war, the world had continued to change at a rapid pace, but Sigrid grounded him with her presence. As the 1920s began, the great pandemic had ended as mysteriously as it had appeared. Now, there was yet another split in the congregation between the old ways and the new. Otto was grateful to hold Sigrid's tiny hand in his, keeping him steady even as circumstances changed around them.

Immediately after the service, the congregation was abuzz with the news.

"Pastor Fisher's faith seems more well-suited toward the new Church of the Brethren," Otto overheard the woman sitting behind him saying. "It may not be Christian of me, but I won't be sad to see the back of him."

"Several younger married couples of Zion German Baptist Church appear convinced that the more moderate Peru Church of the Brethren would benefit their lives and their children's futures," said her companion in a scathing tone.

"Convenient if the Bible wasn't always taken so literally," replied the first woman.

"A few older church members will no doubt follow their children's direction to avoid family division," the second woman said as Otto strode after Sigrid and his family to the front of the hall. When he got there, Fredrick's face was severe.

"The creed and services will remain much the same in both churches," Fredrick said in a level-headed voice. Sigrid nodded. "The adherence to the Word of God shall remain generally the same at the new church, with the exception of tolerance for modern farming conveniences and electricity."

"Did you know about this beforehand?" asked Greta in a sharp tone. She stared at both her children.

"Not the full story, but this commonality could make things more palatable for both parishes," said Sigrid.

"Goodness!" Greta said. "If you suspected something, why didn't you say anything?"

"We thought it best to wait until we all had the full story," Otto said, shifting his weight from foot to foot.

"How many of you are planning on joining this new church?" Oscar asked calmly, scanning the faces of Lena, Fredrick, Otto, and Sigrid. Seeing the answer written there, he looked at his wife, then to the floor, letting out a sigh.

"By no means will we abandon our faith," said Lena, pulling a giggling Rachel out from under a pew. "Most things will probably remain the same. We all plan to continue to dress in the German Baptist way, though no doubt there will be some transitioning to more progressive ideas and manner."

"Pa," said Fredrick, facing Oscar, "I have already calculated the acquisition of a tractor, feed grinder, and other equipment to reduce our labor and increase the farm's production. This could be good for all of us." He looked at his father hopefully.

Oscar sighed. "If it is God's will that you use such methods," Oscar said, "we shall make the transition. However, we must never lose sight of our reverence and thankfulness for the Lord's blessings."

"Of course not," Fredrick said, relief clear on his face. "Not all change is good. This country struggles with crime and the sin of alcohol, for instance, and that must be kept away from our simple way of life. Teaching our young to love and honor God must always come before all else, even if we use a tractor on occasion on the farm."

Otto reached for Sigrid's hand. It was not ideal to be undergoing such doctrine change just a month before their wedding, but the change had been thrust upon them nevertheless. He knew their families would still come together to celebrate their new life.

Sigrid smiled at him as the families prepared to depart. "I will see you tomorrow," she said. "Perhaps Pastor Fisher will tell us more about the new congregation then."

"Yes," Otto agreed. Since Otto had returned, Pastor Fisher had begun counseling Otto and Sigrid some evenings at Otto's home. They discussed many topics—the shifting direction of the church marriage responsibilities in preparation for the blessed union—but Otto was well aware of Pastor Fisher's larger goal. The young minister, in quiet sessions leading up to the wedding, had begun to dismiss Sigrid partway through the sessions and listen impartially to Otto's descriptions of his actions in France.

Otto set his jaw. Thanks in large part to Kate at the Rockefeller Hospital, he had taken steps toward coming to terms with his time in France. However, he knew he would be forever scarred. Questions about his bravery made him uncomfortable, and he minimized past events, generally refusing to discuss them. Even so, Pastor Fisher was helping him deal with reality and move forward.

Sure enough, the next day, Pastor Fisher asked Sigrid to step out of the room once the marriage counseling session was over.

"Otto, I won't keep you long," said Pastor Fisher. "I simply want to hear how you are getting on with life."

"Well," said Otto, "The war is still never completely out of my mind. That being said, I know now that my reactions are probably to be expected. Reckon maybe I'm not going 'crazy,' like I once told Sigi." He smiled.

"I've seen the same signs of anxiety in many former soldiers," Pastor Fisher said, leaning forward, his dark eyes serious above his bushy brown beard. Behind him, outside the window, a watery winter sun shone through the clouds. "The nightmares, the edginess—it's all par for the course for those who have borne the battle. It's just going to take time and distance from that war to rise above the memories and live life again, I think. I respect that you both were willing to delay the marriage until you felt emotionally settled."

"It was the proper course," Otto said. "I thank God for bringing me home to Sigrid alive, even if I find myself struggling a bit."

"Life has not been easy for you, Otto, but neither are you beaten," said Pastor Fisher encouragingly. He picked up his cup of milk. "Tell me, have you been thinking of Elija lately?"

"Yes, in fact," Otto said. He picked up his cup of milk only to find that he had already finished it. "I 'spect he wouldn't join your new congregation."

Pastor Fisher smiled slightly, but he said nothing as Otto organized his thoughts.

"Faith comes in more than one form," Otto said finally. "Lena, Fredrick, Sigrid, certainly you, Pastor Fisher . . . I believe we are all truly devoted to the Lord. We are all doing what we believe is right. And those who are staying in the old congregation are also devoted."

"I think you're right," the pastor said, setting his cup down.

"It's not that Elija was right or that I was wrong. We were both right, and we were both faithful."

Pastor Fisher nodded. "The power of your faith in the Lord and your love for Sigrid will prevail over all evil," he said. "Each new day God sends you is a step closer to healing."

* * *

December 17, 1921, dawned in a snow flurry. As usual, Oscar and Greta rose at daybreak. Greta busily readied breakfast as Oscar tended the livestock.

"The Lord has blessed this day," Greta said as she brought Oscar a plate of ham, eggs, and mush. The room smelled of wood-smoke and sizzling food, and Oscar gratefully took the plate.

"Sigi and Otto have waited patiently for God to bring them to this place in life," Oscar said as he doused his fried mush with butter and honey. "I do wish they could have remained in the Zion Church, though."

"At least they are getting married at Zion Church," said Greta from the stove. "That must count for something." Indeed, honoring their parents, Sigrid and Otto chose to have a traditional German Baptist wedding and reception in the new Zion Church building. It seemed the right setting since Otto and Sigrid had both grown up there.

"That is true," Oscar said, eating a forkful of his steaming mush.

Greta set down her plate and pulled up a chair next to Oscar. "It is a blessing that we all serve the same God," she said. "The Zion German Baptist Brethren Church will go on, just with fewer brothers and sisters. I have no doubt we will grow once again."

"'They that wait upon the Lord shall renew their strength,'" Oscar agreed.

"Perhaps the young should move in different directions," Greta said, cutting a piece of ham.

"Within reason," Oscar said.

The couple sat silently for a moment, eating their breakfast. Sigrid was sleeping in preparation for the big day. Oscar took a moment to gaze at Greta, who was eating her meal thoughtfully. It was hard to believe she was now past fifty years of age; though wrinkles bracketed her mouth and fanned from the corners of her eyes when she smiled, Oscar still thought she was the most beautiful woman he'd ever laid eyes on. Oscar knew his brown hair had thinned, and his face was creased and sagging, but Greta didn't seem to mind.

"I am going to miss Sigi," Greta said.

"So am I," Oscar admitted, placing her hand atop Oscar's. "At least she isn't going far." The couple would live in the added extension of Hans and Ruth's home, where Otto would help Hans and his brothers farm, and Sigrid would join Ruth in managing the home. The plan was for Otto and Sigrid to take over the main house when Hans and Ruth could no longer manage it themselves. It was a simple life, but it would glorify God and give the newlyweds purpose.

Oscar wiped a bit of mush from Greta's cheek. "Sweet girl," he said, "it will be just the two of us again."

Greta smiled. "That doesn't sound so bad," she said. Then, her expression sobered.

"I was just reminded of Kezi suddenly," she admitted. "Without her, it might have only been you here on Sigi's wedding day." Greta reached out, and Oscar put his arm around her. Just a few days after she had said goodbye to her dear friend, public health officials had driven to the Gypsy encampment only to find it deserted; the quarantine notices and handmade wooden crosses placed over five recently dug graves were the only signs that the group had been there at all. The county coroner and sheriff were notified of the public health report. Still, since all county funeral gatherings had been suspended and the circumstances of the Gypsy deaths seemed straightforward enough, it seemed the county didn't plan on taking any further action.

"We owe Kezi much," Oscar said. "She has been on my mind recently, too."

"Has she?"

"Amos' neighbor is a Methodist," he said. "Apparently, the local Catholic, Methodist, and Presbyterian churches are set to buy the land where Kezi's grave is located. They mean to erect five permanent gravestones and a wrought-iron fence around the small burial plot. Perhaps they are acting out of guilt or striving to alleviate the rumored hex they believe the Gypsies left on the town. Though, of course, we don't believe in such things as curses."

Greta sniffed. "That is good to hear. Even if Kezi were capable of such a thing, she would never go out of her way to harm anyone. I would very much like to visit her at a proper gravesite." She wiped a tear from her face and took a sip of water. "I still think of Manfri sometimes. I doubt very much that we'll ever see him again." She knew that after it had been devastated by the Spanish flu, the caravan was thought to have traveled south by the river, avoiding contact with locals as much as possible.

"When the new burial plot is done, we will be sure to visit," Oscar said.

"Now that our children have left the nest, I don't have to worry as much about scrutiny," Greta said with a small smile. Oscar looked at her knowingly, his eyebrow raised.

"My Greta, we may be older now, but you are every bit as curious and ornery as when I first married you," Oscar said. Greta couldn't help but laugh.

Afternoon came quickly. Some congregants brought hearty winter dishes and covered sweets to the reception area, while others found their place in the pews of the Zion assembly area. Greta and Oscar, dressed modestly as usual, each went to their side of the aisle. Greta sat next to Ruth, who was flushed with joy.

"I've made up the new bedroom, especially for the wedding night," Ruth said quietly to Greta.

"I am happy for the both of them," Greta sighed. "Have they decided what they will do tomorrow?"

"They have agreed to attend Zion worship one final time," Ruth said. "If it pleases you, Fredrick, Lena, and you and Oscar can join us for breakfast together before going on to church."

"That would be proper," Greta agreed. Hans, who had clearly been listening from the end of the pew on the men's side of the aisle, sighed.

"It feels like our church is being torn asunder," he said. He and Ruth were remaining at Zion with Greta, Oscar, and many of the older generation.

"And a new one is being made," Greta said brightly. "It is wonderful that Otto's brothers and their wives also joined the Church of the Brethren." Just then, Pastor Fisher strode up to his place in front of the congregation, accompanied by Otto, dressed in his dark collarless suit. A hush fell over the room.

Otto felt as if his feet were nailed to the floor as he awaited

Sigrid. When she finally made her way down the aisle, he realized he'd been holding his breath for quite some time, and he released it in a rush. She looked lovelier than he'd ever seen her before in her handmade linen wedding dress. The ring gleamed openly on her hand.

The sermon passed in a blur for Otto, who gazed deep into Sigrid's eyes. After all the pain he'd been through, all the violence and sacrifice, he reveled in a deep sense of peace within him.

"Will you, Otto Bowman, have Sigrid be your wife?" asked Pastor Fisher. "Will you love her, comfort and respect her, and forsake all others to remain true to her until death separates you?"

"I will," Otto said, trying to keep his emotions from overcoming him. The wait and struggles they had both gone through seemed now only a distant memory. Their lives together would not be without trials, he knew. However, as they now had each other near, nothing seemed too daunting.

"Will you, Sigrid Beck, have Otto be your husband?" asked Pastor Fisher. "Will you love him, comfort and respect him, and forsake all others to remain true to him until death separates you both?"

Sigrid's gaze was riveted to Otto's, her eyes filled with anticipation and excitement. "I will," she said.

"As we all have waited long to celebrate the love that the Lord has bestowed upon Brother Otto and Sister Sigrid," Pastor Fisher said, "I will dawdle no longer. I now pronounce you man and wife." Amens erupted from the congregation as the newlyweds were joined together at last in the sight of God.

Part Three

The Lost Generation (Die verlorene Generation)

25
The Tides of Change
(Die Gezeiten des Wandels)
July 1926

Fredrick took Lena's hand as they walked their property after evening chores. The slightly overcast sky was welcome after a full day of blazing July heat. Eight-year-old Rachel and three-year-old Daniel ran in circles around their feet, laughing and hollering.

Fredrick smiled as Daniel tripped, caught himself, and gave his parents a wide-eyed look before barreling forward with screams of laughter. Daniel had been bright and strong from the day he was born. "Such an energetic little boy," young Dr. Miller had said as Daniel squirmed and flailed after his birth.

"Praise God, how this view has changed over the past few years," commented Lena, adjusting the picnic basket slung over one shoulder. Fredrick nodded, looking at the gently swaying green orchard grass where the windmill had once stood. The Aermotor wind pump and new well had rendered the old windmill obsolete, and with the help of his church brothers, Fredrick had disassembled the structure. He'd filled in the area where the well casing had been, but he'd be careful to leave the six standing stones his father had placed there years before.

"It was a group effort, to be sure," he said. "Silas and Titus are both skilled workers."

"The new German arrivals have been a true blessing to our community," agreed Lena. "A silver lining to the turmoil in the old country."

Looking over the fertile landscape and hearing the happy sounds of his children, it was easy for Fredrick to forget that during the 1920s, the grip of the Great Depression had pushed the congregations to move toward even more conservative and frugal living. Between 1922 and 1923, Germany had fallen into an especially dire state of economic turmoil, and many overseas congregants had been left floundering. Their small farms rapidly failed as the government's commodity needs for the Great War dissolved, and the extreme payments demanded at the Treaty of Versailles left post-war Germany printing devalued currency.

The struggling German people made poor investments, crime became rampant, and inflation ravaged the economy. Naturally, those with connections to the overseas German Baptist communities had flowed into America as Germany faltered. The Zion Church had sponsored several new German arrivals looking for a familiar place of worship, including Silas and Titus, two strapping, unmarried brothers.

The increase in new members was welcome; it nicely offset the loss resulting from the separation between Zion and the Church of the Brethren. The new blood further reinforced the

Anabaptists' need to bond together as a means of communal survival.

Fredrick and Lena made their way slowly into the circle of stones, pausing to admire a meandering groundhog before the children's shrieks sent it hustling away through the thick grass.

"Do you suppose they will remain with us or eventually move to the old church?" Fredrick asked. "Many of the immigrants seem uncomfortable with the liberal manner of dress and behavior the new Brethren Church allows."

"I think they are fine with us," Lena said, her hand moving up to touch her traditional bonnet. "Though I doubt they will go so far as joining the Dunkard Brethren congregation."

Fredrick nodded as they stepped into the circle of stones. By 1926, Pastor Fisher had found a third of his congregation leaving for a newly formed Church of the Brethren in Peru, while others in his congregation gravitated to the more conservative Dunkard direction. The original church had begun calling itself the "Old German Baptist Brethren Church" to signify its adherence to the old ways and rejection of modern machinery as they awaited a new leader.

"Even Otto and Sigrid seem to feel Pastor Fisher's Church of the Brethren has gone 'too far' in his progressive reformation," Fredrick noted as Lena spread a blanket on the grass. Circling the gently waving grass, the six stones stood tall and serene.

"What do you think?" Lena asked, sitting down on the blanket and patting the spot next to her. Fredrick sat and put an arm around his wife, holding her close.

"I feel God would not object to our use of new machinery," he said. "Especially if we continue to follow the rest of the old ways."

Together, the couple watched Rachel hiding behind one of the large rocks. A cluster of butterflies had landed there, bright wings opening and closing. Daniel, laughing, tried to find Rachel. Swirling her skirt, Rachel darted out of Daniel's sight, singing a song she'd learned in Sunday school.

Red and yellow, black and white,
they are precious in his sight
Jesus loves the little children of the world.

"Actually, on that subject," Fredrick said, "I believe Pa is finally willing to go in on purchasing a tiller attachment for the Fordson tractor."

"That would make work a bit easier for all our families," Lena agreed, pulling a cool bottle of buttermilk from her basket.

Fredrick smiled, accepting the bottle of milk. Although the two families lived on separate farms, the three women—Greta, Sigrid, and Lena—pooled their efforts in keeping the households while Oscar, Fredrick, and Otto all pitched in for the farms. Chores, raising children, and worshiping God left time for little else.

"Would we need to go into town to order the tiller?" Lena asked.

"Most likely, I suppose. Speaking of going to town, would you and the children like to watch the Fourth of July circus parade tomorrow in Peru?"

Lena's face, lit by the diffuse evening sun, glowed. "The children would enjoy that very much," she said. "But do you think it's safe for us?"

Fredrick took a swig of milk and swished it around his mouth, watching as Daniel gently tried to touch a butterfly. It was confirmed that the larger Midwest cities were changing identity rapidly, and many so-called "concerned citizens" were looking to stop America from being used as a "dumping ground" for Europe's problems, as they saw it. There was a growing anxiety among threatened whites in the lower economic class. While Germans continued to be accused, they had plenty of company on the list of problematic groups. Black folks moved north to find factory work, and large numbers of southern and eastern immigrants from Europe fled the post-war destruction of their economies. Catholics, who many believed to have allegiance to Rome and not America, also troubled self-appointed national guardians.

"We will be careful," he replied, watching as the butterfly fluttered away from his pouting toddler. Daniel ran over and plopped into Lena's lap, reaching for a glass bottle of water. He looked up at Fredrick with indigo eyes identical to his Grandma Greta's.

"The old manner of dress is difficult for German Baptists to let go," Lena said, carefully helping Daniel take a sip. Fredrick knew what Lena was saying: if it would be better to dress less conspicuously when they went into town.

"Otto and I were just talking about this," Fredrick said. "He thinks at least a version of the dress customs of the German Baptist Brethren Church should be preserved to bear witness for God and openly show our faith." Lena squeezed his hand and nodded her assent as Rachel leaped onto Fredrick's back, laughing.

The following day dawned bright and fair, and the family settled into their buggy for the trip to town. Fredrick smiled as his children played quietly in the back of the buggy. Next to him, Lena adjusted the collar of her plain dress.

The buggy passed two Zion members on the road, who smiled and waved at them. Lena waved back, and Fredrick tipped his head, busy with the reins.

"I am glad there continues to be such strong communion between our churches," Fredrick said. "So many of the Brethren are related to those in the Zion congregation, after all."

"There is no animosity between the two parishes these days," Lena agreed, passing a wooden toy to Daniel in the back seat. "I do wonder what the new pastor will be like, though."

Fredrick nodded, enjoying the play of the warm morning breeze across his face. After his last sermon at the Church of the Brethren, Pastor Fisher announced that a new pastor would take over his responsibilities at Zion.

"Pastor Muller is a devoted German Baptist minister, and the district has recommended him highly," Pastor Fisher had told his flock.

"I hope he recognizes that some changes in farm operation are inevitable," Fredrick said. He suspected the approval of the district meant Pastor Muller generally rejected modernization and the worldly temptations it brought. "We have made many changes on our farm. We cannot return to the old ways now."

"It's not just us," Lena said. "Many within the Brethren Church have already purchased gasoline-run farm equipment and automobiles. It would be difficult to go back, although some continue to argue that the new machinery is too dangerous."

"Farming accidents do occur," said Fredrick. "But you can just as easily be killed by a horse as with machinery."

"Rachel, please stop kicking the front bench," Lena said.

"Sorry," came the reply from the back of the buggy, followed by giggles.

"Times are changing; it can't be denied," Lena said to Fredrick, glancing into the back of the buggy with a grin before her face grew serious once more. "There are other changes, though . . . changes that are not so welcome. Perhaps Pastor Muller can help with those."

"What do you mean?"

"The Spiritualist movement," Lena said in a hushed voice.

"Ah," said Fredrick, guiding the buggy to the side of the road as a wagon traveling in the opposite direction approached. "I disagree with it, but I do understand why it's happening. As Pastor Fisher says, people deeply mourn all those lost to the war and the influenza." He thought of Elija and Pastor Yoder, and a weight seemed to fall on his chest.

"Naturally, people desperately long to reconnect with those lost souls of family members or friends," Lena said, her voice a bit tight. "And yes, the new Spiritualist Church in Peru is just following that trend. But that doesn't make it right." Glancing behind her to make sure the children were occupied, she leaned close to Fredrick. "Did you know that our neighbors a mile north, the Puterbaughs, have purchased a Ouija board? I heard the wife speaking of it the other day in town."

Fredrick pursed his lips. "They lost their son in the war."

"And I lost my brother because of that war," Lena said curtly. "Even so, such actions cannot be in accordance with God's laws."

The pair fell silent as a noisy automobile passed them, swiftly disappearing into the distance. Occult practices gained popularity worldwide after the war. At first, the trend seemed just for novelty and entertainment, but now, seances and tarot readings have become a source of hope for connection and communication with lost loved ones for many outside the Brethren.

"Do you remember the scripture Pastor Fisher referred to when he spoke to us at last Sunday's service?" Lena asked.

"Whosoever practices sorcery, soothsaying, looks for omens, or speaks to the dead is a-bomb-nation to the Lord and will be driven from Him,'" recited Rachel from the back seat.

"That's very close, sweet girl," Lena said. "Can you say, 'abomination?'"

"Abobinjin!" cried Daniel. Rachel started laughing.

"The point is," Lena said, turning back to Fredrick, "The district elders are clearly demanding that attention be drawn to the 'scourge.' You know the Brethren, Dunkards, and German Baptist Districts are united about the danger of dabbling in the occult. There are a few other local churches rumored to be engaged in such activity."

"The Church of the Brethren would never succumb to such blasphemy," Fredrick said. "There's no need to worry about that, even with more liberal leaders like Pastor Fisher."

As the city of Peru came into view and the roads became more crowded, Fredrick drew inward. He thought of Elija, dead at twenty-one, and the haunted look in Otto's eyes. Which fate would have been his had he not been married with a child on the way when the war started? He thought of his mother, of the grief she'd shown at the passing of a Gypsy known for her fortune-telling. In the bright July sunshine, he wondered at how complicated life sometimes was.

The young family parked their buggy at the train station. Rachel held Lena's hand, and Fredrick kept little Daniel in his arms as they wended their way through the crowd, a conspicuous German Baptist island in the sea of modern garb.

Ahead of him, Lena stopped to look at a newspaper stand.

Fredrick saw that she was examining the "The Fiery Cross," a newsprint circulated by the local Klan chapter.

"Look at this," she said to Fredrick. "Rachel, please stop tugging for a moment. This paper says the Klan is recruiting here at the Fourth of July celebration. There's a quote . . . 'Any self-respecting Indiana citizen would be well advised to join such a fine organization as the Ku Klux Klan.'"

"Governor Jackson said that," said a voice behind her. She turned to see two men, one red-faced and rotund, the other tall, slender, and bald.

"Right here in Peru, a couple of years ago during the election," the red-faced man continued. "Damn, good advice, too, by gyp."

Lena gave the man a watery smile, saying nothing. As they walked away, Fredrick heard the bald man mutter, "cheek turners."

"They don't pay taxes," the red-faced man responded. Fredrick swallowed, stepping closer to his family. Had coming here been a mistake?

The family walked toward the main street, sliding between shrieking children and gossiping townspeople to await the beginning of the parade. Fredrick eyed the blooddrop cross of the Klan warily. It seemed to be everywhere: in store windows, on posters, sewn onto citizens' clothing. The Klan numbers in Indiana had swelled to 250,000 substantial, and many savvy business owners, he knew, saw an advantage to serving the organization's members.

The air grew stifling as Fredrick and Lena found seats on the curb of the brick street. Despite the heat, as the parade began, Fredrick began to relax. Rachel and Daniel were delighted by the horses, camels, and elephants that passed by. However, when a Ford Model T pickup drove by with robed Klansmen riding in the back, they instinctively drew back. A robed Klansman rode in the passenger seat, dangling a hangman's noose from the open window.

As the truck passed by where Fredrick and his family were sitting, the hooded Klan member's eyes drifted to the German Baptist family. He lifted the noose and pointed his bony finger at them. Even under the July sun, Fredrick felt a chill travel down his spine.

"Perhaps the children have seen enough of this kind of parade," Lena said quietly. She began to pack up her blanket and the children's belongings. Fredrick helped her in tacit agreement.

"But the parade!" Daniel whined. Rachel's dark, sharp eyes darted to her brother, then to the distancing Klansmen in the truck.

"Let's go," she said, holding out her tiny hand. "I have a surprise for you at home." Daniel, delighted, took her hand.

The young family made their way back to the train station where their buggy was parked.

"I thought the Klan had no quarrels with Anabaptist people," Lena whispered to Fredrick as the crowd thinned. "They think we work harder and cause less trouble, even if that's unfair . . . or at least, I thought they believed that."

"It's not our work habits the Klan are concerned with," Fredrick said quietly, scooping up his lagging son. "It's our stance on war and our acceptance of all people as being 'God's children.'"

The trip back home seemed to fly by as the children, tired from the excitement, dozed in the back of the buggy. Sigrid and Otto had just stepped out of their wagon when Fredrick and Lena pulled up.

Sigrid smiled and reached out her arms to greet them. Lena

handed a sleeping Daniel down to her sister-in-law, then picked up Rachel, who had also fallen asleep. The two women went into the house while Fredrick and Otto took the horses to the barn.

Lena laid Rachel down atop her covers, then peeked into Daniel's room. Sigrid was tenderly stroking her boy's cheek, looking at him with affection. Lena felt a pang, and as the two women went down the stairs, Lena silently prayed that Sigrid would experience the joy of motherhood soon.

"You're home earlier than expected," Sigrid commented. With the curtains drawn against the heat, the kitchen was dark and relatively calm. "Otto and I had planned on doing some chores for you."

"Kind of you," Lena said as she removed her bonnet, which was damp with sweat. Sigrid peered at Lena's face.

"Lena, did you like the parade? "Sigrid asked. Wetting a handcloth and wiping her face and hair, Lena told Sigrid what had happened in town.

"Maybe Pastor Fisher is right. Maybe we should dress less as German Baptists and more as the new Brethren," Lena lamented, seizing a clean bonnet from a basket of laundry by the door. She looked at it for a moment, then slid the familiar garment over her head, tying it on just as Fredrick swung the door open. "Maybe if we didn't stand out in the crowds so much, it would be better. I don't think God would love us any less if we dressed like everyone else."

"Lena, those Klan members at the parade are doers of evil," Fredrick said as he and Otto placed their wide-brimmed hats on wall pegs. "We can't change who we are or what we believe to appease such people. Our Lord calls us to be in the world, but not of the world."

"But anyone who does not behave or dress like them becomes their object of hate," Lena said, her voice a little higher
than usual. "It was different when it was just us, but now we have
the children's safety to consider." She started bustling around the
kitchen, avoiding Fredrick's eyes. "Our children don't understand
why people single us out. Rachel has already noticed. Did you see
her face? How can we explain to her that this is what God wants
for us? Sigi, would you mind getting the milk from the cooling
tank downstairs?"

"Not at all," said Sigrid, exchanging a look with Otto before
walking out of the room. Otto sat down, resting his elbow on the
table and propping his chin up with his hand.

"Fredrick told me what happened," he said to Lena. "Despite
the hardships, I think we must be true to our beliefs and witness
God's word. Our manner of dress shows obedience to God and
bears witness to our faith."

"Pastor Fisher's Brethren beliefs about dress modification
and using automobiles instead of horse carriages ... perhaps it
is something to think about at least," Lena countered, carrying
several servings of cherry cobbler to the table and placing them
on the worn surface with a clatter. "When a third of the people in
town agree with those men in the white robes, all I am saying is
that maybe we would be less at risk if we were to blend in more
and avoid making ourselves such easy targets."

"It sometimes feels as if the ideological gap between the
two churches is becoming a chasm," Otto said, rubbing his beard
thoughtfully. "Let us not forget that though there is separation
in the local Anabaptist denominations, the Brethren are still one
group. As you said yourself, we have much in common. Our cloth-

ing helps to solidify that bond even as we diverge in other parts of our lives."

Sigrid strode back into the room, a porcelain pitcher in hand. She set it down on the table, then went to the cabinet for glasses.

"It's easy for some to see only a person's external appearance and overlook their soul," she said in a subdued voice. "As our God told Samuel, 'Man looketh at the outward appearance, but the Lord looketh upon the heart.' Lena, you can contemplate wearing more worldly clothing, but it is much harder for those who have different skin colors and cannot change their appearance. They have no choice but to continue despite all the hatred around them. Perhaps we can show solidarity in our faith and dress." Lena, who was carrying more cobbler over, paused for a moment before continuing, her eyebrows drawn together.

"Nothing will be resolved today," Fredrick said as Lena sat, passing out napkins. "There is injustice and evil in the world, no doubt. Let it only serve to strengthen the Brethren to be more prudent in honoring God through lives of peace, forgiveness, and daily prayer."

As the four began to eat, there was a stirring from upstairs. Rachel's high, sweet voice flowed down to the dark kitchen.

Like Samuel, let us say,
Whenever we read His Word;
"Speak, Lord, I would obey
The voice that Samuel heard;
And when I in Thy house appear,
Speak, for Thy servant waits to hear.[31]

---

31 *The Sunday School Child Hymn Book: When Little Samuel Woke,* Revised. (Philadelphia: American Sunday School Union, 1900), p.45.

26
Accepting Reality
(Realität akzeptieren)
March–June 1929

"**C**ousins!"

Lena and Fredrick couldn't help but laugh as Paul rushed up to them at the train station, his bags bursting. He was thirty-one now, but the boyish glee in his sparkling eyes hadn't changed a bit.

"It's good to see you again, Paul," said Lena warmly. "What was Europe like?"

"Lena, I have so much to tell you," said Paul, smiling broadly.

"Paul," Fredrick said, slapping Paul on the shoulder. "How long has it been?"

"Thirteen years," Paul said. "Gosh, but it feels good to be home." Paul had been serving the German Baptist Church faithfully as a missionary since Fredrick Sr. had endowed the church with enough money for the trip. Home at last for a visit, Paul was to stay a few days with Fredrick and Lena, discussing his work in a series of meetings at the Zion Church. He would then journey on to Indianapolis, where his parents had moved some years before.

"And it's good to have you back," Fredrick said. "Shall we? Our daughter is eleven, so she can keep an eye on her brother for a time, but I don't want to leave her for too long."

"I'm so pleased to meet my new little cousins finally. Where's your buggy?" Paul said, gratefully handing one of his bulging bags to Fredrick. Fredrick proudly pointed to a Model T parked in the lot, gleaming in the weak March light. Paul whistled.

"When did you get that?"

"Summer 1926," Fredrick said. The trio, all dressed in traditional German Baptist clothing, approached the modern vehicle.

As promised, their conversations throughout the afternoon were intriguing. The children immediately took to Paul, and Greta, Oscar, Sigrid, and Otto, who also had many questions concerning Paul's adventures, came to join them for supper.

"Paul, tell us how you've been spending your time," Greta said eagerly, passing him a bowl of red kraut.

"I've been working at the church in Copenhagen, but my grand achievement is the satellite mission in northern Sweden," Paul said, heaping more sauerkraut onto his plate to go with his sausage, gravy, and mashed potatoes. "We've been ministering to the 'Lappers,' the indigenous people there."

"That sounds so respectable," Lena said, taking the bowl of kraut from Paul and raising an eyebrow.

"Yes, I know I've had a bit of a reputation for traveling among the 'publicans and sinners' in the states," Paul said, loading his fork with mashed potatoes and gravy. "But that has actually been an advantage in Copenhagen. I've become well connected and trusted among the street people there."

"I don't know if that's something to be proud of, Paul," said Otto, chuckling.

"In Copenhagen, such people are typically looked down upon as offscourings of society," Paul said with a shrug. "But that's where the real salt of the Earth is. They have a feel for what is really taking place in the city and Europe. They know there's a change in the wind, especially in Germany." Paul's face grew somber. "Word on the street has it that an ugliness and anger caused by the Great War and the way Germans were treated afterward has caused quite a volatile mood."

"Perhaps you should minister to them," Sigrid said, trying unsuccessfully to stop Daniel from seizing a handful of mashed potatoes.

"What about the Swedish Laplanders? I don't have time for everyone," Paul said.

"Are they more devout than the people on the street?" asked Lena, wiping Daniel's hand with a wet napkin.

"The Sami only paint a thin veneer of Christianity over themselves," Paul confessed. "The tribes are much like our native Indians, but there is strong government pressure for them to practice the Christian faith and become 'Swedified.' Even so, they have many of their old shamanistic beliefs buried deep inside." He gulped down another bite of his potatoes before continuing, a drop of gravy quivering in the corner of his lip. "I can't say that I've done too much to change that. Browbeating people into religious submission hardly seems ethical. They will come to Christ at their own pace."

"That makes sense," said Otto, nodding and tapping the corner of his lip meaningfully. "You shouldn't force people into believing what they don't truly understand." Paul seized his napkin and wiped his face unabashed.

There was a pause, and the clatter of forks filled the room. Rachel, clearly bored by the conversation, was drawing faces in her mashed potato. Lena swatted her hand.

"I am envious of your travels, Paul," Greta said. "I would so much like to revisit the old country. My mother was originally from Sweden; she moved when her family joined the Baptist Brethren in Germany."

"I still have an uncle living in Germany," Oscar said. "We correspond with him through letters a few times a year, though it has been more than twenty-five years since Greta and I have seen him face to face."

"Uncle Dieter?" Fredrick asked, a bite of sausage poised on his fork.

"Yes, exactly," Greta said. "Your namesake's brother. He is a good man."

"I will give you my information before I leave next week in case you ever want to contact me," said Paul.

"Leaving so soon?" asked Sigrid.

"I'm not looking forward to the boring eight-day voyage after visiting my family in Indianapolis," Paul confirmed. "But, alas, duty calls. In any case, you have an open invitation to visit me in Denmark, even by way of Germany, if need be. I must warn you, though, that the Germany of today may not be the Germany you recall. Like I said, a foul mood is in the air."

"Let us all pray that it comes to nothing," Greta said.

"Foul mood or not, the family connections to the old country still hold a special place for us," said Oscar, putting a hand on his wife's shoulder. She nodded. "We know that the chances of either one of us returning are quite unlikely, but even so, we thank you."

"Well, I do have something that will make you feel like you've done some traveling," Paul said, scooping the rest of his food in his mouth and rushing from the table without asking to be excused.

"Not one for manners, even now," mumbled Sigrid, smiling despite herself as she wiped gravy out of Daniel's hair.

"What about Uncle Fredrick's gift?" asked Lena quietly, looking at Greta. "You could surely afford a trip to Germany."

"It's prudent to be frugal," Greta said, but there was a glint in her eye. Lena wondered if another voyage might take place someday.

"Voila!" Paul said, re-entering the room with his arms full of carvings and stitchwork from Sweden and Lapland. And, for a time, everyone forgot about traveling to Germany.

* * *

A few months later, Sigrid, Lena, and Ruth sat on Lena's front porch, cleaning garden peas as they watched Rachel and Daniel playing in the stone circle near the woods. Rachel had built a sophisticated little hut out of sticks, placing a little carved Dala horse she'd received from Paul inside. She was trying to prevent Daniel from knocking the whole structure down, waving him away with a small white pine branch tipped with long, soft needles. A little family of wrens watched the activity curiously from atop one of the stones, and a few squirrels ran through the circle at intervals, chattering at each other. As she watched the children amiably squabble, Sigrid couldn't help but feel a deep longing.

"Lena, are you planning on having any more children?" Ruth asked.

"I don't know," Lena answered. "We're happy with Rachel and Daniel. Daniel is a handful and keeps us quite busy," she added with a huff of laughter.

"Well, if you want more children, you'd better have them soon," Ruth said, throwing peas into the pot. "Once a woman reaches thirty, it becomes more difficult with each passing year to conceive." She glanced meaningfully at Sigrid, who looked away. Sigrid loved Ruth, but she wished her mother-in-law, who had gotten into the habit of saying things like this at every opportunity, would give her and Otto a rest.

Ruth opened her mouth to continue, but Lena, seeing the look on Sigrid's face, swiftly interjected.

"Sigrid, how are you enjoying the new vehicle?" she asked. Otto and Sigrid had recently purchased a pick-up truck.

"It has been nice to have," admitted Sigrid, trying to ignore Ruth's disappointed expression. "Otto and his brothers planned to invest in a John Deer D steel-wheeled tractor soon."

"It seems to me," said Ruth, "that little time was wasted considering whether the purchases were 'too worldly,' but only exactly where and how the new horsepower could be put to use."

"Sister—" said Lena, but Ruth plowed on. "Through saving some physical effort, labor-saving machinery has created time for worldly diversion. In the eyes of many, the Church of the Brethren has become a reflection of the nation, consumed with only production and building capital."

Ruth began waving a peapod wildly about as she aired her grievances. "Lindbergh's transatlantic flight . . . Amelia Earhart's exploits . . . our country is thrilled with what possibilities lie ahead. It seems now some of the Brethren are as well rather than focusing on serving our Lord."

Finished with her speech, Ruth cleared her throat and turned back to her peas. There was an awkward silence as Sigrid tried to think of something to say, watching Daniel dart closer and closer to Rachel's stronghold. Around them, the trees showed the first blushes of fall color.

"Such change is concerning for elders in our church as well," said Lena diplomatically. "Subscribing to more labor-saving methods of farming or transportation was one thing, but many feel other steps go too far." She paused to scrape some dirt off a pea pod. "I worry that the cultural results of the more progressive direction of the Peru Church of the Brethren may begin to force some to look elsewhere for fellowship."

"Yet another division," Sigrid sighed. "Why do you think Otto and I, after much soul-searching, decided to change church affiliation to the Dunkard Brethren Church at Loree? We like that traditional dress is still the standard there, but modern conveniences are also permitted for farming. It suits our desire to publicly bear witness and reverence to God while modernizing methods of labor."

"And what was your justification for staying with Pastor Fisher, Lena?" asked Ruth, raising her eyebrows. Lena met her gaze without guile.

"Pastor Fisher's goal is, as he put it, 'not to conform to Lucifer's plans or become more worldly, but to simply adapt with the times,'" she said, throwing hulled peas into the pot beside her. "No one thought it sinful to begin hunting wild game with a rifle instead of spears or arrows. No one thought it sinful to travel by train across America rather than by covered wagon."

"I know he has a point," said Sigrid, yanking too hard on a pea pod and snapping it in half. "And yet, it is easy to go too far." She waved a fly away from the pot; thankfully, with the cooler September weather, many of the insects had dissipated. "To be frank, my parents' dedication and deep convictions have left their mark on me. As my pa likes to say, 'The consequences of straying too far from plain and humble reverence through dress and manner could be a loss of witnessing and honor for God.'"

"Wiser words rarely are spoken," said Ruth with a nod.

"On the other hand, don't forget that farm prices have fallen during this decade," Lena said. "It's getting harder to scrape up the money for mechanical investments." There were several clinks as more peas were tossed into the pot, and Daniel let out a squeal as Rachel dropped her branch and started tickling him. "The Dunkard Brethren Church is good for those who have no misgivings about using mechanized farming or transportation but who strongly object to liberalizing how we dress and behave, especially for women. Like you and Otto, Sigi. But Fredrick and I have decided that we would like to stay where we are."

"Fine by me," Sigrid said. "We must all choose our way to honor and worship God."

"Let's turn to more practical matters then," said Ruth. "Sigi, have you heard that Sister Reynolds has become pregnant with her fourth child? At age twenty-five, it's quite—oh my stars—" Ruth stood up abruptly and ran towards Daniel, who had run away from Rachel's tickly fingers and fallen headlong into a bush. Sigrid rubbed her forehead in frustration.

"Listen, Dr. Miller is coming by in about an hour to see the children," Lena said quietly. "Why don't we see if he has a few minutes to spare?"

"Yes, I think I would like that," said Sigrid, removing her hands from her forehead, her face flushed.

That afternoon, Sigrid found herself in Lena's guest room with the young Dr. Miller. Sigrid knew that this man's father had delivered both her and her brother. Could he now help her conceive a child?

"Are your menstrual periods regular?" he asked, his eyes kind, behind heavy spectacles

"Yes."

"Pain?"

"Nothing out of the ordinary, no."

"History of injury or illness?"

"I don't believe so. However, I do know my mother initially had some trouble conceiving. Small families are common in our bloodline."

"I see. How old was your mother when she had Fredrick?"

"Twenty-five, I believe."

"I don't think that's cause for concern." Dr. Miller looked at Sigrid, smiling his soft, crooked smile. "I can draw some blood and test hormone levels if you like, but I wouldn't recommend it. I think I know what is going on here."

"You do?" Sigrid asked, her eyes wide.

"I need to ask about Otto."

Sigrid blanched. "What about Otto? What could be wrong with Otto?"

"Would Otto allow an exam?"

"I don't know." Sigrid shook her head. "I don't really see why he would need one. Everything seems fine with him."

Dr. Miller pursed his lips under his trim mustache. "Sigrid, was Otto exposed to mustard gas during his time in France?"

Sigrid thought for a moment. "Yes, on several occasions, from what he has told me. Why?"

Dr. Miller's brows drew together, and he sat back, looking at Sigrid. "There are no sure tests available to determine this. However, we do know from recent cases in France, Britain, and the U.S. that there seem to be very high rates of infertility in families of soldiers who were exposed to sulfur mustard toxin."

Sigrid felt her stomach drop. She carefully chose her words. "You cannot speak of such things to Otto," she said. "Placing this upon him after all that he has been through would cause him only more pain. Learning he may not be able to father children due to a war he now feels such guilt over would destroy him."

"I would not ever do anything that would harm Otto," Dr. Miller reassured her. "Unless you change your mind, Mrs. Bowman, I will not broach the subject with him."

Sigrid said an abrupt goodbye to Lena, Ruth, and the children and returned home feeling nauseous. Should she continue to pray for a miracle? She nearly lied to Otto when he asked what was wrong, but when he pressed, she finally told him that she'd seen Dr. Miller at Lena's house to ask about her fertility.

"Does Dr. Miller believe that you are able to have a child?" Otto asked carefully, moving closer to her on the porch bench. Sigrid hesitated, looking out over the lush fields at the lowering sun.

"He is not sure," she said. "Since he cannot say what the problem really is for sure, I guess we can only wait."

"Sigi, we could always adopt a child if we cannot have one of our own," Otto said, rubbing Sigrid's back.

"I suppose," Sigrid said noncommittally, placing her head on his shoulder. She did not want to consider adoption except as a last resort; she saw it as an admission of failure, the death of all hopes of giving birth to a child of her own. However, she also didn't want to give Otto cause to believe that their infertility was due to anything other than her medical issues. Squeezing her eyes shut, she tried to rid herself of the image of the beautiful child who may never be.

"There may be little or nothing that can miraculously change our parental status aside from adoption," Otto said. "I understand if you don't wish to adopt. In that case, we will leave conception in the hands of God. Life will go on regardless of whether we have a child."

"I won't stop praying for a miracle," Sigrid said, trying to hold back emotion. "But neither will I stop thanking God for all we have."

"God will find a way, Sigi," said Otto reassuringly, looking off into the glowing orange sunset. "He always does."

27
The Sojourn
(Der Aufenthalt)
1931–1932

Greta extracted the dog-eared envelope from its hiding place inside a Sears and Roebuck catalog. After one glance at the return address, she rushed to the house to open it, nearly stepping on the calico cat's tail in her haste.

"Oh, sorry, Leah," Greta said as she closed the door behind her to keep the chilly spring air out. She seized the letter opener, her mind racing with what news the letter might contain. The stock market crash that had ripped through the United States had been devastating for Germany as well. Many of the new German congregants at Pastor Muller's Zion Church, still strongly attached to their homeland, had expressed concern and redoubled their efforts to send money back home. American loans to Germany were now being recalled, sending the already struggling post-war country into an economic collapse. Massive unemployment meant desperation, and the effect on German Americans was symbiotic.

As Greta pulled the letter from the envelope, she hoped against hope its message wasn't as bad as the economy.

This took almost two months to find its way to Indiana, she thought, peering at the date at the top of the letter. *And this isn't Uncle Dieter's handwriting . . .*

Greta quickly scanned the letter, then read it a second time, her heart sinking.

February 12, 1931

Dear Mr. and Mrs. Beck,

It has been many years since we met. I was your Uncle Dieter's masonry apprentice and had the pleasure of meeting you before you departed for America in 1895. I am now married and have the masonry that my son Max, age 21, and I established after taking over Dieter's workload when he retired.

Upon Dieter's retirement, I moved my business to the outskirts of Berlin, as more work was available there than in Butzow. Following the war, my business in the building and subcontracting trades flourished. Though I am not particularly political, I have been able to pick up government work based mainly on word of mouth and the skills I gained from my excellent mentor.

I will never forget Dieter's kindness and willingness to teach me all he knew of masonry when I was beginning. He is more of a second father to me than simply a teacher. So it is that I am writing this letter on behalf of my honored friend, cohort, and mentor, your Uncle Dieter.

It has been very much my pleasure knowing him all these years, but as you are well aware, he is getting on in years. Dieter has been showing a decline in health and vitality for some time now. At ninety years of age, he considers you two his only actual relatives. He still has a few cousins living in Denmark, but since the war, they have broken all contact.

It is Dieter's most fervent wish that he be allowed one last visit with his only nephew and niece before his rendezvous with death. Dieter is concerned with the political direction in Germany despite my reassurance that our current nationalism is a positive development. I believe a visit from you might restore his calm.

Although the depression has depleted resources, as it has for so many, I would be most agreeable to assist with travel plans and itineraries if one or both of you should take the opportunity to visit. I have included a telephone number where I may be contacted upon your arrival.

Your most humble servant,

Rudolph Bach

Greta started as the door swung open, admitting Oscar, his face flushed from the cold. Wordlessly, she held the letter out to him. Oscar read it, then looked up, his expression serious.

"What shall we do?" asked Greta.

"I cannot see how we can go there, especially now," Oscar said, stepping over to the woodstove in the kitchen and rubbing his hands together.

"Especially now?" Greta prodded.

"Black Tuesday," said Oscar.

"That was two years ago now," Greta pointed out. "And we were fortunate to be spared the worst of it." The memory of the stock market crash, however, was still fresh. Banks had failed, and without insurance, many patrons had lost their life savings. Thousands of financial institutions eventually closed their doors as bankruptcies multiplied. It had been a tumultuous time.

"The fact that our community never put much faith in banks served us well during the crash," Oscar said. "However, we did not come out unscathed either."

"We haven't exactly had great experiences with banks even before that," Greta pointed out, putting the kettle on.

"Witnessing that botched bank robbery certainly made me wary of putting money where I can't see it," Oscar said, sitting down at the kitchen table. "But even so, Greta, we have not been immune to the Great Depression."

"We haven't fared so badly," Greta said, pouring sassafras root bark into a sieve. "We've survived an economic disaster where many others, who were not so frugal, did not." Indeed, their family had stayed relatively comfortable thanks to the food they produced, the earnings they continued to accrue, and the inheritance they had secreted away.

"And we have been blessed to be able to help so many," Oscar said quietly. "Thou shalt love thy neighbor as thyself."

"Indeed," Greta said. "I am proud of our community and our children."

"Welfare plans, food distribution, and charities may be a nationwide and governmental effort," Oscar said, "but it was Christ's words, 'whatsoever ye do for the least of my brothers and sisters you are doing for me,' that motivated love and good deeds among the faithful within the three congregations."

Greta approached Oscar and took his hand, now warm from the stove.

"Wise words," she agreed, thinking back over the past few years. The Zion, Dunkard, and Brethren communities had, of course, seen the economic disaster as an opportunity to do God's will. There were no relief or welfare programs to be had, so it became the mission of the Anabaptist community to gather and distribute food and clothing to neighbors in need. With Fredrick and Lena's help, Pastor Fisher organized a food bank in the Brethren Church basement, and word of mouth led the members of the three congregations to those most in need. Greta smiled as she thought of how Sigrid when she encountered those who would not openly accept church help, found creative ways to leave parcels from the Loree Dunkard Brethren Church on their doorsteps.

Greta looked into Oscar's eyes. "Our lack of extravagance and planning for a rainy day has served us well and allowed us to help others," she said. "However, that doesn't mean we cannot ever find something worth spending on. This is about family, Oscar."

Oscar frowned, turning the envelope over to examine the German postage stamps. "I can't just leave for weeks and expect Fredrick and Otto to do everything while I'm gone, especially now that we've decided to become an official partnership."

The kettle began to sing, and Greta stood to pour the hot water over the bark tea Kezi had introduced her to years before, pondering Oscar's words. It was confirmed that the Becks and the Bowmans had consolidated their efforts and the profit based on acreage in an effort to survive the challenging economic times. However, she suspected Fredrick and Otto could easily handle the workload, and she and Oscar certainly had saved enough money to make the two-week trip comfortably.

Greta glanced at Oscar, who was absentmindedly running a thumb over the stamps. Perhaps Oscar, who had loving memories of his strong and capable uncle, would have difficulty seeing Dieter nearing his deathbed. With his deep attachment to family, the loss of Uncle Fredrick had been very difficult for Oscar.

As Greta mulled over the situation, something else struck her. She knew Oscar was embarrassed about his inability to go long periods without urinating, a condition Dr. Miller called "prostate obstruction." Greta never mentioned the problem, as there seemed little could be done. "Just part of growing older," as Dr. Miller put it. However, a condition like that would make traveling very difficult for Oscar.

Greta cleared her throat, then turned to her companion of so many years.

"I must go there," she said. "Someone from the family should be with Dieter before he passes on."

Oscar stared at her, but she nodded as if the matter had been decided.

"I will ask Sigi to come with me. She has often talked about meeting Uncle Dieter and visiting the place where you and I grew up. We can arrange steamship passage for a reasonable price, I think."

"It will be very steep, I reckon," Oscar said.

"Dorcas had relatives from Hoboken who booked a steamer to Hamburg a few years before," Greta said. "She told me they had a very positive experience. The total price was $350 or thereabouts for two people, as I recall. Though costly, that would be manageable for such an important trip."

"You have been thinking of going to Germany for a while now, haven't you?" Oscar asked, his eyes fixed on Greta.

"I have told Sigi many stories of Germany, and I know she would like to see it for herself," Greta said, carrying the teapot and two cups to the table. She was already mentally planning an itinerary.

"It is a lot of money to throw away in such hard times," Oscar said. Greta sat down and smiled as she poured the tea. The couple had saved their money for nearly forty years, and Greta knew precisely what they could and could not afford.

Seeing her expression, Oscar let out a long sigh.

"My Greta, once you have your mind made up, trying to change it is a fool's errand," he said. Greta laughed, pushing a cup of tea toward him.

In the end, it took a year to plan the 1932 trip. Greta first conferred with Pastor Muller, who gave his blessing, as did the church elders. They agreed that "bringing comfort to a relative in their final time on Earth is a noble gesture, and the expense for travel is justified." Correspondence with Rudolph sped up as they discussed logistics, and Rudolph passed on Dieter's greetings and eagerness to meet his grandniece for the first time.

"It seems that Dieter now has a purpose," Rudolph wrote in one of his letters, and this made Greta sure she was making the right decision.

Greta often walked to Lena's house, where Sigrid joined them to discuss the train travel plans from Hamburg to Berlin to meet Rudolph. Dorcas asked her cousins to assist with booking passage on the steamship for Sigrid and Greta, and she began meeting Sigrid and Greta at Lena's house to make arrangements. One chilly fall day, they all sat at Lena's kitchen table, poring over travel options.

"I must admit that travel by Zeppelin intrigues me," Greta said. "It has become quite popular. But we will need to keep our expenditure as low as possible, which rules that out."

"People in the community no doubt would condemn any extra expenses and worldliness," agreed Lena, placing steaming slices of apple bread on the table.

"The Leviathan seems the most practical option," said Dorcas, leafing through page after page of information. "It's a former German ship originally named the SS Vaterland. This says it was seized and renamed by the U.S. government early in 1917 during the war."

Greta peered at the back of the page Dorcas was reading and frowned. "This says alcoholic drinks are served on the ship. The passengers may be rowdy,"

"We can plan on staying in our cabin most of the trip, so no real contact with such behavior will be necessary," Sigrid assured Greta.

"It served as a troopship but was turned into an ocean liner following the war," said Dorcas, ignoring the exchange, immersed in the history of the liner. "The ship routinely travels to Hamburg from its U.S. port."

"It will be a much better experience traveling by sea now than when you and Pa first came to this country," Sigrid said, trying to ease the anxiety she saw on Greta's face.

"I very much want to see Dieter and Germany again, Sigi," said Greta, taking her daughter's hand. "But to think about departing from my home that I have known for forty years . . ." She looked out the window at the blue sky, the crisp white of yesterday's light snow. "Outside of one church trip to Ohio, I have done no traveling in all this time."

"I believe it is time for such a trip, then," Sigi said, smiling. "I yearn to see our homeland finally after all your years of stories and descriptions of food, scenery, and customs. I can't wait for you to show me everything." Her eyes shone with anticipation. Greta swallowed hard and squeezed Sigrid's hand.

"You're right," she said with resolve. "Dorcas, the Leviathan sounds perfectly fine for us. And thank you very much for making arrangements for us to stay with your cousin in Baltimore."

"It is my pleasure," Dorcas said, breaking a piece of the apple bread and popping it into her mouth. "Now, we will have to make a trip to the local train station to put a final travel schedule from Peru to Hoboken. That should just about do it. Lena, this apple bread is a gift from our Lord."

In March of 1932, two weeks before departure was scheduled, Greta and Sigrid met at Fredrick and Lena's farm. The early spring sun soaked the ground, and the tulips and crocuses peeked out from under the remaining snow. As the sun warmed the woods, the three women walked to the nearby stone circle.

Greta felt a deep sense of calm as she stepped into the ring of stones. She always seemed to gain solace there, standing in a circle and holding the other women's hands as they prayed. She reached one hand out to Lena and the other to Sigrid, and the three women closed their eyes.

"Lord, grant us a safe journey to Germany and bless Oscar and Otto while Sigrid and I are away," she prayed. "Amen."

"Amen," intoned the two other women. The three stood clasping hands in silence following the prayer, bathed in birdsong and sunshine, as if to allow Greta's words time to reach heaven. Greta felt Sigrid's grip tighten, and she breathed deeply through her nose as a soft breeze played about her. She had a feeling she knew precisely what Sigrid was silently praying for.

After another few moments, the women opened their eyes. As they made their way back to the house, Greta took her daughter's arm, saying quietly, "With the Lord, a day is like a thousand years, and a thousand years is like a day. In His own time, He will answer your prayer." Sigrid gave a tight, sad smile.

28

The Fatherland

(Der Vaterland)

April 11, 1932

Greta watched Sigrid peer out of the train car, her cheeks pink and her eyes wide. The city of Berlin was coming into view, and Greta felt a thrill. The moment her foot had hit German soil, memories had flooded back. The sounds of voices speaking her first language as they showed their U.S. passports and exchanged dollars for marks, the smells of local food, and even the unique shape of the streets made Greta feel she was home again.

From Hamburg, they had immediately boarded a train for a half-day journey to Berlin, where Rudolph would meet them. Now known as the "world fashion center," Berlin was full of stylish buildings that appeared as the train approached.

"What do you think?" she asked Sigrid.

"It's all so . . . new," Sigrid said, scooting closer to her mother. Greta smiled reassuringly. Sigrid was thirty-three years of age, but this was her first trip, even a few hours away from home.

Sigrid stretched, turning away from the window. "I can't wait until we don't have to sit around," she said. "How long is the trip to Uncle Dieter's house from Berlin?"

"Oh, sweet girl," Greta said. "It is not very long. And trust me when I tell you this trip was so much better than the voyage your papa and I went on." Indeed, Greta had mused on the ship that despite the fact that she had more than doubled in age since her first journey, she was pretty comfortable. The train trip and arrival in New Jersey went without complication. Dorcas had arranged everything, and her cousins helped the two pilgrims to the port of embarkation. On the ship, aside from meals and an occasional walk on deck to take in the air, Greta and Sigrid spent eleven days praying and reading the Bible in the small but cozy cabin. The ship had made its routine stops around England before docking in Hamburg on Monday, the 11th of April.

The train let out a terrific whistle as it slowed and finally stopped at the crowded platform in Berlin. Greta and Sigrid, bags in hand, stepped off the train and into the crowd. Greta was smiling to herself; it had been over forty years since she had been to Berlin, and it felt wonderful to be back.

"Everyone seems to be in a hurry," Sigi said as they walked towards the wide front doors after visiting the modern toilets at the train station. Greta was about to explain it as simply the bustle of the city, but as the flat city air hit their faces, it became undeniable that something had changed. The smile fell from Greta's face as she took in the scene.

Stores were boarded up, and personal belongings and furniture were piled in front of the buildings. A Jewish star of David had been crudely painted in white on the side of the abandoned shops. At both sites, the word "Jude" had been scrawled under the six-pointed stars. "Juden Raus" posters hung in the public squares.[32] In the distance down the street, Greta and Sigrid could see a group of men marching and singing, all wearing brown paramilitary clothing.

"Perhaps one of the political factions that Rudolph wrote about," Greta mumbled to Sigrid, hoisting up her bags and walking faster. "Sigi, you are right. This is not exactly the Berlin I recall."

Sigrid pointed out a blue-and-yellow telephone call box across the way near a legless soldier in a World War I uniform, seated on the ground and begging for change.

"Come," Greta said, tightening her grip on her bags and striding forward.

"Watch out!" Sigrid cried.

Greta started as someone ran right past her, wheezing and almost knocking Greta over. As Greta dropped her bag and grabbed Sigrid's shoulder for balance, another man appeared not two feet from them.

"Herr Hitler is our rightful leader!"

Both women jumped back as a younger man, who sported a red swastika band on his left sleeve, struck his fleeing quarry. The older man fell, stumbled to his feet, and fled once again.

"Hindenburg! Hindenburg!" shouted the man as he sprinted, a hand clamped to his streaming nose. Cursing, the other man resumed his pursuit.

"Hurry," Sigrid said. Looking carefully from side to side, the women rushed to the telephone booth. Greta waited until she was safely inside to collect a few German coins from her purse and make a phone call to the business number Rudolph had sent

32   "Jews Out"

her. Nervously, she watched Sigrid through the glass panes of the booth door; Sigrid was standing in front of the pile of luggage, her back up against the phone booth.

In one ring, the receptionist answered.

"Hello, is Rudolph Bach there?" Greta asked.

"May I take a message?"

"Yes, I am Greta Beck. My daughter and I—"

"Oh, yes, Herr Bach has been waiting for you. One moment, please." A few seconds later, Rudolph answered the phone.

"Greta, welcome," he said. "Where are you?"

"We are across the street from the Central Station by the blue-and-yellow telephone box. We are wearing black dresses and white head coverings," Greta told Rudolph.

"Okay, just stay there," said Rudolph. "I will be driving a blue sedan, an Audi. I'm in a brown suit and blue tie. I will be there in forty minutes."

"Rudolph, Berlin seems to have gone mad," Greta said. "It does not feel safe. Please hurry."

"Ah," Rudolph said. "I should have guessed some upheaval after Hindenburg's win. I will do my best. Please try to find a quiet corner." Greta could hear him shuffling papers off his desk as they said their goodbyes.

Outside the telephone booth, Greta and Sigrid camped out on a bench with their luggage. Luckily, the weather was warm and comfortable, with a slight breeze redolent with unfamiliar sour city smells. Sigrid gazed at the disabled war veteran sitting on the sidewalk.

"It seems there is large-scale unemployment here," she said to Greta.

"The economic depression has taken a toll, no doubt," Greta

said. "But I feel it is more than that. Rudolph mentioned that Hindenburg won the election against Hitler yesterday."

"Oh," Sigrid said. "I am not quite sure what that means."

"I know we do not pay attention to such things, but with our trip on the horizon, I did do a bit of homework," Greta admitted. "Paul's letters have also been informative, and you've read those as well. Do you remember him mentioning the National Socialist Workers Party, no?" Sigrid, who was watching as a wave of new passengers exited the station, shook her head.

"They seem to want to rid Germany of Communists," Greta explained quietly, deliberately speaking English. "Most Americans feel any movement that could dissolve the Bolshevik's ascension in Germany is worth supporting, having seen what has happened to Russia since 1917, so they support the socialists. That is the party that just won the election, thanks to Hindenburg."

"Then who are all these angry people?" Sigrid asked, gesturing in the direction of the shouting and singing. "They support Herr Hitler?"

"Yes," Greta said. "The leader of the Nazi Party. Apparently, certain audiences find him mesmerizing when he speaks. Though his writings condemned Jews, in America, that is dismissed as just repeating what has been repeated for centuries . . . something done to appease some German antisemitism and nothing more."

Greta glanced nervously at the vandalized buildings with their anti-Jewish graffiti. "The few in America who have read Hitler's book don't seem to take it too seriously, either. Even those who agree with his views feel he'll never be given the power to act upon his racial purity campaign, according to some of Paul's letters."

"It seems they were wrong," Sigrid said.

"At least he lost this election," Greta said.

The women waited anxiously, staying alert, looking out of place as usual in their austere clothing. Finally, a shiny auto rolled to a stop in front of their bench. Out stepped a man in his mid-fifties dressed in a fine mohair suit and a matching hat over his graying hair. On his lapel, he wore a small enameled black, white, and red flag pin, and a broad smile caused his eyes to crinkle.

"Welcome back to Germany," he said in accented English, then switched immediately to German as he walked around the front of the car to greet the women. "Greta, you look much the same as when I last saw you!"

"How good to see you," Greta said with a relieved smile. "It's wonderful to be here, Rudolph."

Rudolph placed the women's bags in the back of the car, then settled Greta in the passenger seat. As they left their post, Sigrid tapped the disabled veteran on the shoulder and handed him a coin. Rudolph frowned at this but said nothing.

Circling the city to the motorway and heading northeast out of Berlin, the three-spoke easily about America, Dieter, changes in Germany, Rudolph's wife and son, and Greta's family. Sigrid could hardly keep from pressing her face to the window as the fantastic buildings and people rolled past.

"I am sorry the city is in an uproar today," Rudolph said. "We should come back to shop before you leave when things are a bit calmer. Anna and I come here regularly, and I've never seen it like this."

"I think it would be wonderful for Sigrid to experience a real German city under better circumstances than today," Greta agreed.

"We noticed certain shops in the city are boarded up and have furniture piled outside," Sigrid said.

"Jewish-owned businesses," he replied. "The National Party—you may have seen them, the SA, wearing their pressed brown shirts marching in the streets—they have taken to confronting the 'undesirables': Jews, Gypsies, and Marxists."

Greta made eye contact with Sigrid in the rear-view mirror as Rudolph stopped at a stop sign. "Those groups are being challenged for their lack of unity and love of this country," he said. "These ideas are beginning to become popular mostly in Berlin, but occasionally in the North too, where Dieter lives."

"I see," Sigrid said into the awkward silence. Rudolph took a hand from the wheel to adjust his thinning hair.

"I can't say that some of those outliers don't deserve the harassment," he said. "I find myself arguing over such things every time I visit Dieter, discussing who is right and who is wrong. He has extreme opinions and can get quite upset with me."

"As true Anabaptist believers, we try not to harbor opinions about political affairs," Greta said, keeping her voice neutral.

"Then we should get along very well indeed," Rudolph said with a laugh.

The two-hour ride to Dieter's small farm near Butzow passed quickly. Sigrid, used to glacier-flattened Indiana, marveled at the rolling hills of the German countryside. As Rudolph's car traveled by the forest area south of Butzow, a Gypsy wagon trundled by them on the other side of the road headed west.

"Look, Sigi!" said Greta. "A Jenische wagon."

"Yes," said Rudolph. "The northern vagrants are beginning to leave for Poland, Denmark, or anywhere else that will take them.

You see them moving out more in the larger cities, but those who live in the countryside are beginning to get the message, too. I know one subcontractor working for the Nationalists; he says they may build small centers to help with the Gypsies' reeducation, teaching them real work skills that benefit the fatherland. The drifting rabble doesn't seem to value the same things most loyal Germans do, after all." He snorted.

Greta's mouth fell open, but she quickly closed it as Sigi said, "Is that so?" from the back seat. Subtly, Greta found herself glancing back at Sigrid's reaction. Sigrid's eyebrows were drawn together as she watched the colorful wagon pass. Then Greta glanced at Rudolph, who was humming to himself as he traversed the long, straight road. She did not wish to insult her host, so she said nothing. She stared out the window, the sun playing comfortably over her face as the car rumbled beneath her.

"Ah, here we are," Rudolph said. Greta jerked awake, not realizing she had dozed off. Looking ahead, they could see Dieter's home by the woods.

"Much has changed since I last saw this place," Greta commented sleepily as Rudolph pulled into the drive.

"Yes, we have made many improvements since you last were here, though Dieter would have been just as happy to have left everything just as he had built it fifty years ago," Rudolph said with a laugh as he stopped the car.

"Hello," a querulous voice said as they stepped out of the auto. Greta turned, and in the doorway of the remodeled home at the Tarnow forest edge stood Dieter. Greta was shocked to see how much he had changed. He was much more frail now, and his hair and beard were snow white. He slowly limped with his cane to the drive where the car was parked, then stood holding open his arms out to embrace Greta.

"It is such a happy day for me," he said as he held Greta and gently patted her back. Tears welled in his eyes as he looked over Greta's shoulder and saw Sigrid holding her bags.

"Sigrid," he called out in his hoarse, raspy voice, "you are as beautiful as your mother." He reached his hand to her, and watching Sigrid take Dieter's hand, Greta felt tears slipping down her cheeks.

This was the right thing to do, she thought. *Had we waited another few months, it might have been too late.*

"Come," Dieter said, gesturing for everyone to enter his home. "Rudolph's wife and son are making supper. Rudolph helped me clean and prepare for your visit as well. He and his family are a godsend, to be sure." Greta looked around the home, breathed in the smells of German food, and found herself suddenly re-energized and looking forward to an evening of companionship.

Over a rich dinner of Eisbein pork hock with sauerkraut, mashed peas, and mustard, Dieter proved that he was eloquent and well-informed despite his advancing years. He had a good memory and spoke of growing up with Carl and Fredrick while Sigrid listened with sparkling eyes. The conversation started in a pleasant and family-oriented manner, and Greta enjoyed speaking with Anna. However, Max, who looked barely out of his teenage years, was quite shy and hardly spoke two sentences. However, the mood soured when it turned to the day's tumultuous political events.

"Though Hitler's rhetoric may not always prove popular with all of the Germans or the establishment, Hindenburg could still appoint Hitler as chancellor," Rudolph said as he cut off a slice of steaming pork and dipped it in the juices on his plate.

"I do not trust Herr Hitler at all," Dieter declared, his voice seeming to strengthen. "I have seen these types of men before. If he rises to power, it will be bad for everyone."

"I think what the Brownshirts are doing needs to be done to help Germany," Rudolph said. Anna and Max nodded. Greta, who took a large bite of peas to stop herself from saying something she would regret, was surprised to hear Sigrid pipe up in her stead.

"I don't believe it's so very Christian that Hitler and the— Brownshirts, is that what you called them?—are taking it upon themselves to harass Gypsies and destroy the Jewish people's ability to earn a living."

Greta swallowed, looking at her brave, clever daughter. Perhaps her tongue had been still for too long.

"We are commanded to love our neighbors as ourselves," Greta said, picking up her glass of water. "It becomes all too easy to discriminate one day and physically attack the next." Dieter nodded his wizened head in agreement.

"My personal experiences during the Danish War taught me that," he said a little too loudly, holding up his last forkful of pork and sauerkraut. "'Whoever sheds the blood of man, by man, his blood will be shed.' All this forced reeducation, rumors of people disappearing in the night and closing people's businesses in the cities . . . it can only end badly for Germany."

Dieter's face was turning red, and the rest of the guests had suddenly become quiet. Greta gently cleared her throat, then reached out to pat Dieter's frail arm.

"Sigrid and I would like to walk tomorrow in the woods if you don't mind," she said with an artificially bright smile. "It is still a bit early for mushrooms, but the flowers are beginning to bloom now, and the weather is beautiful."

"Tomorrow will be a good day for a hike," said Rudolph, lighting a cigarette and seeming relieved at the change in conversation. "There is no rain on the horizon. My goodness, dear, you look tired," he said, looking up at Anna, who was stifling an enormous yawn and staring down at her empty plate. She looked back sheepishly.

"I think it is time we returned home, dear," said Rudolph to Anna. "You and Max must be tired from cleaning all day. Sigrid and Greta, let us plan a sightseeing trip to Berlin in a day or so. Things should be back to normal there by then."

"That would be welcomed," said Sigrid.

"If you want," Dieter added, "you can take my horse and wagon tomorrow on your forest adventure. I don't travel much anymore, and when I do, Rudolph usually takes me. I won't be needing the mare or wagon tomorrow anytime." He smiled, his grin yellow and missing a few teeth but brimming with kindness. Greta smiled back, grateful for the gift of these precious days with Dieter.

29

The Answered Prayer

(Die Erhöhten Gebete)

April 12–15, 1932

Sigrid and Greta had already begun preparing breakfast when Dieter hobbled into the kitchen the following day.

"How is my little family this morning?" Dieter asked, smiling to see Sigrid frying eggs on the stove.

"Wonderful," Greta said, bringing Dieter a fresh cup of buttermilk from his wooden, zinc-lined ice box. "The weather is beautiful today. Sigrid was up and exploring your farm early this morning. She fed the pigs and gathered eggs before I even went outside." Facing the window, she closed her eyes, letting the morning sun warm her face.

"We did so much sitting around on our journey," Sigrid said, her eyes bright as she placed a basket of rolls on the table. "I am ready to explore today."

"My goodness, thank you for doing all my morning chores," Dieter said as the two women joined him at the table in front of a spread of eggs, thinly sliced ham, and rolls with butter and preserves. "I will get the wagon for you after breakfast so you can go on your adventure. I need to check on the two calves in the pasture, but it shouldn't take long before you'll both be off."

After saying grace, Dieter pulled his plate toward him with enthusiasm.

"I went to a restaurant once in Berlin," Dieter said, spreading a thick layer of butter onto his dark roll. "The waitress came to me and said, 'I have calf brains, frog legs, and pig's feet.' I said, 'Oh, you should see a doctor immediately.'"

Dieter began to laugh hysterically, gasping as he set his roll down. Greta and Sigrid stared, then burst into laughter as well. The whole table was unable to take a bite for some time.

As the three ate, joked, and talked of their relatives in Scandinavia, Germany, and America, Greta felt herself warmed from the inside out.

"I feel so welcome here with you again in my home country," Greta said. "It is clear that despite all you have been through, you have managed to stand by your beliefs and values all these years."

"You remind me much of Uncle Fredrick in many ways," Sigrid said. "I feel so fortunate to have met you."

Dieter paused as he brought a forkful of eggs and ham to his mouth. "That is very kind of you," he said. "And you are so welcome. Both of you."

"I only wish Oscar could have joined us," Greta said.

"I wish I could have seen Oscar again," Dieter admitted, reaching for his buttermilk. "But it means the world to me that the two of you are here." He smiled warmly at Sigrid, who beamed back.

After breakfast, Sigrid and Greta loaded the wagon with

cheese, bread, and milk for their lunch, along with oats for the mare's lunch. The air was cool, but the sun warmed their faces as Greta took the reins and automatically guided the wagon on the route to the forest. She had replayed the route many times in her mind over the last forty years.

"Around this bend is the spot where your father and I encountered Gypsies decades ago," she said to Sigrid as they rounded the corner. Neither woman was surprised to see a small vardo wagon parked at the edge of the road.

"It must be an established spot of theirs," Sigrid said quietly, waving to the old man who had unhitched his wagon and was tending his horse. Greta slowed her wagon, stopping next to the trailer.

"Good morning," she said cheerfully.

"Are you lost?" the old man asked, looking up with a somber expression.

"No," Greta replied. When the man continued to stare, she went on. "My daughter and I are visiting my uncle. We live in America now, but I have been here before, many years ago. I once met a Jenische woman here when I was young."

"Does something make you think I would know such a woman?" the man asked, furrowing his brow.

"I only thought perhaps you might know what became of her," Greta answered carefully. Was she scaring this man?

"What was her name?" the man asked as if he doubted her story.

"Tshura."

The older man's face suddenly relaxed. His body language shifted, and he patted his horse on the nose.

"Yes," he said, removing the bridle from his horse, whose

chestnut coat shone in the spring sun. "She was well known; may God grant her eternal peace. I am sorry to have been so coarse with you; it's just that one cannot be too careful of people who ask questions."

"I understand," Greta said, remembering the hostility in the city. As the man tended his horse and Sigrid listened, Greta told the man of her encounter with Tshura years ago and how many of her predictions had come true.

"Tshura was blessed, but some say also cursed," the man said, nodding as he bent down and grabbed a coarse brush. "Knowing the future, she foretold to us that a day would arrive when evil people would take over Germany and come for the Gypsies. They never have accepted us fully, but now most believe that the time she spoke of has come."

"We have not been here for long, but we have also noticed that the people here seem defensive and frightened," Sigrid said.

"Most Jenische can no longer just blend in," the man affirmed, running the brush over his mare's coat and earning a soft snort of pleasure. "Many are trying to leave Germany, but it is too late for some. My wife and I are going to Denmark and away from this country in two days. All the arrangements are in place. I know we will be safer there."

The man looked tired as he patted his horse's flank. Greta listened, hearing the sadness in the older man's voice. She wondered if the horse would be going to Denmark, too.

"We must go now," Greta said. "May God keep you safe. We will stop to talk again if we see your wagon before you leave."

"Thank you for your kindness," the man said. He waved as Greta drove her mare forward on the winding forest road.

"I remember the story of your encounter with the old

German Gypsy fortune teller," Sigrid said as they rode. "I am glad to see real Jenische people finally."

"Yes, although I wish they weren't so unwelcome here," Greta said, glancing around as she approached another bend in the road. The forest was not the same as she'd remembered; what had once been small trees were now fully grown, and new ones had filled the once-empty spaces.

"Hmm," she said, spotting the small stream where Oscar had once parked their buggy. She recognized the hill beside it that they had climbed together. "I think this is it."

The two women climbed down from the wagon, and Sigrid securely tied the mare by the brook.

"How strange to finally be in the place that inspired Papa to arrange our stone circle," Sigrid said quietly, looking around.

"It should not take us long to find the original," Greta said, looking up the steep hill, which was colored with new spring flowers and green grass. After feeding the mare her oats, Greta seized a sturdy stick to help her climb the rise as she and Sigrid began ascending.

Midway up the hill, Greta stopped to rest. "The hill has become higher than it was all those years ago," she laughed, breathing hard.

"No doubt," said Sigrid. After a minute, she reached back and took Greta's hand, and together, they reached the top of the ridge.

"This seems like a fine place for a picnic," Greta said. "It has already been quite a while since breakfast, I believe."

Sigrid obediently opened her cloth sack. She was eager to continue to the stones, but she didn't want to rush Greta, who looked glad for the rest. Mother and daughter shared dark rye bread, butterkäse, and dried apple rings under the clear April sky, enjoying the singing of the spring birds and the light breeze that played across their faces.

"The foliage is not so different from Indiana," Sigrid commented as she finished off a piece of bread.

"No, it is not," Greta said, beginning to pack up the remains of their picnic. "That was a surprise when Papa and I arrived in Indiana. Now, let us move along. I think the stones are a bit further ahead." She stood, adjusting her dress and pointing.

Sigrid's heart pounded as she and her mother walked forward for a few minutes. The memories of Greta's stories at bedtime flooded back to Sigrid, and she suddenly looked about, on the watch for wolves.

"Still too early for pilz," Greta said wistfully, looking at the mushroom-free ground as they walked. "Ah, yes, right up there." Just as Greta had remembered, there stood the six moss-covered stones evenly spaced in a circle.

Sigrid felt her heart sink a little. *Sure, they're big, but they look like common boulders covered with lichen*, she thought. Not wanting to disappoint her mother, however, she pretended to be enthusiastic about the monoliths.

Greta took Sigrid's hand and walked forward into the circle. Sigrid watched her mother close her eyes and tilt her head back, a slight smile on her lips. Sigrid followed suit and closed her eyes, still feeling a bit disappointed. The sweet smell of the woods hung in the air as the old trees above creaked, moaned, and gently swayed in the wind.

As the breeze moved about her, Sigrid felt the temperature shift. Soft hands seemed to touch her head. A lightness overtook her, and a sweet cinnamon cookie smell filled her nostrils. Without meaning to, she found herself saying a silent prayer:

"Lord, please help me have a child of my own.

Lord, please help me have a child of my own."

Sigrid could not tell how much time had passed when Greta gently squeezed her hand and slowly began to move from the circle. Sigrid unconsciously followed her, feeling dazed. A few small white feathers blew past her in the strange breeze.

"It is very peaceful, don't you think?" Greta asked, gazing up at the slowly dancing tree branches.

"What?" was all Sigrid answered, still not sure what had just taken place. Greta gave her a knowing glance, saying nothing more as they started their descent down the hill to the waiting wagon below.

The two women made their way through the woods and down the hill, both lost in their minds. Sigrid untethered the mare, and the two climbed back into the wagon and drove through the winding forest.

"It is, just as you said, very beautiful here, Ma," Sigrid said as the mare clomped her way back down the path. "I know now why you have missed this forest so much."

"It is special to me," Greta said, smiling.

In the circular trip, the two took a cross-country path across a field to a road leading back to Dieter's farm. Dieter was splitting kindling for the stove as the women pulled the wagon into the barn, the sun straight above him.

"Did you have a good jaunt?" he asked in his grandfatherly manner.

"Oh, yes," Sigrid said.

"No wolf encounters," Greta added.

"Seems the only wolves in Germany these days are the two-legged kind from Berlin," Dieter said with a laugh, whacking a piece of kindling in two.

"I think it's time to prepare lunch for you," Greta replied, eyeing Dieter's thin frame. "Make sure you wash before you come in." Dieter happily waved his calloused, soiled hands at her.

* * *

A few peaceful and companionable days had passed when, soon after sunrise, Rudolph's Audi pulled into Dieter's lane. Sigrid was returning from the barn, and she strode over, egg basket in hand, to greet him.

"Good morning," Rudolph said to Sigrid. "Would you and Greta care to join me in the city today?" He looked up at the sky to check for any possibility of rain; it had poured the day before, but today, the sky was clear and bright.

"Yes, very much," Sigrid replied. "Please come in to eat. Ma is cooking plenty of food, and Dieter will be happy to see you."

As the four sat down to breakfast, Rudolph outlined their plans for the day: shopping and a meal at his favorite restaurant.

"The trip won't take long, and we'll be back by evening," Rudolph assured Dieter. "Perhaps you'd like to join us."

"No, thank you," Dieter said. "I will be just fine here. Please be careful, though. The city can be dangerous nowadays."

"I think the day you arrived was extraordinary because of the election," Rudolph said, looking at Greta and Sigrid. "As long as we stick together, the city will be safe today."

Greta looked at Sigrid, a question in her eyes. Sigrid smiled brightly, showing she was not concerned. She had enjoyed spending time with Dieter, but she was excited Rudolph had offered the trip. Berlin, on a typical day and without the burden of luggage, would provide a welcome excursion and a look into German culture before they left the following week.

By ten o'clock, the trio had arrived in downtown Berlin. Parking his automobile, Rudolph set about taking Greta and Sigrid to the various street shops. This part of the city appeared more normal to Sigrid than the chaos she'd witnessed upon arrival. Some passersby looked harried as they walked past, but others appeared unconcerned and even happy. People with shabby clothing and looks of desperation loitered in corners, but there were also friendly shoppers examining the dry goods, furniture, and foodstuffs available for sale. Sigrid had fun picking out small gifts from a number of shops for Rachel, Daniel, and the rest of their family.

"Mama, is this part of the city quite different from what you remember?" Sigrid said, leaving a store with a beautiful little painted top for Daniel wrapped in paper.

"Yes, it is," Greta said in a faraway voice. Sigrid's spirit dampened a little when she saw the look on her mother's face.

"How has it changed?" she asked. "I want to know."

"The Great War seems to have quelled the people's spirits, I think," she said slowly. "An air of seriousness and uncertainty hovers, even over the various shop owners trying to be cheerful."

"Things are tenuous now," Rudolph agreed as they made their way down the street. "With the economic depression and the German struggle for identity, no one really knows what to expect day to day. I believe it will eventually be the ruin of the Weimar Republic. But that doesn't mean we can't have an enjoyable day out," he added with a smile, pointing at a small stationery shop and bookstore across the street.

After a few hours of shopping and lunch at a lovely traditional restaurant with an outdoor garden, Greta adjusted her growing cloth sack. It now contained a few items of clothing for Dieter as well as groceries for the evening meal.

"Perhaps returning to check on Dieter would be best," she said.

"Yes, I believe we've seen quite a bit of the city now," Rudolph said. "This way." He strode ahead to check on his car while Sigrid and Greta came more slowly behind.

"Mama, what do you suppose will happen here?" Sigrid asked in English, wanting to be discreet. "Do you think Dieter and Rudolph will be safe?"

"That is a good question, sweet girl," Greta said, also in English. "I am glad Dieter lives in the country. He is away from any turmoil that may take place here, and I believe he is too old to leave in any case."

"And Rudolph?" Sigrid asked, scooting closer to Greta. Neither woman noticed the disheveled young lady who followed at a short distance.

"Oh, I don't think he wants to leave, do you?" Greta asked with a pointed look. Sigrid nodded, understanding her point, as the two women reached the car.

"All set!" Rudolph said. But before the women could enter the car, the young woman who had followed them stepped in front of Sigrid. She had wide, frightened, dark-brown eyes like a deer's, matted, dark hair, and a dimpled chin that quivered as she pushed a large, filthy bundle into Sigrid's arms.

"Please!" she said in English in a hoarse whisper, her arms

shaking. Sigrid stood frozen, looking into her arms at the stunned little girl she was now holding. The little girl was a miniature version of her mother, down to the dimpled chin, dark hair, and luminously pale complexion. Upon her worn frock lay a small silver Star of David pendant.

"What is it you want from us?" Greta said to the woman in German. The woman quickly glanced around her as if she was being pursued.

"Please take my child," the woman said in rapid German with a heavy Slavic accent. "Her name is Yanna. I cannot take a small child to where I'm going." The woman looked over at Rudolph, who had approached and was glowering at her.

"They are Jews," Rudoph blurted out, looking at Greta and then Sigrid.

Sigrid looked back at the woman. The desperate mother stared intently back, her large eyes red with tears. Deep inside, Sigrid felt something click into place. Her arms closed around the child.

"I will take care of her," Sigrid said in German. "I promise."

The woman stared and nodded. She slid a dirty cloth bag over Sigrid's shoulder.

"Clothes," she said. "Thank you. God bless you."

Bending down, she kissed her daughter on the forehead. Then, tearing herself away from the tiny grabbing arms, she fled down the street.

Removing her shawl, Sigrid wrapped the cloak around Yanna, whose cries of "Mama!" were drawing stares.

"Please get in the car, Ma," Sigrid said. Greta, who had been standing quite still, opened the door without hesitation and got inside. Sigrid quickly handed the crying child to her.

"Get us away from here, Rudolph, please," Sigrid said before sliding in and closing the car door. She watched through the window as Rudolph stared after the mother for a moment before closing his eyes, then opening them as if in resolve. He slid into the driver's seat.

"We are going back to Dieter's home, I assume?" Rudolph asked.

"Yes, quickly, please," Sigrid replied. She peered out the window as they drove away, but the girl's mother had already disappeared.

"Mama!" wailed the child.

"Hush, dear," Sigrid said, rubbing the girl's bony back. "You're safe now." With a start, she realized she hadn't even asked the woman's name.

30
The Bargain
(Das Schnäppchen)
April 15–24, 1932

R udolph drove quickly out of Berlin northward toward Butzow, the afternoon sun shining harshly through the west-facing windows of the sleek vehicle. Yanna, who seemed exhausted, was quickly lulled to sleep by the soothing and unfamiliar movement of the auto.

"How old do you think she is?" Sigrid asked Greta.

"No more than fourteen or fifteen months, I would think," she answered. "We need to be careful around the stairs at Dieter's home with this little one." In the front seat, Rudolph remained stoic, his eyes fixed on the road.

At Dieter's home, Sigrid and Greta hastened inside while Rudolph parked his automobile in the barn. Yanna had awoken and seemed confused, though not frightened, by the situation. Dieter, throwing the door open to greet them, immediately focused on Yanna.

"And who is this?" he asked.

As Rudolph came in to join them, laden with the day's shopping, Greta relayed all that had happened that morning in Berlin. Sigrid placed Yanna in her lap and offered her some water. The girl drank insatiably as Greta brought their tale to a conclusion.

"Such things occur more and more now in the cities, at least according to passersby and the neighbors," Dieter said. "The SA has harassed and terrorized Jews and anyone else that they feel burdens society. They blame Jews for all Germany's financial problems instead of the damned warmongers that got us into that losing war to begin with." Dieter scowled at the window as though the warmongers were peering inside.

"Try not to get too riled, Uncle," Greta said.

"Yanna must be very hungry, and it is time for our supper also," Sigrid said, standing. "Would you mind holding Yanna while Greta and I make something to eat?"

Dieter eagerly reached for the little girl, who blinked shyly as she was passed to him.

"Whew!" he exclaimed, tickling Yanna's ribs. "You smell!" Yanna giggled a high, sweet sound.

"I will give her a bath and change her after she eats," Greta said. "Poor thing."

"No need to wait," Dieter said, getting up and limping from the kitchen with Yanna. "Rudolph and I can handle that." Rudolph, wrinkling his nose, followed.

Greta prepared a simple meal of stewed vegetables and potatoes in some chicken broth. At the table, Sigrid mashed some cooked vegetables and meat into a bowl and spoon-fed Yanna, who was now clean and wearing a rumpled but unsoiled change of clothes, while they all ate.

"What do you intend to do now?" Rudolph asked as he swallowed a spoonful of the soup. He had been uncharacteristically quiet since they'd met Yanna.

"We must be very cautious about asking for help, I imagine," Sigrid said.

"We can't tell anyone outside this house about Yanna," agreed Rudolph. Yanna, hearing her name, looked at him, then looked around the room.

"Mama?" she said.

"Here, Yanna," Sigrid said quickly, offering Yanna more mashed vegetables. The hungry child took the proffered food eagerly.

"The authorities, especially the police, are in collusion with the Brownshirts," Dieter said. "They work together. Even though they say they want the Jews to leave Germany, I believe they want to be the sole force that ensures their riddance."

"That's about the sum of it," Rudolph said. "You will never be able to hide the girl here for long."

"Of course, we won't," Sigrid said, wiping some mashed vegetables from Yanna's chin. "She is coming to America with us. I am going to adopt her."

There was silence about the table for a moment as everyone absorbed this. Greta looked at her daughter's face, at the mouth set in a thin, determined line.

"Trying to get her back to America will also be impossible without papers," Rudolph said, his spoon clattering back to the table. "The port authorities have recorded that the two of you were alone when you came to Hamburg and will not permit you to take the child. In fact, if they discover she is a Jew, they will probably detain you or possibly worse." Everyone looked at Yanna, whose features were clearly Mediterranean and starkly unlike Greta and Sigrid.

"The best we can do is take the child to the police station and simply say that we found her abandoned while in the city," Rudolph said, lifting a spoonful of soup.

"No!" Sigrid said, setting Yanna's water glass down a little too hard and propelling droplets across the table. "I promised her mother that I would take care of her, and I will keep my promise."

"Sigrid and I met an old Jenische man yesterday who mentioned that he was going to Denmark in a few days or sooner," Greta said, stirring her soup without eating it, her gaze fixed on a spider making its lazy way across the ceiling. "How do you think he will get there?"

Rudolph scraped the bottom of his bowl with his spoon. "Most folk here know a farmer or two who lives north on the back roads by the canals," he said. "Those farmers run boats to Denmark for a price. There are safer spots for Gypsies and Jews in Denmark, France, and Poland, or so we've heard." Swallowing his last spoonful and leaning back in his chair, Rudolph eyed Greta. "They usually end up taking anything of value Gypsies or Jews have, including wagons, horses, or jewelry, as payment for a trip to Denmark. Since German currency has devalued, they'd rather have merchandise or animals than cash."

Greta glanced down at Sigrid, then nodded. "Thank you. I will go there now before they leave," she said, pushing back her chair and standing. "We happen to have a German Baptist from our church doing some work in Copenhagen. With a little luck, he can take Yanna from the Jenische and help arrange her transport to America."

"Ma, you are right," Sigrid said, jumping up. "I will go with you."

"There have been SA informers recently about this area, rural though it may be," Rudolph said. "The fewer people, the better, and remember, you are not a citizen. It might be an issue if the wrong people were to question us."

Sigrid could see arguing was futile. Leaning over, she said quietly into her mother's ear, "How are we going to pay them?"

"We will manage," Greta replied in a whisper as Dieter abruptly got up and limped out of the room.

"Dieter, we are going to leave," Rudolph roared, standing up from the table as well. "Where have you gone off to?"

"Wait a moment!" Dieter said. Sigrid, helping Yanna finish the remainder of the meal, listened to the sound of rummaging and the creaking of floorboards. Greta stood by the kitchen door, putting on her coat and bonnet, while Rudolph slipped back into his jacket, looking in puzzlement at the ceiling.

"What in the world is that man doing?" he said as they heard the terrific creak of a floorboard being pried up. Sigrid helped Yanna down from her chair just as Dieter came back into the room and walked up to Greta, taking her hand and passing her something cold and round. Greta looked down at what he'd handed off to her and gaped at the three Swiss 117-gram gold ingots in her palm.

"Jenische always wants something for their services," Dieter said. "Try to barter with these."

"Oh, Dieter," Greta said. Dieter closed her hand around the ingots and kissed her closed knuckles, smiling. Greta stifled a sob.

"I'll get the car," Rudolph said gruffly.

In a few moments, Greta once again entered Rudolph's automobile. She smiled at Rudolph, then felt a jolt of panic when a gleam around Rudolph's waist caught her eye.

"What is that for?" Greta asked, pointing to the Luger pistol partially concealed in a shoulder holster under his jacket.

"I travel to dangerous places at times," he answered.

"You do not intend to threaten the Gypsies, do you?' she asked.

"I will not threaten them," Rudolph said, pulling onto the road. "If they do not want to help the child, then there is little we can do to force them. Even if they agree, using Gypsies to transport and protect a small child is a bit like asking a wood fox to guard your laying hens." Rudolph glanced at Greta, his eyes glittering. "This way, right?"

Greta said nothing, simply giving Rudolph a curt nod. She knew that placing Yanna's safety with Jenische was the only chance she had to remove the child from a worse fate. The SA groups marching in Berlin, the panicked behavior of Jews and Gypsies—it all felt wrong.

Greta held the gold ingots tightly as Rudolph pulled into the Gypsy encampment. It was nearly six o'clock now, and clouds were beginning to mar the cheerful spring day. There were two other wagons now present, and several other Gypsy men and women were obviously preparing to leave. Greta recognized the older man that she had talked with during the prior encounter; he had been talking with who appeared to be his wife as they transferred some of their wares to another wagon, but now he and the other Gypsies straightened and looked warily at the car.

"Here," she said, passing Rudolph two of the gold ingots. "I will be back in a moment." Then she stepped from the car, waving to the Jenische group.

"Friend," she called out to the man. "I need to talk with you." The man's expression cleared, and he immediately came forward, gesturing for his comrades to carry on.

As quickly as she could, Greta explained the situation to the man, whose name turned out to be Luca. He seemed surprised, then sympathetic as she described Yanna's plight. When she was done, he waved two younger men over and started speaking in rapid Romani, gesturing to Greta. Greta nodded, guessing he was retelling her tale.

"Some of us are headed to Poland tonight," Luca told Greta in German. "We can help, but it will be risky."

"That's wonderful," Greta said, feeling something in her chest loosen. "I can't thank you enough. We will get Yanna and bring her right back here. And, of course, we are willing to pay." She handed Luca the ingot, and he immediately bit it and put it in his pocket with a nod.

Luca looked behind Greta and seemed to stiffen. Turning, Greta saw that Rudolph had climbed out of his car and was walking toward the group, casually tugging his jacket over the bulge under his left arm.

Oh, Rudolph, she thought, trying not to shake her head.

"What have you decided?" Rudolph asked, stopping beside them.

"They have agreed to help us take the child to Denmark, just like we discussed," Greta replied. "I will write a letter to one of my church members there for them to bring along."

Rudolph grunted, then took the younger male Gypsy's arm

and pulled him aside. He went just out of earshot and then began jabbering intensely to the man while Greta looked apologetically at Luca.

"I am sorry," she said.

"We are used to it," Luca said, shrugging. He watched as Rudolph walked back, swaggering slightly, while the younger Jenische trailed behind, looking annoyed.

"We must go bring the girl back now," Rudolph said to Greta. "The Jenische leave soon, and we don't have much time."

With a quick wave and a look of apology to Luca, Greta followed Rudolph to the car. As they drove away from the encampment, Greta turned to face Rudolph.

"What did you say to the young man? I hope you did not threaten him."

"No threats," answered Rudolph. "I just made it clear that I had friends on the police force in Denmark who would find out if the little girl arrived safely or not. They can make many lives uncomfortable if she doesn't." He unconsciously lowered one hand toward his gun. "I also promised to give another two ingots to his partner, who will be leaving for Denmark next week. They can split them any way they want."

Greta took a deep breath through her nose. His methods may be questionable, but at least Rudolph was attempting to protect Yanna. It was the most Greta could hope for.

As soon as they pulled up in front of Dieter's home, Greta rushed out the door and back into the house. Yanna was sitting on the floor, playing with some wooden spoons. A small smile spread across her face as she closed her hand around one of Sigrid's fingers.

"Quickly! I need to write a letter," Greta said. Dieter hastily fetched the needed supplies, and Greta scribbled out a note to

Paul along with an address of the German Baptist Church in Copenhagen.

"How did it go?" Sigrid asked, approaching with Yanna on her hip.

"It's all arranged," Greta said. "However, we must hurry. It is time to say goodbye to Yanna for now, sweet girl."

Sigrid bustled Yanna out to the car along with her clothing, which was now placed in a fresh sack with some food. Greta got in the back seat, and Sigrid passed Yanna to her, holding back tears. Yanna looked back at Sigrid with wide eyes as the car pulled away, and Sigrid stared back. The sun, now getting lower, found a hole in the clouds and bathed the scene in gold.

Holding the little girl close, Greta knew that so much now rested on the fate of this little child. Yanna may not have known Sigrid for a long time, but it was clear that Sigrid had already accepted the role of Yanna's mother. Yanna, for her part, stood and pressed her face to the car window as they rolled into the street, letting out a small whimper.

"Don't worry, sweet girl," Greta said. "You will see Mama Sigi again soon." Yanna sniffled, and Greta gave her a gentle squeeze.

At the vardo, Luca's wife carefully took Yanna from Greta. This last exchange appeared to be Yanna's breaking point, and the little girl, who had had a tremendously long and fraught day, began to cry. As she did, Luca's wife smoothed a hand through Yanna's hair, looking hard into her scrunched face. She said something quietly in the Yenish language.

"My wife says she believes this child to have some Jenische blood," Luca said, looking at Greta.

"I have reason to believe she is Jewish," Greta replied. Luca shrugged.

"Perhaps," he said, nodding. "And perhaps she is both. Nevertheless, we will care for her as if she is one of our own."

The older woman began singing a song in her Gypsy dialect as she and a younger woman took the child into a waiting vardo.

"Thank you," Greta said, staring at the spot where the women had disappeared into the vardo. "We have not had much time to get to know one another, but Gypsies have guided and protected me throughout my life. I am very grateful."

"We are good friends," Luca confirmed with a smile, "to those we recognize in kind."

From within a hidden pocket of her gown, Greta withdrew a simple wooden rosary. She handed it to Luca.

"This was given to me by a dear friend who saved my life," she said. "I now give it to you to protect you on your journey."

Luca's hand closed around the beads. He nodded, then looked up at Greta with renewed determination in his dark gaze.

"She will be safe."

Rudolph and Greta watched as the wagon pulled away through the forest, headed northwest underneath a sky thick with gray clouds.

"Do you think you will see Yanna again, truly?" Rudolph murmured.

"I know I will," Greta said.

* * *

Sigrid held Dieter's wrinkled hands in hers, looking into the clouded eyes that had become so dear in such a short time.

"I am so grateful for the final opportunity I have had to visit with my family from America," Dieter told her, squeezing her hands. "I am now at peace."

Sigrid tried hard not to cry, but she found that tears were slipping down her face nevertheless. She laughed as Dieter wiped them away with his thumbs.

The truth was that Sigrid had been crying a lot since Yanna had gone several days before. They had kept busy since then, helping Dieter organize and clean, preparing food, mending clothing, and generally putting things in order. After all, both she and Greta knew this would be the last time they would ever see their only direct living relative in Germany, and they tried to cherish every moment.

Sigrid had thrown herself into the manual labor of daily farm chores as much as possible, trying to distract her concerns. But every time her mind wandered, she saw Yanna's thin, pale face, and her mind flooded with all the horrible possibilities of what might be happening to her child.

"Here," Dieter said, handing Sigrid four small, heavy gifts wrapped in parchment. "For you and my dear nephew."

"Thank you, Uncle," Sigrid said. "For everything."

"Come along, now," Rudolph said, closing the trunk on their luggage. "I want to make sure we get there in plenty of time."

Greta and Sigrid both waved at Dieter as they pulled out of the drive. Sigrid tried to imprint the stooped older man and his pleasant grin deep into her memory. She never could have guessed how much this trip would change her life.

As they began the drive south towards Berlin, Rudolph cleared his throat.

"I made a phone call to the police department in Copenhagen yesterday," he said. Sigrid practically jumped out of her seat, trying hard to contain her fears.

"Please tell us, Rudolph," Greta said, reaching back to clutch Sigrid's hand. "Don't conceal anything."

"I can report that I paid the Gypsies last evening," he said, smiling even as he negotiated the highway ahead.

"So Yanna arrived safely?" Sigrid asked breathlessly.

"Yes, Sigrid, she is safe," Rudolph said. "My constable friend contacted your missionary, Paul, in person. Yanna is being well cared for. He told my friend that he will be contacting you soon."

"Oh, Rudolph," Sigrid said, unable to contain her emotions. "I know we haven't agreed on everything, but I can't begin to tell you how greatly this means to me."

"I think I understand, at least a little," Rudolph said, his eyes creasing at the edges as he smiled. "I, too, have a child."

As Sigrid sat in the back seat, staring in a daze out the window, Greta looked at Rudolph.

"Thank you for all that you have done for us and Uncle Dieter," she said. "God will bless you for your kindness."

"Dieter was my teacher," Rudolph replied. "It is I that should be thanking your family for sharing such a man with me all these years."

31
The Next Generation
(Die nächste Generation)
May–December 1932

"What if Paul finds trouble? What if he can't arrange to get Yanna out of Denmark?" Sigrid said, wringing her hands. "Rudolph said the SA has spies in Scandinavia who will turn in Jews for a price. What if this is all somehow tracked back to Dieter and Rudolph?"

Sigrid glanced at her mother, who was sitting in the window seat. Next to her, the Indiana landscape was a blur as the train sped along.

"Our Lord has told us that He will rescue those who love Him and will protect those who trust in His name," Greta said calmly, patting Sigrid's arm.

Sigrid squeezed her eyes shut, trying to breathe evenly. The voyage back to America had been anticlimactic; the two women had talked only superficially about Dieter, the German food they had eaten, and how calm the sea was during the return cruise.

Greta seemed too apprehensive to discuss the possibilities of what could happen to the child they had left in Europe, and Sigrid was not eager to bring it up either. But now that they were almost back home, she couldn't help but speak what she knew was on both their minds.

"But what if . . ."

"Now, sweet girl," Greta said. "You must have faith in our Lord. And, of course, in Paul. He does have a unique way of figuring these things out." She grinned, her eyes sparkling. Sigrid felt a little better despite herself.

"Next stop, Peru," the conductor said, walking through the car. The train began to slow, and Greta leaned closer to the window as the landscape solidified. It was now May, and the land was bursting with greenery adorned with cherry and redbud blossoms.

"Look," Greta said, and Sigrid leaned over her mother to peer out the window. Fredrick, Lena, and their children; Otto and his parents; and Oscar seemed to grow larger and more prominent on the platform as the train approached. The women's bonnets made them easy to recognize, even among others waiting at the station. Sigrid felt herself smiling at the sight of her beloved family. She'd waited on that platform so many times, but she'd never seen anyone waiting there for her before.

At the station, the two weary travelers were welcomed with pats, handshakes, questions, and endless jabbering about all that had happened while they had been away. Otto gently wrapped his arm around Sigrid's shoulders, and she fought the desire to clutch him and sob. Next to them, overcome with emotion, Oscar kissed Greta's cheek; they'd been apart for a month after having been constantly together for decades. The group held hands and bowed their heads, thanking God for the safe return of their loved ones.

"Come," Fredrick said, hoisting his mother's bag up and heading toward the car. "We will have a noon meal at my house."

"That's perfect," Greta said as the families got into two vehicles and started the short drive to the farm. Sigrid found herself in Fredrick's vehicle with her parents and Rachel, who, at fourteen, was already as tall as Sigrid.

"You must tell us everything," Rachel said animatedly as she slid into the back seat with Greta and Sigrid. "Was Uncle Dieter well?"

"He was. How good it was to see Dieter again," Greta said fondly. " He sends good wishes to his family in America. I feel, though, that we should save our story for when we are all together at lunch. Otherwise," she said with a laugh, "we will need to tell it too many times over. So, tell me: what has been going on around here?"

"Everyone is healthy, and the crops are good," Oscar reported as Rachel pouted. "However, three more farmers from the Zion Church are being forced to sell their farms. The depression is devastating our community, I'm afraid."

Sigrid, who had been staring out the window trying to pull herself together, looked sharply at her father. Zion Church had taken on many new immigrants who had little capital, and the once-thriving community now appeared teetering on closing its doors. The loss of membership to the Church of the Brethren, which had brought forth the Dunkard Brethren Church, seemed to mark the Zion Church for extinction. Next to Sigrid, Greta shook her head.

"Oh dear," said Greta. "How many is that now?"

"It's up to a total of twelve farms, with others on the verge of bankruptcy," he replied. "Pastor Muller told me that the church district has decided on the matter. If the German Baptist church is to survive in North Central Indiana, there needs to be a consolidation of congregations and farms."

"That makes sense," said Sigrid. "A much larger unified community will stand a better chance for survival. It is essentially what our families have done—banding together to find strength in numbers but on a larger scale."

"Exactly," replied Oscar. "The district has asked the Old Order German Baptist Church in Camden to help with the situation. The parishioners who are financially struggling or who wish to 'sell-out' have been invited to join the New Zion Church forty miles away in Camden."

"It appears that now nearly half of the Zion Church is considering the move, and Deercreek Church has already made its plans," Fredrick added, his eyes fixed on the cloudy landscape as he drove.

"If the exodus occurs, and it now appears that it will," Oscar said, "Zion will not have enough membership for the district to recognize or support."

"I suppose the Brethren must do what is best for them and the church," said Greta. "However, I don't feel our congregation is able to move or sell only to try to purchase land elsewhere. It makes no sense." Sigrid nodded; the thought of uprooting their whole community, she thought, would be too great of a leap of faith for many in the Zion Baptist Brethren parish.

"I wonder if a reunification would help," Sigrid mused. "The Dunkard Church beliefs are practically the same as Zion's."

"It would be nice for us to all worship together," Rachel added with a smile, appearing to have recovered from having to wait to hear about the trip to Germany.

"There have indeed been several families from Zion and the Brethren Church who have switched and begun attending and worshiping with us over the past two Sundays," Oscar said. "The Dunkard Brethren at Loree have at least tried to hold to the old ways of dress and manner."

"We will all just have to see where God sends us," Fredrick said as the car pulled into the familiar drive.

"Sigrid, would you join me for a moment?" Greta asked. Sigrid, who was once again staring out the window, turned and nodded.

"We'll get your bags inside," Fredrick said with a nod.

Greta and Sigrid walked to the stone circle at the edge of the woods, where they stood facing each other and held hands. The scent of lilacs wafted from the nearby forest, and the warm spring sun shone down on the two women. Sigrid found that now that she had been to the original stone circle in Germany, this place had become even more meaningful to her.

"Dear Lord, thank you for the safe trip we had and for the visit with Dieter," Greta prayed.

"God, please bless Yanna's mother and keep her from harm," Sigrid said.

"Please reunite us with Yanna soon and protect her and Paul on their journey. Amen."

"Amen," said Sigrid, stepping closer to her mother and placing her head on the older woman's shoulder. They stood there for a moment as a flock of barn swallows swooped by, chirping sweetly. Then, hand in hand, the two women walked back to the house to help prepare lunch and catch up on all the events that had occurred since last seeing their families.

"I can't wait to give the children their presents," Sigrid said, looking a little happier than before. Greta squeezed her daughter's hand.

"Me neither, sweet girl."

There was much to do and many people to see after their arrival, and ultimately, it took two days before Sigrid mustered up the courage to tell Otto and Oscar about what had happened in Berlin. She knew her mother would not say anything until Sigrid was ready. In preparation, she invited Greta and Oscar over for lunch, making a batch of dumplings accompanied by the last of the fall pickles.

After everyone had eaten and was enjoying cups of butter-milk, she looked meaningfully at Greta.

"I'm ready," she said.

"I know," said Greta, setting down her milk. "I figured that's why you had us over. It is time to tell them."

"Tell us what?" said Otto and Oscar in unison.

The tale took nearly an hour to divulge. Oscar and Otto's expressions ranged from surprise and delight to fear and worry as the story progressed.

"I am concerned about the risk you took in helping to smuggle the child out of Germany," Otto finally said, his brows drawing together. "The repercussions might fall upon your uncle."

"Uncle Dieter had not only agreed with the adoption but also paid the Gypsies for their services in taking Yanna to Denmark," Sigrid said, trying her best not to sound defensive. "He acted of his own free will. And Rudolph has coordinated wiring money from Dieter to Paul to assist with Yanna's adoption arrangements under the same circumstances."

"Since Uncle Dieter is still as sharp as ever, we must trust his judgment," Greta said, the corner of her eyes crinkling as she smiled.

Otto smiled, too, his face glowing for a moment before the frown returned. "There is so much that could go wrong with such a plan and so many issues to consider," he said, holding up a hand. "The Danish and American governments will no doubt be suspicious of an adoption without provable family lineage of some type," he said, extending one finger. "There is no documentation to attest to the child's lineage; she could well become a ward of the state and end up in an orphanage or somehow even be sent back to Germany, where her ethnicity will soon be discovered," he said, raising a second finger. "Not to mention, it may be difficult even to find passage from Denmark at the moment," he said, raising another finger.

Greta sighed. "I do have my doubts that the plan we put into play may not be possible," she told her husband. "However, now we must put our faith in God."

"And in Paul Kunkle," mumbled Oscar. "I certainly hope he knows what he's doing."

* * *

Paul, in fact, did know what he was doing. While the Beck family sat discussing him on one continent, he reclined in the shabbily opulent sitting room of his friend and associate Pierre Delacroix, mentally running over his plan.

"Here you are, my friend," Pierre said, handing Paul a glass of red wine with his signature dashing smile. Pierre's dark hair was slicked across his head with ample pomade—Paul suspected this was to hide a growing bald spot, though he would never mention this—and his fine brocade jacket gleamed in the light of the fireplace on this unseasonably cool and drizzly spring evening.

Paul smelled the wine automatically, swirling the vermillion liquid.

"Exquisite bouquet," he said, peering at his glass. "Petrus, 1921?"

Pierre tilted his head. "1919. From my home in Bordeaux, of course. Domestic wine is dreadful."

"You are such a French snob," Paul said with a snort.

"Of course. Always. And how is Helga?" asked Pierre, taking the second upholstered chair by the fire, a once-fine hardwood antique that now featured some holes in its scarlet velvet upholstery.

"Helga is a smart, funny, and fetching young vixen," said Paul dismissively. "Perhaps at twenty, she is more than I can handle."

"You talk as if you were eighty," Pierre said with a laugh. "Mid-thirties is hardly ancient. Anyway, you seem to have more in common with her than you admit." He took a sip of his wine, raising his eyebrows at Paul. "I remember the night you met her at the pub. The two of you wouldn't shut up about politics, even with your poor Danish. You seem to share the same points of view on most things."

"Perhaps," Paul said, smiling.

"You find her so desirable despite her Jewish heritage?" Pierre asked, his bushy eyebrows moving even higher.

"And what of your Jewish heritage?" Paul asked.

"Hmm," Pierre said, raising his glass slightly. "I'm staying alive for now, at least." Paul leaned back in his chair, which groaned in response.

"Can you guess where Helga is right now?" Paul asked.

"I haven't the slightest theory."

"She is watching little Yanna, a child who needs your help, Pierre."

Pierre, who had been leaning casually against a wall and studying his wine, stood abruptly upright and stared at Paul.

"A child? Please indulge my curiosity."

Pierre stared into the fire as Paul laid out the difficulty.

"Monsieur Delacroix, I know you're no stranger to lineage modification," Paul said. "I remember what you did for those Nazi administrative hopefuls from Munich, blurring their Jewish heritage and creating a Scandinavian document trail. It was flawless."

"I do what I can," Pierre said, a flash of a smile playing across his face.

"I must ask if you're having any second thoughts about helping the Nazis now," Paul added.

"Prior to 1929, the Nazis had yet to expose their true selves in Denmark," said Pierre. "I didn't really know who or what I was helping back then."

"You're a mystery unto yourself, Pierre," Paul said, sighing and swirling the dregs of his wine. "Sometimes, it seems like you place fast cash ahead of ethnic loyalties."

"Don't insult someone you're trying to get help from, *mon ami*. Anyway, many Nazi collaborators, ironically enough, are Jewish," Pierre said, shrugging. "I suppose we believe it will help inoculate us from persecution somehow. Even so, in order to preclude any kike speculation, it is always wise for ambitious little Nazis to be in possession of a written testament of their Nordic extraction."

Pierre leaned back in his chair. "But now, this kind of work is commonplace. People are beginning to read the proverbial tea leaves. They're asking for assistance to create new identities and escape from what is beginning to become a genetic nightmare, much like your Yanna."

"Well, you can add Yanna to the top of your list, then," Paul said. Pierre frowned.

"Look," Paul said, standing and seizing the wine bottle from the table, then stepping over to refill Pierre's glass. "If you help me, I'll testify to everyone I know that you really are related to Eugene Delacroix, the 'celebrated artist,' as you claim."

Pierre laughed. "Oh, but I am!"

"Of course you are." Paul looked pointedly at his old friend. "You are an artist after a fashion; there is no question. You can duplicate almost anything in such a convincing manner that even those who are considered experts in document authenticity have difficulty discerning your forgeries from original works. You must have inherited that talent from somewhere."

Pierre took a sip of his refreshed wine as Paul poured more into his glass. "Flattery, *mon ami*? I am as much an artist as you are a pious German Baptist. You seem to know a little too much about wine and women, my friend, to be the temperate missionary you claim." Pierre grinned, glancing toward the window and past the dusty crimson drapes into the dark street. "Besides that, my 'art skills' have gotten me into a bit of trouble with the French authorities."

"I am a touch happy for your misfortune, for without that trouble, we would never have met," Paul said. Pierre raised his glass.

"Alright. I will help your Yanna," Pierre said.

"Thank you, Pierre," Paul said, leaning forward. His chest, already warmed by the wine, flooded with relief. "You will be saving a child's life. God will bless you." Pierre rolled his eyes.

"You will bless me with a hefty payment."

"Of course. You can name your price. But how will we do this?"

"Easy," said Pierre. "I have friends at the city morgue. They find a nameless, recently deceased street woman and assign her an identity with a relationship to the Beck family. This, along with the creation of a birth certificate for Yanna, a will, and a few carbon copies of letters—strategically notarized by a local lawyer who owes me a favor—acknowledging an American relative as a designated caretaker for Yanna. That should be convincing enough."

Paul couldn't help but look impressed. Pierre sipped his wine, impassive.

"That does sound convincing," Paul managed.

"Most Danish civil servants and port authorities are much too lazy ever properly to authenticate family relationships or heritage," Pierre said with a shrug of his slim shoulders. "If the child's pedigree appears authentic, the bureaucrats are more than likely to sign off and approve passage to America without a second look."

Paul nodded thoughtfully. "Perhaps clearing U.S. immigration authorities for entrance will be more difficult than departing Europe, then."

"I still have connections in New York. You know I lived there during the war to avoid the half-witted French Army conscription," Pierre said, leaning back and stretching out his legs. "These contacts can easily make notification of social services in Indiana for arrangements and official adoption."

"I am amazed by you," said Paul. "You have friends everywhere."

"I'm a popular artist, after all," Pierre said, nodding sagely.

"Now, what name would you like on the birth certificate? 'Yanna' won't do; it sounds too Jewish."

Paul looked at the ceiling, thinking. "What about Annie? Like Annie Oakley from *Buffalo Bill Cody's Wild West*? It sounds a little like Yanna so that it won't confuse her too much."

"Hmm. I don't think that's a proper name," Pierre said.

Paul snorted. "Anne, then. Queen Anne of Denmark it will be."

"As she should be," Pierre said, chuckling.

"I will arrange with the German Baptist mission sponsors in Indiana for passage once we arrive," Paul said, his chair giving another groan as he sank back into it. "I'll be sure to write to Sigrid to detail our plan. In all seriousness, I can't thank you enough, my friend."

Pierre smiled and drained his glass once more. "I hope Queen Anne enjoys America."

* * *

"Sometimes, I think it may have been easier to have been honest that Annie is Jewish. It certainly would have been cheaper," Paul said to Pierre about six weeks later, speaking in heavily accented Danish for the benefit of Helga. They were all sitting together at The Erik, their favorite pub. Yanna, who they now called Annie, sat placidly in Helga's lap, playing with a small wooden top Paul had purchased for her.

Paul pulled an envelope—money from Annie's benefactor—out of his coat pocket and handed it to Pierre. "We could have merely said Annie is escaping from the nightmare in Germany."

It was now late June, but the day had been cool and rainy. Paul looked out the window at a homeless woman who was trying futilely to shelter her two children under an awning. Denmark's government was rapidly falling into collapse, with thirty-two percent unemployment. The depression had fiscally ravaged the economy, and the evidence was everywhere in the form of dazed people huddled on the streets.

"Don't deceive yourself," Pierre said in much better Danish than Paul's, his glass of pilsner hitting the table with a soft thud. "Antisemitism is just as strong in America as it is in Europe. I've experienced it there; I know. Anne would find no rest from those who wish to torment her and her family were her true origin known." He glanced at Anne, then back at Paul. "It is best that neither you nor her new American family mention her roots."

"Goodness," said Helga. "That seems rather sad." She tossed a lock of her long, dirty blonde hair over Anne's face, causing the little girl to laugh and bat it away.

"It can't be helped," said Paul. "I may return home or even move to Sweden after all this is over. The Nazi party is not yet popular enough to take over Denmark, though rumors are spreading."

"Yes, perhaps New York is in my future as well," Pierre said, staring into his glass.

Helga adjusted Anne in her lap. "I suppose I'll just stay here and rot while the two of you enjoy America, then," she said. "I can't go anywhere with my parents, as their health is poor, and they are resistant to leaving Europe."

"Don't worry," said Paul. "You will hear from me." Helga brightened, her smile wide and welcoming.

"So romantic," Pierre said, rolling his eyes in mock disdain before his eyes landed on Anne again. "I truly enjoy special projects like this one, you know. I even got to choose Anne's new birthdate."

Paul flipped to the right page. "September 1, 1931?"

"I thought it had a nice ring to it."

The conversation stalled as a server set down hearty plates of smorrebrod—Danish open-faced sandwiches topped with cold cuts and cheeses. Paul thanked the server, hastily grabbing Anne's hand before she could seize a handful of cold cuts. Handing the child a single cold cut, he turned back to Pierre as everyone tucked in.

"I've sent a letter to the church to make travel plans," he said through a thick bite of rye and roast beef. "It had been several years since my last visit to America, and the district was quite busy. However, they respect foreign missions and want to help."

"It's a good thing your American church sponsors don't know of the company you keep here in Copenhagen," said Pierre, wiping pilsner foam from his lip.

"Ah, I've always been drawn to people like you," said Paul.

"Con artists?" said Helga teasingly.

"Creatives," Paul said, giving her a pointed look. "I am still faithful to God."

"Whatever you say," Pierre quipped, picking up a smorrebrod topped with pork and pickles. "Now, let's discuss something important. Are you and Anne both packed?"

"Oh, yes," said Paul, watching Annie break bits of bread off and stack them on the table. "I enjoy packing, actually. I've packed many photographs of the Sami people; I took them with my box camera. I collected many cultural items from them. I'll use them to present the results of my work after I deliver Annie to her new home."

"It's just like you to take full advantage of your travels," said Helga, holding a piece of bread to the child's mouth. Annie opened her mouth to protest, and Helga took the opportunity to stuff the bread into Annie's mouth. She immediately fell silent, chewing the bread and glowering.

"Why not?" asked Paul. "I've already received funding to travel back to America to present my work. I'll present to the German Baptist Brethren Church in Camden now that my original church home at Zion will be joining them. It's not an easy trip, but I'll do what I can."

The meal progressed in warm conversation, and afterward, Pierre and Paul shook hands.

"I wish you well, *mon ami*," said Pierre to Paul in fluid English. "You and your little fugitive." He winked at Annie, who buried her head in Paul's shoulder.

"We may see each other yet again," said Paul. He watched for a moment as Pierre turned, his slim, blade-like frame disappearing into the gathering darkness.

A week later, Paul's plan, with the help of Pierre's impeccable documentation, had commenced. Paul and Annie had had no trouble working their way through the port bureaucracy and securing a small cabin on the SS Frederik bound for New York. The ship would meander to ports in Oslo and Kristiansand. However, Paul and Annie never left the ship, instead staying much to themselves in their tourist second-class cabin. Other than a quick walk for fresh air, Paul only left the cabin for food. He knew the less he interacted with strangers, the better things would go.

At lunchtime, about halfway through the voyage, Paul, with Annie in his arms, was heading to the dining area.

"Walk," Annie said in German, pointing to the floor.

"Annie, I'm sorry," said Paul. "It is safer this way." Annie made a sad face, and Paul planted a kiss on her forehead. Despite the fawning passengers showering attention upon the cute little girl with the dimpled chin and round, dark eyes, Paul returned no more than ordinary superficial courtesy. Until Annie was safely in Sigrid's arms in America, Paul could not let his guard down.

Paul set Annie down at the food line.

"Hold onto my coat, Annie," he said, helping her grab the side of his jacket so he could seize two plates and soup cups. He shuffled along as surly-looking kitchen hands loaded up with potatoes, herring, and a gray liquid that Paul guessed was supposed to be soup.

Steering the little girl towards two seats at one of the long, narrow tables that filled the room, Paul set the dishes down. He hoisted Annie up into a chair and took a seat beside her.

"Here, have a potato," he instructed, spearing a small one for hers and handing her the fork. She chewed the potato as Paul began to take quick bites of his bland meal.

"Auntie?" asked Annie. Paul froze.

"Auntie Helga's in Germany," he said quietly. "We're going to go see your new mama in America. Do you remember Sigrid? She is going to be your new mama."

"Mama?" Anne's eyes grew huge, and Paul sighed.

Paul sighed. "No, I'm sorry, Annie. Let's talk about this in the cabin, okay? It is confusing for me, too."

Paul popped a piece of herring into Annie's mouth. "Would you like to help me write a letter to Auntie when we get back to our cabin?"

Annie nodded, smiling and chewing.

"Then afterward, we can work on more English, okay?"

430

Annie gulped down her soup. "Yes," she said in English. Paul grinned, then picked up his soup cup and took a big gulp, trying not to taste it too much. He had just decided to continue to correspond with Helga and perhaps ask if she would be willing to join him in America after he wrapped up his affairs in Europe. He knew America would be a safer place to serve the church now, as politics in Denmark and Germany were obviously headed in precarious directions.

Paul glanced at Annie, who had copied him and was sipping from her soup cup, holding it carefully in her tiny hands. Taking care of Annie was difficult, but she seemed content to have Paul read stories to her and play with small trinkets and toys most of the time. Paul felt a deep sense of accomplishment building within him as he watched her drink her soup, wrinkling her little nose slightly at the taste. It felt as if a void in his life was being filled.

I may have a knack for this, he thought as he helped Annie set her cup back on the table. For the first time in his life, marriage, and children seemed like a good idea.

32
Our New Sister in Christ
(Unsere neue Schwester in Christus)
August 1932–May 1933

Otto nervously paced back and forth as he waited for Sigrid to don her bonnet and coat. Looking around to make sure he wasn't forgetting anything, he saw the neat assortment of wooden toys he'd made over the past few weeks, working primarily with his left hand. They sat there, patiently waiting for their new owner.

The wait is finally over, he thought.

The couple left their modest farmhouse and drove to pick up Greta and Oscar for the much-anticipated reunion with their new daughter, Yanna. They'd received word that Paul and Anne would be arriving that day, the third of August, at half past twelve.

"I cannot believe how our Lord has blessed our lives," Sigrid said to Otto as the fields flew by. The day was already quite hot, and the windows of the car were halfway down to allow a breeze in.

"It is a bit like a dream that we will soon have a child of our own," Otto agreed.

"We must make sure to get to the hospital for Yanna's medical assessment by three o'clock," Sigrid said, jiggling her foot uncharacteristically as she sat in the passenger seat. "Monday morning, the Children's Bureau caseworker will visit as well . . . I must clean the house again."

"We must remember to call her Anne," Otto gently said. Sigrid nodded, blinking rapidly, and Otto put his eyes back on the road. There was no denying antisemitism had taken root in Indiana after the Klan's founding in 1920. So many politicians had become active members that political prominence had become nearly impossible without a Klan endorsement in the state. Thus, Otto knew a slip like uttering the name "Yanna" could be dangerous. They had to remain as close-lipped as possible regarding Anne's arrival and historical identity.

Turning into the Becks' driveway, Otto nodded to himself, then waved as Oscar and Greta came hurrying out of the house.

"Looks like she finished it," Sigrid said, pointing. Otto saw that Greta was holding a meticulously crafted hand-sewn doll, complete with shiny black buttons for eyes.

"Anne will like this," he said, hoping his voice sounded steadier than it felt.

Soon, Otto and Oscar stood waiting in the sweltering air at the train station for their first look at Anne while Sigrid and Greta buzzed with anticipation of seeing her once more. Otto glanced around the train station; as usual, he and his little group were conspicuous due to their garb and beards. After he and Sigrid left the Church of the Brethren in Peru for the small brick Dunkard Brethren Church at Loree, Otto had again grown his beard as a sign of marriage and a lifelong commitment to God. Likewise, Sigrid again wore her bonnet and cape. The Dunkard church, while having no issues with using modern conveniences, did commit to wearing plain clothing.

"It seems," Otto mused as he scooted closer to his wife, "that many of our life's pivotal moments have taken place here." As though in a trance, he looked out at the platform, thinking of the voices of soldiers singing a funny modern song he didn't know, of Elija's thin, white lips pressed together as they pulled out of this station, of silver snowflakes caught in Sigrid's golden eyelashes as she cried tears of happiness. How was it that such joy and such sorrow could concentrate on this place?

Sigrid slipped her hand out from the folds of her dress and took Otto's outstretched hand for a moment.

"That is certainly true," Greta said. "Although, Sigi, did you know your father and I didn't arrive by train when we first came?"

"No," Sigrid said. "How did you arrive?"

"Why, by buggy, of course," Greta said. "All the way from New York City. It took weeks and weeks . . . it seems so long ago now."

"We have spent enough time on this platform since then," Oscar said, wiping away a trickle of sweat. "Ah, look!" Oscar waved, and Otto turned to see two bearded German Baptist Brethren men walking over.

"They must be the district representatives from Camden," Sigrid said quietly. Otto nodded; these men had come to greet Paul and transport him back to his parent's home before his arranged church missionary meeting.

The welcoming committee stood huddled together, lost in their thoughts. Sigrid had begun to tap her foot again by the time the telltale whistle of the train sounded. Otto's stomach flipped.

He knew that this time, the familiar sound heralded a new life for him, Sigrid, and their new child.

The train was ready to offload its passengers before again meandering its way through Indiana. Otto watched with bated breath, taking Sigrid's hand surreptitiously as the doors opened. A few passengers stepped from the Pullman car, one of them quickly lighting a cigarette while still on the platform.

Otto felt his breath hitch as Paul emerged, holding a little girl tightly in his arms. The girl, little more than a baby, was surveying her surroundings with round, dark eyes, her face framed with a crown of little dark curls. Otto felt as though his heart had stopped.

Paul's face turned toward them, and a wide grin transformed his features. He looked older but seemed very much the same pleasant boy Otto remembered.

"Welcome, Brother Paul," one of the church district representatives from Camden called out, stepping forward enthusiastically to shake Paul's hand. Lena also hurried to welcome her cousin, touching his arm affectionately.

"Paul, I can never thank you enough," Sigrid said. Otto stepped behind his wife, looking down at Anne. He exhaled, blinking away tears.

Oh, my heart. My child. How we have prayed for you.

Sigrid looked down at Anne and smiled, her eyes filling with tears.

"Hallo, Liebchen," she said quietly, holding out her arms. "It's Mama Sigi. Do you remember?"

Anne's round eyes widened even further. She reached out for Sigrid, clinging to her neck as Sigrid embraced her. Placing the blanket around Anne, Sigrid began to cry softly. Greta, unable to contain herself, rushed forward and put her arms around them both. Anne smiled shyly at Greta as the older woman planted a kiss on the child's forehead.

"Welcome to your new home, Anne," Greta said, holding up a small hand-sewn doll. Anne's little smile turned into a giggle as she reached for the doll.

"Thank you," Anne said in English. Sigrid sniffed loudly.

Greta joined Sigrid and the two church district representatives as Otto and Oscar laid their hands on Paul's shoulders.

"Thank you, God, for the safe passage of Paul and Anne," Oscar said.

"May you protect and guide Anne as she builds a life here with us," Otto said.

"And may you continue to guide Paul in your service," said one of the congregants.

Everyone fussed over the newest member as Paul loaded his luggage into the farm truck Fredrick had lent him. Sigrid clung to Annie, and Otto protectively stayed by her side.

"Pastor Fisher has arranged a simple welcoming noon meal at the church for you," Oscar said. Paul patted his belly.

"Great," he said. "I'm starving." In less than fifteen minutes, the whole group had driven into the lot.

"How was your arrival in New York?" asked Pastor Fisher, warmly shaking Paul's hand. The Church of the Brethren in town continued a close rapport with the German Baptist district, and his genuine interest shone on his face.

"It was quite efficient, actually," said Paul. "My associate in Copenhagen contacted the New York Children's Aid Society through his Danish government representative before our arrival. All our paperwork was in order, and the passenger service already anticipated Annie's arrival through the emissary."

"Praise be to God," said Oscar. "Your journey sounds divinely guided."

"Divinely guided by St. Pierre," Paul muttered under his breath as he took a bite of a roasted carrot. He groaned with satisfaction at the flavor of fresh Indiana vegetables.

"Annie, eat the carrot. It's so good."

Annie, sitting next to Sigrid, looked up.

"More carrots, Mama?"

"Oh, my sweet girl, of course," said Sigrid, piercing a bite of carrot with her fork. Her lip quivered. "Paul, you have done a good job with her English." Paul nodded, his mouth too full of food to respond.

"What happened once you left New York?" asked Lena.

Paul hastily swallowed. "We were shuttled to arranged living quarters of a parishioner from where we began the train ride to Indiana. They said they'd sent a telegram."

"Yes, which is how we all knew you were coming," said Otto. "What a blessing to have such a wide network of Brethren."

Following the meal and prayers, Sigrid, Greta, and Annie took Fredrick's car to Miami County Hospital while Otto drove the rest of the family home. Wide-eyed and clinging to Sigrid, Annie watched as Dr. Burkybile, a local on-call physician, entered the small exam room carrying a bag. The middle-aged physician with thinning hair and a protruding belly didn't so much as crack a smile as he set his bag down and turned to his patient.

"So, this is a medical examination as part of adoption protocol, eh?" he said. "Let's see what we have here."

Both Sigrid and Greta sat with some apprehension as they could not be sure of Anne's health. Though she had been examined in Denmark and at the New York port, there was always the uncertainty of exposure to tuberculosis while being in close proximity to shipboard travelers.

The doctor took Anne from Sigrid and placed her on the exam table. Anne did not move as the doctor checked her eyes and ears and listened to her heart with the stethoscope that dangled around his neck.

"Not what I would have expected in appearance for a girl from Denmark," he said in an offhand manner.

"What do you mean?" asked Sigrid, her heart pounding.

"Her hair and eyes are quite dark, aren't they? She's not your typical Scandinavian model."

"Many people from Denmark and Germany have dark eyes and hair," Sigrid countered. Greta nudged Sigrid's foot with hers, and Sigrid clamped her mouth shut.

"Maybe your Viking relatives got mixed with the mud races during some of their pillagings," the doctor chuckled as he finished testing Anne's reflexes. Greta scowled at the doctor's back, but neither woman said anything further as Anne solved a simple wooden block manipulation puzzle.

"Well," the doctor said, "she seems healthy enough. From her responses, her mental development even appears advanced, though we'd have to do further tests to know for sure."

The doctor picked up Annie's files and flipped to a page, scanning. "Her papers confirm she's a herring-choker, so eugenics aren't really my concern. Now, were she part nigress or had Jew blood, then I'd want to test further or explore sterilization. In this case, though, the agency will seal her records once the court signs off." He scribbled on a form and handed it to Sigrid.

"Take this down the hall," the doctor said. "Room 107. Get the child's TB X-ray done. I'll report the findings as soon as I get them to the social service agency." He waved his hand carelessly and turned from the room, leaving the door open.

Showing themselves out, Greta and Sigrid led Annie down the hall to room 107.

"I like young Dr. Miller much better, Ma," Sigrid said as she protectively guided Anne through the X-ray lab door. Greta nodded her agreement.

"Let's just get through the rest of this," she said, "so we can finally get Anne home safe."

"Annie," the little girl said.

"Oh! Yes, then Annie, it shall be, sweet girl," said Greta warmly.

After a very long hour of medical tests, Greta and Sigrid finally escorted Annie to her new home, enjoying the cooling breeze from the windows of the car. As Sigrid turned down the familiar road, Greta looked over at her daughter.

"I must admit, I never thought I'd live to see the day when my daughter could operate a motorcar," she said, adjusting Annie's sticky and sleeping form on her lap.

"Otto and I agreed it was more practical for both of us to know how to drive," Sigrid said. "I believe he was right. I enjoy it now, sorta."

"How times change," Greta mused as Sigrid smoothly pulled into the drive. Fredrick's farm truck sat outside the house, and Paul was getting out. As the car slowed, Annie's eyes fluttered open.

"Well, hello!" Paul said, hoisting Annie up and setting her on his lap. "I just arrived from my meeting with the district vestry."

"What did you talk about?" Sigrid asked, watching Annie burrow her face into Paul's shirt.

"I hinted to the district that I see a return to the States as a priority," Paul said.

"Why don't you simply stay here, then?"

"Well, I have some affairs to close up," Paul said. Anne looked up at him sleepily.

"Aunt . . ." she started to say.

"Shh," Paul said, patting Annie's mouth so she made a "wa-wa-wa" sound. She started to laugh. "The district elders also relayed that this was a critical time to spread the gospel in the outer regions of Scandinavia."

Sigrid looked quizzically at Paul, but before she could say anything, Greta came outside, wiping her hands on an apron where she'd been putting a kettle on.

"Did I hear you say Scandinavia? Greta asked.

"Yes," Paul said stoically. "The fascination with the occult and spiritualism in many elite circles of Europe is problematic to the church. Such fads as astrology and mysticism should not go unchallenged."

"That is seen as a problem here also," Greta said.

"Proselytizing to Northern Swedish Laplanders seems a good counter strategy to the return of shamanistic beliefs that are beginning to threaten Christianity there," Paul said, nodding. Looking carefully at him, Sigrid narrowed her eyes. Seeing her expression, Paul laughed.

"Okay, the district may have offered a substantial raise and a cleric position upon return from Denmark following a few more years of service."

"I knew it," Sigrid said with a chuckle. "So, did you accept the new position?"

"I will need to go back to Copenhagen and discuss it with Helga."

"Auntie!" Annie cried.

"Yes, Auntie Helga," Paul said, looking resigned. "I suppose the cat is out of the bag." Greta and Sigrid shared a knowing look.

"Now, darling, that means I will need to leave you for a time," Paul said. He set Annie down and knelt, taking her tiny hands. The little girl stuck her lower lip out.

"No," she said. "Stay."

"I have to go see Auntie Helga, Annie," Paul said. "But I will try to come visit, and maybe Auntie Helga and I could even come to live here someday. What do you think of that?" Annie's tiny face glowed, and she nodded vigorously.

The following day, a Children's Bureau nurse representative visited Sigrid's immaculate home. Sigrid vibrated with nerves as she followed the visiting nurse from room to room, but Annie seemed content and sat playing with her new, expertly carved wooden toys. The nurse seemed satisfied with Annie's new surroundings, and her interview with Otto and Sigrid allayed fears of abuse or adoptive parent health issues.

"I understand Anne received her pertussis vaccine in Denmark," the nurse said. Sigrid nodded.

"Good," the nurse continued, pushing her spectacles up onto the bridge of her nose. "Dr. Burkybile would have told you by now if he suspected any health concerns about Anne. I understand your Dr. Miller is to come around in a few months to perform a routine scheduled examination."

"Yes," Sigrid said, glancing at Annie. "We want to take the best care of her." The nurse, nodding in approval, jotting something down on her form.

"I'll be in touch," she said, standing and smiling. "You seem like a fine family for this little one."

Showing the nurse out, Sigrid sat down on the floor beside Annie, who automatically snuggled up to her as she built a tower with her blocks. Sigrid ran her hand through Annie's dark curls, smiling to herself. A new life would now begin for this girl. Annie would grow up to learn the domestic and farm skills needed for their way of life, and she would grow up to love their Lord. She would learn Brethren ways, wearing modest clothing and a head covering as she said her daily prayers. Sigrid knew she and Otto would lavish all their patience, attention, and love upon this child, the answer to their many years of prayer.

* * *

In May of 1933, a year after their journey to Germany, Sigrid received a letter from Rudolph. It was the first time they'd heard from him since their visit, and Sigrid felt a sense of dread as soon as the envelope touched her hands. Without opening it, she rushed over to her parent's house with Annie, entering just as her parents were sitting down to lunch.

"Look," she said, holding out the letter with a trembling hand. Oscar took it, his face scrunching with worry.

"Let's read it together," he said. "Annie, would you like to play with Samuel on the porch?"

Oscar opened the letter and shook it out while Greta and Sigrid each stood over one shoulder so they could see the letter. As they read, their faces grew more and more drawn, even in the cheerful light of the kitchen on a beautiful spring day.

June 4, 1933

My dearest Sigrid and Greta,

In my foregone letters I had mentioned as of January 30th, Adolph Hitler was pronounced Chancellor of Germany. It seems now he has begun further implementation of his policies of the most extreme nature.

It is no secret in Germany that Jews, Gypsies, and any other groups that Nazis deemed "undesirable" are no longer merely being harassed and threatened. It has become law that Jews will no longer be allowed to conduct or run businesses in Germany. They are also banned from holding any civil and academic appointments. Hitler has also replaced the SA with a secret Gestapo, which is rumored to be pursuing those he has deemed as being of inferior blood. They are being rounded up and sent to a new specific "camp."

Unfortunately, I must also pass on news that is perhaps even more saddening to us on a personal level. On May 23, Dieter peacefully passed away in his sleep. Do not consider or think of sending money for Dieter's burial; I have already covered all the expenses. It was well worth the honor of having known your uncle.

It is in light of Dieter's death that I retrospectively assume some sense of shame for naive political positions to which I ascribed during your last visit. It has become clearer now to me what Dieter was trying to warn against before his passing. I take some redemption in the deed of assisting you with Yanna's extraction to America and expediting and coordinating your uncle's monetary assistance to Paul. I trust that Yanna is safe and well in America.

This will be my final letter for now, as things are becoming more unsettled day by day. There is no longer any assurance of confidentiality in our communication.

Your most humble servant,

Rudolph Bach

There was silence for several minutes, broken only by the sounds of Annie talking animatedly to the dog on the porch. Finally, Oscar broke the silence with prayer.

"Praise God for Dieter's life and final good works," Oscar said. "We ask for Rudolph and his family's safety and give thanks for bringing our Annie to America."

There was a moment of quiet, and then Greta strode purposefully to the other side of the kitchen.

"Annie, sweet girl, come wash up," she said. "You and Ma must be hungry."

"It sounds as if you were lucky to have gotten Annie out of Germany when you did, let alone to have her mother suddenly find you at such a critical time," Oscar said as everyone settled down for a simple meal of dumplings, kraut, and sausage.

"Yes, and fortunate that Uncle Dieter was willing to pay the Gypsies and send money to assist Paul's efforts on behalf of Annie," Sigrid said.

"Otherwise, who knows what might have become of our precious little girl?" Greta added, patting Annie gently on the back. Annie took Sigrid's hand.

"Mama, potty," she said.

"Okay, sweet girl," said Sigrid with a smile. She helped Annie outside to the outhouse. Oscar watched them go, then sat for a moment, chewing a biscuit and looking upwards.

"Just out of curiosity, when you visited Dieter, did you, by chance, also visit the stone circle in the forest near his farm?"

Greta hesitated. "Yes, I thought Sigi might enjoy visiting the standing stones we once saw." She paused, taking a bite of knackwurst. "I was sure she would find them interesting, just as we did."

"Did you two pray while you were there as you do by the stones by Fredrick's woods?" Oscar asked, looking sidelong at his wife.

"Yes."

"You knew what Sigrid was going to pray for, didn't you?"

"I don't know what you mean," Greta said. As she returned to the stove to bring more sausage to the table, Oscar could have sworn she smiled at him.

"Seems to me that Annie's mother finding you and Sigi might not have been such a coincidence after all," Oscar said, chuckling.

Greta sat back down at the table and touched Oscar's hand. "The good book tells us that all things work together for the good of those who love the Lord," she said. "I thank the Lord for blessing us with Annie. I never give much mind to the details of how it all came about."

Part Four

The Greatest Generation (Die größte Generation)

33
Begin the Beguine
(Beginne die Begine)
September–October 1942

"How is it you're still in college?" the coed said with a laugh, scooting closer to Daniel. He looked down at her, his palms suddenly moist with sweat. He'd found himself looking down a lot these days. At twenty, he had somehow grown another inch and now towered above most of his peers at Purdue University, including this coed, though she was tall and athletic. With her auburn hair, she reminded Daniel of a picture of Maureen O'Hara he'd once seen in the dorm in a movie magazine.

Daniel turned his body diffidently away, feeling his face redden as he looked around at the other attendees of the campus bonfire, a celebration of Purdue's undefeated football team. There was no denying the dwindling number of men on campus. One by one, military-age males were being drafted or enlisting.

"I don't think the Army is for me," he said before the silence stretched out too long, still looking away from the woman. "I don't think I could handle the violence. I have considered the possibility of working in the Defense Department after college, though."

"Conscientious objector?" she asked.

"Yeah, something like that," Daniel said, scratching the back of his neck. "My church affiliation allowed me to apply for CO status since I can no longer claim a student deferment. But my engineering degree could also provide the credentials to work in construction to serve the country without wearing a uniform."

"Sure," said the coed, sticking out her hand. "I'm Melodie, by the way. I'm a sophomore." Daniel hoped the firelight hid his rapidly reddening face as he took the young woman's soft, warm hand in his cold, clammy one.

"Where are you from, Melodie?"

"North Manchester, originally. Ever been?"

"Actually, yes, I have," Daniel said. "My cousin Conrad teaches at the Brethren college there. I've visited with my folks before. Do you like living there? It seems nice enough."

"It was nice enough, but I don't live there anymore. I moved to Indianapolis when I was thirteen, attended an Episcopal girl's school there," Melodie told him. "So, where are you from?"

"Peru," Daniel answered.

"Oh! Do you know Cole Porter?" she asked. Her expression changed to one of disbelief when Daniel looked quizzical.

"You don't know who Cole Porter is?" she said incredulously.

"I'm a descendant of Brethren farmers," Daniel said, rubbing the back of his neck again. "Normally, we shun the material world. No card playing, alcohol, dancing, cigarettes . . . you can guess all the rest. So, I'm not so knowledgeable about such things."

"Gee," Melodie said, her eyes wide. "I'd think your dormies would have mentioned that Cole Porter is from Peru, at least."

Daniel shrugged. "Outside of my roommate and a few professors, I don't have many friends on campus. I don't belong to a frat or social club. Just don't have the time."

"Okay, well, you need to know at least who Cole Porter is," Melodie said. "I'll have to play some of his records for you."

Daniel's stomach tied itself into knots. She wanted to see him again. There was an awkward silence before Melodie jumped back in, saving him.

"My pop is a bank president. His entire family are bankers. What do your parents do?"

"My folks farm near Peru," Daniel answered.

"Oh, yeah?" she said. "I was raised in town, so I don't have much experience with county life. But my Grandpa Rubert, on my mom's side of the family, still farms."

"What are you studying?" Daniel asked. "Finance like your pa?"

"Biology, actually," Melodie said. "But I'll transfer to Indianapolis into IU Medical Center for nursing next fall."

"Mel!" someone called from the other side of the fire. Daniel looked up and saw a group of girls waving.

"Duty calls," said Melodie, shrugging. "I hope we meet again, Daniel from Peru." Daniel couldn't help but watch as she ran over to her friends, turning back to wave at Daniel before she was immersed in conversation.

"I hope we meet again, Daniel from Peru," said a mocking falsetto voice behind him. Daniel turned and frowned at Edgar, his roommate, who had snuck up silently and was lurking a few paces back. Edgar was a scrawny philosophy major and one of the most intelligent people Daniel had ever met, though his social skills were somewhat lacking.

"You're bad at flirting," Edgar said bluntly.

"Thanks," said Daniel. "You didn't have to listen in, you know." Edgar just stared at Daniel as if to say he hadn't had a choice.

"I had not expected to be approached by someone of the opposite sex," Daniel admitted. "My focus for the last two years has been engineering, not meeting girls."

"Looks like that's about to change," said Edgar, looking over at Melodie and her friends' backs across the fire. Daniel glanced over to see one of Melodie's friends pointing at him and giggling until Melodie slapped their hands, laughing. He pressed his lips together.

"Doubtful. I don't know if I'll ever even see her again."

In fact, Daniel did see Melodie on campus a few times over the next couple of weeks, exchanging hellos and having conversations, some of which extended into hours of wandering and chatting if they had the time. Daniel felt himself becoming more interested in Melodie every time he saw her. Melodie seemed much more mature than other girls Daniel had known; she was a witty, gregarious, straight-A student who didn't try to hide her capabilities. However, having never dated, much less socialized with girls on a one-on-one basis, Daniel was unsure about progressing the relationship. It soon fell to Melodie to take the first step.

"Hi there! I was wondering when I'd see you again," she said to Daniel by way of greeting one beautiful fall day in October. In the sunlight, her smoky blue eyes sparkled like deep water. "Let's not keep leaving this up to chance, okay? I'm in Duhme Hall, room 207. Hang on a second."

Melodie pulled a notebook and pencil out of her book bag.

Hoisting the bag back high up on her shoulder, she began scribbling something.

"I've heard it's a swell place to live," Daniel said, rubbing the back of his neck nervously.

"Well, its only notoriety is that Amelia Earhart once roomed there as a faculty member," Melodie said with a laugh.

"Odd how her plane just disappeared," Daniel said, wishing he'd come up with something cleverer to say.

"Yes, isn't it?" Melodie said. She handed Daniel the piece of paper. Daniel looked down to see her name and the hallway phone number.

"Oho," a deep voice said. Looking up, Daniel saw a tall man with broad shoulders and hair so blonde it was nearly white craning over Melodie. Melodie, for her part, let out a huge sigh and turned.

"What do you want, Ross?

"Is that your telephone number?" Ross said, pointing at the scrap of paper clutched in Daniel's hand. "Wouldn't you rather give that to me?"

"No," Melodie said firmly.

"You really like this palooka?" Ross said, flashing a set of overly large, white teeth as he slung an arm around Melodie and nuzzled his face into her neck. Daniel felt his face redden. He took a step forward and opened his mouth, but before he could say anything, Melodie cut in.

"Your dad's a minister, right?" Melodie said, bending her knees to squat and maneuver herself neatly out of the man's reach. "I wonder what he'd say about your behavior."

"Do you have class soon?" Daniel exclaimed, looking straight at Melodie.

"No, just got out. You?"

"Same. Why don't we go for a walk?" he said.

"Swell idea," Melodie said. She began walking down the sidewalk at a brisk pace, the diffuse light through the tall maples and oaks around them sparkling in her auburn hair. Daniel followed behind, turning to make sure Ross wasn't following. He was standing there with his arms crossed, scowling.

"Goodbye, Ross," Melodie roared without turning.

"You're not even all that good-looking," Ross shouted. "I can do better!"

After the pair had turned a corner behind a tall historic building, they slowed, going nowhere in particular.

"Well, that was unpleasant," Daniel said.

"Unfortunately, such behavior is nothing out of the ordinary," Melodie said, tossing a lock of her auburn hair behind her.

"That's unfortunate," Daniel said. "I am sorry you have to put up with that, Melodie. Please let me know if I can ever help."

"You're already helping," Melodie said, glancing over at him and smiling. They were silent for a moment, but then Daniel found he couldn't quite help himself.

"He was wrong, you know."

Melodie looked at him quizzically. "What do you mean?"

"You are quite good-looking. In fact, you're beautiful."

As Daniel turned away to hide his burning face, he felt something touch his palm. So casually, Melodie had reached over and grasped his hand. Daniel's heart seemed to stop momentarily, and unbelievably, his face grew even hotter. His first reaction was initially to pull away, but something stopped him from doing so.

Perhaps I've reached the point in life where finding female companionship is essential, he thought. He had to admit he enjoyed

Melodie's company, and being with her felt better than being alone or with grumpy Edgar. Smiling to himself, he squeezed Melodie's hand gently. A gust of a breeze blew past, and orange and yellow leaves swirled down past their faces to dance about their feet as they walked.

"Daniel, what are your plans for fall break?" Melodie asked as they approached an intersection.

"I am not sure."

"Would you like to come spend the weekend at my parents' place in Indianapolis?"

"Oh!" Daniel said, his mood rising even higher. "Sure. Thanks."

"Great! You can meet 'President Harrison,'" Melodie said with a laugh.

"President Harrison?"

"My pops," Melodie said frankly, taking a seat on a ledge. "He can be a bit of a snob. He graduated from Purdue. He's a Pi Kapp and alumni donor."

"Ah," Daniel said, sitting beside her. "That doesn't sound much like my folks."

"They might be a bit surprised about you," Melodie said. Daniel glanced at her to see that she had a pensive look on her face.

"How so?"

"You're not the kind of person who usually runs in their social circles," Melodie said, shrugging. "They can be picky about pedigree and social connections. You were raised in a different world, it seems, without sarcasm or prying into others' affairs. It's refreshing."

"What you're not saying is that I'm what most would call a

'bumpkin,'" Daniel said with a self-deprecating smile. "Academically capable but socially clumsy."

"You know," Melodie said, turning toward him and fixing him in her smoky blue gaze, "that's what I find most attractive about you. Your lack of pretense or concern for social status . . . it's honest and pure."

Around them, students walked back and forth, chatting amiably, but Daniel only had eyes for Melodie. With the glittering sunlight and eddying leaves, the day felt very romantic to him. Despite the chill in the breeze, he knew he was beginning to blush again.

"Thanks, I guess," Daniel said. "I'd been wondering what the heck you saw in me. Clearly, you get plenty of interest from other boys, even with this depleted population."

"That's true," she said with a chuckle. "But I think I intimidate most undergrad males. They try to engage intellectually with me, but they're never happy when they realize I might be as smart as they are."

"Or smarter," Daniel said, thinking of Ross.

"You don't seem to mind, though," Melodie said earnestly. "You don't seem to have the ego so many men here have, and you don't make attempts at trying to be overly charming. Guess that's why I'm talking to you instead of them."

"Well," Daniel said, "I'm happy for your approval." Melodie's soft, warm chuckle filled his ears, and he felt genuinely content.

As it turned out, Melodie's parents' house was on the west side of Indianapolis, easily accessible by bus. When Daniel entered the Harrison residence for the first time, the radio was playing an unfamiliar hit parade song, though, of course, most songs were unfamiliar to Daniel. The house was neatly arranged, and a small fire smoldered in the fireplace. Daniel could smell the lingering aroma of pipe tobacco in the air as he and Melodie walked into the living room.

"Hi, Pop," Melodie said, walking over to hug her father as he rose from the brown tufted leather sofa. He was a distinguished-looking man of middle age, with his salt-and-pepper hair starting to recede.

"Melodie," the man said in a deep, resonant voice. "How was the ride down?"

"Not bad. Pop, this is Daniel," Melodie said. Her father extended his hand to Daniel as he approached. Disconcertingly, his smoky blue eyes were identical to Melodie's.

"It's a pleasure to meet you, sir," Daniel said, trying to be as formal as possible. Melodie had reminded him as they traveled to Indianapolis that her parents valued good manners.

"So, Melodie tells me that you plan on becoming an engineer," her father said, pointing toward a matching leather chair for Daniel to sit in.

"Yes," Daniel said, taking care to measure his words before speaking. "I'm studying civil engineering with a minor in math." He observed Melodie's father's reactions as he sank into the chair, which was very comfortable.

"I'm going to go find Mom," Melodie announced. Daniel tried not to look crestfallen as she walked away, leaving him stranded with "President Harrison."

"Well, engineering is a fine field," Mr. Harrison said. "So, your parents are farmers, and your sister is married?"

"Yes," Daniel said. "My folks are cattle, hog, and grain farmers, though we have a few chickens too. And my sister and her husband are having a child soon."

"I know farming is a hard life," Mr. Harrison said, crossing his arms and giving Daniel a severe look. "Melodie may have mentioned to you that her mother grew up on a farm near North Manchester."

"Yes, she did tell me that," Daniel said. Mr. Harrison nodded.

"It's back-breaking work, but it's much easier now that things are becoming mechanized," Mr. Harrison said as his wife entered the room with Melodie.

"Daniel, welcome to our home," she said. She was pretty and thin, with peroxide-blonde hair and a stern gaze that belied her words. "Would you like some tea? Dinner will be ready in ten minutes."

Soon, the four of them were seated around a cherry wood dining table, eating off of much fancier flatware than Daniel was used to. He tried to keep his elbows off the table as he answered the seemingly endless barrage of questions from the Harrisons.

"So, you were raised Baptist, is that right?" Mrs. Harrison asked a small piece of chicken speared on the end of her fork. "They are quite strict, aren't they?"

"I was raised in the Brethren Church," Daniel said, carefully cutting his chicken into small pieces, "though I don't take the Bible as literally as my German Baptist grandparents or my moderate Brethren parents."

"Is that so?" Mr. Harrison asked, sipping wine from a crystal goblet. "Why is that?"

"The war is hard to ignore," he said, patting his mouth with a linen napkin. "I believe I have to consider our national situation as well as my personal beliefs."

"That seems a wise perspective," Mrs. Harrison commented, her rigid eyes warming a little.

"What are your religious affiliations?" Daniel asked before popping a bite of the chicken into his mouth. He savored the flavorful meat, keeping his expression politely interested.

"Well, we're not overly religious," Mr. Harrison said. "We have attended Christ Church Episcopal on Monument Circle for years.

"Several other bank trustees attend mass there," Mrs. Harrison interjected. "The men like to get together after mass for lunch."

Daniel nodded, swallowing his chicken and hoping there was nothing in his teeth. "It is nice that you share faith with those you work with," Daniel said. "It seems our families have that in common."

Daniel was very much relieved when he and Melodie captured a moment of privacy in the pair of chairs on the front porch. Wrapped in blankets, they breathed in the crisp fall air. Daniel let out a sigh.

"I think that went well," Melodie said. "You even remembered the difference between the salad fork and the dinner fork."

"I'm not usually socially awkward unless I'm talking to a pretty girl," Daniel said, grinning.

Melodie laughed and took his hand. Then, her face grew serious.

"Have you changed your mind about joining up? The way you were talking in there . . . it made me think you'd perhaps reconsidered."

Daniel looked out into the darkening night. There was a bit of a bite to the air now that it was October, but he and Melodie were cozy inside their blanket. "I haven't planned on it, though I probably will have to cross that bridge soon."

Melodie nodded somberly, and the two of them shared a quiet moment, staring into the darkness, lost in their thoughts. Daniel stared at the first stars, his thoughts drifting to the lazy Sunday morning the year before when everything had changed.

On that fateful day, Daniel had been lying on his dorm bed, doing some last-minute reading for class. It was December, still early in the morning, and the window was glazed over with frost.

"We've been attacked!" someone running past the door had screamed. Daniel had heard other shouts and the stamping of feet. Abandoning his book, he'd shuffled to the door and poked his head out.

"What's all the commotion?" he'd asked a red-faced boy.

"Japan just bombed the hell out of Hawaii," the student had panted, his pajama top askew. "This is it! We're all going to war. We can kiss college goodbye!"

Daniel had gone back into his room and closed the door firmly behind him, leaning against it. Then, he'd walked briskly over to the Silvertone radio on Edgar's shelf and turned it on, dialing through the stations until he found the news.

"Did I say you could use my radio?" Edgar had said in his deadpan voice. He'd been sprawled on his dorm bed, face planted into his pillow.

"May I use your radio?" Daniel had asked. Edgar had grunted.

Daniel had listened to the news, feeling the blood drain out of his face. He'd known what this meant, though he'd never given military service much thought before that moment.

"What do you think of this?" Daniel had asked Edgar, who had flopped over onto his back and was staring at the bottom of Daniel's bunk.

"I always thought war was inevitable," Edgar drawled. "This will just speed shit up."

"It's a good thing we have some time off coming up," said Daniel. "My family is going to want to talk about this."

"Talking won't change anything," Edgar had said. "It looks like 'the war to end all wars' didn't ensure shit."

Daniel grimaced. He, like many others, had believed World War One had meant an end to war on a global scale. He'd heard stories of his Uncle Otto's sacrifice. He was aware that most Anabaptists in his church community regarded his uncle as a hero, whether they admitted it out loud or not, and he thought that had meant his family had done its part. But at that moment, he'd known the hopes that another world war could be avoided had been futile.

Now, as stars popped up in the clear sky and Melodie snuggled against his side, Daniel recalled his father's expression when he'd gone home for the holidays.

"There is no need for you to stop attending college, son," Fredrick had told Daniel, staring at him seriously over the dining room table.

"You aren't even eighteen yet," Lena had blurted. "You need to finish school, Dan. By then, maybe all this war foolishness will be over." She'd passed soup bowls fragrant with steam around the table.

"In one act of violence, a divided country—those for and those against America entering the war—have become united to defend the nation," his father had said. "But anything can change at a moment's notice, Dan. Stay out of it as long as you can."

"As long as I can," muttered Daniel to the emerging stars.

"What?" asked Melodie.

"My pa told me to avoid the war as long as I could," Daniel explained at a normal volume. "Now, I have a feeling that time may have come when it can no longer be avoided." He leaned back in his chair and heaved a huge sigh. "I thought I was where I was meant to be, you know? I worked hard in grade school and got fine recommendations when applying to Purdue. Now, it looks like all that could be upended."

"I agree," Melodie said, holding his hand tightly. "All the same, the daily news from the front lines can't be avoided no matter how many times the radio plays *The Lone Ranger* as a distraction."

"Who?"

Melodie chuckled. "We probably are going to have to listen to a lot of radio over the next few days." Then, her tone grew somber. "You are right, Daniel. The war is knocking at our door. It's not a question of if, but a question of when."

The rest of the visit to Indianapolis went surprisingly well. Daniel enjoyed Thanksgiving dinner with Melodie's small, polite family, and he and Melodie listened to enough music to make his head whirl. He was feeling quite comfortable by the day of their departure when he stole downstairs to gather up his toiletries from the bathroom. However, he still felt the need to stay silent when he overheard Melodie's mother speaking in the kitchen.

"Normally, we would have been more critical of Daniel's lineage," her mom said frankly.

"Mom!" exclaimed Melodie in a hiss.

"But," Mrs. Harrison continued, "since you seem sure and Daniel is a sincere and honest young man, your father and I have chosen to place your judgment above our typical scrutiny."

"Well . . . okay. Thanks, I guess."

"He has good manners . . ."

Daniel continued on his way to the bathroom, not wanting to eavesdrop, feeling strange but somewhat relieved that he'd passed the test. He stood looking at himself in the bathroom mirror for a moment. Above his athletic shoulders and the blue eyes he'd inherited from his grandmother, his blonde hair was sticking up in all directions. Glad he hadn't seen anyone in the hallway, he opened the tube of Brylcreem from his shaving kit and tried to bat it down. He wouldn't want to ruin his excellent impression now that he'd been deemed at least partially worthy.

34
Life Transitions
(Lebensübergänge)
December 1942

At Purdue, the fall colors and sweet Indiana air protectively cradled the campus, shielding it from the mayhem of the outside world. As Melodie and Daniel spent more and more time together, occasional servicemen in uniform passing through campus reminded them of what one of Daniel's professors had called the "elephant in the living room." Regardless of how protective or noncommittal the campus culture sought to be, Daniel felt the reality of national anxiety pressing in.

Following the finals of the fall semester classes, Melodie and Daniel celebrated by going out for cokes and hamburgers at the campus union. However, the occasion was not a joyful one.

"I'm going to miss seeing you," Melodie said, picking up a French fry.

Daniel nodded, his hamburger pausing halfway to his mouth.

He knew Melodie was going to transfer to IU Medical Center in January to begin her nursing program.

"Nurses must really be needed now," he said. "I will miss you too, but I understand."

Melodie nodded, stuffing the rest of her fry into her mouth. "There is such a shortage of nurses that the government has mandated schools to accelerate the training programs," she said as a cluster of female students passed by on their way to the counter. "I should be able to complete my training in two and a half years or less by early '44, I hope."

Melodie picked up her hamburger, paused, then looked up at Daniel. "I'll complete the course rather than consider the safer option of taking a minimal amount of training and becoming a nurse cadet," she said, setting her burger down. "Cadets only seem to stay stateside to backfill positions, but most fully trained nurses are getting sent overseas to support the war if they volunteer. I want to get my commission after my training."

Daniel felt a spasm of fear. He looked away from Melodie, staring at a hand-drawn charcoal of Gary Cooper that someone from the art department had hung on the wall.

"Then what will become of us?" he asked, the word "us" seemed to stick in his throat. Melodie reached across the table and took Daniel's hand.

"Well," she said, "I'll write to you every day from Indy. You could come to visit my house for the holidays, or I could come to yours. I want to meet your folks."

"No, I mean, will you eventually find someone else?" he said, his other hand shooting out automatically to grasp hers, food forgotten. "We both know long-distance relationships are difficult under the best of circumstances. And what happens if you join up and are sent somewhere that's really dangerous?" He swallowed, trying to clear the choking sensation that engulfed him.

"Look," Melodie replied, "There are no certainties in life. If I can play a minimal part in helping the war effort or ease some poor soldier's pain, that is what I want to do."

Melodie released Daniel's hands, then stood up and slid into his side of the booth, forcing him to hurry over. "This is one of those times when we shouldn't overthink about the 'what ifs,'" she said. "The news of the war isn't exactly painting a rosy picture of success for the home team. This isn't World War I, where everything neatly stays in Europe. There have already been attacks on the West Coast, and it's only a matter of time until the Nazis or the Japanese figure out how to invade our cities."

Sighing, Melodie placed her head on Daniel's shoulder, watching the students meander by. "I feel like if I don't at least try to do my part, no one's children in America, including ours, will have any future."

Daniel put his arm around Melodie, trying to breathe deeply. He had not seen her this sad before. He knew that the events of the war in Europe and Asia bothered her but had never fully considered that she intended at some point to jump headlong into the situation herself. The thought of her overseas made him feel sick with worry. *Perhaps I'm taking this relationship far more seriously than I'd first imagined I could after just three months,* he thought.

"Look, who knows?" Daniel said, turning to Melodie and trying to smile. "Maybe in two years, the war will be over, and there will be nothing for us to worry about." His smile dropped when he saw the expression on her face. "We'll just plan on writing to each other and take things as they come day by day."

Melodie was quiet, and then she nodded in subdued agree-ment.

"I'm going to finish my hamburger before it gets cold," she said with a sniff, pulling it over to her new side of the table.

"Good idea," Daniel said, trying to shake off his feeling of dread. But just as he pulled his tray toward him, a familiar song came on the radio.

"This Love of Mine," he said. "Frank Sinatra."

"You recognized it," Melodie said with a pale smile. Daniel brushed her tears away with his thumbs, staring into her eyes.

"It can be our song," he said. As if magnetized, their lips met in their first kiss. Daniel knew as soon as their lips touched that he would never forget this moment.

He was still thinking about that moment a few days later as the bus rolled to a stop in Peru. Daniel shook his head vigorously, trying to get his brain to focus on the present moment. Peering out the window, he was pleased to see that both his parents and his Grandpa Oscar were waiting by the family car, easy to spot thanks to their plain German Baptist clothing. The sky above was gray, and the threat of snow lingered in the air.

Daniel looked down at his coat and slacks; he knew he would look out of place until he got the opportunity to change. Although some of the Anabaptist churches had adopted more modern dress, most stood by the simple beliefs through manner and discipline, which had also remained a priority for the Becks. They still ad-hered closely to their beloved German Baptist Brethren principles and customs while adopting their new church. Daniel, for his part, felt that his modest, modern clothing was okay while he was on campus, but slipping into his plain farm clothes always made him feel like he was home.

"Peru!" called out the bus driver, putting the large vehicle in park and swinging the doors open. Daniel joined the students, filing out of the bus, heavy-laden with bags full of books and clothes, and happily walked up to his smiling family.

Daniel looked around at the faces of his beloved family. His father, now nearing fifty years old, still seemed as vigorous as ever despite the deep smile lines beside his eyes and the gray hue his once-brown hair had acquired. His mother had similarly maintained her looks and strength, although deeper lines had appeared between her eyes of late. Daniel, who knew having a son his age during wartime was causing her strain, felt guilty as he looked at her. Meanwhile, at seventy-three, Oscar's face was lined, and his gait was starting to slow. Even so, Daniel thought his grandfather's kindness radiated from his eyes and wide, bright smile.

After the subdued greeting customary to most Brethren, Daniel fell into step with them as they walked to the 39 Ford his father had recently purchased.

"Grandpa, why did you come to pick me up in the cold?" Daniel asked. "I would have been seeing you soon enough. You needn't have troubled yourself."

"Your pa and I were finishing some work on the tractor, and I just thought I'd come along," Oscar said in his German accent, turning and smiling fondly at his grandson.

"I'm glad we can use farming machinery without feeling guilty about it," Fredrick commented, patting his father on the shoulder. Daniel gazed fondly at the two men, so alike in height, as everyone clambered into the car. In 1939, the Zion German Baptist Church consolidated with Deercreek, as many folks questioned the Church of the Brethren's liberal direction. Daniel's family had stayed at the Church of the Brethren while the rest of their relatives were affiliated with the Dunkard church. However, both churches agreed that farm machinery should be allowed. This had been a point of tension between Daniel's father and grandfather for years, but everyone at last seemed to agree.

"It is a relief, I reckon, that we all recognize that farming in the old manner, without machinery, makes life too difficult without a large group of farmers to help each parish survive," Fredrick said, pulling out into the street among a bevy of other motor vehicles. "I reckon the church divide underscored that."

He slid into the back seat next to his mother, who patted his hand affectionately.

"There is no denying that farm machinery is a blessing, especially when you're getting on in age," Oscar said with a chuckle. "Farming in the old ways is full of good memories, but it isn't possible nowadays for most of us."

"Too true. Pastor Graber over at the Dunkard congregation is a level-headed man," Fredrick added. "He understands that you can keep the old dress and manner and still use machines to farm, though some don't choose to own them."

"It is good that he's a former Old Order Brethren," Oscar said. "He seems to strongly draw from the book of Proverbs: 'Many plans are in the minds of men, but it is always the purpose of the Lord that will stand.'"

"He knows making work easier is important, but abandoning the use of conduct and appearance as a tribute to honor our God is not necessary," Lena said.

Daniel, who had heard similar conversations before, interjected. "The Zion German Baptist Brethren Church completely moved to Camden, right?" he asked. "Do you know how they are doing without the use of machinery?"

"They are doing well enough, I reckon," Oscar said. "Your grandmother and I received letters from friends in that congregation not too long ago. They are managing to farm without machines or even electricity, but only due to the large numbers of Brethren working as one."

"I don't believe such a move, due to the distance and upheaval, is an option for our family," Lena said. "I would hate to leave the land you and Grandma worked so hard for."

"It is dear to all our hearts," Oscar said. Daniel nodded; he couldn't imagine his family living anywhere else.

"Grandpa, how is Grandma? How are you spending your time these days?" Daniel asked as Fredrick made a turn onto a long stretch of dirt road. He knew he would have to speak of the inevitable soon, but listening to Oscar talk of his daily life was soothing. His grandparents' life revolved around the joy of children, grandchildren, and soon-to-be great-grandchildren these days.

"Even in the cold, Grandma takes her afternoon walks to your house, especially if she knows Sigrid or Rachel is visiting," Oscar said. "Sigi also often brings Annie over to our house. You know how Grandma loves to bake with Annie and teach her how to sew and whatnot, all the while telling her stories about our family."

"That is good to hear. So, Annie is thriving, I take it?"

"Oh, yes," Oscar said, the affection evident in his words. "Anne loves playing with her cousins and other Christian children, and she is as interested as ever. Afternoons playing outside, feeding the livestock, gathering eggs, doing other chores . . . it all comes sort of naturally to her. I have never heard her utter a word of complaint."

"Rachel is so intrigued by Annie's way of knowing what is about to happen before it does," Lena said with a chuckle. "That girl always knows where the banties hide their eggs in the barn. She even knew exactly where Boots went to birth her last litter."

Daniel laughed. "Very perceptive, our Annie. How's my sister?"

"Her expectancy is all well," said Fredrick. "Only a few months to go. She and John will come tomorrow to see you."

"I still think she could have married a good German Brethren boy . . ." Oscar said ruefully. Daniel blanched. Rachel had married the son of a Catholic neighbor she'd known since childhood; it was the first time anyone from the family married outside of Anabaptist faith.

"But we all believe in the same God," Lena said firmly. "And if it is something that Rachel is willing to accept, then it is her choice." Daniel touched the back of his mother's hand in solidarity, feeling somewhat reassured. Fredrick and Lena had never seemed alarmed about Rachel's choice of a husband, which only served to make Daniel respect them even more.

"Does she seem to take well to her new life?" Daniel asked.

"She seems content to live a simple life as Ma and Grandma did," said Lena. "Rachel has settled into married life and is learning her husband's Catholic beliefs."

"Um, so," Daniel said, his hand creeping up to the back of his neck. "On a related note, I have something to tell all of you." Lena and Oscar both turned to stare, and there was a pregnant pause.

"Come out and just say it, son!" Fredrick said from the driver's seat.

"I . . . I've been sorta seeing someone at school. For most of this semester."

There was dead silence in the car.

"Well, I can't wait to hear more about her," Lena said finally. "But look! It will have to wait. We're home now."

Daniel sighed and stepped out into the chilly air, ready to be interrogated. However, he was distracted when he saw Sigrid and Otto's car a few paces away.

"Are Sigrid and her family here to have dinner with us?" he asked hopefully.

"Not sure," Lena said. "I did not know they were coming, though; of course, they are welcome. I think they showed themselves inside already."

When Daniel opened the door to the house, eleven-year-old Annie, her dark eyes sparkling, threw her arms around him.

"Daniel!" she cried.

"Cousin Annie!" Daniel said, laughing. "My goodness, you have shot up like a weed!"

Annie laughed. "I'm the shortest kid in my grade!"

"Applesauce," Daniel said, looking down at her. The top of her head was level with the middle of his torso. "I won't believe it for a second."

"Come, Annie," Otto called from the living room, waving at Daniel. "Let Daniel get settled and speak with everyone. We should finish our ciphering."

Annie gave Daniel a wide grin. "You'll have to tell me all the interesting things you learned at Purdue later," she said.

"Of course," Daniel replied, lifting his heavy sack of books. "There's a lot to tell."

Stepping into the kitchen, Daniel's smile instantly fell from his face. Sigrid and Greta were sitting at the dining table, ashen, with cups of steaming bone broth. Lena slid into the chair next to Greta.

"Daniel is glad to see you, of course," Lena said, and Daniel nodded. "But it is clear this is not a social call. Are the two of you all right?"

Sigrid began to cry from swollen, red eyes. She pulled a letter from her bag and slid it over to Lena. Fredrick and Daniel both came to read over Lena's shoulder, the blood draining from their faces as they read the German words in the unfamiliar handwriting.

Dear Sigrid and Greta,

I am writing of someone I loved very much and to whom you were also so critical. I found your address in Paul's old notebook. I am his wife, Helga.

While it grieves me to tell you that Paul passed away and has been gone for two years now, may it bring you some solace that he died honorably. When the Nazis invaded, we attempted to leave Denmark. A Danish group Paul had worked with organized an evacuation plan. Paul joined them after learning of an internment camp to be built in Denmark.

My parents and I escaped to Sweden with Paul's assistance. Paul's fortune, however, was not as providential. He and Pierre Delacroix, the man who helped with Annie's papers, were arrested. They were convicted and executed by the Nazis. My parents and I are now safely in Sweden with our son, who will turn two in February.

I think of Paul every day, and of all the lives he touched: mine, yours, and Annie's. I only regret that my parents were too unwell to make the journey to America in time.

I think of Anne often and hope she is happy in America. Please send her love from Auntie Helga. I am also saddened that we never got to meet. I would love to see her again and meet you someday when the world is quiet again.

In grief and gratitude—
Helga Kunkle

Lena, shaking, finally handed the letter to Oscar, who had located his reading glasses. For several minutes, there was no sound except for Annie and Otto's quiet conversation in the next room. Then Lena, despite herself, began to sob.

"May God bless and keep him in his embrace," Oscar said, placing the letter and his glasses on the worn wood table.

"I feel terrible for ever having thought anything bad about Paul," Sigrid said heavily.

"He may have had his faults, but in the end, there can be no doubt that he was brave and kind," Oscar said in an unstable voice. "He only did what he thought was right. There are at least five people who owe him their lives, and likely many more."

"And our Annie is the most precious girl," Greta said, also wiping away tears. "I cannot imagine life without her. I hope Paul knows how grateful we are."

"We will have to inform the congregation and district," Daniel said, putting an arm around his mother, who had put her head down on the table and was wracked with sobs. He had not known Paul as well as the others—indeed, he hadn't seen the man since he was a child—but he felt chilled to his core nevertheless. "They probably haven't had any communication about this at all. It's good that Paul kept your address and that Helga recognized your name, Sigrid."

"It's a miracle this letter made it here at all," Fredrick said, running a hand through his hair so that it stuck up wildly. "It was a risk for her to have written to us. Have you heard from Rudolph, Ma?" Fredrick asked Greta. She shook her head sadly.

For the rest of the evening, through dinner and afterwards, the subdued and shocked conversation revolved around Paul. The news had completely eclipsed Daniel's announcement about his new girlfriend, but he didn't mind at all.

"Otto, are you feeling alright?" Sigrid asked Otto as she was helping to clear dinner plates. Daniel glanced at Uncle Otto and was surprised to see that he was glowering, staring into space.

"How ironic that Annie's birth date is September the first," he said as Daniel popped his last bite of pork into his mouth and handed Sigrid his plate.

"What's ironic about it?" Sigrid asked.

"The Nazi invasion of Poland in '39 was one interesting birthday gift for such a child." Annie looked at Otto, narrowing her bright eyes in thought but saying nothing.

"Otto!" Oscar said, frowning his brow and putting his index finger to his lips.

"I'm just being frank," Otto said. "We're being pulled into another war." His left hand twitched on the table.

"You are safe now," Sigrid said. "You're nearly fifty—too old to have to go back into the Army. And besides, we have a daughter to think of. Annie, please drink the rest of your milk."

"Yes, Mama," Annie said, still watching her father carefully.

"I am not thinking of myself," Otto grumbled. Everyone's eyes gravitated toward Daniel.

"Just thinking about it keeps me up at night," Otto said, now staring at his nephew. "I am glad you have stayed in school."

Daniel gave his uncle a small smile, but his stomach, full of good food, churned within him. Looking around at the drawn faces of his family, he knew they could all hear the clock ticking slowly but surely towards the inevitable.

35
For God and Country
(Für Gott und Land)
June 22, 1943

With a sigh, Daniel snapped the thick textbook shut. He'd just read the same paragraph thrice without taking in a single word. The warm morning sun shone through his childhood bedroom window, warming his neck and shoulders as he abandoned his summer reading, bending down and pulling a tied shoebox out from under the desk.

Opening the box, Daniel scanned Melodie's most recent letter. He'd received it just yesterday. Unlike many of her other letters, this one was short and hastily scrawled.

June 6, 1943

Dear Daniel,

The Ninety-First has received movement orders. I will be boarding a ship and going to a new destination soon. In five days, if all goes as planned, we will arrive there. There, the process of setting up and managing the evacuation hospital will begin.

I love you, and I will write more as soon as I can.

Melodie

Daniel stared at the words, willing them to reveal more information. He knew Melodie's letter was intentionally vague to maintain operational secrecy around the D-day invasion on June 6. Wondering what destination took five days to reach by ship from the United Kingdom, he pulled out of the box another letter he'd received the month before. This one he'd felt much better about.

May 5, 1944

Dear Daniel,

I'm on my way back to Britain to join the Ninety-First Evacuation Hospital in Bristol. My days are currently full of training and packing supplies and equipment. I am not in harm's way, and if the newspapers are right and treaties are imminent, then the momentum of the war will likely slow.

There is now a good chance that I will be able to remain in the United Kingdom until the war ends. I hope the war will stop much the way World War One ended quickly.

As we do our work here, I often think back on my graduation ceremony. The commencement speaker made a point of reminding the new grads of the "needs of the nation." As you know, I'd already begun my enlistment process that April. I still believe it was the right decision to make, even though it means our engagement will be a long one. It will, I believe, be worth it in the end.

Mom and Pop think you're such a swell guy, and so do I. I so look forward to marrying you when I get home. The world feels topsy-turvy right now; we both have much yet to do before we can be together. However, I can think of nothing more wonderful than marrying one day and starting our lives as one.

I will write again as soon as I can.

Love you always,

Melodie

Leafing through the rest of the letters in the box, the oldest of which were becoming dog-eared, Daniel looked back on the story of Melodie's military service: joining the Red Cross service team, being sworn into active service, going to Fort Harrison in Indianapolis for basic military protocol, field sanitation, physical training, and patient management; transferring to Fort Knox; and, finally, deployment. In some of the letters, Melodie's typical optimism was dulled by the many battle-wounded GIs clinging to life, which she'd treated at the hospital during her long duty hours on the wards.

Daniel ran his fingers over the letter Melodie had sent after he'd attended her commissioning ceremony and even older ones from when Melodie had transferred to complete her nursing degree. He pulled out one that he was particularly fond of; its service was wrinkled and faded from frequent readings.

I treasure the memories of the many summer days I spent on your farm. Fishing for shiners in Pipe Creek, feeding the cattle, and baking blackberry pies . . . it all seems like a dream now. I adore your Grandma and Grandpa Beck (they remind me of my grandparents). You really are the image of your Grandma Greta.

Listening to Greta's stories of relatives, cleaning vegetables, sewing clothes, and doing farm chores were the highlights of my summer, as were the long conversations with Aunt Sigrid during our evenings. I was always struck by the similarities and mannerisms you both share.

I often remember Annie, too; thinking of her brings a smile even on the darkest days. She is so intelligent, and her bobbed hairstyle is so cute. I loved how she followed me around the farm, jabbering questions about anything she could think to ask. I still remember once, out of the clear blue, she looked at me and whispered, "You and Daniel will marry someday and have two little boys," as if somehow she knew our future for sure. The honest and uncomplicated love in your family made me so welcome.

With a frustrated grunt, Daniel tossed the letter aside and looked out at the balmy day. The sky was as blue as forget-me-nots, the foliage so green it seemed to glow, but the world was not well. It was time to accept reality. His naive belief that the war would soon halt was betrayed by what he heard and read in the news. He could no longer focus on farm work or school but rather was consumed by the sacrifice Melodie was making while he sat safely at home, reading her letters for the umpteenth time. He'd known what he needed to do the moment the Zenith console radio that sat in Lena's parlor broadcast the news of the Normandy invasion a week before. Now he had this letter, and his fate was sealed.

Gathering all the letters, Daniel tucked them back into their shoebox with a sense of resolve. He steeled himself, packed a few items into a bag, and went downstairs, where his parents were getting ready for lunch. The smell of freshly baked strawberry muffins filled the air, and the radio quietly gave the latest bleak news on the war, which he tried to ignore.

"There you are," Lena said. "Are you hungry, Daniel?"

"Not really," Daniel said, though he did pluck a muffin from the cooling rack, flinching as it burned his fingers. "Pa, may I borrow the truck? I need to go into town."

"Surely," Fredrick said. "Is everything okay, son?"

"Yes," said Daniel.

"You look worried," Lena said.

"I'm always worried these days," Daniel said, scratching the back of his neck automatically, then wincing. The skin there was rubbed raw.

"Please know that we support you," Lena said, watching as Daniel took a hasty bite of muffin, holding it carefully in his mouth and breathing through it to cool for a moment before chewing. "We pray daily with Grandma and Grandpa for peace. We pray for Melodie's safety and that God will protect her."

"I know, Ma," Daniel said with a halfhearted smile after swallowing a tart bite. "Be back soon. By the way, these muffins are delicious."

"Take another one! And try not to be too late," Lena called as Daniel walked out the door, narrowly avoiding stepping on their tabby cat, who was napping on the porch. "Rachel and John are coming over for dinner tonight, and expectant mothers don't wait for dinnertime stragglers!"

Daniel felt somewhat guilty as he stuffed the rest of the muffin in his mouth and then crank-started the truck. His family was aware that Daniel's status as a student was confirmed by the draft board. They had no inclination that military service was something Daniel would ever consider volunteering for. Daniel tried not to ponder this too much as he drove, blind to the beautiful greenery and thriving crops around him.

Fields soon turned into paved brick, and Daniel's resolve stayed with him as he walked into the towering three-story Miami County Courthouse with its imposing columns. He strode directly toward the Army recruiter's office, hearing the secretaries laughing. The chattering of their typewriters echoed down the long marble hallway as he approached the smoke-filled office.

The room was in disarray and obviously understaffed. Stacks

of files sat on mostly unoccupied desks, with frazzled recruiters and secretaries barely making a dent in the piles on their desks. A tall, thin Army staff sergeant with two rows of campaign ribbons attached above his left khaki shirt pocket was sitting behind his desk with a cane propped next to him. He had a short-stemmed pipe in one hand and a cup of coffee in the other, and he pointed at Daniel with the pipe, motioning for him to come in.

Daniel approached with some caution and stood in front of the sergeant, who casually pointed him to a civilian sitting at the next desk.

"How might I help you, son?" the middle-aged recruiter asked, his dark hair slicked with pomade.

"I want to join up," Daniel answered.

"So, you think you would make a good soldier?" the man asked, shuffling through a file.

"I'm not sure," Daniel replied. Hearing a clomping sound, he looked up to see a captain with a noticeable limp walking through the door, making his way toward a desk at the opposite end of the room.

"More fresh meat!" the captain said, his sharp eyes grazing over Daniel. Daniel, for his part, tried hard to focus on the man sitting in front of him.

"Draft status?" the recruiter asked. Daniel pulled a file containing his last notification along with copies of his grade transcripts from Purdue out of his bag and handed it to the man. The recruiter looked through the papers and began mumbling.

"Civil Engineering, grades are high, three years of college, looks good for a possible commission . . . yes, I think we may be able to use you." Clipping the pages together and placing them in a file basket on his desk, the man looked up at Daniel, holding a voucher.

"Take this chit to the restaurant next door and get yourself something to eat, son," the man said. "Come back in an hour. That will give me time to do some negotiating, and I'll be ready to let you know the next step."

"Okay," Daniel said, getting up and leaving the cluttered room. Feeling somewhat disoriented, Daniel walked next door to a small, smoky cafe, where he sat at the counter and ordered a hamburger and vegetable soup. The lunch crowd drifted in and out as he sat lost in thought and accepted his food from the smiling, pretty waitress without giving her a second glance. He regretted ordering a burger, which reminded him of that last meal with Melodie.

Despite his resolve, Daniel was not sure that he was making the right decision. He stirred and slurped his soup, pondering the many complications that awaited him when he returned home. He would have to confide in his parents and grandparents when he got home, and the thought of their horrified faces made him set down his spoon. He also knew the attitude of the church; CO deferment was an option his pastor felt should be used whenever possible. The Army was now overstaffed, able to draft as many men as needed. A prevailing "the war is won" attitude had crept into recruitment stations, and so the pastor's sentiment wasn't an unusual one.

Nonetheless, as he forced himself to eat his hamburger, Daniel felt better and better about his decision. The final march across Europe would make certain job specialties in which Daniel was qualified a recruitment priority. The better the operations were run, the more likely the war would be won and the sooner everyone—including Melodie—could return home.

At one o'clock, back at the courthouse, the civilian recruiter handed Daniel an itinerary for bus travel to Indianapolis for testing and the entrance physical.

"If this goes right and all is on the square, you'll be on your way to engineering training at Fort Belvoir before ya know it," the recruiter said. "Welcome to the Army, son."

"Thanks," Daniel said, trying to look pleased. *This is for Mel*, he thought—*anything to bring Mel home sooner.*

Greta and Oscar were at the family farm when Daniel turned into the drive just before two. Daniel brought the pickup to a stop by Oscar's barn, climbed out slowly, and walked towards the house and his gathered family with his spine as straight as he could muster.

"Dan," Greta said, coming up to hug her grandson. "Why the long face?"

"Daniel didn't say much this morning about what he was up to," Lena said, her face creased with concern.

"I know," Daniel said. "There is something I need to say now." He hesitated, reached for his neck, then stopped himself. Grandma Greta gave him a searching gaze, then took Grandpa Oscar's hand.

"Let us go look at the cherry tree over there," she said. "I think some of those cherries might be ripe, don't you?"

"Ah," Oscar said, his eyes darting from Daniel to Greta. "Yes, good idea."

As the elderly couple approached the little cherry tree, pursued by three of Boots' progeny, Daniel stepped closer to his parents and closed his eyes.

"I'm enlisting in the Army. I went to the recruiting station this morning," he said. Then he opened his eyes. His parents stood silently, mouths open.

"W . . . why?" Fredrick asked after what seemed an interminable pause to Daniel. "You could be exempted after college to help us here on the farm or even as a conscientious objector."

"It's not right," Daniel said, shaking his head vehemently. "Especially now that Melodie is over there doing her part, and I'm here safe at home. I can't take it." He tried to ignore the trembling of his mother's hands.

"Just because Melodie was called doesn't mean that you need to risk dying, too," Lena said in a quiet, desperate voice. "Helping the war effort here at home is just as important."

"What's done is done," Daniel said. "I may not even be qualified, but I had to try at least to volunteer. I will have to take some tests and a physical in a few weeks, so we'll wait and see. No need to tell Grandpa and Grandma just yet."

Fredrick nodded, his expression strangely blank. Daniel reached out a hand and placed it on his mother's shoulder, trying to silently comfort her as Greta and Oscar's voices came closer. She squeezed her eyes shut, placing her hand over his and pressing it there as though to hold him in place forever.

The next four weeks passed too quickly. A month-old letter from Melodie arrived explaining that her evacuation hospital had been inundated with casualties. She wrote about the suffering she had witnessed, the extremely long hours, and feeling exhausted but proud to serve her country. Feeling now more optimistic than ever that it was suitable to volunteer, Daniel passed all his aptitude and physical qualifying tests with ease and was offered a commission as a second lieutenant. He was to attend OCS and the

Army Engineer training course in Virginia for six months before deployment.

The lovely weather continued, but Daniel's mood was somber when, soon before he was set to leave, the Becks and Bowmans gathered for a family meal. Afterward, full of summer squash pie, pork chops, and slow-roasted greens, he sat wondering what the food in the military would be like. Everyone else seemed to be in a happy stupor, sipping buttermilk and nibbling raisin walnut cookies—everyone except Uncle Otto, who placed a hand on Daniel's shoulder. His aging but handsome features were set in an unreadable, almost blank expression.

"Come stand on the porch with me for a moment, Dan," he said.

"Okay," Daniel said, concerned that he knew where this was going. The two men stepped out onto the porch to admire the clear July sky, which was beginning to grow pink and orange with a brilliant sunset. Boots' orange-and-gray tabby kittens, rapidly growing in size, were taking turns batting at a mouse in the dusty drive.

"I know what you are feeling," Otto said. "I was in your spot not so many years ago."

"Let me guess," Daniel said, glancing at his uncle and smiling to break the tension. "My folks put you up to this."

"Your ma wants me to tell you some bloody war stories that will scare the dickens out of you so you'll change your mind and stay in school," Otto said without flinching, staring out at the sunset. "But you and I both know you don't scare that easily."

"Thank you, Uncle," Daniel said.

"All I will say is that if you decide to go through with this, it will change you, Dan," Otto said, still staring forward. Daniel felt the hairs on his arms stand up. "You will never again be as you are at this time in your life. Your innocence and the peace you feel inside will be taken. But it is your choice, and no one can make it for you."

Daniel swallowed hard. "I know, Uncle Otto."

Otto put his hand on Daniel's shoulder and smiled sadly. Without another word, he returned to the gathering inside. Daniel stood for a moment alone, watching the sky turn red.

That night, Daniel sat down and wrote a letter to Melodie, feeling a sense of pride. He was officially dropping out of Purdue to accept the Army commission and would be going to Fort Belvoir soon. He, just like Melodie, was willing to do his part to end the war. They would work to end the fighting together, even if they were far apart.

* * *

"I'd bet your farmwork and problem-solving served you well during training," Fredrick said in an artificially cheerful voice. "I remember Uncle Otto saying that doing farm repairs helped his understanding of the Army better."

"Yes, I suppose maybe for bridge building or earth moving," answered Daniel, reaching for another piece of cornbread. Outside, the west wind blew flurries of snow against the windows.

"We're so glad you could come home for Christmas," Lena said, giving her son's arm an affectionate squeeze.

"Me too, Ma," Daniel said with a small smile that quickly faded. Scanning Dan's face for the hundredth time, Lena was distressed to see that he already looked older, sterner.

"We are all proud of you, Dan," Fredrick said. Daniel sat quietly, munching his cornbread. Lena and Fredrick exchanged glances, and Lena tried to quell the sinking feeling in her belly. She had barely touched her food, although the rich pork bone soup was quite tasty and perfect for such a cold day.

"Army engineering must be easy for you with your school background," Lena said, still trying to sound chipper.

"No wonder you were the company honor man during training," Fredrick said. "We were proud when we read that in your letter, though we kept it to ourselves." Lena glanced over to see Daniel giving a halfhearted shrug.

"We're close to winning," Daniel said, turning to the window, his skin pale in the watery winter light. "Maybe my enlisting will speed things up a bit."

"Perhaps," Lena said, taking a small spoonful of soup. "You're headed to Kentucky after Christmas?"

"Yes, Fort Knox."

"As a combat engineer?"

"Yes, Eighty-Fourth Infantry Division, 309th Combat Engineer Battalion."

When Daniel went straight to his room after the meal, Lena furrowed her brow and looked at Fredrick.

"He is not very talkative, is he?" she said. "Do you think he is sick?"

Fredrick put an arm around her. "No, I don't think there's anything physically wrong."

Lena bit her lip. "I wish we could simply keep him at home."

"I think that might make him feel even worse," Fredrick said, smoothing a hand over Lena's shoulder. "He needs to help, I suspect."

Lena nodded slowly. The stubborn face of her lost brother

was still crystal clear in her memory. *We all serve the Lord in our way*, she thought.

Over the next day after his arrival, Lena and Fredrick managed to get Daniel to talk more about his training experiences and the people in his company. Lena felt herself becoming more and more aware that she was going to have to be the one to have to mention the real reason for Daniel's malaise.

"Have you heard from Melodie?" she finally blurted as Daniel helped her wash up the lunch dishes.

"Only a couple of times," Daniel said, taking a plate from her and drying it. "She was moved forward with her evacuation unit to France and then went to Holland. Lots of wounded there; most severe and needing to be stabilized." He held the plate awkwardly at his side. "Her unit will keep following the Ninth Division. That's about all she said. No specifics."

"That must be awfully hard," Lena said sympathetically. Daniel just nodded, rubbing at the plate with his already sodden towel.

Over the next ten days, much to Lena's relief, Daniel seemed to perk up a little, though he was nowhere near his usual optimistic and curious self. He visited with Rachel and her husband and met their little daughter, Disa, for the first time. He also spent time with Sigrid, Otto, and his cousin Annie. It was Annie, with her dark eyes sparkling as she talked about Christmas, her school play, and Santa visiting her school, who finally got Daniel to laugh. The sound seemed to thaw Lena's heart as she and Sigrid stood together in the kitchen, mixing dough for cinnamon cookies.

The day after Christmas, an hour before Daniel had to leave for the train station, Greta arrived at the Bowman house for one last visit with Daniel. The temperature had warmed into the mid-forties, and a heavy fog hung over the ground.

"Come with me, sweet boy," Greta said, smiling and reaching out an arm for Daniel. Her posture was still straight and tall, and the resemblance between the two of them, despite the difference in age and sex, was uncanny. "Your aunt and I want to pray for you."

"Of course, Grandma," Daniel said, taking her arm.

Vapor rose as, bundled up in coats and shawls, Greta, Sigrid, and Daniel walked to the stone circle by the woods. They kicked up eddies of fog as they talked of family, church friends, and childhood events on the short walk. The sparrows perched on the stones watched as Greta took Daniel's right hand and Sigrid took his left. The three bowed their heads.

"God, we pray for mercy for Daniel," Greta said. "Please send your angels to watch over and protect him wherever he is sent. We also send a prayer for Melodie that you would also watch over her and keep her safe from harm."

As the prayer ended and the trio opened their eyes, the birds took flight, circling briefly overhead before they became specks of color in the slate-gray sky. Despite what may lie ahead, Daniel felt his heart rise slightly with them.

36
Never Again
(Nie Wieder)
April 10 – December 1945

It was hard to read the letter in the dim light of the moving vehicle, but Daniel managed. He quickly scanned the words he'd written to Melodie the day before, making sure there were no errors before he sealed it in its envelope. Imagining Melodie reading it and perhaps tucking it away in a particular spot gave him some comfort.

My Dearest Melodie,

I love and miss you. Our Eighty-Fourth "Railsplitters" have stopped the German offensive in the Rhineland. The battles have been pretty bloody, and my engineering battalion has had to prove itself over and over. We've assisted the division in bridging rivers, cleared lots of mines, and even conducted civil missions to get civilians out of danger.

Currently, I'm serving as a forward adviser. I primarily coordinate the engineering needs of the battalion. Seeing all the casualties has

*made me determined to put this all behind me when I get back home. I
try not to*

The vehicle he was riding in hit a bump, and Daniel looked
up. This morning, the Eighty-Fourth Division was rolling toward
the Neuengamme satellite camp. Around him, members of the
company were silent on the ride, exhausted by the horrors they'd
seen thus far. Knowing time was short, Daniel looked back down
and finished the letter.

*I try not to obsess over what is going on here but instead think of
the life that will be waiting for us in Indiana and how good it will be
to be with you again finally.*

*I carry your picture with me wherever I go to remind myself of
how much I love you and what we are fighting for. There is much we
have to look forward to when this all finally ends.*

*I hope you are well, my darling, and staying safe. Please be care-
ful, and write soon.*

All my love,

Daniel

Satisfied that there were no misspellings, Daniel folded the
letter and licked the seam of the envelope, sealing it and wondering when it would reach Melodie. Though the post had been
slow, Daniel found a sense of shared purpose in supporting the
infantrymen of the 335th that helped him cope when contact
from Melodie wasn't possible.

Putting the envelope safely into his inner pocket, Daniel
looked out the window and watched as the captain leaned out
of the lead vehicle. The man's distinctive Gable-style mustache
and slight build made him instantly recognizable. Despite being
seasoned, Dallas Samson, Captain Promotable, appeared younger

than his twenty-seven years, often being mistaken for a newly enlisted man.

"Want a chaw?"

Daniel looked beside him at Sergeant First Class Milo Bradley, whose oversized ears were red along the edges. He was proffering a twist of chewing tobacco.

"No, thank you," Daniel begged off.

"Suit yourself," said Milo, stuffing some into his cheek. "Say, there's the camp."

With Neuengamme looming in the distance, Daniel mentally ran through what they'd been told during Captain Samson's briefing the day before.

"The Hannover-Ahlem concentration camp is the brainchild of the Himmler SS," Captain Samson had explained to the stern-faced group in his West Texas twang. "Jew prisoners there are forced to work in the tunnel factories cranking out military aircraft parts. We've got to go in and liberate their asses."

Captain Samson had looked each of his men in the eye, conveying confidence and power. "Y'all remember the crap we've seen getting to this point," he'd said with a broad gesture of his hand. "The scouts tell me this camp we're headed to is a real royal shithole. We need to cover each other's asses and stay alert. There may still be krauts left who want a fight, stupid bastards that they are."

The captain had glowered, his hatred palpable. "This mission has a political and propaganda importance, I suppose. But remember: I'll never ask anything of you that I'm unwilling to do myself. Let's get through the bullshit and liberate the camp. The Army's mission is to win this war; mine is to make sure y'all get back home alive, limbs intact."

Daniel's gaze wandered back to the captain, who was holding his helmet on with one hand, squinting into the sun. Daniel wondered what this formidable leader had in store for the enemy. The captain had a distinct and obsessive hatred of the Nazi command and staff but in particular, the SS. Though he never was reprimanded or questioned by his superiors, it was well known that he gave his men carte blanche when it came to shooting captured members of the Nazi officer corps, who often "tried to escape."

The scouts had warned the battalion of what was inside the gates of Ahlem, but nothing could have prepared them for what they saw. As the American and allied forces drove forward, a horrible smell of death and decay met them. They immediately closed the windows of the vehicle.

"Shit," muttered Sergeant Bradley.

"Poor souls," Daniel said.

"We know they death-marched those healthy enough to walk to camp Bergen-Belsen," Milo said, chewing his plug of tobacco with browned teeth. "But the Nazis probably left a few soldiers behind to burn and cover up the shit they did before the American or Brit troops arrived. The rest of them hightailed it . . . chicken shits." Milo spat tobacco juice into a tin, then wiped his mouth on his sleeve. His ears were redder than ever.

Daniel looked out the window at the sick, weak prisoners literally dying before his eyes. A large pile of bodies rose like a nightmare outside of a nearby red brick building, with scattered corpses of men too weak to march who had likely died during the hastily planned retreat. Although Daniel had grown up on a farm and had seen and smelled rotting livestock from the time he was small, the inhumanity of this situation overshadowed anything he could have ever imagined. Everything his religious upbringing had taught him was being tested by the results of the incarnate evil he witnessed around him. Feeling sick, Daniel hoped Melodie was somewhere much better than this.

"Here we go," Milo groused as the vehicles came to a halt. The soldiers came filing out of their vehicles, eyes watering from the putrid smell of decomposition.

"Jesus," Captain Samson said as he placed a towel over his nose and mouth to breathe through. "These poor hebe[33] bastards! FUBAR[34], this is FUBAR bullshit!" He started barking orders while his troops, already gagging and coughing, carried out as best they could.

"Round up those damn strays," Captain Samson barked, pointing at a few German soldiers who were attempting a break near the back of the compound. "Make sure to get them all." The group he'd gestured at immediately went off in search of any remaining German guards.

"Sergeant Malone, get these people out of that goddamn cage and get them some water," the captain said, gesturing around at the Jews who were still locked behind the fence, ignoring the dead bodies rotting at their feet. "Go easy. I've got chow trucks twenty minutes out."

As Sergeant Malone, accompanied by Daniel's team, started breaking into the gates and handing out small amounts of water, the captain coughed through the cloth covering his mouth.

"Now, get up here and put a wire perimeter around the krauts," the captain said to a group of MPs as Daniel fought to keep from losing his breakfast. "The medics have been raggin' my

---

33   Slang for Jews
34   Military slang for "f***** up beyond all recognition"

ass all the way here about not overfeeding these poor bastards. We'll just end up killing 'em," Sergeant Malone said, retying the cloth around his face with shaking, pale fingers as the Jews began stumbling out of the cantonment. His complexion, usually very pink, was now blanched as bone.

"Water and armored cow[35] only," Sergeant Malone said, tossing an empty can of PET Milk[36] sitting on a jeep's fender. "We don't need to add puke to this stench, boys. Unless the docs say something different, give 'em only small amounts."

As Daniel reached for a case of the canned milk, Sergeant Malone let out a wheeze, fixing Daniel with his watery eyes.

"We're lucky in a way," he said. "The weather's been cold enough. Otherwise, this place would be swarming with flies."

"Small blessing," Daniel agreed, his watering eyes brimming over.

As it turned out, only around 300 of the male prisoners had survived the beatings, abuse, and starvation. Daniel, like many of his colleagues, had to take a break to vomit in a corner but was soon back rationing water and milk, trying to be encouraging to the haunted-looking, gaunt Jewish captives. One older man knelt and began praying a Hebrew prayer, tears falling from his badly infected eyes. Several prisoners spontaneously attempted to embrace and kiss the hands of the liberating American soldiers that mingled among them, thanking them in German and Hebrew.

Nearby, the military police quickly formed a temporary holding pen. Soon, American soldiers shuffled the remaining twenty Nazi soldiers into retention. As Daniel went to the truck to unload more supplies, his bandana tied securely over his mouth, Captain Samson's powerful voice rang out.

---

35   WWII slang for canned milk
36   Brand of evaporated canned milk

"Isolate that Nazi bastard," Captain Samson was saying to the military police detachment. "I want to question his ass."

Daniel looked into the enclosure. Among the enlisted enemy soldiers was a hardened-looking young SS lieutenant. He appeared to have tried to remove his rank and uniform before being captured upon the American's camp entry; there were several faded spots on his coat where patches had clearly been hastily torn off, and he was missing his cap.

Turning, Captain Samson saw Daniel staring.

"Lieutenant Beck, get your butt over here," he said, motioning for Daniel to join him. "We might need a translator."

Leaving the water, Daniel did as he was told. He had earned the captain's confidence early on, and he and his squad often were requested by Captain Samson to assist in whatever the mission called for.

As Daniel approached, the first sergeant strode over to the captain, whispering and pointing to three standing boxcars sitting on the train rails outside the camp fencing by an entry gate.

"We'll check it out," the captain said. "Sergeant Phillips, send me over two enlisted kraut P.O.W.s and bring that SS asshole with them. Lieutenant Beck, follow me. We got to make sure public affairs documents this shit."

Captain Samson, Daniel, and three other enlisted U.S. soldiers walked outside the camp perimeter to the parked rail cars. Unbelievably, the smell became even more overwhelming as the five soldiers approached a sitting boxcar. Daniel held a rag over his bandana as they walked closer; the thin cloth was not nearly enough.

"I pour Aqua Velva inside the towel I breathe through, sir," one of the T5s said to Daniel as they stood waiting, holding out a small bottle. "Give it a try." Daniel gratefully held his rag up to receive a little of the liquid.

"Thanks," he said with relief, breathing in the slightly lavender scent.

"Welcome, sir," the tech sergeant said. "Now, here comes trouble."

Daniel stood at attention and saw that the captain was approaching the group with two disheveled-looking German soldiers and the SS lieutenant. A buck sergeant prodded the prisoners forward with his M1 carbine.

The captain turned toward Daniel, cupping his hand around a K-ration Lucky Strike. He lit the cigarette and pulled the cloth from his mouth, taking a long drag and surveying the scene before him with bloodshot eyes rimmed with dark circles.

"Tell the krauts to open the railcar," he said, stifling a cough. Daniel had never welcomed the smell of cigarette smoke more as it wafted toward him, cutting through the stench of decay.

"Offne die Tür," Daniel said to one of the young, frightened-looking enlisted Nazi soldiers.

The German soldier turned and looked at the SS officer, who nodded for him to proceed. Pulling the outer latch counterclockwise, the two German soldiers tugged the sliding door open. As they did, Daniel saw a sight that would plague his dreams for decades to come.

Steam and swarms of spring gnats and flies escaped from the car, and a gelatinous soup of bodily fluids began to drip onto the Earth. The open door exposed a large number of decomposing human bodies stacked like cords of wood. The maggot-infested dead, even in their degraded state, had visible wounds and broken bones. It appeared that the severely malnourished prisoners had been tortured and starved to death.

The three young American soldiers began to gag uncontrollably. Daniel shoved the Aqua Velva rag as far up his nose as it would go and squeezed his eyes shut, saying a silent prayer for all these people who had been so needlessly slaughtered.

Please take them into your care, O Lord. Give them peace and rest.

Daniel heard a snort. Opening his streaming eyes, he saw that the SS lieutenant was unbelievably smirking as he watched the young American soldiers' convulsive reactions.

"Your men are veak, Captain," the German officer said in accented English.

"That kraut officer speaks English, sir," the buck sergeant said.

"Yes, I can see that," the captain growled. His face was a dangerous shade of crimson.

"Your soldiers lack discipline and understanding vhy ve are needing to do zese sings," the Nazi said with a laugh, the sound grating and harsh.

Captain Samson slowly turned and stared at the SS officer. Sparks flew as the captain flicked his lit cigarette at the German officer's forehead. The officer, to his credit, didn't flinch as the captain unbuttoned his hip-holstered ACP, drew it slowly, and strode forward, pushing the barrel of the pistol to the man's pointy nose.

"All aboard, buttercup," he said, tilting his head toward the open boxcar door.

For the first time, fear shone in the SS lieutenant's eyes. He shook his head as if to say, "I don't understand."

"RASCH!"[37] the captain screamed in the lieutenant's face, spittle flying.

The Nazi slowly turned and seized the open boxcar. Daniel had to turn away and retch when the man slipped in the gore and fell to the ground.

"Get your nancy ass up!" the captain shouted. Head swimming, Daniel turned to see that Captain Samson had locked the hammer of his weapon to the rear and forcefully shoved his pistol into the back of the Nazi's head.

Daniel had to turn away once more to dry heave into the dirt. When he was able to get to his feet again, the German soldiers were kneeling to pick up the SS Nazi and hoist him into the railcar. The captain stood by, his gun trained on the Nazi lieutenant.

Once inside the train car, the officer pulled himself upright and stood, defiantly staring at Captain Samson, up to his ankles in the wet remains of his victims.

"Shut the fuckin' door," the captain barked, motioning to the two German soldiers. He glanced at Daniel, who once again had the rag pressed to his face.

"Schließ die Tür," Daniel said in a hoarse, muffled voice.

The two men looked at each other, then rolled the railcar door shut and secured the latch. The officer inside made no sound. Daniel swayed on his feet. Next to him, the soldier who had given him the Aqua Velva was sitting unabashedly on the ground, hyperventilating.

"First Sergeant, get those two enlisted krauts back to the holding area," the captain demanded, lifting his rag off his face to speak between bouts of coughing. "You can leave that SS son of a bitch locked inside for a half hour or so while he admires

---

37   German for "quick"

his work. If he survives the stench, goose-step his ass back to the cantonment wire." He checked his watch: "The Ritchie Boys will be here around 13:00 for interrogations, though I suspect Tinker Bell may try to escape before they get here."

Daniel tried to stand up straight when the captain's blood-shot eyes met his. "Lieutenant Beck," he said. "How soon can you get a couple of D7 Cats[38] in here?"

"The 309th is an hour west, Captain," Daniel said as clearly as he could through his bandana, glad to have something to think about other than the abomination around him. "I can get on the horn and have them here probably by this afternoon."

"Make it happen, Beck," the captain said. "I want all these bodies underground by 18:00 on Friday. There's a group of kraut civilians being trucked here from town this afternoon. They can start cleaning these train cars out and . . ." there was a pause as the captain coughed violently, then wiped his mouth. ". . . moving bodies to bury," he finally finished as he looked with disgust and rage at the scene around him, his eyes nearly popping out of his head. "Brigade is sending the light colonel to take command in the next two days, ahead of our six, Colonel Parker, so the sooner this shit hole is cleaned up, the better, Lieutenant. I don't want the O-5 having to deal with this bullshit any longer than he has to."

"Yes, sir," Daniel replied in his muffled voice. As he returned to the prison compound, searching for the rest of his squad, two mess trucks pulled inside and began unloading the food containers. The weakened Jewish prisoners struggled toward the trucks, and Daniel tried to focus on the relief on their faces, the light returning to some of their eyes.

---

38 · Military armored bulldozers used during WWII

This may be hell, Daniel thought, *but at least we are trying to do God's work here.*

The troops continued to do God's work as best they could, and in four days, the satellite camp had been at least superficially remodeled. The civilian force of German townspeople arrived, tasked with burying the dead. Most of Daniel's fellow soldiers thought the townspeople had turned a blind eye to the camp atrocities and were now obligated to do their share. Daniel tried to listen to their stories. Some argued the Nazis had threatened them with death if they'd intervened; some were remorseful; others seemed terrified or indignant. All were afraid of what the Allies would do to them if they refused to comply with the order to bury the dead, and so there was little resistance to the orders.

The German civilians worked through the night to fill the mass graves. The once-ordinary townspeople heaved and sobbed as they carried the decomposing bodies of the slaughtered Jews to the open lime pits that Daniel's engineer battalion had scraped into the earth with their dozers. The overwhelming, now sickeningly familiar smell of death hung in the air as a German interpreter hired by the U.S. Army shouted orders over a megaphone.

Early Sunday morning, Daniel was busy cleaning Hannover with the rest of his team when he was approached by the new commanding officer's radioman and driver. Captain Samson's brigade commander had taken charge of the camp the day before, bringing med teams and supplies.

"Sir, Captain Samson on the horn," the radioman said, passing Daniel the handheld walkie-talkie.

"Lieutenant Beck," Daniel said.

"Beck, Captain Samson. I need your ass here yesterday," Captain Samson's raspy voice barked over the handheld radio.

Daniel wondered what was in store for him now. The new brigade commanding officer had advanced Captain Samson to lead a team at another satellite camp a few miles away at Salzwedel; this camp was primarily for Jewish women who had been transferred from other camps.

"I got two bean wagons en route, so we need to get these Jew dames organized," Captain Samson said. Daniel held the radio away from his ear as the captain's voice volume intensified. "Otherwise, they'll stampede when the dispatch arrives."

"Wilco, Captain," Daniel replied. "Just need to grab my gear and get the battalion commander's driver to shuttle me. Over."

"Roger, he's got the coordinates. Pronto, Lieutenant! Time's wastin'. Over."

Daniel greatly enjoyed the short reprieve from the putrid smell at Hannover during the jeep ride to the new location. As Daniel and his cohort approached the next satellite camp, however, this break abruptly ended. Nearly 3,000 women had been interned at Salzwedel, and boxcars full of rotting corpses idly stood near the camp entrance.

"Dear Jesus," the jeep driver muttered under his breath as the vehicle entered the front gate. Daniel closed his eyes and silently prayed for all those in the camp who had suffered and died, praying also for the strength to carry on with this gruesome task.

"There you are," Captain Samson coughed as Daniel and his companions approached. "Lieutenant Beck, I've got the perfect job for you," he said, taking a drag of his cigarette.

Daniel was quickly assigned a group of soldiers to command, using his rank and German language skills to organize the situation. The women were given small amounts of water and blankets while awaiting the arrival of the kitchen trucks. The temperature was cool, and many of the emaciated women stood shivering, uninsulated from the morning chill. A few ragged-looking children were also scattered among the women, some looking scared, others looking hollow.

As he bent to get more water, the skin on the back of Daniel's arms prickled. He had the distinct feeling that someone was staring at him. Turning, Daniel saw a haggard woman with unkempt dark brown hair and a dimpled chin protectively clutching the hand of a highly malnourished young girl of perhaps thirteen. Daniel suspected the woman was in her late thirties, though she had the posture and demeanor of someone much older. Much like the other women, she was emaciated and dressed in blue-and-white, striped, lice-infested prison rags. However, unlike the listless faces of the other women, this woman's expression was sharp as she stared hard at Daniel.

"Entschuldigung," a voice said, and Daniel felt a tug on his arm. Momentarily looking away, Daniel resumed his duties, handing out water and blankets. The prickling feeling, however, did not go away. Daniel shook his head, doing his work, wondering what was going on. There was a curiosity many civilians seemed to have with American soldiers; it could also be a form of mental illness manifesting from the stress and abuse the women had no doubt endured.

Daniel looked back at the prisoner, who still stared. He was beginning to have a strange feeling that he did actually recognize her. Their eyes met, and for an inexplicable and surreal instant, it was as if a shared, acknowledged recognition flew between them. It was a thing of beauty in an ugly place.

The spell was broken when the drone of the food trucks emanated from the camp's front entrance. The sight of the conveyances sent the survivors into a frantic rush toward the vehicles. The woman disappeared into an uproar of desperate and starving women and children.

"Lieutenant," Captain Samson yelled from a nearby brick barracks, fighting his way through the melee. "Sorry, Beck. The LTC at Hannover needs your ass back there. The regimental commander wants the Jerry tunnel factory[39] demolished. Need your engineering know-how. We'll get the situation here under control. Colonel P is waiting."

"Understood, Captain," Daniel said. He weaved his way to the front of the crowd as he and the lieutenant colonel's driver were soon bumping away in their jeep, relishing the fresh air and April sunshine.

Staring out into the war-torn landscape, Daniel turned the face of the woman over and over in his mind. Then, suddenly, he sat upright as though he'd received an electric shock. The woman's hair, eyes, and distinguishing dimple clicked into place in his mind.

"Dear God," he whispered to himself.

"What now?" said the driver.

"Nothing, nothing," Daniel said, reaching distractedly for the back of his neck, then pulling his hand back and sitting on it instead.

As he rode the jeep towards Hannover, Daniel found himself haunted by the thought. Perhaps it was just his deep longing and separation from his family that caused him to grasp any reminder of home. But, even so . . .

Staring out into the spring greenery in the distance, Daniel remembered the conversation he'd had with his mother in which

39   German underground factory

she'd confidentially shared with him the circumstances by which Sigrid and Greta first encountered Annie in Germany.

The chances of that being Annie's mother are so slim, he told himself sternly. *And anyway, how would the woman have recognized me?*

The answer came to him in an instant. Daniel had always been told he was the spitting image of his Grandma Greta. Aunt Sigrid also shared the same features and coloring. They were three peas in a pod.

Daniel pressed his palms to his face and heaved a huge, shuddering sigh. If the woman was Annie's mother, that meant Annie's mother was alive. Perhaps not well, perhaps not healthy, but alive. He wished he could turn around and find her, but instead, he had to listen to his captain. The woman was already receiving the best care she could. She was, at least, safe.

37

Reunited

(Wiedervereinigt)
November–December 1945

Melodie was chatting with some members of her Ninety-First Evacuation Hospital unit, walking to the Post Officers Club for lunch, when she saw him.

"Oh," she said in a small voice, stopping in her tracks. Beth, a short, stocky nurse who had saved more than her fair share of wounded soldiers, walked straight into Melodie's back.

"Oof!" Beth said, peering around Melodie and looking at her face. "What's the matter with you? You look like you've seen a ghost."

"Not . . . not a ghost," Melodie said. "My fiancé."

The group of women followed Melodie's gaze to the young man in uniform who was standing stock-still in front of the club, staring back at her.

"Well," Beth said, interlocking arms with Marylin, who was

509

laughing with delight, "I believe you have better things to do than have lunch with us. Come on, ladies."

The nurses disappeared into the building, their cold weather uniforms blending in with the drab November day. Melodie and Daniel strolled toward each other until they stood about three feet apart. Daniel was as handsome as ever, Melodie thought, but every trace of boyhood had left his face. A hardened soldier looked back at her, dark-circled blue eyes seeming to stare into her soul. She wondered if she looked as hardened as he.

Of course, Melodie had known the home of record for both the Ninety-First and Eighty-Fourth Regiments was Fort Knox, Kentucky. She'd known a rapid reduction of forces meant many soldiers, including Daniel, would be passing through here. But she was practical, and she'd never expected to run into him like this on a cold November forenoon, unplanned and unprepared.

"You've lost weight," Melodie said as she stood trembling.

"I've missed you," Daniel said. Then, as if pulled by some tremendous unseen force, the couple were lost in each other's embrace. Military personnel streamed by them as they stood outside the busy club as though welded together, and a passing major guffawed.

"Do us all a favor, Lieutenant, and you two go rent a room?"

Melodie reluctantly released Daniel from her grasp, loathe to feel his arms leave her. They continued to hold hands, unable to take their eyes off each other.

"I missed you too," Melodie said, her voice weak. The words hardly felt adequate, and she was almost surprised to feel tears falling from her eyes.

"My unit is scheduled to depart for Fort Harrison this afternoon," Daniel said, brushing a thumb across Melodie's cheek to wipe the tears away. "But it looks as if I'll be back home by early next month. We can spend Christmas together if it's okay with my folks."

Melodie nodded, wiping the rest of the tears from her face.

"Have you had lunch?" she asked.

"No, but . . . it sounds like a good idea," Daniel replied.

Entering the club, the two sat at a small table in the corner, luckily out of sight of Melodie's fellow nurses. The club was crowded with lunchtime chatter and smells, and the smoke of cigarettes filled the air.

"Tell me everything," they said to each other simultaneously, then laughed.

"You first," Daniel said, but then a pretty blonde server interrupted them to take their drink orders. As Melodie scanned the menu, she felt her whole body trembling with excitement.

"Well, you know some of it," she said after she and Daniel had ordered. "From my letters and the news."

"Your letters were my lifeline," Daniel said, his eyes shining. "I kept every single one. I'm afraid some of them are quite worn."

"That makes two of us," Melodie said with a laugh. "I have a fat manila envelope I kept all your letters in. Found two pieces of cardboard to slip in there to keep them nice and protected when I was on the move."

"Before I enlisted, I used a shoebox," Daniel said, nodding as the waitress put their cokes down on the table. "After, I rolled all the letters up in a piece of pipe that was left over from an engineering project."

"Creative," Melodie said, taking a sip of her sweet, carbonated soda. The taste brought her back to other meals with Daniel, far back before they'd been forced to grow up so fast.

"It's hard to believe that not even a year ago, my unit crossed the Rhine and triaged, treated, and evacuated hundreds of soldiers," she said. "When the war in Europe ended, we were sent to Paris . . ."

". . . ah," Daniel said. "I wondered where you had disappeared to."

"I wish it had been a happier visit," Melodie said wanly. "We were waiting for reassignment orders to the Pacific."

"Orders never came, I suspect," Daniel said with a smile. "I also fully expected orders to the Pacific when the Germans surrendered, and the war drew down."

"We celebrated the news of VE-Day in May but weren't too eager to find out what came next," confirmed Melodie, drumming her fingers over the wood tabletop. "Japan's surrender in September was some good news. But we both know all that. Tell me what you've been doing."

Daniel drummed his fingers against the table as well, then reached for Melodie's hand. Melodie clasped his hand without hesitation, relishing how well it fit into hers.

"Whenever I heard our song, it always made me cry," Melodie said. "You were on my mind no matter where I was sent."

"There is so much I want to say to you," he said. "Everything feels so different now . . . so confusing, like I've lost my innocence. Guess my Uncle Otto was right after all." He smiled sadly.

"I know the feeling," Melodie said, trying not to think about the screams of the wounded soldiers, the deaths she'd witnessed and not been able to stop. Daniel reached across the table and took her hand. "I know the feeling. I know for sure that I'm still very much in love with you."

"Don't make me cry again," Melodie sniffed.

The meal flew by all too quickly as the couple shared food and stories and reaffirmed their devotion. When she and Daniel stood outside the O Club afterward with the November breeze whirling snowflakes around them, Melodie felt a deep reluctance to leave him again. She looked at the new hardness of his face, wondering again what horrors he'd seen, what nightmares would follow him into their new life. She squeezed his hands in determination.

"No matter what's been lost, it was worth the price," Melodie said, a smile flickering across her face. She gazed into Daniel's eyes, tightly squeezing his hand. "We are safe again. We have the rest of our lives ahead of us to make sense of it all and help each other heal."

Daniel nodded, seemingly at a loss for words.

"I love you, Daniel Beck," Melodie said.

"And I love you, Melodie Harrison. We will soon be reunited for real."

It seemed to Melodie that the next month passed in a blur. Saying goodbye to her unit was harder than she'd imagined; they all promised to keep in touch. When she arrived in Indianapolis, she saw her father cry for the very first time as they all embraced on the platform. Her little room, filled with all her things, looked somehow small and foreign now. And, each day, as the weather turned colder and snow piled on the ground, she eagerly anticipated taking the bus to Peru.

At last, it was Christmas Eve, and she was once again in Daniel's arms. Greta, Lena, and Sigrid had prepared a large supper at Oscar and Greta's home, and the family gathered with all the children and their spouses for a feast. As they sat together in the front room, the scent of the upcoming heavy meal permeating the air, Melodie smiled contentedly. She'd tried to help in the kitchen, but she'd been shooed away with the admonishment that "heroes deserve a rest." She was surrounded by people she loved. The house, though plain, held a charm and fascination for her. The handmade furniture and the shagbark hickory logs burning in the fireplace made her feel warm and connected to this new life.

"Tell me again why Grandma and Grandpa have no Christmas decorations or a tree," Annie asked Daniel as she stroked Boots, who was stretched out by the fireplace. Melodie reached over and took Daniel's hand, eager to hear his reply.

"Our grandparents believe in the old order tradition that our Savior's birthday should be kept sacred, with no trappings of the world," Daniel said, gazing at Annie. "They celebrate with hymns and prayers to thank God for the gift of His son."

"Come, dinner is ready," Greta called.

Around the large table, created by shoving two smaller tables together and covering them with a crisp white tablecloth, Melodie took a moment to look around and take in the whole family, feeling very much at peace. Before them sat a meal of beef brisket, chicken and dumplings, pumpkin pie, mashed potatoes and gravy, pickled beets, deviled eggs and green beans, pumpernickel bread, pretzel rolls, and ham and beans slow-cooked with pork fat and onions.

Following prayer, the plates were circulated around the table. Annie excitedly talked about school with Lena; she wanted to be an engineer just like her cousin Daniel. Greta, Sigrid, and Rachel dandling little Disa in her lap, discussed plans for Daniel and Melodie's upcoming wedding. Oscar, Otto, Fredrick, Daniel, and John, as usual, discussed church, farming, and fishing in Pipe Creek while passing plates and baskets around the supper table.

The sound of the evening wind and snow could be heard striking the windowpanes of the house, which somehow made the scene even cozier. No one mentioned war or politics; the only thing that mattered that night was the family being together for Christmas.

As Melodie accepted a dish of mashed potatoes, she listened to the friendly chatter and felt her heart warm from her core.

"It is such a blessing to be here with all of you," she heard herself say.

"The Lord guides the steps of those who are godly," Oscar said in his thick German accent. "We are blessed that you have made it back to us."

Greta reached across the table to touch Melodie's hand. "Sweet girl," she said. "Have you heard the story of how our family came to Indiana?"

Epilogue

In the summer of 1953, at eighty-four years of age, Oscar quietly passed away in his sleep. He had helped Fredrick and Otto bale hay one hot afternoon, complained of "feeling a little tired," and gone to bed early that evening with his beloved wife.

Lena and Fredrick moved to Kokomo, Indiana, in May of 1956. Daniel completed his degree in civil engineering at Purdue University, and Melodie continued her nursing career at the Bunker Hill Air Force Base Hospital after marriage. They moved into Fredrick and Lena's old farmhouse, where they raised their twin boys and continued to check on Greta each day.

Annie did not discover how she came to be part of Otto and Sigrid's family until high school, when Sigrid, at last, convinced antisemitism had died down, finally confided the story to her. She included the painful news of Paul's demise and gave Annie the Star of David necklace that had been hidden away for nearly two decades. Upon hearing this and weighing his conscience, Daniel struggled with whether or not to tell the story of the young woman at Camp Salzwedel. In the end, after much soul-searching and talking it over with Melodie, Daniel did indeed share the story of his encounter in Germany with Annie and Sigrid.

Annie received her engineering degree from Purdue University, and Sigrid and Otto proudly attended her graduation. Annie went on for an advanced degree and later established a career in aerospace in Houston, Texas. She sometimes wondered about the woman Daniel had seen, though, with hundreds of survivors of the death camp and no knowledge of the woman's name, the chances of finding her were remote. She couldn't help thinking, however, that someone who had been at Salzwedel might well remember a kind, middle-aged woman with a distinctive dimpled chin. She never gave up writing letters and researching the matter.

Greta had seen two world wars and technological advancements, all while watching her children and grandchildren raise children of their own. However, it was the reminiscence of how God had blessed and watched over her and her family that she spoke of most often. In the final years of her life, she often walked the distance to the stone circle near the shade of the woods, where she would sit on a blanket, lean her back against one of the large rocks, and close her eyes. In these moments, she remembered family, travels, and friends' past and often spoke aloud to Oscar as though he was sitting beside her.

On the third of June, 1960, during her ninetieth year on this Earth, Greta laboriously lowered herself to the grass within the stone circle one last time. She breathed in the warm summer air, thinking over her long, prosperous existence. She thought of her children and grandchildren. She thought of the many beloved ones who had preceded her in death: her parents, Carl, Dieter, Sarah and Bauer, Kezi, Paul, Uncle Fredrick, Pastor Yoder, and the love of her life. She longed to see them all once again.

"Oscar," she said, her eyes closed, a smile spreading across her face. "I am ready to join you, my love."

As she spoke, two gray wolves emerged from the edge of the woods. No such species had been seen in the area in over fifty years. Silently, the animals walked into the circle and lay on each side of the old woman. Their ears flattened as Greta gently laid a hand on each of their heads, her crooked, arthritic fingers softly caressing their fur. Then, with a peaceful sigh, she ascended from her full and blessed life.

Character Profiles

Beck

NAME	DATES	PARENTS/ SIBLING	APPEARANCE
Carl	1838-1895	Danish German extraction	brown dark hair blue eyes 6' 1 140
Dieter	1841-1933	German/Dane	dark brown hair brown eyes 6'2" 180
Fredrick Sr.	1840-1916	German/Dane	dark brown hair brown eyes 6' 3" 190
Oscar Carl Beck	1869-1953	Carl and Petra (Hansen) Beck	brown hair blue eyes 6'1 175
Greta Alsa Beck (nee Hock)	1870-1960	Jurgen and Alsa (Ivarsson) Hock	blonde hair indigo eyes 5'9" 130

NAME	DATES	PARENTS/ SIBLING	APPEARANCE
Fredrick Jr (Fredrick Jurgen).	1895-1975	Parents Oscar and Greta Beck. Sigrid Beck (sister)	light brown hair blue eyes 6' 175
Lena (nee Kunkle)	January 21, 1895-1978	Parents- Dorcas and Amos Kunkle Brother is Elija Kunkle	dark brown hair brown eyes 5' 6" 125
Rachel Beck (Mooney)	1918-2009	Lena and Fredrick Beck Daniel is sibling, Husband is John Mooney, daughter is Disa	blonde hair, brown eyes, slight build
Daniel	1923-2005	Lena and Fredrick Beck Rachel is sibling	dark blonde hair Indigo eyes 6'0 180
Melodie (nee Harrison)	1923-2019	Mr. and Mrs. Harrison of Indianapolis, Indiana.	auburn hair smoky blue eyes 5'7 125

Kunkle

NAME	DATES	PARENTS/ SIBLING	APPEARANCE
Dorcas (nee __)	1872-1963	German lineage	dark brown hair brown eyes 5' 7 140
Amos	1862-1951	German lineage	brown hair gray eyes 5'9" 165
Elija	May 1, 1896- November 1917	German lineage Dorcus, Amos Kunkle	brown hair green eyes 5'7" 140
Paul	1898-1940	Father: Dorcas' unnamed brother	light brown hair blue eyes 5'10 168
Conrad	1889-1970	Father: Dorcas' unnamed brother	blonde hair blue eyes 6' 182
Helga? (nee __)	1913-1996	Danish lineage	brown hair brown eyes 5'5" 130
Paul Jr.	1939- ?	Paul and Helga's son	?

Bowman

NAME	DATES	PARENTS/ SIBLING	APPEARANCE
Ruth	1874-1952	German descent	light brown hair blue eyes 5'9" 145
Hans	1871-1959	German descent	light brown hair gray eyes 5'10" 165
Otto	1896-1979	3 brothers Ruth, and Hans Bowman	light brown hair blue eyes 6'1" 193
Sigrid	1899-1989	Fredrick Oscar, Greta Beck	strawberry blonde hair indigo eyes
Annie	1931-?	Jewish/ German/ Jensche?	dark brown hair brown eyes dimpled chin

About the Author

GREGG HAMMOND is a decorated veteran, a father, grandfather, teacher, and healer. He is retired and lives on a small farm in North Central Indiana with his wife and terrier.

Bibliography

Barry, John M. *The Great Influenza: The Story of the Deadliest Pandemic in History*. Penguin UK, 2020.

Brumbaugh, Grove Martin. *History of The German Baptist Brethren in Europe and America*. Mount Morris, Illinois: Brethren Publishing House, 1899.

Charles River Editors. *The Roma: The History of the Romani People and the Controversial Persecutions of Them Across Europe*. Independently Published, October 18, 2019.

Crane Jeanne. "Portals." *Celtic Spirit Books,* October 21, 2019. Accessed March 1, 2023. https://www.celticspiritbooks. com/blog/2019/10/21/portals

Davenport, J. Matthew. *First Over There: The Attack on Cantigny, America's First Battle of World War I*. illustrated. St. Martin's Publishing Group, 2015.

Dick, Harold, and Douglas Robinson. *The Golden Age of the Great Passenger Airships: Graf Zeppelin and Hindenburg*.

Washington, D.C. and London: Smithsonian Institution Press, 1985.

Falkenstein, N. George. *History of the German Baptist Brethren Church*. Original from the University of Virginia. New Era Printing Company, 1901.

GG Archives. "Cabin Class Passage Contracts & Tickets." Accessed March 1, 2023. https://www.ggarchives.com/Immigration/ImmigrantTickets/PassageContracts-CabinClass.html.

Glazier, Ira A., and Percy William Filby, eds. *Germans to America: July 1894–October 1895: Lists of Passengers Arriving at US Ports*. Vol. 66. Scholarly Resources, 1989.

Hussey, Kristin and Pomeroy, Luke. "The addictive history of medicine: The curious case of the 7 percent solution." *Science Museum*, May 11, 2012. Accessed March 1, 2023. https://blog.sciencemuseum.org.uk/the-addictive-history-of-medicine-the-curious-case-of-the-7-percent-solution/.

Klimczak, Natalia. "The Nazi Temple of Pomerania: Exploring the Mysterious Odry Stone Circles." *Ancient Origins Magazine*, Updated June 26, 2016. Accessed March 1, 2023. https://www.ancient-origins.net/ancient-places-europe/exploring-mysterious-odry-stone-circles-pomerania-006175.

Kuo, Michael. " *Boletus edulis*," MushroomExpert.Com. Accessed March 1, 2023, https://www.mushroomexpert.com/boletus_edulis.html.

Lee, Patrick Jasper. *We Borrow the Earth: An Intimate Portrait of the Gypsy Folk Tradition and Culture.* Ravine Press, 2015.

McGowen, Tom. *The Battle of Cantigny: Cornerstones of Freedom.* Illustrated. Children's Press, 2002.

Stone, Dan. *The Liberation of the Camps: The End of the Holocaust and Its Aftermath.* Unabridged. Bedford Square, London: Yale University Press, 2015.

Sweden.se. "Sami in Sweden." Last updated on January 16, 2023. Accessed March 1, 2023. https://sweden.se/life/people/sami-in-sweden.

The National Museum of American History. " Aboard a Packet." *The National Museum of American History,* Accessed March 1, 2023. https://americanhistory.si.edu/on-the-water/maritime-nation/enterprise-water/aboard-packet.

The Old Farmer's Almanac. "Weather History for Indiana." Accessed March 1, 2023. https://www.almanac.com/weather/history/IN.

The Sunday School Child Hymn Book. Revised. Philadelphia: American Sunday School Union, 1900.

United States Holocaust Memorial Museum. "NEUENGAMME." *Holocaust Encyclopedia,* Accessed on March 1, 2023. https://encyclopedia.ushmm.org/content/en/article/neuengamme.

Walter P. Reuther Library. " (11165) Base Hospital # 17, Main Building, Dijon, France, 1917." July 22, 2014. https://reuther.wayne.edu/node/12026.

Water Science School. "Water Dowsing." *United States Geological Survey,* June 6, 2018.

Weyrauch, Walter O., ed. *Gypsy law: Romani legal traditions and culture.* Univ of California Press, 2001.